THE SILK FIST CONSPIRACY

THE SILK FIST CONSPIRACY

DAVID STEDMAN

Matador
9 Priory Business Park
Kibworth Beauchamp
Leicestershire LE8 0RX, UK
Tel: (+44) 116 279 2299
Fax: (+44) 116 279 2277
Email: books@troubador.co.uk
Web: www.troubador.co.uk/matador

ISBN 978 1783063 185

British Library Cataloguing in Publication Data.
A catalogue record for this book is available from the British Library.

Printed and bound in the UK by TJ International, Padstow, Cornwall
Typeset in 11pt Aldine401 BT Roman by Troubador Publishing Ltd, Leicester, UK

Matador is an imprint of Troubador Publishing Ltd

For Sharon and Teresa
with love

Visit David Stedman at his website:

www.gradgrind.co.uk

1

Dundalk Research Institute, Dundalk, Ireland, February 12th

The most beloved woman in the world was murdered at ten minutes past noon.

Christopher Wyatt had been watching the opening ceremony of the research institute from a vantage point several metres away. He was watching with alert concentration but also with pleasure. This was one of the easy assignments, the enjoyable assignments. He sensed no threat from the throng of Dundalk citizens cheering the Princess Royal.

Wyatt saw the Garda chief superintendent pushing through the crowd. The chief smiled broadly. 'Hello, sergeant. Everything is going well. No reports of any problems. The sniffer dogs have done the rounds inside the building.' He looked up at the cloudless sky. 'We've a grand day for the opening ceremony. It's not usually this mild and sunny in February.'

'We're very lucky, sir.' Wyatt sensed that the chief superintendent was itching to ask the question that everyone asked.

'I had the honour of being introduced to the princess a few minutes ago. Such a beautiful and charming woman. You say you've been her protection officer for over two years?'

'Yes, sir.'

'Is she as kind and gracious in private as in public?'

Wyatt gave the reply he had given so many times. 'Before I took this job I was indifferent to the monarchy but now I'm delighted that the princess will one day be my head of state. I've travelled with

1

her to many different countries. I can assure you that her charm is unfeigned and her concern for the less fortunate of all races and creeds is entirely genuine. I'm privileged to serve her.'

The chief superintendent nodded, well pleased with exactly the answer he had wanted to hear. 'That's excellent. This is a real red letter day for Dundalk. The new institute looks magnificent.'

'Indeed it does, sir, although a bit too much chrome and glass for my taste. I'm more enchanted by your country, the scenery, the unhurried pace of life, the friendliness of the people.'

'I'm glad to hear that,' the chief superintendent replied. 'If you don't mind me saying, you could pass for an Irishman. You have the dark brooding look of a Celt. Have you never been to Ireland before?'

'No, this is my first visit, which is strange because my mother is Irish and often talks about the old country.'

'Aah, there you are. Ireland is in your blood, sergeant.'

'You're right, sir.'

'Well, I'd better do the rounds again. I'll see you at the reception later on.'

'Thank you again for your support today. Your officers are doing an excellent job.'

The chief superintendent nodded in acknowledgement. 'So are yours, sergeant.'

A large contingent of Garda officers was keeping the crowd well back from the princess and the director of the research institute. The two of them were standing either side of a commemorative brass plaque at the entrance to the institute. There was a silk ribbon draped across the doors waiting to be cut. The director was holding the ceremonial golden scissors.

The Princess Royal stepped up to the lectern to begin her speech. Wyatt noted that the princess had decided not to wear an overcoat. It was, he thought later, a decision that may have cost the princess her life.

The children were waving their little Union Jacks and little Irish tricolour flags with unrestrained excitement. The adults murmured their approval of the princess's hopes and prayers for co-operation and reconciliation between the two countries. No, there is no threat here, Wyatt thought.

He allowed himself a second to look away from the ceremony and beyond to the undulating blue hills rolling along the horizon. Closer, the reflected sunlight sparkled along the ripples of the Castletown River as it swirled and flowed out into the bay. The air was full of the iron salty smell of the Irish Sea. Wyatt was viscerally enchanted. Ireland was, indeed, in his blood.

There was a loud shout, almost a scream of anguish. Wyatt turned back quickly. The director was shouting and brandishing the golden ceremonial scissors above his head. Wyatt reached for the firearm holstered inside his jacket.

The director grabbed the princess by the hair, drew her roughly towards him and plunged the blades of the scissors into her neck. A spurt of blood sprayed up and then fell to stain her pale blue dress. There was a collective moan of horror from the crowd.

The director, shouting the same word again and again, raised the scissors and stabbed the princess in her breast. The princess was blocking Wyatt's line of fire. Police officers were moving forward, screaming children all around. Wyatt ran several steps to adjust his position and fired one shot on the move as the director's head bobbed into view. The director dropped the scissors and clutched his neck as blood spurted from the bullet wound. He collapsed on to concrete paving. The princess, released from his grip, fell backwards. Her head thumped the concrete and she lay as still as a statue.

The medical team rushed forward. Wyatt pushed his way through the crowd and glanced at the princess as he kneeled down. The medics were working frantically but Wyatt could see from her lifeless face and blood-soaked dress that it was too late. He was filled with a murderous anger he could scarcely control. He grabbed the director by the lapels of his jacket, raised him up and through gritted teeth said: 'Why? Why did you do it?'

The director feebly plucked at Wyatt's lapels. There was no hatred in his eyes. There were tears, contrition and pleading desperation. His throat was gurgling and filling with blood as he spoke.

Wyatt struggled to understand. 'Hate you?' he replied. 'She didn't hate you. She didn't hate anyone.'

The director was frantic to make Wyatt understand.

Wyatt said: 'I don't hate you either. What do you mean?'

The director whispered his last words, then his eyes clouded with death and his breathing stopped. Wyatt lowered him gently back on to the ground.

Wyatt stood up and looked at the two bodies. He became aware of the chief superintendent standing beside him.

'Holy mother of God,' the chief superintendent whispered. An ambulance had arrived and the bodies were being covered. 'Come away now, sergeant. There's nothing more you can do.'

'I've been in the army,' Wyatt said, aware that he was in some state of shock. 'I've seen wounds and carnage but I've never seen anything like this.'

The chief superintendent took his arm. 'Come away now, son.'

Wyatt did not move. 'It was my duty to protect her. She was the heir to the throne and now she's dead.'

'There'll be many, many questions to answer, sergeant. What did the director say before he died?'

Wyatt considered what to tell the chief superintendent. He had been shocked and bewildered by what the director had whispered with his dying breath. He decided to guard the information carefully, that it must not yet become public knowledge, and that this tragedy could be part of something more evil and threatening than an isolated political assassination.

Wyatt lied: 'I couldn't understand what he said.'

Wyatt allowed the chief superintendent to guide him away from the scene. He realised, with a sinking heart, that life, for him and for countless other people, could never be the same again.

2

Apartment 6, Dominion Building, Sugar Hill,
New York City, February 12th

Linda Marquez finished packing, closed the lid of her travelling case and fixed it on to the trolley. Her husband stood at the bedroom door. Michael O'Brien's eyes were glazed with resentment, his expression mean, his attitude sarcastic and hurtful. She braced herself for his next outburst.

Michael said: 'So you're not going to change your mind? You're leaving me again?'

'We're flying to Hawaii tomorrow. It's only for two days.'

'That bitch must have dozens of flunkies who can look after her.'

Linda Marquez winced. 'It's the First Lady you're talking about in that disrespectful way. What's gotten into you lately? You used to approve of what she stands for. You used to support her… and me.'

'That's before I realised how much time you would be spending away from me because of her. Can you imagine what it's like to be a cop in this city and come home after a long shift to an empty apartment because your wife is away cosying up to the high and mighty? I eat takeout meals on my own surrounded by nothing but all this depressing wood and coloured glass and fancy plasterwork in this goddamn mausoleum.'

'A nineteenth century masterpiece you used to call it. You said you hated modern apartments, and I agreed. You loved this place when we bought it.'

'*You* bought it, Linda, you and your family money. We could never have afforded this place on my cop pay or your Secret Service pay.'

'Is it such a bad thing, to have a wealthy family?'

'No, but I still suspect that's the reason you didn't take my surname. Marquez of the Florida orange dynasty has a lot more clout than wife of a cop with a mick surname like O'Brien.'

'I keep my own surname for my job simply because it's easier. I'm equally proud of the names Marquez or O'Brien.'

'So why don't you junk that job and stay home with me? You don't need the Secret Service pay.'

'I don't do it for the money, Mike, you know that. President Logan is halfway through his second term. In two years there'll be a new President and then I'll retire and we can start a family, but in the meantime I want to complete my tour of duty with the First Lady. This is the culmination of my career.'

'Career?' Mike said. 'You're a frigging sergeant. Some career!'

'I'm also Marty's personal protection officer and assistant,' Linda said patiently. 'I love my job and I believe that Martina Logan is a real force for good in America. I'm serving my country. Marty needs me.'

'Marty!' Michael spat. 'She feels safe with you because you're another spoilt spic bitch like her.'

Linda's stomach turned over. She was determined to stay calm and answer calmly. 'My mother is of Mexican heritage, same as Mrs Logan. My father is of Spanish heritage. Proud as I am of both of them, I am simply American, as is the First Lady, and honoured to call myself American. I wouldn't refer to you as a mick or a paddy or whatever. Why have you become so filled with hate?'

'I don't know,' Michael said. There was a fleeting look of contrition on his face.

'Are you taking drugs or drinking behind my back?'

'No.'

'You're not yourself, Mike. You've changed in the last few weeks.'

'You keep saying that. You think I've changed because I get angry

7

when you disappear for weeks at a time with Martina frigging Logan. It isn't me who's changed, Linda, it's you. You'd rather be parading around the White House waving your gun and your badge playing the chosen special agent rather than making a home for me.'

'That's not true, Mike. I love being here with you more than anything. Perhaps the strain of your job is getting you down? Why not get a check-up with the doctor or make an appointment with the counsellor or the psychiatrist?'

'What! You gotta be kidding! Pour out my worries like some fairy faggot with the guys at the precinct laughing behind my back? Besides, there's nothing wrong with me.'

'Well, remember that I love you dearly. I'm proud of you, Michael, and I'll be back as soon as I can, then I'll take some time off. I promise.'

Michael looked back at her with something of the old pride. 'You are beautiful, even wearing that regulation issue black suit and those damn glasses. I do love you.'

Linda took off her spectacles and put them in her jacket pocket. She wanted to go to Mike, to hold him and be held, to bring back the good times. She moved towards him but a sudden sneer changed his expression to a mask of hatred. Linda held back. Michael took an object from the pocket of his shirt and held it up. 'Do you know what this is?'

'It's your lucky silver bullet,' Linda replied, deflated and depressed, yet again, by her husband's sudden change in demeanour.

'Yes, my lucky silver bullet,' Michael said. 'I think I'll use it on Mrs Marty Logan the next time you get me in to meet her. That will solve all my problems. That will keep you at home. With her gone you'll be nothing again. Two Sweet Briar prom queens who mean nothing.'

Linda forced herself to answer rationally. 'The fact that we both went to Sweet Briar is not why Marty chose me as her special assistant.'

'No? Just a coincidence was it, like you both being in that same sorority? What was it? Sigma Phi Beta? Sigma Phi Bitch more like. Sigma Phi spoiled spic bitch.'

Linda's cell phone rang. She picked up and answered.

The doorman said: 'Your cab is here, Mrs Marquez.'

'Thanks. I'll be right down.' To Michael she said: 'I have to go. My cab is waiting.'

Linda took hold of the luggage trolley handle and moved towards the bedroom door. Michael did not stand aside.

'What are you going to do, Michael? Keep me here imprisoned? Beat me up? Shoot me? I'll be back as soon as I can. We'll have to talk about all this. You've got serious problems, Michael. Please think about what I've said.'

Michael, with a show of reluctance, stepped aside. Linda wanted to kiss him goodbye but knew he would not allow it. Instead she said: 'I'll see you, Mike.'

'You two Sigma Phi Beta bitches have a good time in hula hula land.'

Linda opened the door of the apartment. She turned and said: 'It was Sigma Phi Kappa, Michael.'

'What?'

'Kappa, Michael. Sigma Phi Kappa.'

Michael became tense and wary. His expression lost the look of malice and became watchful and alert. 'Okay, so it's Sigma Phi frigging Kappa. You're all spoiled little rich bitches who deserve one of these.' He held up the lucky silver bullet. 'What do you want me to do?'

Linda could no longer control her pent-up anger. 'Right now, Michael, I wish you'd shove that bullet up your ass and go jump off the Brooklyn Bridge.'

Linda Marquez sat in the back of the cab and fought back tears and an overwhelming sense of loss and bewilderment. Something had gone terribly wrong with her marriage or, more specifically, her husband. Was Michael right? Were her frequent absences on duty driving them apart?

Michael's character had changed. The Michael she loved was no longer there. Whatever the reason for Michael's behaviour, Linda berated herself for the nasty comment she had hurled at him as she left the apartment. She had to stay sane, calm and rational for Michael's sake, for her own sake, for the sake of their marriage, and not be drawn into a vicious war of words against the man she loved, a man battling with psychological demons he clearly could not understand or control.

Linda Marquez would regret her hateful final comment until the day she died, but in a way she could not begin to imagine.

3

Room 115, Research and Analysis Wing headquarters,
New Delhi, India, February 12th

Premendra Dhawan looked up from his laptop when the security door opened. Colonel Ashok Chatterjee entered the room. He was in uniform and his sudden presence caused a flurry of activity among the staff of cryptanalysts and computer hackers.

Premendra Dhawan made to stand up but Colonel Chatterjee waved at him to keep still. Chatterjee pulled up an office chair and sat down beside Prem.

'Well, Prem, what's the verdict?'

'I'm afraid the verdict is guilty, sir. I'm guilty for keeping all these good people from their homes on a wild goose chase. We cannot find any evidence of any danger to India or establish any link between this recent series of events.'

Chatterjee frowned. 'So you persuaded me to authorise all that extra overtime and resources on a "wild goose chase"?'

'I'm afraid so, sir. My instinct was wrong.'

'Your instinct has served us well for many years, Prem, but I have to say I'm disappointed. I have a security meeting with Prime Minister Mishra and the other chiefs this afternoon. I'd hoped that you could give me something positive to report. Can you give me anything?'

'There are certain similarities, as I outlined in my preliminary report, but we have been unable to build on them. Over the past few weeks we have captured billions of emails and electronic transmissions from around the world. We seeded our analysers with key words such as "attack" or "revenge" or "terrorist" but no common threads have emerged. We've penetrated intelligence and police files in the countries where these attacks have taken place and there are general similarities. All the attacks have been against democratic countries, Europe, Canada, USA, one in Brazil. Nothing in Africa or any Asian country except Japan, but that's a democracy, like India. I still think India will be a target soon, that's why I was so eager to complete this exercise as soon as possible.'

Chatterjee sighed. 'Are you sure all these events are not coincidence, Prem? They are all so different in nature. A Canadian tanker explodes in port, a dam bursts in France, the wealthiest industrialist in Germany shot to death, a power black-out cripples industry for days in California, and the latest one, a British princess assassinated by a lone madman. Where's the connection?'

'Don't forget the several attacks on top political and business leaders.'

'I haven't forgotten. I ask again, where is the connection?'

Prem accepted the rebuke. 'I cannot tell you, sir. It was my hunch, my instinct. At this point we can't find a connection. My apologies.'

'No need to apologise, Prem. The espionage trade is as elusive as catching mist in your hand. You can keep a small team on this project but we had better turn our attention back to China, Pakistan and the Naxalites.'

'I've already arranged for that, sir.'

'Good. That's where we know the threats are coming from. You look exhausted, Prem. I want you to take the rest of the day off.'

'I'm okay, sir.'

'That was not a suggestion. That was an order.'

'Very well, sir. Thank you. I had planned to walk to South Block and have lunch with Rhea. I haven't seen her for three days.'

'Good. Then go and see her, Prem. I suspect that you also have a soft spot for all that pseudo-Indian Imperialist architecture over at the Secretariat. That's why you go over there so often.'

'Let's say that I find it interesting, sir, but I find my wife even more interesting.'

Chatterjee nodded. 'It's a fine day outside. Perhaps I will leave my official car in the garage and walk over with you, if you would not object to my company?'

'Not at all, sir.'

Colonel Chatterjee smiled and patted Prem on the back. He stood up and addressed the twenty or so staff within the room. 'Listen everyone! Thank you all for your efforts last night and over the past few days. You are a vital element in the security of our land. I'm allowing your boss to have the rest of the day off. He is considerably older than you youngsters and needs his rest.'

There was a ripple of laughter in appreciation of the jest. They all knew that Premendra Dhawan's energy in defence of his country was inexhaustible.

'Come along,' Colonel Chatterjee said to Prem. 'Are you taking your briefcase home?'

'Yes, sir. I'll go over those reports again when my mind is fresh.'

'Then let me carry it for you while we get through the door. Let me help you with your jacket as well.'

'Thank you, sir.' Premedra Dhawan stood up and allowed Chatterjee to slip on his jacket. Prem fastened the buttons with his right hand. The left sleeve of the jacket hung empty.

As they walked out into the sunlight Colonel Chatterjee asked: 'Are you aware that your boys and girls call you the Hawk?'

Prem had to walk fast to keep up with Chatterjee's tall spare frame. 'I am aware of my nickname, sir. They think I don't know. I'm secretly pleased with it, unless it's a reference to my fine aquiline nose.'

'Don't be disingenuous, Prem. It's because you watch over our country like a bird of prey, relentless, watchful, concentrated. They're devoted to you.'

'I'm devoted to them. They're the cream of India's universities and you've made sure they have the best equipment to work with.'

'Because our department is ultra-secret most officials have no idea that we exist, let alone what we do. I've had to fight many battles to make sure we have the best.'

'Is that why you always wear your uniform to work? You've no need to.'

'Why do you think I wear it?'

'I'm not sure. To impress the staff?'

Chatterjee smiled. 'The explanation is much simpler. After nearly forty years in the army I don't feel comfortable in civvies.'

They discussed department business until they turned to walk past India Gate and on to the Rajpath leading to the Secretariat South Block.

Prem said: 'I have to admit you're right, sir.'

'What about?'

'I do enjoy the look of this Imperialist architecture. It's more pleasing to the eye than the ugly modern concrete eyesore in which we have to work. I envy Rhea her working environment, that elegant suite of offices, as well as the excellent staff restaurant. The food is much better than our canteen. That's why we meet for lunch so often here.'

'How long have you and Rhea been married?' Chatterjee asked.

'Next month will be our thirtieth anniversary. I marvel at the fact that, after all that time and after merely three days apart, I am excited to see her again.'

'You're a lucky man, Prem.'

'Indeed I am, sir. Do you ever wish you were married or regret not marrying?'

Chatterjee shrugged. 'I am abstemious and ascetic by nature. I'm impatient and I don't suffer fools or liars. I regarded my service in the army as a mystical mission. That has made many people afraid of me. I appear cold and distant. I've enjoyed the company of women on many occasions but my needs are not great in that direction. I haven't been as fortunate as you, Prem, to win the love of a remarkable woman. Perhaps my character is forbidding to love but, as I grow older, I do harbour some regret about being alone.'

Prem did not know how to respond so he kept silent. He was not afraid of Chatterjee but he did find his commanding officer formidable.

Chatterjee said: 'The Prime Minister speaks highly of Rhea. He approves the fact that she wears the sari while most of his staff have gone over to Western dress. Like Rhea, he is a traditionalist in the best sense. He relies on Rhea heavily.'

'That is good to know. She was lucky to get the job.'

'Nothing lucky about it, Prem. Rhea's formidable intelligence and energy won her that job.'

'I know,' Prem said. 'I didn't want to brag on Rhea's behalf. She loves her job but her devotion and commitment to our marriage and our two sons has never wavered.'

The guards at the entrance to South Block snapped to attention as Colonel Chatterjee presented his security pass. They had once waved him through without checking his pass. The resulting blast of disciplinary action for such a flagrant dereliction of duty had made the colonel legendary.

Prem presented his security pass and they were allowed through into the vaulted foyer.

Chatterjee stopped and said: 'I have to make my report to the chiefs before I see the Prime Minister. I'm going to accept your recommendation, Prem, and request that security in all official and government buildings be tightened severely until we can find out exactly what is going on with these attacks.'

'I'm relieved, sir. I will do my best to find out what is going on.'

'I'm sure you will. Thank you for your company, Prem. Have a pleasant lunch and give my regards to Rhea.'

Chatterjee strode off towards the ceremonial staircase.

Prem turned left into the long sunlit corridor leading to Rhea's office. She must have noticed him walking across the courtyard because she was standing at the office door waiting to greet him. She waved and smiled. She was wearing a green and gold sari. She looked enchanting. Prem waved back.

Someone was shouting. Prem turned around. There was a guttural roar of defiance. Then gunshots. The emergency alarm system blared. Prem stood stock still.

A tall and powerfully built white man, well over six feet tall, ran into the corridor. He was waving a pistol and shouting. He was wearing a garish Hawaiian shirt that seemed to balloon out around his torso. Prem realised with horror what was strapped underneath the shirt.

Prem swung his briefcase at the man's head. He caught the intruder with a glancing blow. The intruder slowed and Prem, cursing his missing arm, charged at the man in an attempt to unbalance him. The man checked and stumbled but stayed on his feet. His eyes were wild and he looked confused and distracted as if he barely knew where he was. He shoved Prem aside with massive crazed strength. Prem crashed against the wall and fell to the floor.

Rhea was standing at the door to her office.

'Rhea!' Prem shouted. 'Come out! Run towards me!'

Security guards ran into the corridor and raised their rifles.

'Don't shoot!' Prem shouted. 'You'll hit my wife.'

The guards ignored his plea and fired several shots at the running man. He momentarily stopped, blotches of blood spreading on his back and legs but then, with a bellow like a wounded bull, he charged on.

Rhea stood in the doorway and tried to prevent the man from entering. He grabbed her face in his huge hand and smashed her head against the door jamb. Rhea collapsed. The man bulldozed his way into the Prime Minister's outer office. Screams and cries from within the office. Prem had hauled himself up to run towards Rhea.

A flash of blinding white light and a mind numbing blast. A scorching wave of air pressure knocked Prem on to his back. He was badly winded, groggy, dazed, almost blind and deafened. He had to get to Rhea. Through blurred eyes he could see her lying in the doorway. Smoke and flame billowed out of the office. He had to get to her.

'Rhea!' he called. 'I'm here. I'm coming.'

Rhea did not move. He could not tell whether Rhea was alive or dead.

4

Royal Lani Hotel, Waikiki Beach, Hawaii,
February 14th

Linda Marquez looked out at the rollers thundering on to the beach and the teetering surfers riding the pipeline. A crescent of brilliant white sand swept around to the dark mass of Diamond Head cliffs far in the distance. Under normal circumstances she would be exhilarated by such a view but today she could concentrate her mind on only one thing: her failing marriage. She thought, with melancholy, that today was St Valentine's Day. She had called Michael several times but his cell phone was switched off. She tried to convince herself that he was involved in a police situation during which he could not have his cell phone switched on. More likely, Linda thought sadly, he did not want to speak to her.

Professionally, the day had been successful. The First Lady's two official engagements had both gone smoothly. Linda had even found time to go window shopping along Kalakaua Avenue but the products offered by Chanel, Prada, Dior, Tiffany and Cartier had left her uninterested. All she could think of was Michael.

Linda realised that she had subconsciously made the decision that her marriage was more important than her career. As much as she loved working for Martina Logan, she loved her husband much more. Linda would inform the First Lady of her decision to resign as soon as they returned to Washington. Michael hated the fact that her job with the First Lady took her away from him so often. Her resignation would be the first step in healing the marriage. Michael clearly had problems of some kind, mental or physical, and it was Linda's duty to be there to help him overcome them. The vows she had taken were not optional. Her marriage was going to be for life.

Linda was startled by a knock on the door. 'Come in,' she called.

The door opened. Deputy Chief Isaiah Franklin stepped into the room. He said: 'She's asking for you, Linda.'

'But I haven't showered and changed for dinner, sir. Surely it isn't time yet?' Linda looked at her watch.

'This isn't about dinner, Linda. Mrs Logan is distraught and asking for you.'

'Distraught? Why? What's happened?'

'Haven't you been watching your television?'

'No, sir. I...'

'Then come with me. We have to be on our guard more than usual, Linda. I've drafted in some local agents to beef up the security round the hotel. Be watchful, be vigilant. Something has happened back home.'

They went up in the elevator. Franklin led Linda past the augmented security detail in the corridor and into the presidential suite. Then he left the suite and closed the door behind him.

Martina Logan was perched on the edge of a sofa as she watched the television. She was still formally dressed from the afternoon's speech. Linda was shocked to see tears running down the face of the tough and self-controlled woman she admired so much.

'Marty?' Linda said. 'What's wrong?'

Linda sat down on the sofa and Martina Logan instinctively took Linda's hand for comfort. 'Have you been watching this, Linda?'

'No. What's happening?'

'Some lunatic released some form of lethal gas at the Oscar ceremony in LA. They're saying it was released through the air conditioning system. Some of my favourite actors have been killed and many others are in a serious condition, theatre staff, agents, directors, producers, some of the top names in the film industry.'

The television pictures showed stretchers being carried out of the auditorium and taken to banks of ambulances, blue and red lights flashing, parked along Hollywood Boulevard. The two women watched in silence as the enormity of the crime sunk in.

Linda asked: 'Do they know who did it? Did they get the perp?'

'He's dead. He released the gas and then ran into the auditorium screaming the same word over and over again. Then he shot himself.'

They watched the television coverage in silence for several minutes.

Martina Logan managed to compose herself and said: 'The world is going crazy, Linda. All these disasters happening at once. Thank goodness the Prime Minister of India survived that terrible bombing. I keep thinking of the Princess Royal. The British people are shocked and inconsolable. Joe rang His Majesty to offer condolences on behalf of the American people. He said it was the hardest job he's ever had to do.'

'Did you ever meet the princess, Marty?'

'Yes, three or four times. Some of the other British royals are stuffy and formal, you know, cold in that way the Brits can be, but she was different. She was delightful. As soon as you met her she made you feel like a friend you'd known all your life. The tragedy is that a few years ago the British parliament changed the rules on the succession so she would have been the queen one day.'

Linda spoke without thinking. 'The princess should not have died. It was preventable. It was incompetence.'

Martina Logan showed her surprise. 'What do you mean, Linda?'

'We've analysed the film of the assassination. That British royal protection guy who shot the director took his eye off the ball. You could see him staring off into the distance before he realises something is going on. If he had been watching the ceremony, or if he had stationed himself closer, he could have perhaps stopped the director. He moved too late. He was incompetent.'

'Well, however it should or should not have happened it's a terrible loss to Britain and to the world.' Martina Logan indicated the television screen. 'And now this on top of everything else.'

Linda tried to find some words to comfort her friend. 'I'm sure the President will order everything within his power to find out what is going on and stop it. In the meantime, Marty, you'd better prepare yourself for even more tight security than we're giving you now.'

'I accept that, Linda. It's a great comfort to me that you're here. Even the First Lady needs a friendly shoulder to cry on.'

'You've given me so much, Marty. I'll do anything I can to help you. We Sweet Briar girls have to stick together.'

Linda's remark was rewarded by a wan smile. 'I was at Sweet Briar many years before you were, Linda, and that's not why I chose you as my special assistant, but it does help form a bond, like all great schools do.'

'They were happy days. I hope we'll be happy again, very soon.'

'Amen to that, Linda.'

Linda's cell phone rang. She stood up and said: 'Do you mind if I answer this call, Marty. It might be my husband.'

'Go ahead, Linda. I hope the President remembers that it's Valentine's Day or else he'll be in big trouble.'

Linda smiled and moved to the window. She looked at the number ringing but did not recognise it. It was not Michael's cell phone. She answered: 'Linda Marquez.'

A gruff masculine voice, nervous, hesitant, replied: 'Linda, this is Assistant Chief Dempsey of the NYPD. I'm aware that you're in Hawaii on duty with the First Lady, mam, and I deeply regret having to call you, but it's my sad duty to give you some very bad news.'

5

Briefing Room, Cabinet Office, Whitehall, London, February 15th

Home Secretary Clare Barnard came out of the Briefing Room to the anteroom where Assistant Commissioner Sangita Desai Sherman was waiting.

'Still not here?' Barnard said in a tone that showed she was not pleased.

'No,' Sherman replied. 'I specifically ordered Wyatt to be here at two pm. I'm bloody angry. He's ten minutes late for probably the most important meeting of his life. And mine.'

'Are you nervous, Sangita?' Barnard asked in a more sympathetic tone.

'Yes, I admit I am. This uniform usually gives me confidence and authority but I feel like a nervous schoolgirl. I know I'm going to get a grilling. I've been in the Metropolitan Police for thirty two years but I've met a Prime Minister only twice, and then briefly and informally. Is this one as tough as they say?'

'Yes,' Barnard said. 'But he's also fair and honest. Be yourself, don't let him browbeat you, and answer honestly and you'll be fine. You look good in that uniform but with your figure you'd look good in anything, unlike my matronly shape.'

Sherman gave a wan smile, appreciative of her superior's effort to boost her confidence.

Barnard said: 'Well, we can't keep them waiting any longer. Let's go in.'

Sherman followed the Home Secretary into the Briefing Room.

It was a long and windowless wood panelled room with most of the space taken up by a long wooden conference table with twenty chairs.

Barnard indicated that Sherman should sit down in a chair halfway along the table and directly opposite Prime Minster Murdo Montrose.

Montrose was a Scotsman who was indifferent to his popular image and reputation. He was short in stature, irascible, driven, an angry micro-manager but basically honest and with a growing reputation for getting things done. He was unpopular with his political colleagues but popular with the people because he did not tolerate 'spin' or bullshit as he called it. He was plain-speaking, determined and hard-working. His propensity for wearing old-fashioned three-piece suits gave him the appearance of a diminutive Winston Churchill, a comparison that the Socialist Montrose would emphatically reject.

'Good afternoon, Assistant Commissioner,' Montrose said. 'This preliminary inquiry is to establish what happened to cause the assassination of the Princess Royal, to establish whether there are there any further threats to the royal family, and how to prevent such a tragedy ever happening again. I hardly need tell you that His Majesty will take a deep interest in our findings and I will be reporting our conclusions to him personally. Let me introduce the other participants. On my left is Foreign Secretary Richard Harcourt. You obviously know your own boss, Home Secretary Clare Barnard, and on my right is Sir Derek Llewelyn, chief of the Joint Intelligence Service, and at the end there is Jonathan Schneider, chief of the CIA in the UK.'

Sangita Sherman was puzzled as to why a representative of the Central Intelligence Agency was present. She decided not to be intimidated and said: 'May I ask why Mr Schneider is present?'

'A fair question,' Montrose replied. 'We often invite the head of the CIA to sit in when the matter being discussed may affect the

United States or if we consider that our American friends may be able to help us out.'

Jonathan Schneider was a tall, slim man with thinning light blond hair but whose deeply tanned and lined face suggested he had reached retirement age several years ago. He said: 'I can assure you that there is no hidden agenda in my being here, Mrs Sherman, and I appreciate the Prime Minister's courtesy in keeping me in the loop. The terrible event we're here to discuss has shocked my fellow countrymen almost as much as the British people. We will do all that we can to help find the culprits.'

Sangita Sherman nodded and said: 'Prime Minister, I must apologise for Sergeant Wyatt not being here. I specifically ordered him to be on time.'

'Perhaps not a bad thing,' Montrose said. 'It will give us a chance to ask you about Sergeant Wyatt first. We have your report and the report from the Garda, who interrogated Wyatt after the assassination, but there are many puzzling features. The Home Secretary has expressed her complete confidence in your abilities as the head of the Royal Protection Squad and the Special Escort Group, and we are entirely satisfied that you ordered all necessary measures, in line with standard procedure, to protect the life of the princess.'

Clare Barnard smiled at Sangita Sherman. The Home Secretary was a plump and motherly figure, an appearance that throughout her long career had fooled many people until they realised that her razor-sharp brain and unflagging devotion to detail had outwitted them. She had personally selected Sherman for promotion to Assistant Commissioner and was supporting her out of political expediency but also because of a genuine belief in Sherman's abilities.

The Prime Minister, in his usual abrupt manner, said: 'While he's not here, Mrs Sherman, tell us about Sergeant Wyatt. Speak plainly and honestly. Do you believe he was in any way culpable or incompetent?'

'Sir, he is the person I would trust above all others in the Royal Protection Squad. He has served loyally, efficiently and courageously ever since we recruited him after his career with the Special Boat Service. You will recall that incident in India involving the princess last year. I don't believe anyone on my team could have acted with more speed and skill to have disarmed and disabled that deluded maniac.'

The Foreign Secretary was a tall and distinguished Old Etonian, an unusual addition to the Socialist Cabinet, but he was a jolly, down-to-earth and companionable man, a master of languages and diplomacy, who was well-liked and welcomed by governments and embassies around the world. He asked: 'If Wyatt is so good, why is he still only a sergeant?'

Sherman said: 'Wyatt has been promoted three times but each time he has refused to accept and threatened to resign if such promotions were enforced.'

The Foreign Secretary chuckled. 'As an ambitious politician who is scrambling up the greasy pole, I find turning down promotions strange, not to say bizarre. What were his reasons?'

'Simply that he wanted to remain in the front line where the action was. Promotion would mean more administration, more paperwork, more personnel work, more desk-bound duties. Wyatt doesn't want that and, I have to admit, I was secretly pleased because there is no-one better at his job than he is.'

Sir Derek Llewelyn, whose flamboyant manner of dressing, suspiciously long hair and arrogant attitude belied his shadowy job as overseer of all Britain's intelligence gathering services, commented: 'Perhaps Wyatt has turned down promotions in order to be in place when such an assassination was required by an alternative employer.'

'You're asking whether he might be a traitor?' Sherman replied with unconcealed disapproval. 'I cannot accept that hypothesis, sir. If that was the case then Wyatt could easily have allowed that maniac in India to do the job.'

'Perhaps it wasn't the right time? After all, this time Wyatt was in Ireland and Wyatt's mother is Irish?'

Llewelyn's insinuations and smarmy tone of voice invited a sharp reply from Sherman. 'Wyatt's mother has lived in England for nearly forty years without any suspicion or stain on her character. I would credit Wyatt's mother with raising a courageous and courteous son who is utterly loyal to Britain and without racial prejudice. As you can see, I am a woman of Indian heritage and Wyatt has shown me nothing but support, courtesy and loyal service.'

'Until today…' Llewelyn sat back with a cynical smile. His comment left a suspicion hanging in the air despite Sherman's defence. Sherman had never met Llewelyn before. She sincerely hoped she would never have to meet him again.

Jonathan Schneider said: 'Forgive me if I'm asking an obvious question, I've been sidetracked by the terrible events in Hollywood, but what was the princess doing in Dundalk? She was opening some new science centre but I had to look up Dundalk on a map. It's a little out of the way, isn't it?'

Montrose answered: 'On the contrary, Jon, Dundalk is almost exactly halfway between Dublin and Belfast and already has excellent facilities for scientific research and development. The Irish Prime Minister and I were equally keen on building the research centre to strengthen the excellent relations between our two countries. I sincerely hope that the tragic death of the princess is not the first step in the return of the Troubles. On that subject, what have we found out about this institute director who murdered the princess. Derek, what have your spooks come up with?'

Sherman was gratified to see that Llewelyn was irritated by the term 'spooks' but could not answer back to the Prime Minister.

Llewelyn opened a thin folder. 'We have reports from the Garda and the Irish Secret Service as well as my own people. They give the same picture. Dr Colm Flaherty, aged 55, married with three children. He was born and educated in Cork. There is some evidence that he was an IRA sympathiser while he was a teenager but his talent for chemical engineering won him a place at Oxford University where he fitted in with great success and popularity. If there was any anti-British feeling before then there is not a trace afterwards. During his career he has worked in Dublin as well as the north of England at Imperial Chemical Industries. All his former colleagues speak of him with respect and affection. He was talented, diplomatic, popular and that's why he was selected as the perfect director for a joint Anglo-Irish venture. We have looked at him as closely as we can in the time available. Flaherty's actions have shocked his family, his friends and his colleagues. No-one can offer any explanation as to why he committed such an act.'

Sherman said: 'He was vetted by us, in conjunction with the Garda, after it was decided that the princess would be performing the opening ceremony and would be in close proximity to Dr Flaherty. We could find no evidence to suggest he was contemplating or capable of such a brutal act.'

'Whose idea was the scissors?' Llewelyn asked. 'His?'

'No,' Sherman replied. 'That was agreed by the joint Anglo-Irish planning committee. Dr Flaherty had co-operated fully with all the security measures we requested, including a body search for weapons before the princess arrived. We'd had the sniffer dogs in the new building plus the scanners for explosives. Unknown to the crowd we had marksmen on the roof of the institute. Wyatt's plain clothes undercover team, as well as many Garda officers, were mingling with the crowd watching for threats. You will see from Sergeant Wyatt's preliminary report that everything possible was done to protect the princess.'

Llewelyn said: 'Except the threat from the lunatic director with a pair of sharp ceremonial scissors.'

Sherman sighed. 'Wyatt cannot be held responsible for what was agreed by the committee. There was no reason on earth to think that Dr Flaherty would use them to kill the princess.'

The Prime Minister waved his hand with irritation. 'Mrs Sherman, I've told you that we accept everything was done to protect the princess and we are in no way questioning your procedures. No-one could have foreseen this tragedy. Derek, tell us more about Flaherty on the day of the opening. I believe that his wife reported that he seemed distracted and irritable?'

'Yes. His friends and colleagues had noticed no change in his demeanour but his wife said that Flaherty had seemed faraway and distracted for several days. He had previously had nothing but kind words for the princess but as the day of the opening ceremony drew nearer he made one or two disparaging remarks about her. But she insisted it was only minor criticisms and attributed them to the strain of work. He had been extremely busy organising the new institute as well as rehearsing the opening ceremony.'

'Umm,' Llewelyn mused. 'Someone or some organisation could have got to Flaherty, perhaps blackmailed him. Told him that he must kill the princess or we'll kill your family, that sort of thing. Terrorists are adept at that ruthless sort of threat.'

Schneider said: 'It's possible, and certainly worth following up, but what would anyone or any organisation gain from the death of the princess? She was admired, even loved, around the world, not least in my country. Any terrorist organisation hoping to score points from her death would find themselves utterly reviled the world over. The princess had no real power to affect the political process. She was simply a much loved woman, girl really, doing a difficult job brilliantly in difficult circumstances.'

'Thank you, Jon,' Montrose said. 'You have stated the conundrum behind all this perfectly. Why did she have to die? I have the reputation as a hard-bitten and cold-hearted political operator but I tell you truthfully that, having met the princess on many occasions, I am genuinely and deeply upset by her unnecessary death and I want everyone around this table to spare no effort to find the reason for this callous butchery. I will…'

Montrose was interrupted by a knock on the door of the Briefing Room. 'Come in,' he bellowed loud enough to startle his colleagues.

A Cabinet office secretary stepped into the room and said: 'Sergeant Wyatt is here, sir. He requests that he talks to Assistant Commissioner Sherman before he comes in.'

'Request denied,' Montrose snapped. 'Bring him in here now!'

Sherman noticed that her boss, the Home Secretary, had laid a hand on the Prime Minister's arm in an attempt to restrain his temper.

Wyatt entered the room. The door was silently quietly closed behind him.

Sherman could not help herself saying: 'Good grief, Christopher, you look terrible.'

Wyatt was wearing Levis and a creased white shirt under his jacket. He was unshaven and his eyes were bloodshot. He said to Sherman: 'I'm sorry I'm late, boss.'

Montrose said: 'You show disrespect to all of us by turning up late in such a condition.'

Wyatt turned to look at the Prime Minister. 'No, I show disrespect to Assistant Commissioner Sherman. I made no promises to you.'

'Are you a habitual drinker, Sergeant Wyatt?'

'No.'

'Do you often get yourself stinking drunk.'

'Only on occasions.'

'Such as what?'

'Such as after some politician sitting in a comfortable office has made a cock-up and sent me out to fight and to watch my comrades die for no good reason…'

'Chap must be a Tory,' the Foreign Secretary said.

'… or when I have seen a woman I was proud to serve stabbed to death in front of me for no good reason.'

Montrose said: 'Well, that's what we're here to find out. Sit down next to Mrs Sherman. I doubt you'll find any answers at the bottom of a whisky bottle.'

'Maybe not,' Wyatt said as he took his seat, 'but I've more chance of finding straight answers at the bottom of a bottle than I am from any politician.'

Jonathan Schneider had listened to the exchange and watched the Prime Minister's thunderously angry expression with amused astonishment. He said: 'Just as well you're not interested in promotion, Sergeant Wyatt. When I want my career to end abruptly I'll try your approach with my President!'

Wyatt said: 'I won't be browbeaten by anyone. I will respond to respect and courtesy.'

Sherman whispered: 'Please behave, Christopher. For me if not for you.'

Wyatt nodded. Reluctantly he said: 'I apologise to all of you for my lateness and my… condition.'

'Very well,' Montrose said briskly. 'Let's get on with it.' He introduced Wyatt to the other members of the committee and then said: 'I'm sorry if this upsets you again, Sergeant Wyatt, but we're going to show footage of the assassination on the big screen. Derek, would you be good enough to operate the remote.'

Film of the opening ceremony, taken from some distance away, started showing on the wall screen at the end of the room. They listened in silence to the princess's speech. Wyatt could clearly be seen at the edge of the crowd on the right of the picture.

Montrose said: 'Stop it there, Derek. Can you tell us what you were looking at, Sergeant Wyatt?'

'Yes. I was looking at the sea, the river, the mountains in the background. It was a lovely day. I had never been to Ireland before. I took a second to glance at the view.'

Clare Barnard said: 'Nice travelogue, sergeant. You took your eye off the ball.'

'No, I reject that suggestion.'

'But that's what people are saying,' Barnard persisted. 'You took your eye off the ball to enjoy the scenery. At the very second you should have been looking at the princess, at the moment that Dr Flaherty shouted and raised the scissors, you were daydreaming.'

'I was not daydreaming and I don't think the fact that I was not actually looking at the ceremony made any difference.'

Schneider said: 'Do we know what Flaherty shouted? Some reports say it sounded like "kill".'

'That's wrong,' Wyatt said. 'It was more like "ken".

'Are you sure?' Llewelyn asked.

'Yes.'

Sherman said: 'Several other people in the crowd reported it as "ken" or "Ken" with a capital K.'

'Umm,' Llewelyn said. 'Could be a man's name or ken meaning to understand. I'll get my sound experts to analyse all the footage and see if we can pin down exactly what Flaherty said.'

Llewelyn re-started the film to show Wyatt moving to shoot the director.

'There were children on the other side directly in my line of fire,' Wyatt explained. 'I had to change position.'

'Perhaps you should have thought of that beforehand,' Llewelyn said.

Wyatt ignored him and said: 'People were surging forward and I had to fire through them.'

Sherman said: 'My team are trained exhaustively in moving and firing at targets simultaneously. I consider that Sergeant Wyatt moved and fired as fast as anyone could have done in that situation.'

'If he hadn't been staring at the mountains,' Llewelyn said.

Wyatt decided not to reply. Despite his denial he had considered the same possibility over and over in his mind. He could not come to any conclusion. The guilt haunted him. The slimy chief of intelligence services might be correct in his accusation.

The film showed Wyatt glancing at the princess and then kneeling down beside the body of the dying director. Wyatt watched himself angrily grabbing the director's lapels and raising him up.

Montrose said: 'According to your report, you asked Dr Flaherty why he had done it but Flaherty did not reply.'

'That's what I told the Garda and the preliminary report that would be seen by many people. I decided to save the truth for this committee.'

The Prime Minister looked surprised. 'What is the truth?'

'Remember that my shot had hit Flaherty in the throat. He wanted to say something but had difficulty saying it. I asked him why he had done it. He replied: "Why hate us?".'

'Why hate us?' Montrose repeated. 'What did he mean by that? Who are "us"?'

'That's exactly what I asked him. At first I thought he meant that the princess hated him. I told Flaherty that the princess didn't hate him. She didn't hate anyone. Flaherty repeated what he had said. "Why hate us?" Then he said: "It was Mao" or it might even have been "killer Mao". It was definitely Mao.'

Clare Barnard asked: 'How can you be so sure he said Mao if he was having trouble speaking?'

'Because he spelt it out. He spelt out M-A-O, and then he died. It was if he was desperate for me to understand.'

There was momentary silence around the table, broken by Schneider saying: 'Jeez, was he saying that Maoist terrorists were responsible? Or that he was a Maoist sympathiser?'

'That's why I kept it quiet and waited to tell this inquiry,' Wyatt said. 'I believe that the Princess Royal's assassination could be linked to the series of unexplained attacks that have been happening around the world in recent weeks.'

Llewelyn said: 'My people have been looking at that possibility. There are certainly many similarities. Flaherty's statement about Mao could point to a possible central source of the attacks. As

Jonathan said, if a state such as China is behind all this then we could be in a very dangerous situation. Whether Sergeant Wyatt could or should have acted more quickly is open to debate but he did well to keep this information back from public knowledge.'

After another hour of discussion Montrose said: 'We've made significant progress and this will need careful handling. Sergeant Wyatt, thank you for your evidence. You can leave now.'

Wyatt stood up. Sherman also stood up and asked: 'I'd like a word with Sergeant Wyatt before he leaves. Would you excuse me for five minutes?'

'Go ahead,' Montrose said.

Sherman followed Wyatt out into the anteroom. She whispered: 'You've landed me in one hell of a heap of trouble today. I've stood up for you in there because you've backed me up many times but I can't go on doing so. Go and get yourself cleaned up and get some sleep. Take the rest of the day off and report to me at my office tomorrow, nine o'clock sharp. Don't let me down again, Christopher.'

'I won't. I'm sorry, boss.'

'Okay. Get out of here while the going's good.'

Wyatt left the anteroom. Sherman turned to go back into the Briefing Room but was surprised to find the Prime Minister waiting to speak to her. He took her arm and led her over to the window. They were looking out as Wyatt emerged and walked off down the street.

'An impressive man, that,' Montrose said. 'He had the guts to stand up to me and his service record, until now, is exemplary. I wouldn't want to meet him in a dark alley, as the saying goes.'

Sherman decided to say nothing until she understood why Montrose had come out to talk to her.

Montrose went on: 'When the country recovers from the shock of losing the princess the people will want answers, they will want scapegoats. That means him, you as his immediate superior, and me as the overall commander, the captain of the ship. I have no intention of going down with my ship. You have worked hard and overcome all sorts of obstacles and prejudices to achieve the rank you now hold. You could go all the way to Chief Commissioner. It would be a shame if this senseless killing wrecked your career. Sergeant Wyatt was not concentrating on what he was doing. If he had been truly intent on guarding the princess then he could have stopped Flaherty before he struck. It could be interpreted as gross negligence. I want you to take him apart with a fine toothcomb. The fellow already has a drink problem. See what else you can find.'

'Sir, you're not asking me to invent evidence in order to put the blame on Wyatt?'

'Certainly not,' Montrose replied. 'I'm asking you to make the most of anything you can find, for your sake as well as mine, but especially for yours. We all have our little secrets that we would rather anyone else didn't know about, don't we, Assistant Commissioner.'

'I'm not sure I understand what you mean, sir?'

Montrose leaned forward and whispered in her ear.

Sherman could not hide her shock.

Montrose smiled reassuringly. 'No need for anyone else to know. No need for you and I to have our life's work ruined. When tragic events like this assassination take place there is a need for public expiation, for scapegoats. A Metropolitan Police sergeant is expendable. An Assistant Commissioner is not. At least, not without severe social and political repercussions. Thank you for your co-operation today, Sangita. May I call you Sangita?'

'Yes, of course, sir.'

'Then thank you, Sangita. The Home Secretary thinks highly of you. Let's keep it that way. I'll let you go now.'

The Prime Minister went back into the Briefing Room. He said to Schneider: 'Will you excuse us now, Jon. I need to talk politics with my colleagues. You will, of course, have to report what you have heard to your director and to President Logan but please keep Wyatt's information to yourself as far as you are able.'

Schneider left and discreetly closed the door behind him.

Montrose remained standing. He said: 'Listen to me and listen carefully. This bloody mess has the potential to seriously damage my government and I do not intend to let it. Clare, I'll speak bluntly. You like and support Assistant Commissioner Sherman but I'm wary about her close relationship with Wyatt.'

The Foreign Secretary said: 'She's well worth a close realationship. She's a fine looking woman, tall, elegant, sexy uniform.'

Clare Barnard said: 'For God's sake, Richard, keep it zipped. Your fantasies will be the ruin of you one day. Murdo is right. We have to avoid the fallout from this mess and the last thing we need is you involved in another sex scandal. What do you want from us, Murdo?'

'Find any dirt you can about Sherman and Wyatt. Derek, the same with you. Use all the intelligence methods at your disposal to find any dirt that we can stick to Sherman and Wyatt. Especially Wyatt. I don't like jumped up police sergeants insulting me to my face. I want that bastard brought down.'

6

Office of Colonel Ashok Chatterjee, RAW Headquarters, New Delhi, India, February 17th

Colonel Ashok Chatterjee looked up from his desk and was surprised to see Premendra Dhawan standing in the doorway. 'Prem? What are you doing here? I told you to stay away for as long as you needed, at least for the mourning period.'

Prem remained standing in the doorway, uncertain of Chatterjee's mood. He said: 'I came back to work the day after the funeral. I've been working on the bombing with my team.'

'You disobeyed my specific order? You've been working without telling me?'

'Yes, sir.'

Chatterjee shook his head in exasperation. 'You look terrible, man. Have you looked at yourself in a mirror?'

'Once, sir. I haven't looked again.'

'You're still covered in scars, and your hair…'

'I'm aware of how I look, sir.'

'There are others who could investigate the bombing. Perhaps not as thoroughly as you,' Chatterjee conceded. 'But others can do the job.'

'With respect, sir, I have to do this myself. My wife has been taken away. I have to find out why she died and the reason for the attack.'

Colonel Chatterjee nodded. 'Very well, I understand, Prem. Am I that much of an ogre that you shelter in the doorway? Come in and sit down.'

'Thank you, sir.' Prem pulled up a chair and sat down opposite his boss. 'I was afraid you might discipline me, or order me to go home again.'

'I regard you as a friend, Prem, as well as a most valuable colleague. As an ascetic bachelor myself I cannot imagine how it feels to have such a woman as Rhea torn away from you. If you consider that you can best recover from her loss by returning to work and finding out who was behind this atrocious attack, then I will support you. What have you got for me?'

Prem passed over a copy of his report. Chatterjee opened the folder.

Prem said: 'The bomber's name was Laurens du Preez. He was a white South African, forty-five years old, unmarried, and worked as a farm labourer near a town named Venterstad on the border of Free State and Natal. According to the South African police, du Preez was a huge man, about six feet five inches tall, a rugby player of little talent, and a man of low intelligence. He was frequently in trouble with the law, usually for being drunk and disorderly or for committing violent acts, usually minor. But there is one serious offence, when he broke the neck of a fellow farm labourer, a black man.'

'Did the police consider it a racist attack?'

'Very much so. Du Preez was quite open in his hatred of black and coloured people.'

'That tends to confirm what witnesses, including yourself, have reported about him repeatedly shouting "kaffir", a derogatory Boer term for any coloured person. So that is a possible motive.'

'Yes, sir, but the South Africans do not consider that du Preez had the intelligence or know-how to make the bomb, even though he had access to the type of fertiliser chemical that was the explosive element.'

'So he probably had help to make it?'

'Yes. We believe that the bomb was already waiting for him in

India because he arrived here by air on a standard passport as a holidaymaker. There is no possibility that he could have smuggled such a large body bomb through our security procedures.'

'How did he get through the security gate at the Secretariat? Sheer brute strength as reported?'

'Yes. He simply barged his way past the guards and the barrier. They fired on him but the body bomb protected him, and his bulk and strength allowed him to run, despite being wounded, to the Prime Minister's office where... where my wife attempted to stop him. He was in the outer office and about to enter the Prime Minister's office when he collapsed. He must have detonated the bomb as his last dying act.'

Colonel Chatterjee shook his head in disgust. 'Infamous, useless, racist, pointless. Your wife and five other staff killed, Prime Minister Mishra lucky to have survived, although he was concussed and badly shocked.'

'Yes, sir. According to his few friends and his co-workers on the farm, du Preez had become particularly virulent in his hatred against India and Indians in the last three days before he flew in.'

'Do they know why?'

'No. They assumed it was something that had entered his head to join the general slew of hatred festering inside there. But I think we may have found the reason.'

'Go on, Prem.'

'We have dug deeper, done some hacking, and I have a particularly valuable source who confirms that du Preez was being paid to be a muscleman enforcer. He had been used at least four times to kill or seriously injure black politicians or local officials in different parts of Africa who were deemed to be getting in the way.'

'Getting in the way of whom?'

'That's why I brought this to your attention personally and left it until the end of my report.'

Chatterjee read the last paragraph of Prem's report. His eyes widened. 'I'll have to take this to the Prime Minister immediately. This could be much, much more serious than we feared?'

'Yes, sir. We could be facing an international incident here.'

Chatterjee looked at his colleague. 'At the very least, Prem. This could mean war.'

7

Office of Assistant Commissioner Sangita Sherman, New Scotland Yard, London, February 17th

Sergeant Christopher Wyatt reported to Sangita Sherman at precisely nine as ordered. Sherman had arrived two hours earlier in order to start work on a most important assignment. She realised that she needed the officer standing in front of her more than she cared to admit. She decided to modify her disciplinary approach.

'Sit down, Christopher. Would you like a cup of coffee?'

Wyatt recognised the offer as a conciliatory gesture. 'Yes, thank you, boss.' He pulled up a swing chair and sat down.

'Cream with two sugars, isn't it?'

'Yes, boss.' Wyatt relaxed as he sensed that the expected punishment was not going to be administered.

Sherman said: 'You look much better this morning, Christopher. Nice to see you back in a suit and tie and without bloodshot eyes.'

'I want to apologise again for letting you down at the Cabinet Office. I appreciate the way you stood up for me. The death of the princess has affected me more than I realised. I can't seem to get it out of my mind.'

'Why not accept the counselling on offer instead of drowning yourself in whisky?'

'I've got the drinking under control and counselling is not my thing.'

'Too unmanly for a tough guy like you, sergeant?'

Wyatt shrugged. He was stung but determined not to show it. 'If you like, boss.'

Sherman handed him the coffee. There was a trace of a shake as Wyatt accepted the cup and saucer.

'Let me be blunt, Christopher. It was stupid of you to confront the Prime Minister in the way you did.'

'I can't abide politicians, especially those who use war as a means of distracting attention away from the mistakes of their administration. I have many friends in the army who have had to pay dearly for Montrose's policies. I can't stand the trumped up little…'

'That's enough! You are a civil servant, as I am, and the Prime Minister is our boss, just as I am your boss. I wouldn't tolerate you talking to me in that manner. You have stirred up trouble for yourself and for this department. If you want to change things in politics then resign and stand for Parliament. Until then I expect you to show respect to your superiors.'

Those higher in rank, Wyatt thought, but not my superiors. He said nothing.

Sherman waited for his reply but then accepted she would not get one. She said: 'I've received the autopsy report on the princess. It's top secret so I don't want you to repeat what I'm about to tell you. Do you agree?'

'If you order me to keep it secret, I'll keep it secret.'

'Good.' Sherman opened a folder marked TOP SECRET. 'The autopsy found that *"the stab wound to the neck and left innominate vein and arch of the aorta resulted in an arteriovenous aneurysm that dissected the anterior mediastinum and ruptured into the left pleural cavity where a massive hemothorax was formed".*' I have no idea what that means except that the princess was exceedingly unlucky. Nineteen times out of twenty she would have survived the first stab wound, and probably survived the others before you stopped Flaherty, but the first stab caused a massive trauma and meant that the princess drowned in her own blood. Even if she had been in a hospital trauma unit there is nothing that could have been done to save her. Her life could not have been saved even if you had acted instantly. We do all that is humanly possible to protect our royal family but there is nothing we can do to prevent a sudden crazed attack by a maniac who is obliged by circumstance to be in close proximity.'

Wyatt nodded.

'As far as I'm concerned, Christopher, you are in no way to blame and could have done nothing to prevent the princess's death.'

'That is personally reassuring, boss, but I think the nightmare will stay with me for a long time, especially when I'm guarding other members of the royal family.'

An uncomfortable silence. Then Sherman said: 'That will not be an issue for you in future.'

'What do you mean?'

'I'm taking you off the Royal Protection Squad.'

Wyatt was momentarily too stunned to respond. Then he said: 'Boss, you can't do that!'

Sherman pointed to the crown and crossed batons insignia on the epaulette of her uniform. 'This says I can do whatever I deem best for my department.'

'But I'm…'

'You're being transferred to the Diplomatic Protection Group.'

'What! You're reducing me to guarding embassies and consulates and minor functionaries?'

'If I so order, yes. I intend to use you for guarding important foreign dignitaries. You have skills over and above those possessed by the vast majority of my team. I have need of that skill.'

Wyatt was not mollified. 'I'll bet this is the Prime Minister's doing.'

'No, it is not.'

'The royal family know me. They are used to me. They will still want me around.'

'Christopher,' Sherman said gently, 'this was a request from the highest possible authority in the land, and I don't mean the Prime Minister.'

'You mean, the king himself?'

'Come on, Christopher, you must surely have expected this? The princess was the heir to his throne. More than that, she was his beloved daughter. She was beloved by the entire nation. Have you read the newspapers, turned on your television set, seen the crowds laying wreaths outside Buckingham Palace? The country is clamouring for answers.'

'Clamouring for a scapegoat, that's what you mean, isn't it?'

'Not as far as the king is concerned. He has seen the autopsy report, you are blameless in his eyes, but can you imagine what it would be like for the royal family to see you again, to be constantly reminded that you were the one who should have protected the princess?'

'Why don't you stick the knife a bit further in, boss?' Wyatt said bitterly.

'I'm sorry, I didn't phrase that well.'

'No, it's alright, I understand. I've never thought of it that way.'

Sherman stirred her coffee thoughtfully. 'Talking of scapegoats, we've been able to protect you from the public, so far. They don't know who you are. In fact, you seem to be considered the hero for your swift response, but your name and identity will emerge sometime. The media will want to sensationalise it, sell newspapers, sell advertising on their TV shows. We may well become scapegoats, both of us. In fact, after the briefing at the Cabinet Office, I fully expect it.'

'From the Prime Minister, you mean?'

'Yes, and my boss, the Home Secretary. I get on well with her but it's the nature of politicians to throw their own children to the wolves to save their career. We have to be careful.'

Wyatt nodded. 'I appreciate your frankness, boss.'

'I still have the utmost faith in you, Christopher. I'm going to give you a job vital to the welfare and image of this country. The funeral of the princess is being held soon and the Americans will be represented by the First Lady, Martina Logan, and the Vice President, Cleytus Kefalas. I will be in charge of the overall international security operation but I'm putting you in charge of liaising with the American security team. As Britain's most important and powerful ally, it's vital that we protect the safety of such distinguished visitors. It's been arranged that the two of them will stay at the American ambassador's residence.'

'Where is that?'

'It's Winfield House in Regent's Park. It's a good choice because there is already considerable security in place. It will be a lot easier to protect them than if they stayed at a hotel or whatever. They will be in the country for possibly three days and the most important security problem will be when they go into St Paul's Cathedral for the service and then come out again. No other official appointments are scheduled.'

'St Paul's? I thought the funeral was going to be held at Westminster Abbey? That's where state funerals are usually held.'

'That story was put out for the media, to deflect attention from the real venue. Any terrorist planning to use the funeral for an attack will have wasted time before learning of the change of venue. But the real reason is that St Paul's, being surrounded by other buildings and narrow streets, is much easier to protect from a security point of view.'

Wyatt nodded. 'That makes sense. But why have you chosen me to liaise with the Yanks? I mean, it's a risky top level assignment. The Prime Minister doesn't like or trust me. What will he think about you entrusting me with such a sensitive and important job?'

'I'm paid to make such decisions, not the Prime Minister. Without blowing my own trumpet too loudly, I can say that I bring many qualities to this job. I have organisational ability, concentration, attention to detail, and skill at handling difficult and temperamental officers such as yourself.'

'I agree with all that, boss. I have none of those qualities and I would hate to have to deal with someone like me.'

Sherman could not help smiling. She reminded herself firmly not to lose herself in Wyatt's dark eyes. Why did he have to be so damn... likeable? She continued briskly. 'The American Secret Service are the most skilled in the world at protecting their leaders but here, of course, they are on relatively unfamiliar territory. Most of them are ex-special forces, as you are. You can talk their language, in military and security terms, and vice versa. We'll be allowing them to carry weapons. You can deal with these issues in a way, I frankly admit, would be impossible for me, so I'll be relying on you, Christopher.'

'Okay. I appreciate your faith in me, boss.'

'You've earned it. An American security team has already arrived at Winfield House and I've arranged for you to visit them at two o'clock this afternoon, so you've got five hours to prepare your briefing. I'm going to hold the first overall planning meeting at five o'clock, so get back for that if you can. Now, clear off and let me get on with my work.'

Wyatt stood up and opened the office door.

'By the way,' Sherman said.

Wyatt turned back. 'Yes, boss.'

'Take lunch in the canteen, not the pub. That's an order.'

'Whatever you say, boss.' Wyatt went out and closed the door behind him.

Sangita Sherman got up and looked out of her office window. The sound of Big Ben chiming floated across from Westminster. A light rain was falling on the glass and distorting her view of the outside world. It seemed appropriate. She had treated Wyatt more leniently than she would have treated most of her subordinates. As an officer, he was invaluable. As a man, she harboured a deep affection for him, an affection she would never admit to another soul. But whatever her affection for Christopher Wyatt, she was now caught in a neat trap and could not think of an escape without using him as collateral damage. With a reluctant shrug she turned back to her desk and picked up the telephone.

8

Winfield House, Regent's Park, London, February 17th

The American Secret Service agents filed out of the briefing room.

Deputy Chief Isaiah Franklin patted Wyatt on the back. 'A most informative and lucid briefing. Thank you for your input, Christopher. You covered a few things we didn't know about and one or two we wouldn't even have thought of.'

'Thank you, sir,' Wyatt replied as he collated his briefing documents.

'The First Lady and Vice President have requested to meet you before tomorrow's funeral service. I hope you can spare the time.'

Wyatt looked at his watch. 'I really ought to be getting back...'

'It won't take long, they're here in Winfield House.'

'They're here already?' Wyatt said. 'I thought they weren't flying in until tonight?'

'Another deception to fool any terrorist threat. They arrived in total secrecy earlier today. It would be wise to meet them and let them know who you are before the funeral.'

'Of course, sir.'

'Come along then,' Franklin said briskly. 'I'll show you some of the house as we go.'

Wyatt said: 'Hold on a second. I know a lot about the First Lady, she's very popular this side of the pond, but I don't know much about the Vice President, apart from his famous grin. Could you brief me so I don't put my foot in it. We don't see much of him over here.'

Franklin smiled. 'We don't see much of him in the States either. As someone once remarked, the Vice Presidency is hardly worth a bucket of cold spit. What do you want to know?'

'Well, something about his background and career, anything useful that might help me protect him.'

'Okay. The Veep is in his mid-Fifties, I guess, but very fit and active. He comes from Chicago, his ancestors came over from Greece in the nineteenth century. He was a brilliant scholar but gave up an academic career to join the army, so that's some common ground between you and him.'

'Good,' Wyatt said. 'Did he see any action?'

'He saw plenty. He became the youngest full colonel in the US Army. Then he used his distinguished military career to launch his political career. He served two terms as Mayor of Chicago before becoming an Illinois senator. He was apppointed Director of the CIA and then ran for the Presidency. He was defeated by Georgia Joe Logan as the party candidate but Logan was shrewd enough to recognise Kefalas's appeal and offered him the Vice Presidency. You'd think a man with his military background would dress smartly but the Veep favours the casual look and approach. You'll probably find him in an open-necked shirt and Levis. It's an attitude that's made him popular with blue collar and ethnic voters. What else can I say? He's in the prime of life and already the foremost candidate to become President after Logan has completed his second term. He's a widower which, to be brutally pragmatic, has won him a lot of sympathy. His wife died of cancer, I think, some years ago. I like the guy. I think you will too.'

'Okay,' Wyatt said. 'Let's go and meet the future President.'

Franklin said: 'I think you'll also be pleasantly surprised by the First Lady.'

'In what way?'

'You'll have seen on the TV that Mrs Logan is always immaculately dressed and hair-styled and she's also much more attractive in person. You've heard the saying about television adding ten pounds to anybody's weight and it does. She was Miss Santa Fe when she was seventeen.' Franklin grinned. 'I can say it to you, being a heathen Brit, but Martina Logan is a babe, even though she's over fifty. I envy the President.'

As they left the briefing room Franklin pointed out of the window to the long sweep of lawn. 'This is the largest private garden in central London, apart from Buckingham Palace. We Yankees like a lot of elbow room.'

'So does our royal family,' Wyatt said. 'How many rooms in this place?'

'Good question, Christopher. I don't know. The whole place once burned down and was rebuilt in this style, which is Georgian, I guess.'

They entered the entrance hall. Franklin said: 'Leave your weapon and other stuff with the guys here and collect it after you've seen the guests.'

Wyatt handed over his briefcase and Glock pistol as ordered.

Franklin waved his hand at the ceiling and said: 'All this fancy plasterwork is in the Adam style.'

Wyatt was not sure who Adam was, so he kept quiet.

Franklin went on: 'This place was once owned by Barbara Hutton. She sold it to the US government for one dollar. She was once married to Cary Grant, who was a Brit by birth, so it's kinda appropiate that it's now used by the US ambassador.'

Before Wyatt could admit that he had no idea who Barbara Hutton was, Franklin had swept on down another corridor. He stopped outside a door and nodded to the two agents guarding the entrance.

Franklin said: 'This is the Garden Room. The First Lady and the Veep are having a drink, relaxing after the journey. I'll make sure they're ready to meet you.'

Franklin knocked lightly, opened the door and looked in. 'Sergeant Wyatt is here.'

Wyatt heard a familiar female voice say: 'Sure, bring him in, Stack.'

Franklin led Wyatt in to a large room, decorated on a Chinese theme, which overlooked the garden at the rear of the house.

The First Lady was sitting on a sofa drinking a cup of coffee.

Franklin said: 'Mam, this is Sergeant Christopher Wyatt of the Diplomatic Protection Group. He will be in charge of the British contingent guarding you tomorrow.'

Martina Logan smiled.

Wyatt saw that Franklin had not been wrong in his estimation of her attractiveness. He said: 'It's an honour to meet you, mam.'

'It's a pleasure to meet you, sergeant. I'm sure you'll look after us well tomorrow.'

'I'll do my best, mam.'

The Vice President, was standing at the window with a glass of whisky in his hand. As Franklin had predicted, Kefalas was casually dressed in an open-necked shirt. He stepped forward and held out his hand to Wyatt.

'I'm Cleytus Kefalas, sergeant. As one ex-military man to another, it's good to meet you.'

Wyatt controlled a smile as he was given the famous 'Cleytus Grin'. Kefalas was a few inches shorter than Wyatt but he radiated charisma and energy.

Wyatt said: 'My military career was not nearly as distinguished as yours, sir.'

'You Brits with your damn modest self-effacement. I know you were in the Special Boat Service, Chris. They take only the best and there is no finer fighting unit in the world.' He turned to the First Lady. 'We're in safe hands with this guy, Marty.'

A female voice said: 'I wish I could be as confident.'

Wyatt turned around to see who had spoken. A woman, dressed in a dark grey business suit with the badge of the US Secret Service at her waist, had entered the Garden Room by another doorway. She was carrying a laptop and a sheaf of folders.

Isaiah Franklin said: 'Christopher, this is Sergeant Linda Marquez of the United States Secret Service.'

Martina Logan said: 'Linda not only guards me, sergeant, but she keeps me informed and organised. I couldn't do without her. She is my personal assistant. Ladies and gentlemen, won't you please sit down.'

Linda Marquez sat down on the sofa next to her boss. The others selected an armchair except Cleytus Kefalas, who remained standing.

Wyatt said: 'Is it unusual for a Secret Service agent to also act as the First Lady's secretary?'

Linda Marquez was visibly annoyed. She said: 'I am not a secretary. I am a personal assistant. And, no, it is not at all unusual.'

Martina Logan said: 'Sergeant Wyatt, it's important that I have someone I can trust, not only to organise my official affairs but also to protect me. I trust Linda because she is a superb organiser and she is highly trained in personal defence. As you see, we are from the same sort of background and we understand each other. I have complete faith in Linda.'

Wyatt nodded. 'I understand. Will you be helping to guard the First Lady tomorrow, Sergeant Marquez?'

'Yes. I'll be accompanying her.'

'It's just that I didn't notice you at the security briefing. I specifically requested that all members of the American security team be present. It's important that everyone, and I do mean everyone, knows exactly what they are supposed to be doing, where they should be and, most importantly, that if a member of the security team, British or American, tell you to do something, you do it immediately and without question.'

Linda took a deep breath and said: 'I know exactly what I'll be doing, sergeant. I'll be travelling with the First Lady in her limousine.'

'Where will you be stationed when the funeral is in progress? Are you going into the cathedral.'

'No, I'll wait outside.'

'Doing what?'

'Watching.'

'Watching for what?'

'Any threats to the First Lady or the Vice President. What else would I be watching? The scenery, as you did?'

Martina Logan asked: 'What did you mean by that?'

Wyatt said: 'I understand what Sergeant Marquez is implying, mam. She can stand outside with me.'

'I don't need you as a nursemaid, sergeant.'

'If your bite is as tough as your bark I'm sure you don't need any nursemaid.'

'Whoa, whoa,' Isaiah Franklin said. 'Take the gloves off, you two. Chris, Linda is fully briefed and capable. Linda, it's not a bad idea for you to stay with Chris outside. He is, after all, our British liaison officer.'

Wyatt studied Linda Marquez. She had taken off her spectacles. She looked desperately tired, edgy, restless and combative. Her black hair had been inexpertly chopped with scissors. There was a strange faraway look in her green eyes. Wyatt considered whether she had been drinking or was taking drugs. Whatever the reason she was clearly brittle and not in full control of herself. Wyatt decided she was not up to the job. He would have to 'nursemaid' her carefully.

Franklin was saying: 'Sergeant Wyatt made a very valuable contribution to the briefing. His team are fully prepared, as is ours. The security around the cathedral will be watertight. All roads around the cathedral will be closed and blocked off, there will be marksmen on the roof of the cathedral and on all surrounding buildings. All those buildings will be evacuated and manned by British army personnel and they will be thoroughly searched for any conceivable hidden threat. Even the airspace around the cathedral will be protected by concealed ground-to-air missile units and by RAF fighters on standby. There will be hundreds of police officers controlling the crowd, in uniform and plain clothes, watching for threats. After all, it's not just we Americans, there are statesmen and royalty from all over the world coming to represent their countries. I have every expectation that the mourning in the crowd will be profound, and might spill over into hysteria or sudden random acts of imagined revenge or something.'

Kefalas took a sip of whisky and asked: 'So the only time we'll be open targets is when we have to walk from the car and into the cathedral and then on the way out.'

'That's correct, sir,' Franklin said. 'The Beast has been flown over from the States as an extra precaution.'

Wyatt asked: 'What is "the Beast" or whatever you said?'

Linda Marquez ostentatiously shook her head as if appalled by Wyatt's ignorance.

Franklin said: 'The Beast is our nickname for the Presidential Cadillac. It's specially adapted to be bullet proof and bomb proof. We are ready for anything. There is no way anyone can get to you.'

Kefalas made a sceptical harrumphing sound. He said: 'Deputy Chief, have you ever read *The Day of the Jackal*?'

'I understand what you mean,' Franklin said. 'A lone assassin, highly trained, unknown to the authorities, utterly ruthless. It's the worst nightmare. But that sort of operation takes a lot of preparation and it's been only days since the tragic death of the Princess Royal until now.'

Wyatt nodded. 'We've put our heads together and shared our years of experience to assess where any threat may come from. Deputy Chief Franklin and I will prepare our reports and schedule tonight and dispatch them to you tonight so that you all know exactly what is going to happen tomorrow.'

Linda Marquez said: 'It's a pity you didn't do that in Dundalk, Sergeant Wyatt. We needn't be here if you had.'

Wyatt used all his self-control to keep his voice even: 'What do you mean by that remark, sergeant?'

Martina Logan, baffled by the hostile exchange, said: 'Take it easy, Linda. What are you talking about?'

'Mam, Sergeant Wyatt was in charge of the security unit when the princess was murdered.'

Martina Logan looked at Wyatt. 'Was it you who shot that Dr Flaherty?'

'Yes, mam.'

Linda said: 'You were enjoying the scenery, weren't you, sergeant? If you had been on the ball you could have dropped the guy before he had time to act.'

Kefalas said: 'That's harsh, Linda. I've watched the film several times. For Sergeant Wyatt to move and fire as he did was skill of the highest order. No-one could have reacted more quickly. You've never been in a combat zone, Linda. I have. Sergeant Wyatt has. We're all human. The shock of seeing what Flaherty was doing would paralyse anyone into momentary inaction, even a highly trained SBS operative. Sergeant Wyatt's response was exemplary.'

Martina Logan put her hand on Linda's arm. 'Calm down, Linda. I have faith in Sergeant Wyatt.'

'Well, it's more than the royal family has,' Linda replied. To Wyatt she said: 'I understand you've been taken off the Royal Protection Squad by order of the king himself.'

'That's not strictly true,' Wyatt said.

'Not good enough for British royalty but good enough for the colonial cousins. Is that it, sergeant? I don't know if the Brits regard this as a sick joke but I'm not laughing.'

Martina Logan said: 'That's enough, Linda. Just shut up.'

Linda said: 'I'm sorry, mam, but I'm directly responsible for your safety. If Sergeant Wyatt screws up again and is not up to the job then I will get the comeback as well.'

'I'm up to the job, *sergeant*.'

'Just make sure you are, *sergeant*, because if anything happens to the First Lady or Vice President then I'll make sure the only security job you get in future is a night guard in a shoe factory.'

Wyatt stood up. 'If you'll all excuse me I have work to do. You'll receive my report by nine o'clock tonight.'

The Secret Service agents patrolling the grounds looked on curiously as their boss ran out of Winfield House and trotted across the parking lot to catch up with the British guy they had met earlier.

'Chris!' Isaiah Franklin called out. 'Wait a minute, man. Wait a minute.'

Wyatt stopped at his Range Rover and took several deep breaths. He looked up at the grey scudding clouds. The distant roar of the London traffic was like an unbearable cacophony. The murderous anger was like a vice around his heart and his stomach. He could not loosen its grip.

Franklin trotted towards him.

Wyatt said: 'If she was a man I'd have ripped her bloody head off.'

'Listen, Chris, there's something...'

'Doesn't that bitch think I feel grief too? I adored the princess. Doesn't Marquez think that I haven't asked myself that question a thousand times, is there any more I could have done to stop Flaherty?'

'Chris, Chris, please calm down. Have you seen the autopsy report?'

'I've been told about it.'

'I've seen it, so has the Veep and the President, of course. No-one in the know is blaming you, Chris. Sergeant Marquez has not seen the autopsy report. She is not in the loop.'

'The only loop she deserves is a rope around her bloody neck.'

'Stop it, Chris. Linda is a valuable and competent officer, but she is not in her normal frame of mind.'

'Why not?'

'Her husband just committed suicide.'

'I'd have done the same if I was married to her.'

It was Franklin's turn to be angry. 'Jeez, Wyatt! That's a cheap shot. The poor woman's on medication. She went to her husband's funeral yesterday before flying here. Cut her some slack. She's off her head with grief.'

Some of Wyatt's anger melted away. 'Okay. That was a nasty thing to say. I'm sorry, chief.'

'Call me Stack. I'm not your boss.'

'Why do they call you Stack?'

Franklin shrugged. 'What can I say? I like pancakes. Listen, Chris, let me apologise on Linda's behalf. I tell you, she's a good kid. She is an exceptionally competent agent and normally as polite and sunny as can be.'

'A regular Pollyanna, eh? If she is on drink or drugs or off her head with grief she shouldn't be here.'

'We couldn't stop her, and Mrs Logan insisted she came. Linda will do her job. These are strange times, Chris. Something bad is going down. I can feel it in my bourbon. What with the princess, that business in Hollywood, the bombing in India, more attacks in Germany, mass hysteria in Japan over that baby food thing. It's more than coincidence.'

'I agree,' Wyatt said. 'I've been feeling the same in my single malt.'

Franklin said: 'Linda Marquez is right about one thing. If anything bad happens tomorrow then we'll all be working as night guards in that shoe factory.'

9

New Scotland Yard, London, February 17th

Christopher Wyatt looked out of his office window at the traffic moving in the street below. He was still keyed-up and restless. What Sergeant Marquez had said to him earlier had cut him deeper than he would have thought possible. Wyatt recognised a kernel of truth in what she had said, what many people had said, despite the autopsy report. He *had* been looking elsewhere, he *had* almost been daydreaming. And the sense of foreboding expressed by Deputy Chief Franklin also played on his mind. Wyatt sensed that he had been so distracted recently that he had missed something, missed an obvious link or a vital clue.

His mobile phone rang. He answered: 'Chris Wyatt.'

'Chris? Where are you? It's a quarter to ten. You were supposed to be here at eight. Are we going out to eat or what?'

Another mistake.

'I'm sorry, Steph. I haven't been able to get away. I should have called you. I'm still here with the other guys finalising arrangements for the funeral tomorrow.'

The large open plan office was deserted.

'When do you think you'll be finished?'

'Hard to tell, love. I still have to finish the security schedule for tomorrow and send it over to the Americans.'

The schedule had been sent to Winfield House over an hour before.

'I could cook something? Have something ready when you've finished?'

'No, don't go to any trouble. The boss wants to see us all in a few minutes. I could be stuck here for hours.'

'Okay, never mind. Will you be coming over when you've finished work?'

'No. I'd better go back to my place tonight. It's been a tough day, I need to relax and get a good night's sleep.'

'I know how to relax you, darling.'

'Have to go, Steph. The boss is glowering at me, waiting for me to finish.'

'You shit...'

Wyatt cut off the call. How do women always sense when you're lying to them? It was all going wrong with Stephanie. Even so, why had he turned down a chance to spend the night with a beautiful and willing woman? Wyatt put it out of his mind. That conundrum would have to wait for another day.

Wyatt checked that the office door was closed and that no-one was looking through the glass partition. He opened the bottom drawer of his desk and took out a half bottle of whisky. It was against all the rules and all common sense but he could not settle down without a drink. He took a long swig and put the bottle back in the drawer.

Wyatt decided to check his messages for any last minute problems. He did not understand how computers worked and stuck rigidly to operating them in the basic way he had been instructed. He checked, for the sixth time, the schedule and security arrangements for the funeral. He was satisfied that he and his American colleagues had 'covered all the bases' as they phrased it.

Wyatt scrolled down the list of reports. It was now routine for the intelligence services of friendly, and unfriendly countries, to share information of common interest since the upsurge of the scourge of terrorism.

Since the start of the year there had been several instances of attacks or sabotage by individuals who had shouted something at the commencement of their crime. Wyatt had heard Flaherty shouting something like 'ken'. Before the toxic gas attack in Hollywood the perpetrator had been heard to shout 'kisser' or 'kicker' before he took his own life. The baby food poisoner in Japan had also taken his own life but had been heard to be muttering 'fay' or 'flay' before infecting the production line. The Japanese authorities had no idea what it might have signified. Another perpetrator in Germany had shouted 'cop'. A helicopter pilot who had flown a kamikaze mission into a Canadian oil refinery was shouting 'hover' before he died in a gigantic fireball that had also taken the lives of thirty workers. There were many other instances, and they were increasing in frequency and severity.

Not one intelligence or police organisation had been able to fully understand what these perpetrators had been shouting or been able to establish any connection between them but Wyatt sensed, as many others did, that there simply had to be a connection. He was about to switch off when he noticed a new report, the last in the file. It was a long report and he decided to save it for another day. Then a word sprang off the screen and fully caught his attention. The word was 'Mao'.

Wyatt took another swig of whisky, put the bottle back in its hiding place, and decided to read the full report. It had been sent from the Research and Analysis Wing of Indian intelligence and its author was someone named Premendra Dhawan. It was a report on the recent attempted assassination of the Indian Prime Minister by human bomb. The perpetrator, who had died in the explosion, had been shouting 'kaffir' and had now been proved to be in the pay of Chinese agents who had hired him to commit acts of violence against troublesome African politicians and activists opposed to the insidious Chinese encroachment into Africa. The perpetrator was a possible Maoist sympathiser and agent.

Wyatt remembered how Dr Flaherty had struggled to say the word 'Mao' and how he had desperately spelled it out before expiring. Wyatt was excited by this first discovery of a common link.

The implications of such a link were too fearful to contemplate. He did not know whether Indian intelligence had been given the details about Flaherty's dying words. He suspected not but he considered it vital that Premendra Dhawan was informed. They might be able to establish a definite link between the two attacks.

Wyatt picked up the secure telephone to ring Dhawan but then remembered that India Standard Time was six or seven hours ahead of Greenwich Mean Time. It would be the middle of the night in New Delhi. The phone call would have to wait until after tomorrow's funeral.

Wyatt took another swig of whisky and put the bottle back in the drawer. Seconds later Assistant Commissioner Sherman opened the office door. She stood in the doorway and said sternly: 'Chris? What are you doing still here?'

'I've been checking the schedule again, boss.'

'We've been over it several times already. Why don't you go home and get some rest?'

'*You're* still here, boss.'

'I get paid much more than you to be here.'

'That's true. Harry can't see much of you these days.'

Sherman glared at Wyatt and said: 'That's a damn nasty thing to say. That's not like you. Have you been drinking again?'

Wyatt was genuinely bewildered. 'No, I haven't been drinking,' he lied. 'What do you mean nasty, boss? I don't understand.'

'Don't you listen to the office gossip?'

'I still don't know what you…'

'Harry and I separated weeks ago. We're getting a divorce.'

'I swear I didn't know, boss. I wasn't being nasty. I'm sorry to hear that. What caused the break?'

'That's not your business, sergeant.'

'No, no, of course not. You may not want to hear it but I like you as a friend as well as a colleague. I only met Harry a few times but I liked him. I'm truly sorry.'

Sangita Sherman wanted to say something but decided not to. She was visibly upset by the exchange and Wyatt changed the subject quickly.

'While you're here boss, I've found a connection between the attack on the princess and the attack on the Indian Prime Minister. We've received a report from…'

'Chris, for goodness sake, it's nearly ten o'clock. We've got a huge job to do tomorrow. Whatever you've found out can wait until after the funeral.'

'Yes, but boss, this might be vitally important.'

'Stop it, Chris. Switch that computer off and go home. We must not take our eye off the ball tomorrow.'

'But it'll take only a minute to…'

'Go home, Chris. That's a direct order.'

Wyatt shrugged. 'You're the boss.'

'Yes, and don't you forget it.' It was said with a smile.

Wyatt put on his jacket. He brushed past Sherman as she stood in the doorway. He caught a whiff of her delicate perfume. Harry Sherman must be crazy. He said: 'Good night, boss.'

'Don't be late tomorrow,' Sherman said to his back as he walked off down the corridor.

'Wouldn't dare, boss,' Wyatt said as he entered the lift. He turned and smiled as the lift doors closed.

Damn, damn, damn, Sherman thought. That smile almost persuaded her to walk away and let the Prime Minister do his own dirty work. She went over to Wyatt's desk, took a handkerchief from her uniform pocket, opened the bottom drawer and, using the handkerchief to avoid smudges, carefully picked up the half empty bottle of whisky.

10

St Paul's Cathedral, London, February 18th

Christopher Wyatt and Linda Marquez stood at the foot of the steps leading up to the Great West Door, the colonnaded entrance of St Paul's Cathedral. The afternoon was bitterly cold with a light and icy rain falling on the city. The rain was whipping into the faces of the crowd, driven by a gusty wind. Even the weather was in mourning.

Linda had turned up the collar of her long black overcoat and was keeping her hands in the pockets. Even so, she was shivering.

Wyatt was wearing brown leather gloves, his hands crossed respectfully in front of his grey overcoat. Linda was struck by his stillness. He stared straight ahead and he had not moved for at least half an hour. His hair was soaked and rivulets of rainwater ran down his face but he did not move to wipe them away. They had not exchanged words since a perfunctory greeting an hour ago when Deputy Chief Franklin had ordered Linda to stay with Wyatt.

Linda was overwhelmed with sadness, for herself, for the royal family, for the British people, even for Wyatt. This was her second funeral in three days, first for her husband, now for the princess. Life was so fragile, so vulnerable, so eternally confusing.

Across the road, beyond the tight cordon of police officers, the crowd was eerily silent. The funeral service was being relayed outside, sound only, so that they could hear the hymns and prayers for a lost daughter, a lost princess, a lost monarch.

Linda looked up. The vast grey bulk of the cathedral pressed down on her. She could glimpse the marksmen on the rooftops of surrounding buildings. In the window of each building was an armed soldier, each one silhouetted against the artificial light, the only bright light warming the early afternoon gloom.

Linda was startled by a sudden message through her earpiece. She turned to Wyatt and said: 'The service is over. They'll be coming out soon.'

Wyatt simply nodded and did not look at her.

A group of Anglican bishops, church dignitaries and representatives of other faiths, emerged from the cathedral in solemn procession and lined up down the steps, either side of the doorway, to await the coffin of the princess. A black limousine hearse drove slowly around the corner and pulled up at the foot of the steps. The coffin of the Princess Royal, draped in the royal standard and borne on the shoulders of eight volunteers from the Brigade of Guards, all wearing full red and gold uniform, was carried out into the rain.

Linda saw Wyatt move. He took one look at the coffin and then looked away. The pain in his expression was palpable. He stood with head bowed as the coffin was slowly eased into the back of the hearse.

Linda said: 'I'm sorry for the way I spoke to you yesterday. I can see how much the princess meant to you.'

Wyatt did not look up. He said: 'It doesn't matter.'

'Yes, it does. Stack told me about the autopsy report.' Wyatt did not respond, so Linda went on: 'Truth is, I've been on medication and I'd had a drink. Several drinks. The First Lady would can me if she found out.'

Wyatt accepted the olive branch. 'Franklin told me about your husband. It was gutsy of you to carry on with your schedule after that. I can't imagine how hard it must have been for you.'

The royal family, striving to maintain their regal poise in the face of overwhelming grief, emerged from the cathedral to watch the hearse pull away. A group of three black limousines pulled up at the steps to carry away the royals.

Linda said: 'Until yesterday I thought everything I had was secure and settled and good. It isn't.'

'In what way do you mean?' Wyatt asked.

'Something happened last night. I'm not sure…'

The voice of Deputy Chief Franklin came through her earpiece: 'All agents be alert. First Lady and the Veep are about to come out.'

The Beast appeared around the corner and took the place of the royal cars as they drove away.

Linda said: 'My people are coming out, Wyatt. Let's get them safely into the car and back to Winfield House, then we can breathe again.'

Wyatt did not reply. Linda looked around and was surprised to see that Wyatt was answering a call on his cell phone. He said: 'Okay, boss, I'll be right there.'

Wyatt began to walk away.

Linda said: 'Hold on, Wyatt, where are you going? You're supposed to stay here.'

Wyatt called back: 'The boss wants me around the other side immediately. Something's happening. I've got to go.'

Wyatt disappeared around the corner to the north side of the cathedral. Linda found herself swearing under her breath. 'Goddamn stupid prick.'

Martina Logan and Vice President Kefalas were shaking hands with the Archbishop of Canterbury. The archbishop was standing with his back to Linda. He was holding the pastoral staff of office, a heavy silver and brass crozier, in his left hand.

Linda watched in blank amazement as a bishop standing next to the archbishop suddenly stepped up and punched the archbishop in the face. There was a collective gasp of shock from the crowd. The bishop wrenched the crozier out of the archbishop's hand and raised it above his head. With a demented cry he swung the crozier down on Martina Logan's head. The First Lady fell to her knees, clutching her head with both hands. The bishop struck her again, an awkward glancing blow that hit the hands and not the head. Cleytus Kefalas tried to grab the crozier but the bishop kicked him away and jabbed the crozier into his face. Kefalas, blood running from his nose, staggered backwards.

Martina Logan was still on her knees, her face now covered with blood. The bishop let out another demented wail as he raised the crozier to strike Martina Logan on the head.

Linda raised her pistol and fired two shots. The bishop dropped the crozier. It clattered and rang on the stone. The bishop clutched at his back. Red blotches stained his white surplice. He moaned in pain, then pitched forward and tumbled down the steps.

Martina Logan, blood and rain water streaming down her face, was being helped to her feet. An ambulance shot around the corner and screeched to a halt at the foot of the steps. Police and Secret Service agents moved in to form a tight cordon around the ambulance.

Wyatt reappeared around the corner and looked at the scene with astonishment. Linda was still holding the pistol in the firing position. Her hands were shaking.

'What the hell happened?' Wyatt asked.

'I had to shoot the bishop,' Linda whispered. 'He was going to kill Marty.'

Wyatt looked at the prone body of the bishop. The body was being covered with some sort of ecclesiastical cloth but blood was trickling down the grey stone steps.

Wyatt said gently: 'Put the gun down, Linda.'

Deputy Chief Franklin pushed his way through the crowd and said: 'What happened here?'

'Linda had to shoot the bishop,' Wyatt said.

'*Linda* shot him? I thought it must have been you.'

'No. I wasn't here.'

Franklin took the gun out of Linda's hands. 'Wasn't here?' he repeated. 'Why not? This was your allotted station.'

Wyatt said: 'I had a call from Sherman. There was…'

'Something more important around the corner,' Linda said savagely. 'You left me here to deal with this mess.'

'Looks like you dealt with it very well,' Wyatt said. 'Try to calm down, Linda. The adrenaline makes people angry and aggressive in a situation like this.'

'I don't need lectures from you,' Linda said, her eyes burning with fury. 'Perhaps you didn't want to be here, Wyatt.'

'What do you mean by that?'

'Seems like you're always looking somewhere else when people are being attacked.'

'That's not true. My boss called me away.'

'What did she want?'

'I don't know. She had gone by the time I got there.'

'How convenient!'

'You nasty cow. I wasn't…'

'Stop it, you two,' Franklin ordered. 'Linda, I'm going to take you to the embassy. It'll be safer and more secure. The British police will want to talk to you, and so will I. Chris, I want you back at Winfield House for the debriefing. I'll get my guys to give you a lift.'

The traffic away from St Paul's Cathedral was crawling, virtually gridlocked. Wyatt was in the back of the car. There were three Secret Service agents in the car with him. The driver was saying: 'It's true I tell you. That crazy bishop was shouting "bash, bash, bash" as he swiped the First Lady and the Veep with that damn hooked thing.'

Wyatt asked: 'Are you sure he was saying "bash"?'

'Sure as I can be. I was as close as anyone and I'm sure he was shouting "bash", and that's exactly what he was doing!'

The agent in the back with Wyatt said: 'Hey, Sam, if you were so close how come Linda got the drop on the bishop before you did?'

'She was the only one of us with a clear uniterrupted shot,' Sam replied. 'Okay, she reacted quicker as well, I'll give her that. She's already got the softest job in the Service, babysitting Mrs Logan. Thought I'd give the girl a chance for more promotion.'

His back seat colleague said: 'She's a real fox, that Linda. I could wake up in the morning to that black hair, those green eyes and that body. Perhaps there's a chance now that her hubby swallowed the bullet.'

'That's not how he did it,' Sam said. 'I knew Mike O'Brien. He was a good guy, you know, a straight cop and a straight talker, ballsy. I know his captain even better. The captain gave me all the skinny on how Mike got himself promotion to the big precinct in the sky. They told Linda a pack of lies because the real story was too strange to swallow. You guys wouldn't believe how he did it.'

'Why don't you try us?'

'Nah. I swore to the captain I wouldn't breathe a word.'

Sam was finally coaxed into relating the true facts about Michael O'Brien's suicide. The other two American agents mocked him and told him he was crazy if he thought they would buy that load of hokum. Wyatt listened with mounting dismay but also mounting excitement.

The car was stationary, caught in another traffic snarl up. Wyatt said: 'Thanks for the lift, guys.' He opened the car door, leapt out on to the pavement and began running back in the direction they had just travelled.

11

United States Embassy, London, February 18th

Lieutenant Paul Belasco nodded to the two armed Marines guarding Interview Room Five. He went in. Room Five was a small windowless room furnished with a desk and office chairs. The pastel green walls were decorated with prints of landscape scenes from American national parks.

'I'm Lieutenant Paul Belasco. I'm deputy chief of embassy security. You are Constable Ablett of the Royal Protection Squad?'

The man sitting in front of the desk answered: 'Yes, sir.'

'What can I do for you?'

'Well, sir, I believe you spoke to my colleague, Sergeant Wyatt earlier?'

'Yes. He said he needed to speak to Sergeant Linda Marquez urgently.'

'That's right. I understand she refused to speak to Wyatt so we are hoping she'll consent to speak to me.'

Belasco reached inside his jacket and took out a pistol. He ordered: 'Put your hands on your head.'

The British officer did as he was asked. Belasco searched inside the officer's jacket and took out two sets of identity documents and a security pass. Belasco studied the documents and then said: 'I don't like being played for a fool. It makes me angry. Especially in a climate of terrorism such as we're facing at the moment.'

The British officer did not reply.

Belasco said: 'Do you think we are incompetent, Sergeant Wyatt?'

'I see that you are not, sir.'

'Our facial recognition technology identified you at the first gate. You've been to the embassy before so you are on file. You're not armed so we let you come through. Why the subterfuge?'

'I have to speak to Linda Marquez. She refused to talk to me when I rang earlier. I thought if I could get my foot in the door by pretending to be Ablett she might speak to me and I might persuade her to talk to me.'

'What do you want to talk about?'

'It would take too long to explain but I can assure you it might be vitally important, for both our countries. I believe Linda unknowingly has information that is vital to our mutual national security.'

'Listen, Wyatt, why not go through the proper channels, arrange a meeting through our superior officers. Who is your superior officer?'

'Assistant Commissioner Sangita Sherman of the Metropolitan Police at New Scotland Yard.'

'Is she aware that you're pulling a stunt like this?'

'No. I can't afford to tell anyone about what I've found out until I've talked to Linda. I can't go through channels until I'm sure of what Linda knows.'

Belasco considered Wyatt's statement. 'I've checked you out, Sergeant Wyatt. I'm impressed so I'm going to give you the benefit of the doubt. Sergeant Marquez is still in the embassy and her debriefing has been completed so I'm going to ask her to come and talk to you. Please allow me a few minutes to locate her.'

'Of course,' Wyatt said. 'Thank you, lieutenant.'

Belasco opened the door. Then he turned back to Wyatt. 'Being aware of your capabilities as outlined in your service record, I'm going to keep you locked in this room until Sergeant Marquez is found. If you try any funny business, these guards out here are under orders to shoot you dead, no questions asked.'

'No funny business, I promise,' Wyatt said.

It was nearly an hour later when the door was unlocked. The guards trained their carbines on Wyatt as Belasco walked into the room. Linda Marquez was behind him.

Wyatt stood up.

Linda said: 'What do you want, Wyatt?'

'Linda, you must listen to me. You have to talk to me because what you were told about your husband's death was false. You were not given the true facts. You may know something that...'

Linda Marquez looked desperately tired but her eyes blazed with anger. 'What is with you, Wyatt? Don't you ever know when to stop? How dare you seek to get to me by telling a pack of lies about my husband? You should...'

'Linda, I'm not crazy, I'm not lying. I beseech you to believe me. Your husband knew something about what is going on with all these tragic events that are occurring.'

Linda said: 'That's a crock, Wyatt. Michael was a New York cop. He would have told me if he had found out anything. Chief Dempsey of the NYPD gave me all the facts about Michael's suicide.'

'No, he lied to you to protect you from the truth.'

'Enough! You accuse a long-serving New York police captain, a respected colleague of my husband, of telling me lies? You're up to something, Wyatt. I don't trust you, I don't like you and I'm not going to talk to you.' To Belasco she said: 'Lieutenant, this man was present at the assassination of the Princess Royal and at the attack on the First Lady and Vice President today. I believe he may be a danger. I am not going to talk to him. I suggest you contact Assistant Commissioner Sherman and hand the problem to her. This guy is a loose cannon of the worst sort.'

Belasco said: 'That's good enough for me, Linda.'

Linda moved away.

Wyatt said: 'For God's sake, Linda! You saw what happened today. You know better than anyone that there are strange things happening...'

Linda turned back. 'I'll tell you what I saw this morning. I saw a cowardly bastard desert his post and expose my people to danger, a coward who might have protected the life of his own princess if he hadn't been daydreaming. Stay away from me, Wyatt, or I'll take you down.'

Linda was gone. Belasco said: 'You're staying in this room, sergeant.'

Belasco went out and locked the door behind him.

Two hours later the door was opened again. Standing beside Belasco was Assistant Commissioner Sangita Sherman.

Wyatt said: 'Hello, boss.'

'Sergeant, you are in such a world of trouble that I scarcely know where to begin.'

'I accept that I've broken…'

'Shut up, sergeant. You were supposed to go back to Winfield House for the American debriefing. Apparently you leapt out of the car taking you back there without any explanation or apology. Then I saw you back at the Yard and ordered you to attend my debriefing session. You flagrantly disobeyed my direct order and walked out on me.'

'I apologise for that, but…'

'Now I find out that you stole the identity documents of a respected fellow officer in order to get into this embassy for some bizarre reason.'

'Boss, it's not a bizarre reason, it's a very good reason. Linda Marquez may have vital information that she doesn't even know she has. She might hold a vital key to the puzzle of all these strange attacks, as happened today. It's imperative that you get them to make Linda Marquez talk to me. Let me explain. I…'

'Save it, sergeant. You'll have to explain yourself, not to me but to the Prime Minister. He wants to see you… now.'

12

Office of the Prime Minister, 10 Downing Street, London, February 18th

Sergeant Christopher Wyatt and Assistant Commissioner Sangita Sherman were guided through the secure garden entrance into Number Ten Downing Street. They walked through a maze of narrow corridors and cramped office rooms until they arrived at the office of the Prime Minister.

Murdo Montrose was standing but Foreign Secretary Richard Harcourt, Home Secretary Clare Barnard, intelligence co-ordinator Sir Derek Llewelyn and CIA chief Jonathan Schneider were sitting and watching television footage of the attack at St Paul's Cathedral.

Wyatt and Sherman stood and watched Linda Marquez shooting the Bishop of Carlisle.

'It makes entertaining viewing for millions of people worldwide, doesn't it?' Montrose snapped sarcastically. 'Switch it off, Derek. Another bloody mess and, once again, we find Sergeant Wyatt on the spot. Or, rather, not on the spot where he should have been. The media are camped outside the gates of Downing Street screaming for answers, we are in the midst of an international diplomatic crisis but we didn't mind waiting, so thank you for gracing us with your presence, sergeant. I've filled in the time by a long conversation with the President of the United States explaining why his wife and his second-in-command were attacked and severely wounded by an Anglican bishop!'

Wyatt refused to rise to the bait. He asked: 'What's the condition of the First Lady and Vice President? I haven't seen any news reports.'

Clare Barnard replied. 'The First Lady needed stitches in a deep cut on her scalp. The Vice President suffered a sprained wrist, severe contusions to his abdomen and cuts and bruises to his face and scalp. Also a lovely swollen black eye. The bishop died instantly.'

Montrose went on: 'Sergeant Wyatt, I understand that you again went absent without leave. Where did you find him, Assistant Commissioner? In the nearest pub?'

'No, sir. Sergeant Wyatt had been detained at the American embassy.'

The Prime Minister's expression showed his surprise. 'What was he doing at the American embassy and why was he being detained?'

'Sergeant Wyatt had attempted to gain entry to see Sergeant Marquez by using a false identity, security documents that he stole from another officer in the Diplomatic Protection Group.'

This time Montrose spoke to Wyatt directly. 'Why did you want to see Marquez?'

Wyatt was determined to remain calm. 'Sir, I believe Sergeant Marquez has information that may be of value in establishing the cause of the recent spate of attacks, such as occurred today.'

'If Marquez has such information, why hasn't she given it to her own people? Why do you feel the necessity to use deception to get into an allied embassy in order to interrogate her?'

'Because Sergeant Marquez is not aware that she has such information. It concerns her husband and the nature of his behaviour before he committed suicide. I believe it may provide a clue to the cause of these attacks that have been happening around the world.'

Sir Derek Llewelyn spoke up. 'If I may, Prime Minister, our intelligence gathering has found no link between these attacks. There are certain similarities but these incidents are so varied and widely spread that we consider it impossible that they are the work of a single enemy or terrorist organisation. I believe our American friends agree with us, isn't that so, Jonathan?'

'Yes,' Schneider said. 'So far there are no indications that these incidents are the work of a single entity or organisation. We are currently investigating the theory that a new and unknown virus might be the causing the perpetrators to behave in the way they do.'

'I don't agree,' Wyatt said. 'I believe that...'

'Oh, so you don't agree?' Montrose interjected sarcastically. 'One lowly sergeant in the Diplomatic Protection Group knows more that the combined intelligence services of the United Kingdom and the United States?'

'It's possible,' Wyatt said.

'Or perhaps you know more because you are involved in planning these attacks. You've been on the scene for two of them.'

Wyatt said: 'Like most of your ideas, Prime Minister, that is offensive crap. I was proud to serve the princess and it tortures me that I couldn't save her life. If you...'

Sherman laid a restraining hand on Wyatt's arm.

Clare Barnard cut through the tension by saying: 'Sergeant Wyatt, why did you abandon your assigned position at the cathedral just before this terrible attack on the First Lady and Vice President?'

'I responded to a call from Assistant Commissioner Sherman that there was an incident on the other side of the cathedral and that she needed help.'

Sherman looked at Wyatt with astonishment. She said: 'But I made no such call.'

'You must have done, boss. It was your voice.'

'I tell you, I made no such call.'

Barnard asked: 'What happened when you arrived at the site of this alleged incident?'

'There was no-one there,' Wyatt said. 'There was no incident.'

Wyatt looked at the faces staring at him and, with a stomach churning insight, realised that he was under threat in ways he had not previously considered. Schneider, the CIA chief, was measuring him up as if he were a mortician. Clare Barnard looked sceptical,

Montrose regarded him with loathing, Llewelyn was sneering cynically in his usual manner, and Richard Harcourt looked uncomfortable, but no more so that Assistant Commissioner Sherman. She had actually edged away from him. His own boss had set him up as the fall guy.

Barnard said to Wyatt: 'After returning to Scotland Yard you then ignored a direct order from Assistant Commissioner Sherman to attend the debriefing session.'

'Yes, but I decided I had to get to the embassy and talk to Linda Marquez before she flew back to the States.'

'Did Sergeant Marquez talk to you?'

'No. She refused. She doesn't like me and she doesn't trust me.'

'She joins an ever growing throng,' murmured the Prime Minister.

Wyatt took a deep breath. 'Whatever any of you think of me personally, it's my duty to urge you to persuade Linda Marquez to talk about the behaviour of her husband before he committed suicide.' Wyatt turned to Jonathan Schneider. 'Especially you, sir. We British have no power to command Marquez to talk but you, as a senior officer in the CIA, certainly do. I beg you to listen to what I'm saying. If you don't then you will all be guilty of a dereliction of duty more severe than anything you imagine I have committed.'

Schneider looked away and did not reply.

Montrose said: 'Are you threatening us, sergeant?'

Wyatt could make no reply except a contemptuous shake of the head.

Montrose said: 'Sergeant Wyatt, you are free to go. We now have to discuss your situation.'

Wyatt said: 'I suspect my "situation" has already been decided.'

Montrose said: 'I'll get someone to show you out the back way.'

As soon as Wyatt was gone Prime Minister Murdo Montrose slammed his fist on his desk. 'Insolence, insubordination, treason and treachery.'

Sherman said: 'Sir, insolence and insubordination certainly, treason and treachery I can't believe of a man like Wyatt. His record, up to now, has been exemplary.'

'*Up to now* are the operative words,' Montrose said. 'You told me that you have proof that his drinking is out of control.'

'Yes, sir. He has been drinking while on duty. I have the evidence, a half bottle of whisky I found in his desk drawer.'

Montrose brooded for a few moments and then said: 'I want him out.'

Sherman said: 'If you end his career now he'll lose his reputation as well as his pension rights.'

'I want him out,' Montrose repeated. 'Clare, you're the Home Secretary. What do you think?'

Clare Barnard said: 'It's better to have someone inside the tent spitting out rather than someone outside the tent spitting in. I propose that we suspend Wyatt from all duties but on full pay. That way we keep him on a leash, keep control over him rather than cutting him loose to cause trouble.'

Montrose turned to Sir Derek Llewelyn. 'What do you think?'

'Clare, as always, makes sense. Let's keep Wyatt twisting in the wind. I can have him watched on a twenty four hour a day basis if necessary.'

Montrose said: 'What's your opinion, Jonathan?'

'I'm here as an observer but as you ask for my opinion then I back Clare and Sir Derek. Keep Wyatt under surveillance and control. He might even lead us to whoever or whatever is instigating these security breaches. We have ways of monitoring guys like Wyatt so they can't take a… a shower without us knowing about it.'

'Thanks for cleaning that up, Jonathan,' Clare Barnard said drily. 'Do you think that your Sergeant Marquez might unknowingly have useful information about these attacks?'

'It seems extremely unlikely. I don't know what Wyatt is up to, whether he is seeking to divert attention away from his own failings or whether his failure to save the life of the Princess Royal has affected his mind, but it would seem sensible to take him off duty, give him a rest and watch what he does.'

Montrose said: 'Okay, thank you all for the advice, which I accept. But what about you, Mrs Sherman? You are Wyatt's immediate superior. Do you agree with suspension and surveillance.'

'Yes, sir. I'll go along with that rather than outright dismissal. I might be cutting my own throat but I have faith in Sergeant Wyatt. In the years I have worked with him he has never given me cause for a moment's doubt.'

Montrose nodded dubiously. 'Very well, decision made. Wyatt is suspended on full pay with immediate effect. Thank you, Mrs Sherman. You can give Wyatt the news in your own time.'

Wyatt was in his office at Scotland Yard working at the computer. The report was preparing was nearly completed. His mobile phone rang. He looked at the number displayed on his phone and said: 'Hello, boss.'

'Chris, where are you?'

'I'm in the office.'

'Well, stop whatever you're doing, clear out your personal effects and leave the building immediately.'

'So I've been sacked?'

'No, you're suspended from all duties pending further notice. You will continue on full pay but you are not to set foot in the office or communicate with any other members of the team. I'll confirm all this in writing. Is that clear?'

'I understand completely, boss.'

'Go away and have a long holiday, Chris. You've earned it.'

'Okay. You've got me out of the way at last, boss.'

'That's not what I wanted. I...'

'Just answer one question. Why did you set me up?'

'I didn't, Chris. I swear I didn't.'

'It was your number and your voice.'

Silence. Then: 'Don't be there when I get back, sergeant.'

Wyatt ended the call. He turned back to the computer screen and tapped out the three lines needed to complete his report. He sent a copy to his home computer then double checked the email address of the recipient. He was sending his report to the one person in the world who appeared to share his analysis of what was happening. He pressed send, then he deleted all record of the email. He wondered what reaction it would engender. He could not have guessed in his wildest dreams.

13

Boeing 747-400 over the Atlantic, February 20th

Linda Marquez stared out of the cabin window. Outside was blackness, a blackness that mirrored her emotions. She could be travelling at 30,000 feet in the air or 30,000 feet under the sea for all she could tell, or care.

Despite the subdued lighting and the steady hum of the engines she was finding sleep impossible. Whether she looked at the blackness outside or whether she closed her eyes, she could see only one image, burned into her mind, the image of a bishop tumbling down stone steps with the blood from her gunshot wounds staining his back.

Linda had never before shot at a fellow human being, let alone taken a life, and now she had killed a distinguished man of God, a previously blameless and Christian soul. She tried to persuade herself that it had been her duty but she was frightened by how difficult it was to come to terms with. She was overcome with guilt and remorse. The poor guy was obviously mentally ill. Perhaps she should have aimed to wound him but that risked hitting Marty or Kefalas. The bishop's back was a big enough target for her to be confident of hitting it without endangering anyone else.

She thought of Christopher Wyatt, of his wild dark eyes, of his odd behaviour. Linda wondered how many people he had killed during his military service. One? Several? Hundreds? The guilt weighed heavily upon him. Now she understood what he had gone through.

Wyatt. He was a puzzle. The guy was crazy and yet his black eyes blazed with a kind of convincing integrity. Why had he wormed his way into the American embassy and tried to spin her a lie about her dear dead Michael? Or was it a lie? Wyatt was very insistent, and persistent. Even crazy people tell the truth. He was crazy but not creepy. Was there a kernel of truth in his claims?

She looked at her watch. It would be about nine thirty in New York. The Boeing 747, often chartered by government departments, was adapted to allow cell phone calls without danger. Linda looked around. She was well away from her Secret Service colleagues, many of whom were asleep. Linda found the number and started the call.

After several seconds a gruff voice answered: 'Dempsey.'

Linda said: 'Chief Dempsey, this is Linda Marquez, Mike O'Brien's wife.'

'Jeez, Linda, this is spooky. I've just been watching you on television.'

'How do you mean?'

'They were showing the film of you shooting that bishop guy on the news. That was good work, Linda. You're famous now.'

Linda's heart sank. 'I don't want to be famous for that, chief.'

'Well, don't worry, the media don't know who you are and your bosses won't tell them. You're being protected. I won't say anything.'

'Thanks, chief.'

'What can I do for you, Linda?'

'Chief, I'm sorry to disturb you. It's about my husband, Michael. What I was told about how he was behaving and how he... how he took his own life, was that the true version?'

'For Chrissakes, Linda, what makes you ask that?'

'I overheard some gossip, some of the guys were talking. Someone told me that there was more to his death than I've been told.'

'Linda, listen to me. I'm an Assistant Chief of New York City police. Micky was a well-liked and valuable officer. More than that, he was a friend. Do you think I would disrespect you, and disrespect his memory, by telling you lies?'

'No, I guess you wouldn't. I didn't mean to insult you, chief. I had to ask the question.'

'That's okay, Linda. I want to put your mind at rest. Don't listen to those sons of bitches gossiping. It's probably just cop black humour.'

'Okay, chief. I'm sorry to have disturbed you.'

Linda ended the call. Assistant Chief Dempsey was right. There was no reason to become paranoid because of Wyatt's strange behaviour.

Linda decided, before she attempted to sleep once more, to check on Martina Logan. The First Lady and the Vice President were in the upper first-class cabin. The stairway was guarded by two of her fellow agents even though there were no other passengers except Secret Service personnel and a few government aides and officials.

Although the thickly carpeted stairway made no noise, Linda trod softly in case she woke the two distinguished passengers. As she reached the top of the stairs she heard the Vice President say: 'How are you feeling, Speedy?'

The Vice President was leaning over Martina Logan's seat. Kefalas looked around when he noticed Linda at the top of the steps. He smiled and said: 'Hi, Linda. Can't you sleep?'

'No, sir. How about you?'

'No way. My stomach still hurts like a bitch where that maniac rammed his hook into me. I was just checking on Marty.' Kefalas returned to his seat and picked up a glass of whisky.

Martina Logan looked pale and shaky. She had been badly upset by the attack.

Linda knelt down beside her and asked: 'How are you doing, Marty?'

'I'm fine, I guess, thanks to you. I can't sleep. My head aches but there we are.'

'Can I get you a painkiller or a drink or anything?'

'No, just stay with me for a while, Linda.'

Linda took the seat opposite Marty.

'You don't look too good yourself, Linda? Are you still upset about the shooting?'

'Yes. I can't get it out of my mind.'

'Don't be upset, Linda,' Kefalas said from the other side of the cabin. 'That was damn fine work. Probably saved our lives.'

Linda nodded. 'I'm also upset about what that guy Wyatt said about my husband.'

Kefalas interrupted again. 'You don't have to worry about that asshole again. The Brits have suspended him from duty. I'd have court martialled the bastard for deserting his post like that.'

Martina said wryly: 'I thought you said we were in safe hands with him.'

'Judging by his record I thought we were. I misjudged him.'

The Vice President closed his eyes and was soon asleep. Whether it was the low hum of the airplane engines, the subdued lighting, the womblike warmth of the cabin, the lack of formality, or whatever, Linda felt compelled to tell Martina Logan about her troubled marriage. She said: 'Michael hated me working for you, Marty. It was driving a real big wedge between us.'

'But I thought you said he supported your career?'

'He did in the early days. He changed in the last few weeks. He resented me leaving him so often. I probably shouldn't tell you this, Marty, but I was going to resign from the Service after our Hawaii trip and before Michael did what he did.'

Martina Logan did not reply immediately. She looked weary and dejected, her world confusing and fragile despite the power of her husband. Finally she said: 'You would have had to put your marriage before me. Are you still intending to resign?'

'No, mam. I want to stay with you.'

'I can't tell you what a relief that is, Linda. I seriously don't know what I'd do without you. But I think you need a break. You shouldn't have come with me on this trip. When we get back home I want you to take at least a week off.'

'That won't be necessary, Marty. I'll be fine in a day or two. It's just that...'

'Linda, that is not a suggestion, it's a direct order, and I won't listen to any further argument.'

'Yes, mam.' Linda sat back and looked out of the window but then leaned forward again. 'I don't believe what I'm seeing.'

'What?'

'There's a fighter plane off our starboard wing.'

Martina Logan leaned forward to take a look. 'Is it one of ours?'

'Yes, it must be. That's an F-22 Raptor. We don't sell them to any other country.'

Martina Logan smiled. 'You see, Linda, that's why I like you around. You seem to know this stuff without looking it up.'

Linda looked across out of the port window. The Vice President was snoring lightly, head resting on a pillow.

Linda said: 'There's another Raptor on the port wing.'

A voice said: 'Excuse me, mam. I see you've noticed our escort.'

They looked around to see Isaiah Franklin standing at the top of the stairway.

Martina Logan asked: 'What's going on, Stack?'

'No immediate cause for alarm, mam. We are being diverted to another airport. The President ordered the Raptors to escort us as a precaution. I'm afraid there's been another incident.'

14

Feroz Shah Kotla Cricket Stadium, New Delhi, February 21st

Premendra Dhawan found Colonel Ashok Chatterjee in his usual seat outside the new club house next to the West Stand. It was odd to see Chatterjee in civilian clothes, a white tropical suit and Panama hat. Prem was also relieved to see that Chatterjee was unaccompanied with plenty of spare seats all around so that their conversation could not be overheard.

Prem said: 'Good afternoon, sir.'

Chatterjee looked up and sighed. 'Hello, Prem. Have you come to interrupt the one indulgence in my life? Owing to your complete lack of interest in cricket, I suspect you have.'

'My apologies, sir, but there is something you ought to see immediately. What's the score?'

'Do you really care?'

'No, sir.'

'Then suffice it to say that we are winning.'

'Who are we playing?'

'Don't you recognise those baggy green caps? We are playing Australia. I had booked today off in the hope of enjoying this one day international.'

'I realise that, sir, but this is more important than cricket.'

'India and Australia are currently the two best teams in the world. There is nothing more important than that.'

'Yes, sir. I'll only take up a few minutes of your time then you can return to your flannelled fools.'

Chatterjee chuckled. 'A famous saying. I wonder who made such a ridiculous comment.'

'It was Rudyard Kipling, sir.'

'Ah, the arch imperialist.'

'He was born in India, sir. Some say he loved India as much as we do.'

'Umm, I doubt that. I have a feeling, Flight Lieutenant Dhawan, that you are not only going to ruin my cricket but also ruin my day. Sit down, then, and do your worst.'

A deafening roar erupted from the packed stands as the Indian batsman drove the ball high into the West Stand for six runs. Chatterjee clapped his hands and shouted his approval. Premendra Dhawan could not understand why anyone should want to spend a calm and sunny day in a raucous cauldron of noise that looked like a cross between a Roman amphitheatre and the grim multi-storey car parks he had seen in England. England was where his thoughts were today.

Prem said: 'First of all, sir, we have further information about the tragedy at Dulles Airport. It's confirmed that the pilot was Major Spencer Kraft, a long-serving and respected US Air Force officer. He was shouting what sounded like "too low" before his Stratotanker hit the airport.'

'Umm, same pattern then,' Chatterjee said.

'Yes, sir. By some miracle the aircraft missed the terminal but ploughed into aircraft on the ground. It destroyed four airliners and caused a huge fireball that is still burning. The airliners were empty of passengers but about twenty airport maintenance staff were killed. The First Lady and Vice President were scheduled to land at Dulles about ninety minutes after the incident. We are not sure whether they were meant to be targets or not.'

'Do we know any more about this man Kraft?'

'Very little at this stage, sir, but my people are working on it.'

'Very well, Prem. Let me know if and when you find anything

of significance to us. I'm sure you have not interrupted my main pleasure in life in order to tell me that.'

'No, indeed, sir. This is very much of significance to us.' Prem took out three sheets of paper from his briefcase and handed them Chatterjee. 'I received this email from a Sergeant Christopher Wyatt in London. He had read my report about the attack on our Prime Minister and has given me some information that our British intelligence colleagues have, for reasons best known to themselves, kept secret from us. Please read it before I go on, sir.'

Chatterjee did as requested. Prem was gratified to see the mounting interest on Chatterjee's face. 'This might be the breakthrough we've been hoping for, Prem. This man Wyatt confirms our suspicions about a possible Maoist plot behind these vile attacks. So Wyatt was the officer who shot dead the Princess Royal's assassin, that chap Flaherty?'

'Yes, sir. And Flaherty's dying words seem to confirm the Maoist link. Wyatt agrees with our theory about such a link.'

'We must get in touch with Wyatt and perhaps work with him on this.'

'There is a snag, sir. A big one.'

Chatterjee sighed. 'There always is. What is it?'

'Sergeant Wyatt has been suspended from duty with the Diplomatic Protection Group. He was the liaison officer with American Secret Service at the Princess Royal's funeral but he's been accused of abandoning his assigned position just before the assault on Mrs Logan and Vice President Kefalas.'

'Could Wyatt be working with or for the Maoists? He seems to be conveniently present when these things are happening.'

'I think it's extremely unlikely, sir. After all, it's Wyatt's job to be in places where these sort of incidents might occur. He is an interesting character and everything we've researched suggests he is utterly loyal and dedicated to his king and country.'

'Okay, so what do we know about him?'

Prem handed his boss another sheet of paper. 'We've built up this profile. Christopher Sean Wyatt, aged 34, height six feet one inch, divorced, no children. One younger sister, one older brother. Born in north London, now lives in west London. His mother is Irish and his father English. He...'

'Irish mother?' Chatterjee interrupted.

'Yes, but British intelligence reports show that she has lived in England for nearly forty years with no known links or allegiance to any Irish terrorist group, or any other terrorist group. None of the Wyatt family have any links to any dubious organisation.'

'Okay. Carry on, Prem.'

'Wyatt was educated at a comprehensive school, that's a basic school for working class children, where his reports say he was bright but easily bored and restless. Poor marks in all studies except sport, in which he excelled. He was expelled for a time at the age of fourteen.'

'What for?'

'One of the male teachers attempted to molest Wyatt. He was badly beaten and hospitalised.'

'Who? Wyatt?'

'No, sir. The teacher.'

'Wyatt was expelled but was reinstated after proof of the teacher's paedophile activities came to light. After leaving school Wyatt joined the British Army and the records show that he blossomed. The exertion and training channelled his restless nature and the discipline helped to control and shape his personality, although he found it difficult to accept orders he thought were wrong. His commanding officers, however, reported that he was completely loyal. He applied to join the Royal Marines, was accepted and passed their rigorous training course. He played rugby and cricket for the Royal Marines and...'

'Cricket, you say,' Chatterjee said brightly. 'Batting or bowling?'

Prem consulted his notes. 'Useful tail-end batsman and excellent right-arm fast bowler.'

'Wyatt doesn't sound like he would have the patience to be an opening batsman, but I like his style. Those Australians out there could do with a good fast bowler.'

'Yes, sir,' Prem replied, suppressing a smile. 'Anyway, Wyatt was promoted to sergeant and saw action in the Middle East and during the break up of the old Yugoslavia. Then Wyatt applied to join the elite Special Boat Service, that's the naval equivalent of the SAS.'

'I'm well aware of that, Prem.'

'Yes, of course. Sorry, sir. Wyatt was accepted and passed the extremely rigorous entry course with flying colours. As you also know, SBS and SAS operations are usually top secret so we don't have many details about what Wyatt was doing, but during his time with the SBS Wyatt was awarded the Conspicuous Gallantry Cross. It's a relatively new award. The only higher award for gallantry in the British Army is the Victoria Cross. Such awards for members of the SBS are ungazetted, so nobody knows about them, not even his current employees, the Metropolitan Police.'

'Why did Wyatt leave the army and join the police?'

'He was injured in combat. It took him many months to make a full recovery, during which time he decided that his SBS career was over. He spent several months as a freelance bodyguard and security expert but it seems that Wyatt is a disastrous businessman, so he offered his services to the Met police. They grabbed him with both hands and immediately put his skills to use as a member of SO14, the Royal Protection Squad. His service record has been exemplary. You may remember that incident here in India last year when the Princess Royal was attacked.'

'That was Wyatt who stopped that maniac?'

'Stopped him cold, sir, with a minimum of fuss and effort. He is still in jail and still recovering from what Wyatt did to him.'

Chatterjee nodded. 'It seems unlikely then that Wyatt was in any way culpable in her assassination.'

'Yes, sir. Reports show that Wyatt was deeply affected

psychologically by the death of the princess. He was offered counselling but refused. I'm afraid his drinking became out of control, that is one reason he has been suspended.'

'Hmm, do you think he would be reliable if we need to use him?'

'I believe so, sir. It's understandable for anyone to take to the bottle after experiencing such a tragedy.'

'You didn't, Prem.'

'No, sir, but Wyatt doesn't have two sons and the memory of a beloved wife to keep him sane. Rhea would be really angry with me if I went off the rails in such a way but there have been many times when I have been tempted.'

'I understand, Prem. I deeply admire the way you have coped with your bereavement. If this Wyatt is so good, why is he still a sergeant?'

'Met Police records show that he has been offered promotion but Wyatt chose to turn it down. It seems he likes to stay where the action is.'

'Excellent,' Chatterjee said. 'Sergeant Wyatt seems the ideal candidate if we need some muscle somewhere where the colour of our skin would make us conspicuous.'

'Exactly what I was thinking, sir.' Prem held up the empty left-hand sleeve of his jacket. 'I'm no longer any use at that aspect. But look what we turned up last night.' Prem handed Colonel Chatterjee another report. 'It was marked "Top Secret" but we hacked our way in.'

Chatterjee read the report. 'I knew you were going to ruin my day, Prem. Okay, from now on, this information stays strictly with you and I. What I want you to do, as I suspect you came to ask me, is get on the next flight to London and make contact with Wyatt. Get to know him, feel him out, look him in the eyes. You're a good judge of character. Then we'll work out everything you might need as back-up.'

'Perhaps Wyatt will not want to co-operate with us, sir?'

Chatterjee held up the report. 'Show him this report. If that doesn't make him co-operate, nothing will. He doesn't know it yet but his life is in the gravest danger.'

15

Sylvania Hotel, Klosters, Switzerland, 3.58 pm, February 26th

Christopher Wyatt watched as Linda Marquez walked towards the Princess Royal. The princess was smiling. Wyatt could see Marquez's reflection in the glass wall of the research centre. Marquez was brandishing golden scissors above her head. Something was wrong. Wyatt reached inside his jacket and took out his semi-automatic pistol. He raised the gun and aimed at Marquez. Marquez said: 'No, not me, not me.' Wyatt changed position and aimed at the princess. The princess looked back at him, her expression filled with tenderness and regret, and said: 'Why hate us?' Wyatt pulled the trigger. The explosion tore into his head.

Wyatt opened his eyes. His heart was racing and he was sweating. He realised, with a surge of intense relief, that he was awake and that the bang had been caused by Stephanie angrily closing the door of the closet.

Wyatt sat up and then shifted to sit on the edge of the bed. He was wearing a jacket and tie. He could not remember why. His head ached and his eyes were filled with grit. He looked at Stephanie as she bustled around the room packing things into her case. Something *was* wrong, time out of place, the world out of kilter.

'What are you doing?' Wyatt asked.

'I'm moving out,' Stephanie replied. Her face was flushed with anger.

'What time is it?'

'Look for yourself.'

Wyatt picked up his watch from the bedside table. It was three fifty in the afternoon. He said: 'I'm sorry, Steph. I met some guys down in the bar. What do you mean you're moving out? We're in a hotel in Switzerland.'

'We certainly are!' Stephanie said savagely. 'What a bloody mistake this trip was. The idea was to be together and try to patch things up. You've hardly looked at me since we've been here. You were supposed to meet me for lunch at the Gabriella at one. I sat there for an hour, on my own, feeling like a complete idiot. Then I find you snoring on the bed after yet another drinking session.'

'I'm sorry, Steph. Look, I dressed for lunch. I only had a couple of drinks then I came back up here to get my coat. I was tired. I laid down for a nap. I must have dropped off. How was the skiing?'

'The skiing was great. Exhilarating. If you had come with me it would have been even better.'

'I can't concentrate on anything. Things keep swirling around and around in my mind.'

Stephanie looked at him. He was sitting hunched over, his face in his hands. Stephanie's temper cooled. She sat down on the bed and took his hand. 'Listen, Chris, I accept you've had a really rough time since what happened with the princess, but that was weeks ago.'

'Less than two weeks ago, Steph.'

'Okay, but drowning in booze is not the answer. How long have we known each other, Chris? Over a year now. I've never seen you drink anywhere near this much before. A couple of pints or a couple of glasses of wine and that's been it.'

'That was before I saw the woman I was supposed to protect stabbed to death in front of me.'

Stephanie squeezed his hand earnestly. 'It wasn't your fault, Chris. Nobody could have stopped that man doing what he did. Can't you put it out of your mind and come back to the living again?'

'It's difficult, Steph. It's not simply what happened to the princess. There's something else going on, something really big, and I've been suspended. I was getting close to an answer. Now I've been cut adrift. I'm cast out and useless.'

'Whatever is going on is not your problem, Chris.'

'It *is* my problem. What if everyone thought like that, Steph. "It's not my problem. Let somebody else sort it out". It is my problem because I chose a career in which my duty is to protect the security of the country and the people visiting or living in it. Not only that, I'm involved in humanity and I've been caught in the middle of a dangerous threat.'

Stephanie patted his hand. 'You're a special guy, Chris, and you make me feel special. I feel safe and respected and sexy when I'm with you. I love the way you still stand up to greet me when I walk in the pub or restaurant or whatever. I love your strength, your determination, your good manners, your self-deprecating humour, the way you are with your family, with your sister and her kids. They adore you. You're a great guy. Can't we get past this? Why don't you resign from the Met and start afresh in a new job?'

Wyatt slowly shook his head. 'I couldn't do that, Steph.'

'Oh, Chris. There are times when I'm in love with you, then there are other times when I think this is not going to work. Isn't that why we came here? To get away and think and be together and sort things out.'

Wyatt nodded. 'I realise I've been driving you away from me. That's why I thought of this place. I love Klosters. When I used to come here with the princess it always calmed me down and…'

Stephanie let go of his hand. 'You came here with the princess? You didn't tell me that.'

'Not me personally, Steph. Klosters is a favourite resort with the royal family. I was one of the Royal Protection Squad guarding the princess.'

Stephanie stood up. 'That bloody woman keeps coming between us even when she's dead.'

'Don't talk about her like that, Steph.'

'Were you sleeping with her?'

'What!?'

'Were you sleeping with her?'

'No, I was not. Don't talk offensive rubbish like that, Steph. She was a member of the royal family, strictly off limits. My duty was to guard her, not sleep with her. She was simply a very special person.'

'More special than me, it seems.'

'If you like.' Wyatt wished he could bite back the words but it was too late.

Stephanie zipped up her travelling case, anger burning her face red. 'I'll come back for the rest of my stuff some other time. I'll leave you here to stew in your memories of your beloved princess.'

'Where are you going? Back to England?'

'No, I'm staying here with someone else.'

Wyatt did not reply.

'Don't you want to know who?'

Wyatt shrugged. 'It's your life, Steph.'

'Sod you, Chris.'

The hotel room door slammed shut. Stephanie was gone. Wyatt opened the blinds. The clean white light from the mountains blazed into the room. He loved the clean white peaks against the pale blue sky. He watched the skiers run down the slopes like tiny black insects, down into the thick green forests. He watched for a long time. Then he got up, undressed and went to shower. He stood with the stinging hot water pouring over him and with a curious mixture of intense regret and intense relief that another relationship was over. How could he expect Stephanie to understand him when he scarcely understood himself?

16

Sylvania Hotel, Klosters, Switzerland, 6.00 pm, February 26th

Yaroslav Blokhin walked into the bar of the Sylvania Hotel at six o'clock. There were only a few other *après-ski* drinkers. Blokhin ordered his two bodyguards to take a seat at the nearest vacant table while he ordered the drinks.

The barman said: 'Good evening, Mr Blokhin. What can I get you this evening?'

Blokhin rested his stocky corpulent body on a bar stool.

'Vodka, straight. Not that watery Western vodka. Stolichnaya Elit.'

'I'm sorry, sir, but we don't stock the Elit.'

'Call this a five-star hotel?'

'We have ordinary Stolichnaya or the Blue, sir.'

'Give me Blue. A double. And two bottles of beer for my companions.'

'Which beer, sir?'

'Anything. Those apes have no taste.'

'I'll bring your drinks over straight away, sir.'

Blokhin wandered over to the curving floor-to-ceiling windows that afforded a panoramic view out over the observation deck and away to the village and mountains and forests down the valley. The lights in Klosters were being switched on. Revellers were walking up and down the narrow streets. Blokhin turned around and summoned his bodyguards to join him.

Blokhin said: 'I'm going to take my drink out on to the deck and watch the sunset.'

Vladimir said: 'Okay, boss.'

'I want to sit at that table on the far left there.'

Vladimir and Oleg looked out at the deck. Oleg said: 'There are plenty of other tables free, boss.'

Blokhin said: 'Do you think I'm blind? I can see there are other tables free but I want to sit at that one. I'll give you a bonus if you can make that man give up his table.'

'How much?' Vladimir asked.

'Ten thousand dollars, each.'

Vladimir and Oleg looked at each other. Oleg asked: 'What's the catch, boss?'

'No catch, my simian friend. Make that man move and you earn an extra ten grand, as our American friends say.'

Vladimir and Oleg considered the offer. Vladimir asked: 'What if we can't make him move?'

'Then I'll sack you without pay.'

The bodyguards shrugged. Oleg said: 'Okay, boss. It's easy money.'

'Yes,' Blokhin cried. 'It's a doddle, as our English friends say. English friends like him.'

'How do you know he's English?'

'I know everything, bonehead. Don't be too easy on him. If he won't move, rough him up a bit.'

'Anything you say, boss.'

Oleg and Vladimir opened the sliding door and stepped out on to the polished wooden deck.

Wyatt took a sip of his single malt and watched the lights coming on one by one down in Klosters. The village was cobwebbed with light. His mind was in a ferment thinking about the princess, and Stephanie, about what was going on in the world and, oddly, that bloody woman Marquez who was now popping up in his dreams. The hair of the dog was clearing his head but he was exhausted and deeply despondent.

Wyatt had noticed that two men had approached from behind and were standing either side of him. He looked up. Both men were wearing sober suits and ties. The man on the right was stocky, almost as broad as he was tall. His head was shaved like a convict. The man on the left was taller, swarthy, with a black beard, piercing eyes and long black hair. He looked fit and confident.

The tall man, Vladimir, spoke in English with a thick accent. 'Excuse me, sir, but our employer wishes to sit at this table. Would you mind moving?'

Wyatt said: 'That's a strange request. There are many other unoccupied tables with the same spectacular view as this table.'

'Indeed, sir, and we want you to move to one.'

Wyatt asked: 'Who is your employer?'

'He is a rich and important man. He is used to getting his own way, getting what he wants.'

'I see,' Wyatt said. 'What happens if I don't wish to move?'

'Then we have been instructed to move you.'

Wyatt nodded. 'I should warn you that I'm not in the best of moods. I've lost my job and my girlfriend walked out on me two hours ago.'

Vladimir said: 'That is no concern of ours.'

'Well, think hard, comrade, because, in a few seconds time, it might be of painfully serious concern to you.' Wyatt looked at Oleg. 'What do you think I should do?'

Vladimir said: 'My friend doesn't speak English. Are you going to move, or do we have to make you?'

'Okay, okay. You're two big lads. I don't want any trouble. Let me get my drink.' Wyatt leaned forward as if to reach for his glass. He bent his arm and rammed his elbow into Oleg's groin, then slammed the back of his clenched fist into Oleg's nose.

At the same instant Wyatt had grabbed Vladimir's tie with his left hand and yanked down his forehead to strike the sharp edge of the metal table.

As Oleg was dropping to his knees, cupping his testicles and making a strange strangled sound, Vladimir sagged to his knees, blood pouring from his gashed head.

A woman screamed.

Oleg tried to get to his feet. Wyatt slammed his elbow into his nose. Oleg fell backwards clutching his face. Wyatt was still holding Vladimir's head down by his tie. Vladimir recovered his wits. He tried to break free. Wyatt jabbed two fingers into Vladimir's eyes and drove the palm of his hand into his nose. Vladimir, temporarily blinded, staggered backwards.

Both bodyguards were now kneeling on the deck clutching at their faces, blood trickling between their fingers and moaning with pain. The other drinkers on the deck had watched the scene with horror.

Wyatt was gripped by a red murderous rage. He stood up and was about to grab Oleg when a voice rang out: 'Christopher! Please stop!'

Wyatt looked up. He was breathing heavily, the rage rapidly dissipating. 'Mr Blokhin?' he said, as if in a daze. 'Are these your men?'

'They were,' Blokhin replied. To Vladimir and Oleg he said: 'Go and get yourselves cleaned up, you useless apes. Call yourselves spetsnaz. More like little girls. I don't want to see you again. Easy money, indeed.'

The two bodyguards stumbled away, Oleg guiding the temporarily blinded Vladimir away from the scene of their humiliation..

Wyatt asked Blokhin: 'What did you mean about easy money?'

'I made a bet with my men that they could not make you move. I offered them ten thousand dollars each. You have saved me twenty thousand dollars. I see from your face that you are annoyed with me.'

'Why the hell did you do that?'

'I wanted to see if you had slowed down at all.'

'And have I?'

'No, Christopher. You have the same skills that saved the life of my wife and family but this time overlaid with some sort of savage intensity. Please accept my sincere apologies for my stupid prank. Can we be friends again?' Blokhin held out his hand.

Wyatt said: 'I'll shake your hand on one condition, Mr Blokhin.'

'What is that?'

'Give those two bodyguards their jobs back. They probably have wives and families. I caught them by surprise. I've caused enough trouble lately. I don't want their unemployment on my conscience.'

'Very well, Christopher. I rather like those two barbarians anyway. Are you still angry with me?'

Wyatt took Blokhin's hand and said: 'I couldn't stay angry with you, Mr Blokhin.'

The hotel manager and two security men came out on to the deck. The manager timidly approached Blokhin. Before the manager could speak, Blokhin said: 'Please accept my apologies. There was a slight misunderstanding between my bodyguards and this gentleman. It is now sorted out. Please express my sincere apologies to all the guests who had to witness this misunderstanding and serve them your finest champagne and charge it to me.'

The manager bowed, clearly relieved, and ushered his men away.

Wyatt asked: 'What brings you to Klosters, Mr Blokhin? Is your charming wife Anastasia with you?'

'Alas, no, Christopher. She will be mortified to have missed you. I am here with my granddaughters and their boyfriends. They wanted to ski so where better than here. Have you had dinner yet?'

'No. I'm not really hungry, sir.'

'Christopher, you are not in my employ any longer, so please call me Yuri, as all my family and closest friends do. Come and keep me company while I eat.' Blokhin patted his ample stomach. 'You know I like my food. We'll drink and talk about old times.'

'I'd like that, Yuri. Old times were better.'

17

Sylvania Hotel, Klosters, Switzerland, 7.10 pm, February 26th

Yaroslav Blokhin's cheerful company, together with the spectacular view of the village and the moonlit mountains from the best table in the restaurant, revived Wyatt's spirits. He ordered a steak and salad while Blokhin ploughed through course after course, all washed down with Stolichnaya Blue.

Wyatt took another sip of the smooth but deadly vodka. He was drinking too much again. He decided to confront Blokhin before the vodka robbed him of the power of logical thought.

'Cheers, Yuri,' Wyatt said. 'I'd like to propose a toast.'

'Certainly, my friend.' Blokhin picked up his glass.

'Here's to your two granddaughters. They must be very precocious.'

'In what way?' Blokhin asked.

'Irina must be about seven years old and Magda about five. Skiing? Perhaps. Boyfriends? You, and their mother, would consider that rather too precocious, wouldn't you?'

Blokhin had the grace to laugh heartily. 'Congratulations, Christopher. I should have known better than try to deceive you. How did you know?'

'I follow your life and career with interest, Yuri. You were kind and generous to me. I became fond of you and your family.'

'That is touching, Christopher. I'm glad you feel that way because that is why I am here. I want you to work for me again.'

'In what capacity?'

'The same as before, to supervise the security of myself and my family. When we first moved to London you looked after us superbly well. We understood nothing about life in England, still less of life in London. You saved us from those bastard kidnappers. I love London. Yes, I am a proud Russian, but I consider London my home. I want you to come back and look after us again.'

'Why now, Yuri? You haven't needed me for several years.'

'Christopher, let me be blunt, if not downright boastful. When you worked for me before I was a rich man, isn't that so?'

'Yes, indeed.'

'Since then I have become rich beyond the dreams of King Midas. I am worth an absurd amount of money. I have fingers in so many pies that I need a hundred hands. I bestride the world with my network of companies, oil, metals, minerals, shipping, newspapers, media. Name your own salary, Christopher. Money is like confetti to me. I would gladly give you any sum in order to protect my family.'

Wyatt took a long reflective sip of Stolichnaya.

Blokhin said: 'This Russian vodka is good, no? Much better than those Western rip-offs.'

'Actually, Stolichnaya Blue is made in Latvia. And it's going to my head.'

Blokhin laughed. 'That is why I like you, Christopher. You respect me but you are not afraid to "take the piss" as you English say. I am surrounded by yes-men and arse kissers, except for you. You were guarding the Princess Royal. I have seen the film. I recognised you.'

'And you still want to employ me as your bodyguard after seeing that?'

'Do not denigrate yourself. The way you took down Flaherty was remarkable. I said to Anastasia, we need Christopher back with us. Nobody else could have acted with such speed and skill. I'm aware of your troubles with your current employers. You have been suspended, that is why I came here, to persuade you to work for me. Name your salary, Christopher.'

Wyatt was aware that he was beginning to slur his words. 'Yuri, I am immensely flattered by your offer. In different circumstances I would be sorely tempted to accept. But these are not normal times. Again I ask you the question, why now? Why have you come back for me now?'

'You have hit the nail on the head, Christopher. These are not normal times. There is danger everywhere. This recent series of catastrophic events is no coincidence. My intelligence and news gathering organisation is one of the best in the world outside of national governments. There are many other examples of less serious attacks that our leaders have not connected with the others. There is a mind, a plan, a strategy, behind all this. As a wealthy and prominent man I am in danger, my family is in danger, my business is in danger. That is why I want you back, Christopher, to protect me and my loved ones from whoever is conducting this war.'

'I'm excited to hear you say this, Yuri. I also believe there is someone or some organisation planning and linking these attacks. My superiors are reluctant to accept such an idea. I have to take some action myself but I'm not sure what to do. That's why I can't come back to work for you. I have to stay within the system to make my case and help combat this menace. I have personal knowledge about a possible source of these attacks. I have given the information to my superiors but they have suppressed it.'

'What knowledge is that, Christopher?'

Wyatt was aware that he had said too much. He had drunk too much vodka. 'I can't tell you, Yuri. I'm constrained by the Official Secrets Act.'

'Bah,' Blokhin spat. 'Work for me and your Official Secrets Act can go hang. I'll give you all the men and material you need.'

'It's a tempting offer, Yuri, but I suffer from an abiding problem.'

'What is that, my friend?'

'I love my country and I'm loyal to my country.'

'A creditable outlook, but what about loyalty to your friends or to those who love you?'

'That's in short supply at the moment.'

'Yes, I have been informed that the beautiful Stephanie has walked out on you. Such a woman! My wealth would allow me to buy such a delectable woman, if I chose, but she gave herself to you voluntarily and you reject her with your indifference.'

Wyatt could not decide whether to be angry or amused. 'So you've been checking on my personal life as well? Is there anything you don't know, Yuri?'

Blokhin said: 'My final offer, Christopher. Name your own salary and come and work for me. Please.'

'Sorry, Yuri, but I can't.'

Blokhin momentarily looked annoyed. Then he leaned forward and said quietly: 'Let me help you. You said that your superiors are suppressing information. Give the information to me and I can pass it on to other people who might want to do something about it.'

'Like who?'

'Like anyone you want me to. My name opens doors all over the world.' Blokhin poured another glass of Stolichnaya. 'Drink, my friend. If you do not wish to give me facts, give me a theory. Prost!'

Wyatt downed another slug of vodka. Perhaps Yuri was right. Perhaps he should go outside his own people, for the sake of the world. He wished he had not drunk so much. He looked around to make sure they could not be overheard but the restaurant was nearly empty. He said: 'The only connection that has definitely been discovered is to a Maoist group.'

'Do you know which group?'

'No, but I don't believe it is a small group. I believe it might be the biggest group of the lot, a resurgence of Maoist ideals that Western intelligence is not yet aware of.'

'You mean China?'

'Yes. Think about it. China has surreptitiously been moving into Africa. They are gradually getting their hands on the mineral wealth of Africa. They've even built cities in Africa big enough to house thousands of people in which no-one is yet living. China has been stockpiling various rare metals and materials for years. They've been conducting a cyberwar against the West for years. They can't take over the West by military means but they can possibly take over by using their incredible wealth and highly intelligent population in various subtle ways. The Chinese are an old and patient people. It might take them decades, even centuries, to achieve their goals. Perhaps this spate of overt attacks are designed to disrupt or destroy the morale and cohesiveness of Western society.'

Yaroslav Blokhin looked at Wyatt. Wyatt expected him to burst out laughing but Blokhin said: 'Once again you amaze me, Christopher. You have confirmed something that my people have found out, by means I cannot disclose, not even to you. But you have been frank with me. Now I am going to give you something in return, something that will help you re-establish your career. You must go back to your people and make them listen.'

'How?'

'First, and remember that I speak as your friend, you must put the cork back in the bottle of your self-pity.'

Blokhin saw the momentary blaze of anger in Wyatt's eyes and was afraid, but it subsided quickly and Wyatt said: 'You're right, Yuri. What else?'

'You must go back to your superiors with two words.'

'Two words? What two words?'

Blokhin leaned forward and whispered: 'Silk Fist.'

18

Tavern Street, Islington, London, February 27th

The taxi driver stowed Wyatt's case on the step of his black cab and asked: 'Where to, sir?'

Wyatt said: 'Islington. Tavern Street.' He climbed in the back of the cab.

'I know it well, sir,' the cabbie said as he drove away from the railway station. 'Lovely Georgian terrace. Lots of celebrities live around that way. I had that young pop star in the back the other day. You know, the one with the funny name that all the girls scream over these days. And a few months ago I picked up that girl who plays tennis and got herself in trouble with the drugs and what not. Are you a celebrity, sir?'

'Hardly. More like a pariah these days.'

It was past three o'clock in the morning and the traffic was mercifully light. Wyatt always enjoyed a taxi ride through London in the wee small hours. It was a magical time of day, full of lost dreams but new hopes as well, and he had hoped to savour the sights and sounds without conversation. He was unlucky.

The cabbie said: 'You must be doing well for yourself to be able to live in Tavern Street.'

'Not really. A friend of mine let's me live there rent free.'

'I should have such friends! Why does he do that?'

'I helped him out with a problem. Him and his family. He even pays the council tax and utility bills. I told him once how I loved the atmosphere and the social life in Islington and he bought the house until he's ready to use it himself. He'll kick me out one day.'

'What do you do for a living, sir?'

'I'm a sort of lifestyle consultant.'

The taxi driver chuckled. 'I've got one of those. It's my wife. Always have to consult the missus before I do anything. What does that involve then?'

'What?'

'Being a lifestyle consultant. What do you do?'

'Let's say I look at the way someone is behaving and persuade them to change their ways, if necessary.'

'Is that what you've been away doing, being a lifestyle consultant?'

'No. I've been on holiday in Switzerland but I've had to cut it short.' Wyatt thought back to his dinner conversation with Yaroslav Blokhin. He had woken the next day with a ferocious hangover but an equally ferocious determination to stop drowning his emotions with alcohol and make British intelligence aware of Blokhin's information about Silk Fist. He would start with Assistant Commissioner Sherman whether she wanted to see him or not.

'Switzerland you say, sir. Nothing to do with that disaster out there?'

Wyatt was alert. 'I haven't seen any news for a day or two. What disaster is that?'

'Some looney sabotaged one of their biggest chemical and pharmaceutical companies. Dozens killed, the site all but destroyed. This bloke was apparently shouting "glayva" before he went barmy. You know, "glayva", like that liqueur stuff. Sounds like he was pissed. Beg your pardon, sir. Drunk I mean. You would be on that stuff. Dunno what's happening to the world lately. My wife says she's afraid to step out of the door. You don't know what's going to happen next. Here we are, sir. Tavern Street. Which number?'

The street lamps were out with not a light showing in any of the other houses. Wyatt noticed the van immediately. It was parked on the opposite side from Wyatt's house and about thirty metres away.

The plain white van stuck out like a beacon in the quiet residential road.

Wyatt leaned forward and said to the cabbie: 'Slow down as we go past that van.'

'You're the guvnor.'

The large van had a sliding side panel and someone was sitting in the driving seat.

Wyatt said: 'Go the end of the road and turn left. You can drop me off there.'

'You're the guvnor.'

Wyatt considered his options. He was unarmed. His Range Rover was parked outside his house but he did not have the car keys and, in any case, he did not keep any weapons in the car. There was nothing in his luggage to use as a weapon. Then he noticed something that would serve well enough.

The taxi stopped. Wyatt and the driver got out. The driver unloaded Wyatt's case and watched nervously as Wyatt uprooted a hollow iron pole that had been planted in the tiny front garden of a terraced house. Wyatt ripped off the estate agent's 'For Sale' sign. Wyatt said: 'I can't stand the bloke who lives here.'

'Nothing to do with me, guv.' The cabbie was well used to picking up all sorts of eccentric oddballs late at night, harmless and otherwise.

Wyatt said: 'How would you like to earn fifty quid on top of the fare and your tip?'

'Doing what?' the cabbie asked warily.

'Take my bag to number 37 back in Tavern Street. Here's the key. Open the front door and put the bag in the hallway. The house is empty. You won't disturb anyone or get in any trouble.'

'What will you be doing?'

'Best not to ask,' Wyatt said. He leaned the iron pole against the cast iron railings and took out his wallet. He counted out eighty pounds and offered them to the cabbie. The cabbie looked at the money uneasily but greed overcame his uncertainty. He took the notes. He picked up Wyatt's case and started walking back towards Tavern Street.

Wyatt took the iron pole and, keeping low and hidden by parked cars, shadowed the cabbie's progress from the other side of the road. Wyatt moved as close to the white van as possible without being seen by the driver. The cabbie carried the case up the four steps leading to Wyatt's front door.

Wyatt heard the side door of the van slide back and three men jumped out. They were wearing black, faces hidden by black ski masks, and were carrying baseball bats. They began to run, noiselessly on trainer-shod feet, across the tarmac of the quiet street towards Wyatt's house.

Wyatt moved out from behind a parked car and sprinted to intercept them. He swung the iron pole and caught the first assailant on the back of the head. The sinister black clad figure went tumbling forward and sprawled on the road.

Wyatt raised the pole to parry a blow from the second man and then swung it down in an arc to catch him behind the knees. The man screamed in agony, lost balance and fell face down.

The cabbie was watching the scene with disbelief. Wyatt shouted: 'Run, you idiot! Run!'

The cabbie dropped Wyatt's case on the top step, jumped down the other steps and sprinted away as fast as his portly legs would carry him.

The momentary distraction cost Wyatt dear. The second man managed to raise his arm to block Wyatt's swing. The third man brought his baseball bat down on Wyatt's head. It was a glancing blow but enough to stun for a split second. The second man lying in the road used his arm to sweep Wyatt's feet from under him. Wyatt landed bottom first with an agonising thud.

The three attackers had not said a word but now the third man, incensed with anger and blood lust, shouted something in a language Wyatt did not understand. He drew a pistol and aimed at Wyatt's head. The second man shouted something at the third man as if to restrain him but Wyatt could see eyes blazing with lethal fury. The third man rammed the barrel of the pistol against Wyatt's head. Wyatt braced himself for oblivion. There was the whump of a silenced pistol and a red star-shaped hole appeared in the gunman's forehead at the same instant as blood sprayed out of the back of his head. He fell backwards, dead.

Wyatt was momentarily shocked but then galvanised into action. He grabbed the second man and wrenched off his ski mask. 'Bloody hell,' Wyatt breathed.

The van driver had leapt out of the van. He was brandishing a machine gun. He shouted something at his companions. They picked up the body of their dead comrade and carried him back to the van. They tipped the body into the van and jumped in. Wyatt expected to die in a hail of machine gun fire but the driver climbed back into the driving seat, started the engine and the van roared away down the road.

Wyatt, fighting excruciating pain in his lower back, used the support of a nearby car to haul himself to his feet. He looked around to see who had fired the silenced pistol.

A man stood up from concealment behind a parked car. He was pointing the pistol at Wyatt. He said: 'Please come and pick up your case and put it in the trunk of this car. Then put yourself in the trunk. We have to take a short ride.'

19

Pangbourne Road, Harrow, London, February 27th

The trunk was opened and Wyatt, with great difficulty, climbed out. He had been bent double and the pain lanced into his back. The gunman handed Wyatt his case. The car was parked in a long street of large and unremarkable Victorian semi-detached houses. The street was still and quiet and utterly deserted under the pale moonlight.

Wyatt was ushered at gunpoint towards a house with a small overgrown front garden. The gunman handed Wyatt a key to unlock the front door. They went into the house and Wyatt was ordered to turn right off the hallway into a large living room. The room was clean but drab and shabby. The wallpaper was garish brown and orange, the armchairs cracked brown leather, the furniture stained oak. A gas fire was burning on low heat to take the chill off the room.

Wyatt put down his case and turned to face the gunman. He said: 'Do the house owners realise the Second World War has ended?'

The gunman did not lower the pistol as he replied: 'The Indian intelligence budget does not allow funds for fashionable redecoration.'

'That is clearly obvious, Mr Dhawan.'

'Why do you call me by that name?'

'It seems to be a fair bet considering your appearance and accent. Having sent an important email to one Premendra Dhawan of the Research and Analysis Wing, I expected a reaction but this is a little extreme.'

'My profound apologies for having to lock you in the trunk. As you can see, I have only one arm and it is difficult enough to drive in a foreign country without having to protect myself from a man of your capabilities. I assure you it was for your own safety.'

'What are you doing here, apart from saving my life and then kidnapping me?'

'If I put away this gun do I have your word that we can talk without you trying to harm me?'

'Of course you have my word. You obviously know something about me so you must also know that I'm not a savage. Your methods of personal introduction are unusual but no doubt you have your reasons. Where are we?'

'This is a safe house kept by my organisation.'

Wyatt watched as Prem held the pistol between his knees and unscrewed the silencer with his right hand. He put both in his jacket pocket. Premendra Dhawan had snow white hair, a fine aquiline nose, and brown eyes that, Wyatt was already convinced, missed nothing.

Wyatt asked: 'Why have you brought me here when we were standing outside my own house? I would have been pleased to invite you in.'

'I'll come to that in a moment. It was imperative that we meet and talk and compare notes.'

'That's nice, but why not ring me or email me?'

'Because things are a lot more complicated than they seem, Christopher. May I call you Christopher?'

'After taking down that bastard who was about to kill me you can call me anything you like. That was great shooting. Do you mind if I sit down? My back still hurts from falling on my arse.'

'Please do. I wish I could claim the credit for such a good shot but I was aiming to wound. Would you like a drink? I'm going to have a whisky.'

'That's the most sensible thing you've said all night. Sounds good. Have you got any painkillers?' Wyatt gingerly lowered himself on to a cracked brown leather sofa.

Prem went to a cheap sideboard with faux ormulu handles. He took out a bottle of whisky and two glasses. From the top drawer he took a carton of aspirin and tossed them to Wyatt.

Wyatt swallowed three tablets. Then he said: 'Do you know who they were? One of them was Chinese.'

Prem handed Wyatt a glass of whisky and sat down in an armchair. 'They were all Chinese and they were not here to kill you.'

'No, they wanted to kidnap me but I don't like the idea of being snatched by Chinese government thugs outside my own home.'

'They were not Chinese government men.'

'What makes you say that?'

'I heard what they were saying to each other.'

'You speak Chinese?'

'I speak Mandarin fluently, plus several other dialects passably. One of them was saying "no guns, they want him alive". Those men were certainly from Hong Kong. My guess would be Triads.'

'Triads? Hired by the Chinese government?'

'It's possible. They did not expect you to foil their kidnap attempt with such an ingenious solution.'

'I always thought those Kendo lessons would come in handy one day. Cheers.' Wyatt drank a large slug of whisky.

Prem said: 'I had been watching them for hours. I did not expect you to notice the danger. I was not sure what I could do. I have my pistol but I'm a poor shot and a fifty-year-old one-armed man is not much use in a fight.'

'All evidence to the contrary, Mr Dhawan. I'm glad you were there.'

'Please call me Prem.'

'Okay. Why do you think the Chinese are interested in me?'

'We have both found evidence to make us believe that there is a Maoist connection to the recent spate of unusual attacks.'

'How do they know and why should they want to kidnap me?'

'Perhaps you know more than you are telling me yet, especially after your meeting with a Russian oligarch.'

Wyatt could not hide his surprise. 'My compliments, Prem. Your intelligence network is impressive. It was hardly a meeting, more of a chance encounter and a chat between old friends.'

'Men of wealth and power like Blokhin are watched and monitored wherever they go. When Blokhin's two tough ex-Spetsnaz bodyguards are disabled by a mysterious Englishman who did not even need to get out of his chair to do so, that is worth a report. What did Blokhin tell you to cause your sudden return to England?'

Wyatt shook his head. 'Hold on, Prem. You've made an impressive introduction but why should I trust you? You saved my life but you didn't attempt to stop that van, shoot out the tyres or something.'

'The last thing we want is a shoot-out on a quiet London street. I'll soon know where those men came from and who they are.'

'How are you going to do that?'

'I planted a transponder on their van. My men are tracking them with GPS. We'll find out where they are going, pick them up and persuade them to tell us who hired them.'

'Your men? How many men have you got?'

'Hundreds. There is a large Indian community in London, in Britain as a whole. They like living here and, despite what a few racist idiots believe, they appreciate the opportunities that Britain has given them, opportunities such as achieved by your own commanding officer. They do not want thugs, of whatever nationality, polluting the country. There are many sleeper agents here willing to help us out.'

Wyatt nodded appreciatively. 'You're an interesting man, Prem, but I have learned from painful experience to beware of Greeks, or Indians, bearing pistols. My head aches, my back hurts like fury and my neighbours will be wondering what was going on. Why did you force me to crawl into your trunk and come here instead of going into my own comfortable home?'

'Because your assailants had been in your house. They could have planted explosives or bugged the place. Let my men check it over before you go back in.'

'Where do I go then?'

'You stay here, for the time being.'

'I hope the sheets have been changed.'

'They have, with finest Indian cotton.'

'Good, but there are things in my home that I need.'

'You have just returned from abroad. Everything you need, except a change of clothes, is in your case. Everything else I can supply you with. Please believe me when I tell you that your life is in mortal peril, and not only from hired Hong Kong thugs.'

'Mortal peril? From who? Why should I believe that?'

Prem got up and went to a briefcase standing on the dining table. He took out a sheet of paper and handed it to Wyatt. He said: 'That is a copy of an email my team intercepted two days ago.'

Wyatt read the email with mounting disbelief. 'My own people are setting me up?'

Prem nodded. 'It appears you have been selected as the scapegoat.'

'This could be a fake. I can't believe my own people would do this to me. *You* could be setting me up, not *them*.'

Prem sighed. 'Christopher, sometimes we have to trust someone, even if we are not sure of their motives. Why do you think I have flown thousands of miles after exchanging emails with you? I saved your life tonight. We are the only two people in the world, as far as I can tell, who believe that a Maoist resurgence might account for these brutal attacks. Let's work together on this. Help me, Christopher.'

Wyatt looked at Premendra Dhawan and decided to trust his

instinct that Dhawan was genuine. He said: 'Have you heard the term "Silk Fist"?'

Prem took a sip of whisky. 'No, I haven't.'

'Blokhin's news media contacts have come across this term. They think it's the Chinese code name for a new overt war against the capitalist West.'

'Silk Fist?' Prem pondered. 'There are many Chinese words denoting silk. Perhaps "bóo" or "chóu"? Fist is easier, perhaps "quán" or "chui", which means to beat with a fist. This is vital information. We will have to analyse what this term means.'

'Before we do that, Prem, I have to get some sleep. I'm beat, in more ways than one. I'll have to leave you to work on the meaning of Silk Fist. There is something else I have to do as soon as possible.'

'What's that?'

'I have to get to America. There is a woman over there who knows something about what is going on, but she doesn't know that she knows. I have to find her.'

20

Pangbourne Road, Harrow, London, March 1st

Wyatt was carrying his suitcase downstairs when the front door opened and Premendra Dhawan came in carrying an attache case.

'Where the hell have you been?' Wyatt asked irritably. He followed Prem into the living room and put down the suitcase on the sofa. 'I was stuck in this mausoleum all day yesterday and then you disappeared for most of the morning. I should be in the States already.'

Prem was unperturbed by Wyatt's mood. 'Patience, Christopher. I see you are packed. Your flight does not leave for three hours. There is plenty of time. You are a man of action, Christopher. I am a man of thought and reflection. If you insist that it is vital to contact this Marquez woman then it will be better if you are not intercepted by American homeland security. There is not time to secure the necessary papers. That's why we agreed it was best for you to fly to Toronto and cross into the States from there. That will be the most dangerous part of your trip.'

'I don't think so, Prem. The border between Canada and the USA is the longest continuous border in the world. I'll be able to slip across unnoticed somewhere, probably by water. Hundreds of illegal immigrants do it every year anyway and I was trained to do it properly when serving with the SBS, so if they can do it I'm sure I can.'

'And how many years ago was your training with the SBS?'

'Nearly ten years ago.'

'Exactly. Since then American border security has advanced greatly. They now employ heat and movement sensitive devices, drones, and even satellite surveillance to guard their border.'

'I'm aware of all that, Prem. Bloody hell, this is like being sent on a mission with my mother.'

'A most excellent woman by all accounts.'

'How do you know that?'

'We know everything about you, Christopher. That is why we are supporting you on this mission. Tell me, could you be doing this without us?'

Wyatt conceded the point. 'No, I could not.'

'Then please listen to my advice. Do you own a mobile phone, or cell phone as the Americans call them.'

'Yes, of course.'

'Give it to me, please.'

'What for?'

'I will keep it safe for you. You must not take it on this trip.'

'Why not?'

'Because you will be tempted to use it and that will immediately tell the American authorities where you are and what you are doing.'

'Oh, come on, Prem. I don't believe all that stuff about our mobile phone calls and emails being read by the intelligence services. They might do that with suspects but not ordinary citizens.'

Prem regarded Wyatt like a fond uncle teaching a backward child. 'Tell me, Christopher, have you heard of an American organisation known as the NSA?'

'Yes, of course I have. It's the National Security Agency.'

'Have you heard of Operation Shamrock?'

'Not unless it's an Irish Indie band.'

'During the 1970s, Operation Shamrock allowed the NSA to read all telegrams sent from the United States to wherever. All of them, Christopher.'

'We don't use telegrams anymore.'

'But we do use mobile phones, land line phones, emails, and so on. The NSA currently intercepts approximately two *billion* such transactions a day and analyses them for any information that might be a threat to US security.'

'That's still probably a fraction of the number being sent every day.'

'A good point, Christopher, but the Utah Data Centre is about to come on line, if it has not already done so. It's a high security facility, deep in the Utah desert, that will allow the USA to store a septillion bytes of information. A septillion is one followed by twenty four zeroes, or five hundred quintillion pages of text and graphics, more than the estimated number of stars in the entire universe. You British are increasing such facilities in a similar way, albeit on a smaller scale, at such places as GCHQ in Cheltenham, all in the name of the war against terrorism.'

'All very fascinating, Prem, but why are you telling me this?'

'Because this is my speciality, Christopher. Every citizen in your country and the USA is being watched, spied on, monitored, photographed, analysed and categorised, day in and day out. Fortunately such measures have not arrived in my country but, given time, they certainly will. If you want to be found by the authorities, the easiest way is to make a mobile phone call. Technology is simultaneously a secret agent's best friend and worst enemy. But you have an advantage that all the technology in the world cannot overcome.'

'What's that?'

'You have been trained to look after yourself without all this electronic paraphernalia. When you are in the States I urge you to use it as little as possible.'

'But I must have some form of communication. And a weapon would be useful, if I can get my hands on one.'

'I agree.' Prem opened his attache case. 'Here are your flight tickets and here is confirmation of your reservation at the hotel in

Toronto. After you have checked in you will be visited by a "business associate". He will give you a case containing everything you need. There will be a weapon, also a laptop and a mobile phone. Both have been specially adapted by my team to be completely untraceable. Use only that phone and laptop. If you lose them or in case of a dire emergency, buy a pre-paid mobile phone and destroy it as soon as it has been used. Land lines are much safer but still vulnerable. If you have to send an email, use an internet cafe and then get as far away as possible as soon as you have pressed send. And one further vitally important point. Although the mobile phone and laptop are untraceable, do not insert the SIM card and especially not the batteries until you need to use the devices. Mobile phones can be traced even when they are switched off. You must take out the batteries. Do you understand?'

'Yes, mother.'

'I'm not your mother but you are young enough to be my son and I am becoming fond of you, despite your intemperate and impatient nature. I want you to come back in one piece. Oh, and beware of transponders. They can be fixed on your car, your suitcase, your clothes, even on your person. If the authorities are watching you then such devices allow them to know exactly where you are via GPS.'

'Do you think I'm being watched already?'

'Probably not. Your superiors will assume that you are still on holiday in Switzerland. That was another good reason not to go back to your own house. It is almost certainly being watched. After that email intercept you cannot be too careful.'

Wyatt took his mobile phone from his jacket pocket and threw it on the dining table. 'I still can't believe I'm being set up. What did the email say? "The Wyatt problem must be solved an a permanent basis". You say it was sent to several different departments, including my own?'

'Yes, it was at the highest security level. We cannot be sure who sent it. That's why I stopped you from contacting Assistant Commissioner Sherman. There could be a mole or a traitor in British intelligence. The way the email is phrased, it could mean little, such as you are simply to be sacked. It could mean you are to be liquidated.'

'Liquidated? The British government doesn't do such things.'

Once again Prem shook his head at Wyatt's naïvety. 'Do they not? There is an ultra-secret cadre of special forces personnel who are willing to undertake British government sanctioned assassinations. It is known as Increment?'

'I've heard rumours about Increment but I don't believe such an organisation exists.'

'Believe me, Christopher, it exists.'

'Thanks for the pep talk, Prem. If I was worried before, I'm now terrified. Talking of assassins, did you get much out of our Chinese friends?'

'No. We followed the van to a lock-up garage in Chingford. They were, as I expected, Triads hired in Hong Kong to do a one-off job. They were paid to capture you alive and take you to that garage. They had no idea who hired them or why they wanted you kidnapped. It was clear they didn't know anything, so we let them go.'

'Let them go? Was that wise?'

'We know where they are?'

'How?'

'Transponders, Christopher. Remember what I told you. If you are ever seized by the authorities and then released, search your baggage, your clothes, your car, and, if you have been unconscious, even under your skin for transponders.'

'How do I know you haven't planted one on me?'

'I have. There is one on your luggage here and one concealed in your clothing. I want to know where you are at all times. That reminds me of another interesting development. My people swept your house for explosives and bugs. We found a bug, but it had been in place, in your landline telephone, for many years. It is of Russian manufacture.'

Wyatt was surprised. 'So Blokhin was listening to my phone calls ever since he gave me the house, although I rarely use the landline since those bloody things became popular.' Wyatt gestured at his mobile phone and then went to the window to gaze out at the grey London sky. 'Do you think we're on the right track about China? Silk Fist sounds like a Chinese code name but why should they bring a world of trouble down upon their heads? The Chinese are a subtle, sinuous and insidious people. Even if the Maoists are regaining control in China, Chairman Mao died years ago. Surely nobody reads his Little Red Book anymore.'

'On the contrary, Christopher. I have been fighting against Maoist insurgents throughout my career.'

Wyatt turned back, his interest aroused. 'Where? You mean in India?'

'Yes. Have you heard of the Naxalites?'

'No, I haven't.'

'That's because you live in a Euro-centric and US-centric culture. There are several Maoist and Communist insurgency movements in various parts of India. We have lost hundreds killed fighting them in recent years I think it's entirely possible that the Maoists are starting a new offensive against the capitalist West.'

'Is that how did you lost your arm, fighting against these Naxalites?'

'Yes. I was a flight lieutenant in the air force. I was in my F-15 in a dog fight over the Punjab against twelve enemy MiGs. They came at me out of the sun but I turned and twisted and barrel-rolled and looped-the-loop and shot them all down.'

Wyatt frowned sceptically. He said: 'Are you serious?'

'Of course not but I enjoyed the look on your face. I lost my arm in a training accident. I was instructing a new pilot who, to be generous, did not have much talent. His landing did not come up to scratch and that was the end of my flying career… and his.'

'Well, you manage to drive a car okay with that ingenious device that fits on the steering wheel. How did you get into intelligence work?'

'I'd always been fascinated by computers and modern technology. After I was discharged from the Indian Air Force I discovered that I had a real talent for cryptography and computer hacking. It has served me well.'

'You said you were only fifty something years old. Did the flying accident turn your hair white?'

'No, Christopher. Until three weeks ago my hair was black.'

'Really? What changed it?'

Prem hesitated. Then he said: 'I saw my wife killed in an explosion.'

Wyatt, for a moment, thought that Prem may have been joking again but Prem's expression told him otherwise. He asked: 'Do you mean in that attack on your Prime Minister by that crazed South African?'

'Yes. My wife's name was Rhea. She ran Prime Minister Mishra's office. I was meeting Rhea for lunch. She was only a mere few metres away from me. The bomber, du Preez, ran past me. I tried to stop him. Rhea tried to stop him. One moment she was there, a beautiful, vibrant woman, smiling with happiness to see me. The next she lay on the floor like a castaway rag doll. The mother of my children destroyed into a bloody pulp in an instant. I loved her so deeply, Christopher. My life will never be the same again.'

Wyatt nodded. He did not know what to say.

Prem went on: 'On the surface I may seem amiable enough. I am a Hindu. I believe in love and forgiveness and reincarnation. I try to rationalise what I feel, I try to accept it, be a good Indian, a devout Hindu, a man of the spirit, not of hatred. But I tell you truly, Christopher, inside me I seethe like a volcano with hatred for those who blotted out the life of my beloved wife. I want blood, I want death, I want revenge. I want you to be my weapon, my instrument of revenge. You have the strength, the skill, the tenacity, the physical capacity that I don't possess. I have seen the reports of your superior officers from your army days. They all say that your greatest quality is that you never give up. They say...'

Wyatt interrupted, almost angrily: 'Please, Prem, that's enough. I understand how you must feel but I have to keep a cool head. You cannot load your emotions on to me. I nearly lost my way after the princess was murdered. I will do my best for you, and Rhea, for the whole world, but we have no idea, yet, what we are up against.'

Prem nodded. 'You are right, Christopher. I overstepped the mark. I apologise for my outburst.'

'No need, my friend. I've already learned that you're an exceptional man. Rhea must have been an exceptional woman.'

'She was. She was, indeed.' Prem sighed and opened his laptop. 'Time for us to go. I'm flying back to New Delhi this afternoon. It will be easier to monitor your movements from there and order any back-up you might need. I can get my team started on investigating Silk Fist. I'll check the news reports and my emails for any last minute complications. Oh, dear. Here's one already.'

'What is it?'

Prem turned the laptop screen towards Wyatt. Wyatt read the news report with astonishment and mounting alarm.

'Damn,' Wyatt said. 'I didn't expect that. They'll be coming at me from both sides.'

'We have to go. The sooner you get through Heathrow checkout the better. Be extra vigilant and remember what I have told you,'

Wyatt nodded. 'I'll try, Prem, if I can make it across the Atlantic without being killed by one side or the other.'

21

The White House, Washington, March 1st

L inda Marquez was shown into the Family Dining Room. Martina Logan was eating breakfast alone. She said: 'Ah, there you are, Linda.'

'I'm sorry to keep you waiting, Marty. I thought you'd be in the East Wing.'

'No, no. I'm late having breakfast. I should have called you. It's been quite a night.'

The dining table was strewn with newspapers.

'What's going on?' Linda asked.

'Sit down and have something to eat. Keep me company.'

'Just coffee for me,' Linda said.

'Nonsense,' Martina Logan said briskly. 'You'll have something to start the day. I've a feeling you'll need all the energy you can get. You like scrambled eggs, don't you?'

'I guess. Thank you.'

Martina Logan summoned the butler and gave him her order. She scrutinised Linda's appearance. 'How are you bearing up, Linda. You look a little peeky.'

'Just tired, I guess, but I'm okay to do my job, Marty.'

'I regret having to cancel your holiday after the Dulles airport tragedy and... well, everything else.'

'It's no problem, Marty, really. I can deal with it. How are you doing? Is that head wound still bothering you?'

'It throbs when Joe starts shouting but apart from that it's healing well. Have you seen the news today?'

'No, I haven't had a chance.'

Martina Logan selected a broadsheet newspaper and handed it to Linda. 'That's the *London Sentinel*. It's one of Britain's best newspapers and they rarely get things wrong. The *Sentinel* broke the story. The other British papers, and ours, and all the other media, have picked up the story. Joe's been up since five trying to find out what is going on. Read it.'

Linda read the headline aloud. '"*China's Secret War Against Democracy*"? Surely that's absurd.'

'Read the whole story, Linda.'

The butler brought in Linda's scrambled eggs and a fresh pot of coffee. Linda did not touch either. She read aloud again: '"*These astounding claims are based on reliable information received from a member of Britain's security forces who was on duty during the assassination of the Princess Royal and also the recent assault on America's First Lady and Vice President at St Paul's Cathedral. He claims that China has given this secret war the code name Silk Fist. The source has been suspended from duty and has now disappeared.*" That has to be that guy Wyatt. He was present at both incidents and he's been suspended from duty.'

'It seems likely,' Martina Logan said.

Linda threw down the newspaper. 'I knew there was something suspicious about Wyatt. The way he disappeared at the cathedral, supposedly called away by his boss, and the way he tried to get into the embassy in London to tell me lies about how Mike died. Wyatt is on the run and spinning a web of lies to cover his own tracks and pin the blame for his culpability on someone else.'

'I'm not so sure. The *Sentinel* is a respected and reliable newspaper. I doubt whether they would print such a dangerous story unless they were sure of their facts, let alone on the say so of one renegade agent. Eat your eggs, Linda. The President has ordered increased security here and at other government and defence buildings until he finds out what is going on. He's in conference with the intelligence chiefs at this moment.'

'No, I'm not,' President Joe Logan said as he strode into the dining room. 'I've been up since five, I'm starving, and I'm damn well going to have a quiet breakfast.' He kissed his wife. 'Good morning, dear. Good morning, Linda.'

Linda Marquez stood up. 'Good morning, sir. I'll leave you in peace to enjoy your breakfast.'

Logan waved his hands for her to it down. 'Finish your eggs, Linda. I'll enjoy my breakfast all the more with a pretty girl to look at.'

Martina Logan glared at her husband.

'Okay, two very pretty girls to look at,' Logan said.

Linda was uneasy about the President's avuncular sexism but she accepted that he did not mean to be offensive. He was from a different era, a different culture. Martina Logan was looking at her shrewdly, understanding full well what Linda was thinking.

The butler asked: 'What would you like, sir?'

'Cheese grits,' Joe Logan said. 'Then some pancakes with syrup.'

Linda's heart sank at the prospect of having to watch Georgia Joe Logan eat such a breakfast.

Martina Logan said: 'Why not have some eggs, or fresh fruit salad.'

'I need sustenance, not bird food. It's been a helluva start to the day. What are you two looking at?'

'I guess we're both concerned about you,' his wife replied. 'You look tired. You've put on too much weight, Joe. You're too fond of fatty foods and bourbon. You're a tall man and you can carry the weight well, especially hidden by a good tailor, but you should listen to your doctors and try to lose a few pounds.'

'You know, Marty, ever since we came to the White House I've put on twenty pounds, my hair has turned thin and grey at the edges, and I've got considerably more lines on my face, and yet a funny thing has happened.'

'What's that, dear?' Martina Logan asked like a patient parent addressing a toddler.

'I'm actually more popular than when I was first elected, or so the polls tell me. That's not bad for a guy who's held down the toughest job in the world for the past six years. Perhaps Mr and Mrs Average America are reassured by a man would likes his food and drink.'

'I think you're popularity is more owing to your low cunning, your political instincts and your down-to-earth Southern charm, Joe. It certainly worked with me.'

Logan smiled sweetly. 'Best use I ever made of it.'

'Thank you. I'll take any compliment I can get from you these days. It's a good job that Mr and Mrs America can't see how ruthless you can be. You were born into good old Southern money and all your life you've been used to getting you own way.'

'I don't always get my own way and if I'm ruthless then it's against my enemies, both political and international.'

'And your colleagues if they don't make the grade.'

'Goddamit, Marty, are you throwing that in my face again? I'm well aware that you think I'm too afraid of anything radical. You're not the only one who thinks like that. Listen, before I make any decision about this great country of ours I think carefully, slowly, take all the advice I can get, analyse the effect any decision might have, and then I back my judgement one hundred per cent, so get off my back, woman. Where the hell is my breakfast?'

Linda stood up and said: 'I'd better go.'

Martina Logan said: 'Oh, I'm sorry, Linda. We didn't mean to start an argument and embarrass you.'

'Sit down, Linda,' the President ordered. 'We're always having these little spats. Do you think I eat and drink too much?'

'Sir, it's not my place to…'

'I'm asking you. Do I eat and drink too much?'

'Yes, sir, but I can understand why. The stress of the job and so on. It's called comfort eating.' Linda dare not say that she found Logan's eating habits repulsive, a feeling she kept strictly to herself and had not even told Mike about.

'There you go, Marty. Linda understands.'

'But she didn't say she approves. Why do you think Joe is so popular, Linda?'

'Oh, Marty, you can't put me on the spot like that in front of my President and commander-in-chief.'

'I'd be interested to hear your opinion,' President Logan said, almost cruelly enjoying Linda's discomfiture. 'Why do you think I'm so popular. No ass kissing now!'

Linda was relieved that she could reply with complete sincerity. 'It's quite simple, sir. It's nothing to do with the way you look, or where you come from, or your supposed Southern charm. It's the fact that the people, like me, are sure that you're completely honest, that you respect our laws and that you have a deep and sincere love of America. They're convinced you're not a fake.'

President Logan was silent for a few seconds. Then he said: 'Wow, Linda, that's the most succinct and reassuring analysis I've ever heard. I should can my other political advisers and get you on my team.'

'I wouldn't accept, sir, because I love working for someone who is as equally responsible for your popularity as you are.'

'You mean you wouldn't leave Marty to work for me?' Logan asked teasingly.

'No, sir.'

President Logan smiled broadly. 'Well, Linda, I asked for no ass kissing and you certainly didn't. Ah, at last, here's my food.'

The butler arranged the dishes on the table and withdrew.

Martina Logan said: 'Linda and I were discussing this Silk Fist thing before you came in. Are we to expect Chinese tanks rolling on to the White House lawn at any moment?'

'I've already spoken to the Chinese ambassador and he assured me that Silk Fist is a myth. His government knows nothing about it, denies any culpability, and are not directing such overt attacks against us.'

Linda said: 'Isn't that what the Japanese ambassador said the day before Pearl Harbour?'

Joe Logan chuckled. 'They certainly denied planning the attack until it actually started. What do you think about Silk Fist theory, Linda?'

'I find it difficult to believe that China is responsible, sir, especially those claims about brainwashing and all that stuff. What would China gain by taking us on? Not just us, but Europe, Japan, India and other countries as well. They are all democratic capitalist countries but China surely cannot believe that it could bring down our system in such an odd way.'

'You're right, Linda. The investigation of any crime usually starts with motive. We have some evidence of a possible Maoist involvement but I cannot see any possible motive the Chinese would have except to cause some degree of panic or destabilisation. It doesn't make sense.'

Martina Logan said: 'I'm glad our three kids have all got married and moved out of here, in case we get bombed.'

Joe Logan grunted and said: 'Don't worry, Marty, the Chinese would have to get past the entire US air force and that's not going to happen on my watch.'

Linda looked away and studied the room as Logan tucked into to his pancakes.

Once again Martina Logan was looking at Linda shrewdly. She said: 'It's a lovely intimate dining room, isn't it, Linda. Such elegant understated charm and beautiful furniture. We much prefer this room to eating in the bigger state dining rooms.'

The Vice President looked into the room. He said: 'I'm sorry to disturb your breakfast, Joe. Let me know when you're finished and I'll come and report about the briefing.'

Joe Logan waved him in. 'Come and sit down and have some coffee, Cley. I'm not going to get much peace today so let's get it over with.'

Cleytus Kefalas bestowed the Cleytus Grin as he entered. 'Good morning, Marty. Good morning, Linda. How are you?'

'Fine, sir. How are you?'

'Fully recovered and raring to go.'

'I'm glad to hear that, sir.' Linda stood up. 'I'd better leave so you can talk.'

'Will you please sit down, Linda,' Joe Logan said impatiently. 'Stop bobbing up and down. You haven't drunk your coffee yet. If there's anyone in Washington, in the entire country, that we trust more than you then I don't know who they are, and I'm the goddamn President.'

'Yes, sir. Thank you, sir.'

'Now, Cley,' Logan said. 'What do the intelligence boys, and you as their co-ordinator, think about this Silk Fist business?'

'It's possible, Joe, but extremely unlikely. The claim that Maoist elements have seized power in Beijing is frankly unbelieveable and can't be confirmed by any of our sources, and we have many both in and outside of China.'

'That's what I don't understand,' Logan said. 'We've spent billions of dollars on the most thorough and sophisticated espionage and surveillance systems in the history of the world and none of our people saw this coming or can tell us what the hell is going on.'

Kefalas shrugged. 'I hate to agree but that is true. At least now we have these two words "Silk Fist" to search for. I've already ordered all our electronic search and analysis capability to concentrate on those two words, in all known languages. China, especially at the highest echelons, is such a closed and puzzling society that power plays could be conducted behind closed doors of which we have no inkling.'

'But why launch an attack on the West in such a manner? What would they be trying to achieve? They can't bring us down in this way? They could hardly even weaken us to any degree. During World War Two our bomber guys and the Royal Air Force were sending over hundreds of bombers day and night to carpet Germany with explosives but it still couldn't knock out the Nazis until Russian tanks rolled into Berlin.'

Martina Logan said: 'Perhaps they're trying to scare us, to soften us up for some reason. I'm scared ever since that business in London. I now look at people I have to meet officially and wonder if they're going to try to knock my head off. If these claims about brainwashing are true and they caused a bishop, of all people, to try to kill us then who can we trust? When do we know we're safe, any of us?'

'It's a good point,' Kefalas said. 'Psychological warfare can be devastating in the right circumstances. China has conducted a cyber war against us for years. That's caused a degree of destabilisation and uncertainty. Perhaps Silk Fist is the next step in their campaign.'

Logan said: 'This is the United States of America. We're not going to be defeated by a bunch of chicken shit rice farmers, however clever and rich they've become.'

Kefalas said: 'It doesn't pay to underestimate China.'

'It doesn't pay to underestimate *us*. What do we know about this *London Sentinel* paper? Who wrote this story?'

'British intelligence visited the *Sentinel* offices as soon as the story broke. The editor was reluctant to talk but eventually admitted that the story was sent by the owner of the newspaper under strict instructions that it must be printed as written.'

'Who owns the paper?'

'It was bought a couple of years ago by a Russian oligarch named Yaroslav Blokhin.'

Joe Logan sat back in his chair. 'Blokhin? I've heard of him. Can we get to him?'

'He normally lives in London but nobody knows where he is. We think he is back in Russia. Blokhin has interests all over the world, in all sorts of businesses, including the media. It was his media outlets, as well as the *Sentinel,* that broke the story. The editor said that Blokhin had never before been involved or dictated the content of the *Sentinel*. The editor was surprised and highly dubious about the story. He contacted Blokhin who insisted the story was true, that he had evidence from several sources and that it had been confirmed by a British intelligence agent he had met in Switzerland.'

'Do we know the name of this British agent?'

'Not at this point, Joe. The Brits are working on it.'

Linda Marquez said: 'Forgive me, Mr Vice President, but I think the Brits are not telling you everything. They must know the identity of this so-called agent because even I can take a good guess.'

'What was that, Linda?' Joe Logan asked. 'You know who this guy is?'

Before Linda could answer, Deputy Chief Isaiah Franklin entered the dining room. 'My apologies for disturbing your breakfast, Mr President. May I have a word with Linda?'

'Sure. Go ahead.'

As Linda was getting up, she asked: 'This wouldn't be about Sergeant Christopher Wyatt, would it?'

Franklin looked at her in astonishment. 'How the hell did you know that? Pardon me, mam.'

'That's all right, Stack,' Martina Logan said.

Joe Logan asked Franklin: 'Is this anything to do with Silk Fist?'

'I believe it could be, sir. It was Wyatt who gave the *Sentinel* the story about Silk Fist. The British thought he was on holiday in Switzerland but Wyatt had returned to London.'

'Have they picked him up?'

'No, sir, they screwed up. Wyatt booked a flight to Toronto. It took off about five minutes before the Brits put out the word to have him detained. Wyatt is in the air at this moment. That's why I decided I'd better interrupt your meal, sir. His flight arrives in Toronto in about an hour.'

'Then we have to move real fast,' Kefalas said. 'I'll arrange with the Canadians to have Wyatt detained.'

'Why is Wyatt going to Toronto?' Logan asked.

Linda Marquez said: 'It might sound strange, sir, but he could be coming to the States to find me. He attempted to break into the embassy in London in order to get to me. He is under the delusion that Mike's death had something to do with this Silk Fist stuff but I've been reliably informed by Mike's old captain that Wyatt is completely wrong.'

'Yes,' Kefalas agreed. 'Wyatt is an odd sort of guy, a drunk, a loose cannon. He couldn't come directly to the States at such short notice because of our homeland security measures but, as a British subject, he can enter Canada easily. A guy with his sort of training in the special forces could easily slip across the border. We have to pick him up, Joe.'

Joe Logan was deep in thought for several seconds. Then he said: 'Why not let him run?'

'How do you mean?' Kefalas asked.

'This guy Wyatt is obviously up to his neck in whatever is going on with Silk Fist. We're not sure that he is coming to find Linda. He might be coming over to meet other Silk Fist confederates. Why not let him run? Keep close surveillance on him and see where he leads us.'

Chief Franklin cleared his throat and said: 'Excuse me, Mr President, if Wyatt is coming to find Linda then that strategy might expose her to a great deal of danger. That's why I came to warn her now. If he happened to get away from us then Linda's life might be threatened.'

Linda said: 'I appreciate your concern for my safety, chief, but if it helps us to find out what is going on about Silk Fist then I'm willing to take the risk. After all, I am a Secret Service agent. I've been trained in self-defence and can use a firearm. Sergeant Wyatt doesn't worry me.'

Logan said: 'Okay, thank you, Linda. That decides it. We have to move quickly. Cley, will you contact the Canadians and ask them, as a matter of national security and as a personal favour to me, to put their best surveillance team on Wyatt and shadow him wherever he goes. Offer to send our best guys and equipment to help, whatever it takes. Okay, thanks, Cley. Thanks, Stack. Let's get moving on this.'

Cley Kefalas and Isaiah Franklin left the dining room. The President stood up but his wife said: 'You just wait a goddamn minute, Joe Logan.'

'What's wrong, Marty?'

'What's wrong is that Linda is employed as my protection officer and my special assistant. She is also my close friend. I'm not going to let you use her as bait to attract some crazy British hit man. This guy Wyatt, if he is coming for Linda, will assume that she is here at the White House, so I want Linda to be sent away where nobody can find her. I don't even want Stack to know. This is between the President, the President's wife and Linda. Nobody else need know.'

Logan shook his head. 'You're wrong, Marty. If Wyatt is after Linda then she is safer in the White House under close guard.'

'She'll be safer somewhere secret and unknown and where you can arrange for her to be guarded round the clock. What do you think, Linda?'

'Could I go and stay with my parents in Florida? Their house is well away from any towns, it's well protected anyway, and it would be great to see my folks. They've been worried about me ever since Mike died.'

Martina Logan was dubious. 'I don't know whether your parents' house will be safe enough.'

'I don't want to spend days or weeks locked in the White House or in some anonymous safe house on my own.'

'Well, okay,' Martina Logan said reluctantly. 'I promised you a holiday and had to cancel it. Now you can go away for as long as it takes to clear up this mess. Any arguments, *Mr President.*'

Joe Logan held his hands up in surrender. 'Whatever makes you happy, Marty. Linda, I'll order the local cops and FBI office to liaise and send their best men to look after you and your folks. That's not negotiable. That way you'll be completely safe and you can have a good rest away from this slave driver.'

'Thank you, Mr President,' Linda said.

Joe Logan walked out and Martina Logan said: 'I'm glad that's decided. Don't tell Stack or anyone else where you're going. You need a break, Linda, and Wyatt will not be able to get anywhere near you down in Florida.'

22

Silver Lake Motel, near Toronto, Canada, March 5th

G erry Murphy looked around the parking lot. Nobody was watching him. It was late evening and there were few shoppers at the mall. Murphy walked over to the corner of the parking lot as if making for his car. He ducked into the shadows behind a large plain blue van. He tapped lightly on the back doors of the van.

One of the doors opened. Murphy held up his CIA credentials. He said: 'Sorry I'm late. I had a problem finding this place. I'm Gerry Murphy.'

A burly dark-haired man, at least ten years younger than Murphy but already losing his hair on top, said: 'Welcome aboard. Come on in.'

'I went to the wrong mall,' Murphy explained as he climbed into the van. 'I didn't expect you to park this far away from the motel.'

'No problem, you haven't missed anything.' The two men shook hands. 'I'm Jack Leighton, CSIS. I've been given the unenviable task of heading this operation.'

'Why unenviable?' Murphy asked.

'Because the heat coming from my boss, your President and the British Prime Minister is enough to melt my shorts. If we lose this guy we'll all be transferred to Afghanistan or somewhere.' Leighton closed the door.

Murphy looked at the bank of monitoring screens and asked: 'Who is the target?'

'His name is Christopher Wyatt. I've not been told all the details about what he's done or why we have to stick to him, but I have been told that he is British, ex-special forces, possibly armed and extremely dangerous. We have to stay with him and find out where he's going at all costs. Repeat: *at all costs.*'

Murphy nodded. 'Okay. I've brought men and equipment with me, the best we've got. They're holed up in another motel until I find out how they can help. I've been ordered to co-operate fully and give you any assistance you require, although it looks like you've got this guy buttoned down pretty tight.'

Murphy studied the bank of six monitor screens.

Leighton said: 'We've installed cameras at the front and the back of the motel. Two of them are infra red. There's also one trained on his hire car in the car park there, and one on the entry and exit lane in case he slips past somehow.'

'Do you think Wyatt knows we're onto him?'

'I'd say not. Wyatt's been trained to counteract any tails or surveillance but he's been acting in a manner that suggests he doesn't suspect we're observing him. He's been acting strangely but not in a way that makes me think he's blown our cover.'

'How do you mean by acting strangely?' Murphy asked.

Leighton said: 'We've been following him ever since he entered the country at the airport. He checked in to the Hilton and later went shopping for all sorts of stuff, some of which we were able to identify, mainly clothes and tools. He made no attempt to hide what he was doing or to evade any possible tail.'

'What sort of tools did he buy?'

'Small stuff like a screwdriver, pliers and a wrench. That's what we could identify. He also did some shopping in a big department store but we couldn't identify his purchases for fear of spooking him.'

'Could be making a bomb or some sort of explosive device?'

'It's possible,' Leighton said 'He checked out of the hotel and rented a car, the one on the screen. Then he drove straight here and checked into the Silver Lake Motel. Can't understand why he chose the Silver Lake. It's an old-fashioned roach pit.'

'Could be meeting someone here or simply chosen this motel as somewhere more anonymous than the Hilton hotel to prepare some scheme. Do you have any people on the ground in case Wyatt spots the cameras?'

'Oh, yeah. The cameras are well concealed but we've got agents with night glasses all around the place. This small screen here is a motion sensor. We can tell whether Wyatt is moving about in his room. He's on the second floor, in room eight. That's up those steps, along the balcony, about in the middle of the row.'

'He's definitely in there now?'

'Yes. We can tell he's watching the television from the signal and we can see the lights on.'

'Has he been out since he got here?'

'No. He had a pizza delivered. We couldn't interfere with that in any way. We've planted trackers on his car but obviously we can't get close enough to get one in his luggage or in his clothing but whatever this guy does we'll know about it.'

'I'm impressed,' Murphy said. 'You've got him locked down tight. It looks like a busy place. There's quite a bit of movement, many guests coming and going, even though it's late at night.'

'That's because it's cheap with some very dubious characters living here. I wouldn't board my dog in there.'

Murphy looked at his watch and said: 'It's ten o'clock now. I'll ring my guys and tell them to stand down for the evening. I'll stay and observe, if that's okay.'

'Fine,' Leighton said. 'Glad to have the company. Can I get you a coffee?'

'That would be great.'

Murphy made his call. As he was finishing, Leighton said: 'Looks like someone has sent out for some fun.'

The two men looked at the screen. A young woman was

approaching the motel. She was wearing a black plastic raincoat with a large bag slung over her shoulder. Her walk, and the black fishnet stockings, betrayed her occupation.

Murphy said: 'I wonder if our boy Wyatt has sent out for some relaxation.'

'She could certainly relax me, all night if she wanted to. She's walking up to the second floor.' Leighton pressed a switch and said quietly: 'All units, watch for a woman nearing Wyatt's room. She looks like a working girl. Be vigilant.'

The woman walked along the second floor balcony. Leighton and Murphy held their breath, but she walked past room eight and, after looking around, tapped on the door of room nine. The door opened and the woman went into the room.

Murphy said: 'Do we know who's in room nine?'

'No,' Leighton said. 'We had to inform the motel manager that we were putting his place under surveillance but we didn't specify who or what we were looking for. His staff know nothing. We thought it might tip Wyatt off if the manager or his staff started acting strangely.'

'You've done a great job here, Jack. There's no way Wyatt can get out without us knowing.'

Two hours later the door of room nine opened. The working girl came out followed by a black man wearing glasses and a brown overcoat. The pair were laughing. They stopped to kiss as they walked along the balcony.

'What's Wyatt doing?' Murphy asked.

'He's in his room. The television is on, so are the lights and there is movement. He must be in there. Even so, I'm not taking any chances.' Leighton switched on the microphone link and said: 'Sally, check that woman and the black guy in the brown overcoat. They might be accomplices. Follow them, see where they're going, but don't get seen.'

'Roger, chief. I'm on them.'

An hour later the television in room eight was switched off. Five minutes later the lights went out. The motion sensor showed no movement.

'Guess he's tucked in for the night,' Leighton said. 'I'll arrange for another shift to take over from us and the watchers at two. Then we can clock off and get some sleep ourselves.'

It was gone half past one when an agent called in.

Leighton pressed receive on the mic. 'Go ahead, Frank. What's happening?'

The agent said: 'Sir, we've just found Sally. She's okay but she was bound and gagged and locked in a cupboard in an empty store. The black guy wasn't black at all. He was white made up to look black. It was Wyatt.'

'How can you be sure of that?'

'Because he told Sally who he was and apologised for having to put her out of commission. He even left Sally a bottle of champagne to compensate. Quite a charmer she says.'

'Shit,' Leighton said. 'I'll give Wyatt some frigging charm when I catch up with him.' He rang his commanding officer.

An hour later his commanding officer rang back. Leighton said to Murphy: 'We've consulted with the Brits and with your guys and we've received permission to go in.' Leighton switched on the microphone link. 'All agents hear this. The chicken has flown the coop so we're sending in the SWAT team. All agents remain in position until they've been in. Wyatt may have booby trapped the room or have accomplices inside.'

Ten minutes later the SWAT team arrived. They swarmed up to the second floor balcony, followed by Leighton and Murphy. A hydraulic ram smashed down the door to room eight and two stun grenades were thrown inside, immediately followed by two tear gas grenades. The SWAT team, wearing gas masks and oxygen, went inside. Within minutes the leader of the SWAT team came out, took off his breathing mask and said to Leighton and Murphy: 'It's empty. The gas has cleared. You'd better come and look at this.'

Leighton and Murphy went in. They looked up at the toy airplane on a wire, no longer going round and round. 'That was to fool our motion sensors,' Leighton said.

Murphy nodded. 'He put time switches on the television and the table lamp. All the while we thought Wyatt was in here he was long gone. But how?'

The SWAT team leader said: 'Over here.'

Leighton and Murphy walked further into the room. The SWAT leader pointed to a large hole cut through the thin partition between room eight and room nine.

'Now we know why he chose such a cheap motel,' Leighton said. 'The bastard walked out right under our noses and in full view.'

Leighton went over to the dining table on which was standing a bottle of single malt whisky. Underneath the bottle was a handwritten note. Leighton took it out and read: *'Sorry, guys. I hope I didn't keep you hanging about all night. Have a drink on me. Wyatt.'*

'What is it?' Murphy asked.

'Our ticket to Afghanistan,' Leighton said.

23

Danielville, Florida, March 14th

Linda Marquez said: 'Whenever I'm away this is how I think of home. Sitting out on the stoop with you guys on a warm night like this, the sky full of stars, the perfume of the orange groves, listening to the mockingbirds, drinking a daiquiri. I'm so glad to be home.'

Her father smiled. 'So you haven't completely changed into a New York girl?'

'No, pop. I love the city but there is only one place to call home, and this is it. It's done me a world of good to get away and see you both. I feel like I'm sixteen again.'

'Except we didn't allow you to drink daiquiris back then,' her mother said. 'And we didn't have to watch a bunch of cops and FBI guys lurking behind the magnolias and scaring off the fireflies. Honey, can't you tell us why they're here?'

'It's nothing to worry about, mom, really. It's just a precaution after that terrible business in London and with this Silk Fist nonsense going on. Marty insisted that I be given some extra protection.'

'Marty!' her father exclaimed with an ironic tone but also with pride. 'She calls the First Lady of the United States Marty! Our little girl has some powerful friends.'

Linda finished her drink. 'I think I'll turn in now. If we're going to the Strawberry Festival tomorrow we'd better get an early start.' She stood up and kissed her mother and father goodnight.

'Sleep well, honey,' her mother said.

Linda went into the house. She loved her parents and loved being back home with them but sometimes the questioning became a little too persistent, a little too irritating, about Mike, about Marty, about her life in New York, about the agents patrolling the grounds.

Linda opened her bedroom door and switched on the lights. She froze with fear when she saw Wyatt sitting in her armchair over by the window. He was dressed all in black, a black ski mask resting in his lap. The drapes were drawn behind him. He was holding a pistol aimed directly at her. He said quietly: 'Please close the door and switch off the lights, Linda. Don't try to warn anyone.'

Linda hesitated but then closed the door and switched off the lights. The room was illuminated by a single table lamp on her dressing table. Linda's stomach took a somersault. She was fearful but also angry about this invasion of her private space. She determined that if she was about to die she would face her killer boldly. 'What are you doing here, Wyatt?'

'The same reason as before. We have to talk about Mike.'

'How did you get in here? The place is surrounded by cops and Feds.'

'I'm sure they're all nice guys, good family men and tax paying citizens, but when it comes to this sort of operation they're amateurs.'

'What operation, Wyatt? You think you're such a big man, breaking into an undefended woman's bedroom?'

'No, Linda. I'm talking about Silk Fist and the lives of hundreds, perhaps thousands, of people. Mike knew something, or was involved, or was affected. I don't know how, but I suspect you do but you don't know that you do. We have to talk about that.'

'I don't have to do anything. The press are saying that you're involved with Silk Fist, Wyatt. They're calling you a rogue agent, a renegade, that you were involved in the murder of the princess and the assault on my people at St Paul's Cathedral. If you're trying to wriggle out by pinning something on me, or my late husband, then you can go take a flying...'

'I've been set up as a fall guy, Linda. I'm being used by a Russian oligarch. I thought he was a friend. He owns the *London Sentinel*. He took something I said and exaggerated and twisted it into a blatant lie. I'm also being set up by my own people, perhaps even the Prime Minister. Perhaps some of your people are also involved.'

'That's bullshit. You're probably here to kill me and then pin some sort of blame on me. Well, go ahead, Wyatt. You're the expert shot special forces hero. Go ahead and shoot an unarmed woman.'

Wyatt indicated the pistol he was holding. 'Do you know what this is, Linda?'

'It's a Glock Parabellum semi-automatic with a standard fifteen bullets.'

'Very good, Linda.'

'It won't take all fifteen to kill me. Fuck you, Wyatt.'

Wyatt turned the gun around and held it out, butt first, to Linda. 'Take it.'

Linda did not move.

Wyatt said: 'Either talk to me about Mike or take this gun and kill me. Your choice.'

Still Linda did not move.

Wyatt threw the gun on to the bed. He made a show of looking around the room. 'Did you grow up here, Linda?'

Linda did not reply.

'It's a lovely house,' Wyatt said. 'It looks like one of those big haciendas we used to see on *Bonanza* or *The High Chapparal* and all those cowboy shows we used to get in England. I suppose it was built like this in honour of your Spanish ancestors.'

Linda glanced at the gun.

'Go ahead,' Wyatt said. 'Go for it. I won't stop you. I love this bedroom. I say bedroom, it's more like an apartment. Your own bathroom, a big television, music centre, computer and desk, bookshelves full of books, plenty of space. I grew up in a council flat in north London. The whole place wasn't much bigger than this room. I had to share a tiny bedroom with my big brother. My sister slept in my parent's bedroom.'

'Very touching, Wyatt. My heart bleeds for you.'

'I'm not angling for sympathy. You've been lucky to be born into wealth but I can see you've also worked hard. I've been looking at your trophies and certificates, and your photographs.'

'Why don't you look in my closet and my underwear drawer while you're at it?'

Wyatt ignored the comment. 'You're a talented girl. Top of the class in exams, almost top in sports, excellent at languages. More than excellent, a major talent. Plenty of friends in the sorority, whatever that is. Some sort of sisterhood I presume. This Sweet Briar place sounds idyllic.'

'It was. It's a great school. I was privileged to go there.'

'There's one word that caught my attention, Linda.'

'What word?'

'The word "kappa".'

'What about it?'

'It was a word that your husband shouted just before he died.'

Linda said: 'I have to sit down.' She went to her bed and perched on the edge. She put her head in her hands and ordered herself not to weep.

Wyatt said: 'I profoundly apologise for being so brutal but it's the only way I can make you listen to me. Pick up the gun, take off the safety, point it at me if you like, but please let's talk.'

Linda ignored the gun. 'Okay, Wyatt. You win.'

'There's no winner here, Linda. What I have to tell you will be extremely hurtful, stressful and upsetting for you, but I have checked the facts about your husband's suicide and what I'm about to tell you is true. Bizarre but true. Together we may be able to prevent other people from suffering the same tragedy.'

Linda nodded. 'I understand. Tell me.'

Wyatt took a deep breath. 'Your husband did not shoot himself, as you have been told. He jumped off the Brooklyn Bridge and was drowned. When his body was recovered, an autopsy was performed and revealed something very strange.'

'What was that?'

'They found a silver bullet inserted into his anus.'

The memory of her last conversation with Mike hit Linda with a mind-numbing shock of guilt. She did not trust herself to speak.

'Linda?' Wyatt said gently. 'Can you explain that?'

'Yes, I can,' Linda replied. 'I told him to do it.'

'Told him? In what way?'

Linda tried to control the catch in her voice. 'Mike had changed in the last three or four weeks. He had been a loving, supportive and kind husband. He changed into a sarcastic, antagonistic brute, resentful of everything about me, my racial heritage, my family money, my career. Especially my career. He hated the time I was spending with the First Lady. The last time I spoke to him I said something hateful. He had made some comment about his lucky silver bullet. The last thing I said to him, as I walked out the door, was "why don't you take your lucky silver bullet, stick it up your ass and go jump off Brooklyn Bridge". Now you tell me that's exactly what he did. It was all my fault.'

Linda could no longer hold back tears. Wyatt stood up and took a box of tissues from her dressing table. He handed the box to Linda.

Wyatt sat down again and leaned forward earnestly. 'Linda, it's not your fault. I believe Mike had been somehow brainwashed into acting the way he did, just as Doctor Flaherty had been when he killed the princess, or the Bishop of Carlisle when he attacked Mrs Logan and the Vice President. That's why Mike changed from a loving husband into a monster. Linda, you must not blame yourself.'

Linda wiped her eyes. 'What did you mean about "kappa"?'

'According to witnesses who saw Mike jump off the bridge, he shouted "kappa", or what sounded like kappa. I haven't got time to explain all the implications but Mike's behaviour ties in with all the other strange and violent events that have been happening around the world. For instance, I have met a man who was present when the Indian Prime Minister was attacked by a human bomb. They thought the bomber was shouting "kaffir", but it may have been "kappa". Does kappa mean anything to you in relation to Mike?'

'Yes, it does. Before I left for the last time, Mike was ranting about Marty Logan. We both went to Sweet Briar college and we were both members of the Sigma Phi Kappa sorority. Mike was insulting us and called us Sigma Phi Beta bitches. I corrected him by saying "it's Kappa, Michael, not Beta".'

'How did Mike react?'

'When I said "kappa" he sort of became alert. That look of hatred left his face. He asked me what I wanted him to do. That's when I made the nasty remark about throwing himself off Brooklyn Bridge. I'm so ashamed of myself. What sort of wife says things like that to her husband?'

'Linda, Mike was ill, or drugged or brainwashed. We don't know how but we have to find out. When you were going through his effects, did you find anything odd or suspicious or incriminating?'

Linda dried her eyes again and said: 'I haven't been back to the apartment. I haven't been able to face it. I went to Hawaii with Marty and then London and I've being staying in a Washington hotel since then.'

'So your New York apartment is untouched?'

'I'm the only one with a key so I guess it must be.'

'Then we'll have to go and search the place.'

Linda mentally kicked herself to stop the tears and remember that she was a trained Secret Service agent caught in a dangerous situation. 'Hold on, Wyatt. I'm not letting you into our apartment to rummage through my deceased husband's effects.'

'You come with me. You do the rummaging. We might find out why Mike began behaving so strangely.'

'No, Wyatt. I've listened to you and I believe you, up to a point. Now it's time to hand this evidence over to the proper authorities. They can investigate better than we can.'

'I have to disagree with you there, Linda. I don't trust my superiors. One, or two, or maybe several of them are setting me up. Can you trust your people with certainty?'

Linda recalled what President Logan had said about having a multi-billion dollar surveillance and espionage system and yet having no idea who was committing the Silk Fist attacks.

Wyatt was saying: 'If we find evidence in your apartment I swear I'll let you decide what to do with it, but I think you and I should look first, then such evidence cannot be denied or hidden or lost in the system. We could drive up tomorrow and…'

'Whoa! I'm not driving with you.'

'Why not?'

'You might wait until we're in the middle of nowhere and get rid of me permanently.'

Wyatt shook his head with exasperation. 'Don't be ridiculous, Linda. If I wanted to kill you I could do it here and now.'

'There's no silencer on your Glock.'

'What do you mean by that?'

'If you fired that in here there'd be half a dozen Feds on top of you. It would be too dangerous to kill me here but that doesn't mean you won't kill me out in the country if we drive to New York.'

Wyatt sighed impatiently. 'If I wanted to kill you here, Linda, I wouldn't need the Glock to do so. Please believe that I wish you no harm. I can't fly to New York. I've entered your country illegally and I don't have proper identification documents. I could meet you at the apartment?'

'And take the chance that you'd go in before I got there and plant the evidence. No way.'

'Meet me somewhere in New York then.'

'No. You could easily find the address of my apartment. If we do this I want to keep an eye on you. We'll go by Greyhound.'

'By bus?' Wyatt repeated incredulously.

'Yes. There'll be plenty of witnesses on board if you try anything.'

'No way,' Wyatt said. 'I refuse to travel anywhere by bus.'

'We'll take the train then. We can take the Silver Meteor from Jacksonville. You can book a sleeping compartment, one each. It takes a couple of days.'

'Two *days!*' Wyatt exclaimed. 'And I thought British trains were slow!'

'At least it'll be comfortable, if I decide to go.'

'You haven't decided?'

'No. I'm not sure I trust you, but book us two sleepers for the day after tomorrow. I think the train leaves about five thirty.'

'Hold on… why the day after tomorrow?'

'Because I'm going to the Strawberry Festival tomorrow with my mom and dad.'

'Going to the *what?*'

'The Strawberry Festival. It's a family tradition and I'm not going to miss it.'

Wyatt shook his head in mock despair. 'It's taken me several days to track you down and now I've got to wait yet another day while you go and pick strawberries. I've heard of girls playing hard to get but you take first prize, Sergeant Marquez.'

Partly through intense relief that she was not going to die but partly through the expression on Wyatt's face, Linda found herself smiling. 'It's a chance you'll have to take, Sergeant Wyatt. Tomorrow I'm going to make some inquiries and think about what you've said. You wait for me on the platform at Jacksonville the day after. You'll either find yourself surrounded by me and my travel case or by a SWAT team.'

149

24

Amtrak Railway Station, Jacksonville, Florida, March 16th

The Silver Meteor was pulling into the station but Linda Marquez had not arrived. The train was exactly on time. Wyatt accepted that Marquez had decided not to accompany him. All he could do now was travel to New York and find out the address of her apartment. It should be possible to break in and search the place. He took one last look up and down the narrow island platform.

Marquez was approaching, walking quickly and lugging her travel case behind her. She was casually dressed in jeans, blouse and a jacket.

As she drew near Wyatt said: 'I thought you weren't coming.'

'I was here. I've been watching you to make sure you're not up to anything. Have you got the tickets?'

'Yes. What did you think I might be up to?'

Linda did not answer. They handed up their luggage to the attendant, then stepped on board and were shown to their sleeping compartments. Wyatt had made sure they were next to each other. Wyatt gave the attendant a ten dollar tip, hoping it was an appropriate amount. The attendant departed, seemingly satisfied.

'Nice cabins,' Wyatt said, looking in as they stood out in the corridor.

'They're okay. A bit cramped.'

'Perhaps I'm more used to roughing it than you are.'

'Don't start with the poor boy act, Wyatt. You seem to have plenty of money.'

'Thanks to an Indian friend of mine.'

'What Indian?'

'It doesn't matter. How did you enjoy your Strawberry Day?'

'What do you care?'

'Perhaps you didn't go to any Strawberry Festival at all. Perhaps you've been arranging a reception committee for when we get to the Big Apple.'

'Only tourists call it "the Big Apple",' Linda said contemptuously.

'I was simply making a polite inquiry about how you enjoyed your day out.'

'We're not here for the small talk.'

Wyatt sighed theatrically. 'This is going to be a long trip. Let's get settled in then we'll talk about more important things. Your place or mine?'

'You've got to be joking. I'm not letting you into my cabin, and I'm certainly not coming into yours.'

'Come on, Linda! What do you think I'm going to do? Can't we be civil to each other for a day or two?'

'Listen, Wyatt, I don't like you and I don't trust you.'

They braced to steady themselves as the Silver Meteor pulled out of the station.

'What do we do then?' Wyatt asked. 'Stand out here in the corridor and glare at each other?'

'No, we'll talk over dinner. I need to make a couple of calls before then.'

'What? On your mobile? I mean cell phone.'

'Yes. What of it?'

'That's not a good idea, Linda. Cell phones are easily traceable. For the time being we don't want anyone to know what we're up to. Don't forget you're now on the run with a wanted man.'

'No, I'm temporarily co-operating with a wanted man in the hope of finding vital evidence. That's a world of difference. Even so, I take your point. If we have to do this then we'll do it properly and securely. I'll wait until we hit New York and use a pay phone.'

'Thank you.'

'I'll meet you in the dining car at seven. Is that okay for you?'

'Yes, fine.'

Wyatt went into his cabin but a few moments later Linda looked in and said: 'The Strawberry Festival was fun. It was a good day under the circumstances. Thanks for asking.'

The dining car attendant said: 'Good evening, sir. May I have your seat or cabin number?'

Wyatt said: 'Cabin eighteen. I'm travelling with my fiancèe, Miss Marquez. She's in cabin nineteen. Could you give us that table right at the end of the car and make sure we don't have to share with other people? I'd like a romantic dinner with her.' Wyatt gave the attendant a fifty dollar bill.

'Certainly, sir. I'll make sure you'll remain undisturbed.'

Wyatt followed the attendant to the table. Wyatt took the seat from which he could observe the whole length of the carriage. He looked out of the window. The sun had set but there was enough moonlight to see that the Silver Meteor was travelling through low-lying scrubland.

After a few minutes the train passed through the suburbs of a small town. There were lights on in some of the homes. Wyatt could see families sharing their evening meal. Wyatt felt cocooned, strangely peaceful and secure in the rolling silver tube.

Linda Marquez entered the dining car. She had changed into a light blue belted dress. He stood up as she approached.

Linda said: 'Where are you going?'

'Nowhere. I was taught to stand up when a lady enters the room or joins me for dinner.'

'Oh, right, of course.'

They sat down.

Wyatt said: 'I like your dress. It suits your colouring. And your hair has grown out nicely since I saw you in London. You look really lovely.'

Linda sighed with exasperation. 'Cut the crap, Wyatt. This isn't a date.'

'I'm well aware of that. I'm not coming on to you. I was offering a sincere compliment without any hidden agenda.'

Linda looked at him. 'I can't decide whether you're genuine or trying to make a fool of me or trying to smarm your way into my favourable opinion.'

'Time and events will solve that conundrum.' Wyatt picked up a menu card. 'Let's decide what we're going to eat and then we'll get down to business.'

The attendant arrived carrying a silver tray with a bottle of champagne in an ice bucket. He placed the champagne and glasses on the table and said: 'With the compliments of Amtrak. Are you ready to order?'

They ordered their meal then, as the attendant was walking away, Linda asked warily: 'How come we get champagne?'

'I told him that we were engaged and that we wanted a romantic evening without being disturbed. Don't worry, my motives are strictly professional. We don't want anyone joining us while we talk about Silk Fist. We might as well make the most of the champagne. I'll pour.'

Linda held a hand over her glass. 'Not for me. I want to stay sober while I'm dealing with you. Let's talk about Silk Fist. You tell me everything you've found out and I'll tell you what little I've been told.'

They had finished dinner and were drinking coffee by the time Wyatt said: 'The most puzzling aspect is these words that the perpetrators shout before committing the atrocities. Perhaps we could work out a connection. They seem to be code or trigger words that compel the perps to launch their attack. Michael responded to

153

the trigger word "kappa". All the trigger words are odd or unusual words that probably wouldn't come up in everyday conversation.'

'What other trigger words have you got? Let me write them down on this napkin. Spell them out as you think they were said.' Linda looked in her bag. With a trace of self-consciousness she put on her spectacles. 'Damn, I haven't got a pen.'

Wyatt took a ballpoint pen out of his inside pocket and handed it to Linda. He said: 'There's "kappa", which also may have been the word used in India instead of "kaffir". There's "bash" as used by the Bishop of Carlisle.'

Linda shivered at the memory. 'Pour me a glass of champagne. I'll have one glass.'

Wyatt poured the champagne and went on. 'There's "ken" as Doctor Flaherty used. Others have included "fay", "cop", "kisser" or possibly "kicker", "hover", "holder", "glayva" and one that was reported as "burro" or "borough". Some words have been used in more than one attack, some in just one. There are probably many more used that we don't know about or when the perp has been killed in the act. You're good at words and languages. Can you see any link?'

Linda studied the list but shook her head. 'Some, like "ken" could have double or multiple meanings. Ken meaning to understand or Ken as a male first name. Or perhaps a place name. "Fay" could be a female name or it could be spelt F-E-Y.' Linda's eyes lit up. 'Yes, "fey" is an old Celtic word meaning possessed with magical powers. It can also mean crazy, and also marked for imminent death.'

'That's good,' Wyatt agreed. 'Isn't "ken" a Celtic or Scottish word.'

'Yes, it is. It's also the name of Barbie's boyfriend.' Linda smiled but then quickly remembered who she was dealing with.

'We shouldn't rule out any possibility,' Wyatt said.

'Well, "kappa" is a Greek word, or course. There was also Frank Capa, the famous war photographer.'

'Umm, a bit tenuous.'

'Let's use the internet to look up some more of these meanings.'

Linda rummaged in her bag but Wyatt said: 'Use mine.' He took out the secure mobile that Prem had given him.

'Why do you want to use yours but not mine?' Linda asked suspiciously.

'Because mine has been specially adapted to be untraceable.'

'What do you mean? You were given it by some boffin, like that guy in the Bond movies?'

'Sort of. He certainly has white hair like Q and he's certainly very clever. Let's start with "kappa". Oh, it can be a Japanese water sprite.'

'Try "bash".'

'There's hundreds of definitions.'

'All right, what about "holder".'

'Again, there's hundreds. Noddy Holder the pop singer, Vanburn Holder, the great West Indian fast-medium pace bowler.'

'What the hell is that?'

'It's cricket, Linda. It's a game too complicated for you Americans to understand, that's why it never caught on over here.'

Linda looked at Wyatt sharply then realised she was being sassed. She hardly dare admit to herself that she was enjoying this game. 'Is there any champagne left?'

'Sure,' Wyatt said.

After two hours Wyatt said: 'I'm mentally exhausted. We're getting nowhere. I can't see any link or connection.'

'No,' Linda agreed. 'I think it's best if we leave it until another time. I'm going to get some sleep.'

'How about a nightcap?'

'No thanks.'

'Come on, it's still early, don't leave me on my own. Tell me about Mrs Logan and all the secrets from the White House.'

'You've got to be joking, Wyatt.'

'Have a brandy and tell me about the First Lady.'

Linda considered for a moment. 'All right. One brandy.'

Wyatt summoned the attendant and ordered the drinks.

'What do you want to know about Marty?' Linda asked.

'Well, why are you so devoted to her? Is it simply because of your Hispanic heritage?'

'No, of course not,' Linda answered irritably. Then more calmly: 'Our shared background was a common bond that brought us together but it wouldn't make any difference if she was white, black, yellow or purple. Marty has done so much good work, not only for Hispanics but for all the people of America. She supports as many charities as she can, campaigns tirelessly for equality and for better conditions for poorer people. She is terrific.'

'What about the President? What do you think of him?'

'I'm not going there, Wyatt. He's my commander-in-chief.'

'That's his office. What do you think of the man?'

Linda said: 'He eats and drinks too much. I don't know how Marty puts up with him.'

Wyatt waited for more but it was clear that Linda would say no more about her President.

The attendant came with their drinks.

Wyatt picked up his glass and said: 'Cheers.'

Linda did not respond.

Wyatt said: 'What about the Vice President, that Cleytus whatever. That's some set of teeth when he flashes that Cleytus Grin. Many people would have preferred him as President. Would you?'

'Enough, Wyatt. What I think of the Veep is irrelevant.'

'Okay. Touchy subject. What about your family. Your parents must be proud of what you've achieved.'

'I'm not sure. Mom and dad are proud, but they worry, especially after these recent incidents. I had to lie to them as an excuse to hook up with you today. That feels bad. My sister, she's older than me, she thinks I'm wasting my life, that I should have got married and raised a big brood like she has. That's her idea of a worthwhile life. I'd like to have kids one day, but I want a career first.' Linda chided herself for talking too much. To deflect away from herself she asked: 'What about you? Are you married, or ever been married?'

'I was married once. It didn't last long.'

'What happened?'

'She didn't like my strict mistress.'

'You had a strict mistress?'

'Yes. I love that stern look of disapproval on your face. My mistress was called the British army. I got myself wounded and the army looked after me. My wife couldn't be bothered.'

'How did you get yourself wounded?'

Wyatt shrugged. 'It happens in combat. One day you're bound to come across an enemy a bit faster, tougher and smarter than you are.'

Linda nodded. 'I understand, you don't want to talk about it. How do you cope with having to kill people?'

'Bloody hell, Linda. That's a blunt question but I understand why you're asking.'

'You do? Why am I asking?'

'Because every time you try to sleep or try to relax you see the bishop falling down the steps of St Paul's.'

Linda took a sip of brandy. She regretted asking the question but could not help asking another one. 'Does it get any easier?'

'Yes, but it takes time. You did your duty, Linda, and did it well. Take comfort in that.'

Linda nodded. Change the subject. 'Ever been close to marrying again?'

'I've fooled myself into thinking so a couple of times but neither situation was right.'

'Touchy subject again. What's your family like?'

'My dad's a good bloke. He's retired now but he used to be a train driver on the London Tube, what you call the subway. It was a solid job but he never got rich, except by meeting my mother. She had come over from Ireland to visit relatives, met my dad and never went back. They're solid and decent people, hardworking. I have an older brother but we don't get on well. He suffers badly from the worst English disease of them all.'

'I'm sorry to hear that. What disease?'

'In England, as soon as anyone makes money they assume they've stepped up a social class and are above everybody else. It's called being a bloody snob. He lives in East Hampstead with his stuck-up wife and holds his nose when he has to visit us in north London.'

'Hell, Wyatt, I thought you were going to tell me he was dying from some incurable disease!'

'My kid sister is exactly the opposite, really down to earth. She's a good mother. I love her to bits and I miss her, and her two boys. I teach them how to play rugby and cricket and take them to watch Arsenal, that's a soccer team in north London. I also show them ways to defend themselves but under strict orders that they musn't tell their mother. She would kill me if she found out. She hates violence. I have fun with my nephews. Believe it or not, I'm a great uncle.'

'I can believe it.' Linda said. She looked away from Wyatt's dark eyes and reminded herself again that the man sitting opposite might be a dangerous killer, or at least a deluded renegade. She finished her brandy and said briskly. 'Okay, I'm going to get some sleep. What time do we get into New York tomorrow?'

'Just before noon,'

'Okay. Shall I see you back here for breakfast at nine?'

'Suits me,' Wyatt said. He watched as Linda Marquez walked away. He debated whether he should trust her completely. He wanted to trust her but it was always easier to give the benefit of the doubt to a beautiful woman, to be duped by a lovely face and enchanting green eyes. Was that what somebody intended? Was he being played like a violin?

It had been easy to get inside her family home, perhaps too easy. Did someone want Linda Marquez to make contact with him, to win his trust, to find out what he was up to or what he might find out? He decided to be extremely careful when they visited her apartment. He had already been set up by Yaroslav Blokhin and by the British. Was he now being set up by the Americans? When all was said and done, he was now completely on his own.

25

Oval Office, White House, Washington, March 17th

President Josiah Logan looked out at the White House garden while he drank his morning coffee. His chair was fitted with a rocking facility and the motion soothed him, as it always did when he was sitting out on the stoop back home in Georgia. The morning reflection was a solitary habit he had developed during the years of his presidency. He would sometimes order no interruptions for fifteen minutes while he drank his coffee and considered the myriad duties and responsibilities that weighed on his shoulders. Today that weight was heavier than he had ever known and the morning had already been filled with problems. Some had been easy to solve. Other problems seemed insoluble despite the incredible wealth, power and ingenuity of the nation he was proud to lead.

Logan sighed as the intercom buzzed. His fifteen minutes of solitude were up. He pressed receive. 'Yes, Amy?'

'Sir, the Vice President is waiting.'

Perhaps Cleytus Kefalas would provide some solutions. Logan was not optimistic.

'Please ask him to come in.' Logan switched off the rocking chair. Back to business.

Kefalas entered the Oval Office carrying a sheaf of folders. 'Good morning, Joe. How are you today?'

'I feel like boiled crap. Perhaps the doctors are right. Perhaps I should watch what I eat and try to lose some weight. Pull up a chair, Cley.'

'Tough trip?'

'I hate flying, even in Air Force One. The British Foreign Secretary and their chief of intelligence services are arriving any time now. There's something I have to tell them as well as you so you can make your report when they get here.'

Cley Kefalas grinned. 'Knowing that guy Harcourt he'll probably ask you to get him a girl after we've had the meeting.'

Logan chuckled. 'He certainly likes the ladies. I'd better lock up my secretaries. But he's a smart cookie and I like him. I wish he wasn't here with that smarmy asshole Llewelyn. He dresses like an aging hippy but speaks like a toff, always with a cynical sneer on his face. I tried to persuade Prime Minister Montrose to come over but he's got a mountain of his own problems.'

'I'm surprised you get on so well with that socialist. The Brits are a strange bunch. They elect a party that supposedly believes in social equality and yet they love their unelected royals and aristocrats with all their Lord-this and Sir-that. It's as if they enjoy being downtrodden peasants looking up from the gutter at their so-called betters. Thank God America broke away from that nonsense.'

'I agree, but I like Murdo Montrose. Politically we're worlds apart but he tells it like it is and doesn't mince his words. Also he likes an occasional cigarette, like me. I remember us standing out in the garden at Downing Street. We laughed at the thought of the Prime Minister of Great Britain and the President of the United States relegated to the garden to smoke like naughty schoolboys, both victims of our own legislation.'

Kefalas said: 'I like Britain but it's a quaint and peculiar country. They're useful patsies to give our policies a veneer of legitimacy whenever necessary. They suck up to us because they can't accept that their empire's gone and they're a piss ant country like any other now.'

'The Brits can still punch above their weight when necessary, Cley.'

'They sure can, but we have to consistently punch below our weight because of the jealousy and mistrust of lesser countries, all that Great Satan crap. We could wipe them off the planet if we wanted to.'

Logan was relieved when the intercom buzzed.

Amy said: 'Excuse me, sir. The Foreign Secretary and Sir Derek Llewelyn are here.'

Logan said: 'Show them in, Amy.' He got up and went to the door to shake hands with the visitors. 'Richard, great to see you again. Sir Derek, welcome. Have you ever been in the Oval Office before?'

'No, sir,' Llewelyn said. 'It's very exciting. Please just call me Derek. I don't insist on my title.'

Cley Kefalas looked away to hide an involuntary smile.

Logan noted that Llewelyn's palm was warm and wet. Harcourt's handshake had been dry, firm and confident.

Logan said: 'Derek, I usually sit behind the Resolute desk here which, as you probably know, was a gift from Queen Victoria to President Hayes in 1880. It's made from timbers taken from HMS *Resolute*, which was one of your Arctic exploration vessels.'

Llewelyn glanced at the Resolute desk and murmured his appreciation.

Logan said: 'Gentlemen, let's sit down on the sofas. I'll order a pot of coffee. Or would you prefer tea?'

Harcourt said: 'No. Coffee would be most welcome,'

President Logan lowered himself carefully on to the sofa. 'My goddamn back is stiff from all this travelling. Gentlemen, I'll cut to the chase. My trip to Thailand was sold as a goodwill state visit but that was a crock. The king of Thailand co-operated in the cover story. I went there to meet the Chinese premier. I couldn't tell you, Cley, because we figured that the less people knew the more secure and secret the meeting would be.'

'No problem, sir. That's standard security. How did it go?'

'I waved the big stick. We already have the fleet on manoeuvres in the South China Sea and the premier was aware of the build up of our forces in strategic bases around China. I told him in no uncertain terms that we are well aware of their cyberwar and their compromise of our interests in Africa but this overt Silk Fist strategy would not be tolerated and that if China had instigated Silk Fist, or was backing it, the consequences would be catastrophic. China has invested a lot of their wealth in our financial system but I warned the premier that we were not prepared to tolerate lethal attacks on our country, or those of our allies, under any circumstances.'

Harcourt asked: 'What was the reaction?'

'He assured me that China was not responsible, that he knew nothing about Silk Fist, and genuinely appeared anxious to assure me that, despite hysterical media reports, China was in no way involved. I have to say, gentlemen, that having looked him straight in the eye, I believed the guy. You look sceptical, Cley.'

'I suppose my study of post-Second World War military history makes me distrustful of China.'

Logan said: 'Our analysts at the State Department have found no evidence of Chinese involvement. None of our intelligence assets or allies can find anything to link China with Silk Fist. Richard, the British have close ties with China through your old colony of Hong Kong. Can you tell us anything?'

'I regret to say, Mr President, that I cannot. Our sources, and they are planted deep in China, confirm what the Chinese premier told you. We have no evidence that China is involved in Silk Fist.'

'Damn,' Logan said. 'It's a relief that China is probably not involved but disappointing not to find some sort of lead. Before I went to Thailand I asked Cley to make a report on everything that US intelligence sources have found about Silk Fist. Cley was the director of the CIA for many years. His expertise and knowledge is tremendously valuable. Give us your report, Cley.'

Kefalas waited while Amy came in with a tray of coffee. Richard

Harcourt watched appreciatively as she bent down to place the tray on the coffee table.

'Thanks, Amy,' Logan said. 'We'll help ourselves.'

Cley Kefalas handed each man a thin folder.

'This is it?' Logan said. 'This is all we know about Silk Fist?'

'All apart from Operation Cardinal. As agreed with our British friends here, nothing has been written down about that.'

Logan pursed his lips. 'I gave presidential approval to Cardinal but you're all aware that I was unhappy to do so. It certainly contravenes the Constitution as well as the law.'

Harcourt said: 'I think we were all uneasy, we are not savages, but sometimes unusual and illegal methods are necessary for the greater good.'

'I know, I know,' Logan said tetchily. 'Cley, give us your report on Cardinal.'

'Since the start of this year we have identified nineteen events that have borne all the hallmarks of, and been classified as, Silk Fist. There are no doubt more that have gone unrecognised. Most of the perpetrators of the Silk Fist attacks died as a result of the attack or killed themselves afterwards. Of the survivors there are five in US custody and three in the UK. There are, of course, a few others in custody in other countries. All our survivors, under normal interrogation, claim that they have no memory or awareness of the crimes they committed, and that is also the case with the British survivors, isn't that so, Derek?'

'Yes. Our psychiatry boffins tried all sorts of ploys to trip them up but we have had to accept that they genuinely do not remember what they did or why.'

'Okay,' Kefalas went on. 'We identified two of our subjects and one British as suitable for rendition to our special facility.'

'What do you mean by suitable?' President Logan asked.

'Suitable by the fact that they did not have a family or legal representatives who might ask questions if our special procedures went wrong.'

'Jeez,' Logan said. 'Spare me the details. Did we get anything?'

'We tried various psychotropic drugs and so-called truth drugs. One of the subjects was tested with pain inducement techniques.'

'Torture, you mean?' Logan said.

'Yes, sir. I regret to say that the subject did not survive. The two other subjects suffered severe psychological reactions. They have now been returned home but are under permanent medical care.'

'Did we get anything out of them?' Logan said.

'I regret to say that we didn't, sir. It's clear that whatever methods we may try, the perpetrators are unable to give us any useful information after the event.'

Logan said. 'Close down Operation Cardinal immediately, Cley. We had to try but I want no more of that barbarity. Do you agree Richard, Derek?'

'We do, sir,' Richard Harcourt said, with evident relief.

'Okay,' Logan said. 'Let's return to good old espionage and electronic surveillance. What have we found?'

'I hate to say it, Mr President, but we have found hardly anything. This report mainly deals with the similarities between the Silk Fist attacks and the perpetrators. I've spent the week with the directors of all our intelligence services. Between them they have re-analysed literally billions of emails, and cell phone calls looking for key words such as, obviously, Silk Fist. They've also tried the strange code words that the perpetrators shout before committing the crimes but that has proved fruitless. Apart from electronic espionage, they've been re-investigating every known terrorist, religious and criminal organisation. They've tried everything. They've come up with diddly squat.'

President Logan leaned forward. He looked drained and weary. 'You can't be serious, Cley. Billions of dollars worth of staff and equipment and they can't find anything?'

'No, sir.'

Llewelyn said: 'I regret to report that I have been involved in a similar exercise with British intelligence. We also are stumped by Silk Fist.'

'We must have found something?' Logan said impatiently.

Kefalas said: 'We've established the pattern of the attacks, the use of the lone perpetrator, the words they shout before carrying out the attacks. There is evidence of isolated incidents of such attacks going back several years but on a small scale. Since the start of the year such attacks have exploded, sometimes literally, into a worldwide epidemic. We have established what is happening but not how or why. The perpetrators are certainly being brainwashed or drugged in some way but we cannot establish how that is being done. There are autopsy reports included in my report. All the men, and with one exception they are all male, have high levels of testosterone. The most baffling aspect is that they also show the presence of monoamine oxidase inhibitors.'

'What are they?' Logan asked.

'They're a group of drugs once used for the treatment of depression. Tests show an old form of MAO inhibitor that is no longer used because it has a potentially fatal interaction with some types of foodstuffs or other drugs.'

Harcourt said: 'MAO did you say?'

'Yes, sir. I know what you're thinking. MAO. Mao, could that be the origin of the Chinese Maoist theory? It's what Dr Flaherty said as he was dying.'

Harcourt said: 'Could these MAO drugs alter someone's personality and drive them to commit these acts?'

'Not according to the doctors. No way.'

Llewelyn said: 'Our findings completely agree. We've also had our cryptanalysts and language experts working on these words that the perpetrators shout before each attack but we cannot establish any link or pattern.'

Logan said: 'So if we haven't yet established how it is being done, are there any further theories about who might be doing this, apart from China. Al-Qaeda?'

Kefalas said: 'No, sir. They are a busted flush. They don't have the resources for this scale of operation.'

'The Mafia? Colombian drug barons? Some sort of criminal organisation?'

'To what purpose, sir?' Kefalas replied. 'There have been claims from small and insignificant terrorist organisations seeking to take credit but whoever is behind Silk Fist must have massive wealth and massive resources. It almost has to be another state inimical to the USA and other democracies.'

Llewelyn said: 'We have found no indications that an actual state or country is involved. Why should another country risk incurring the wrath of the USA, Europe, Japan and India? It doesn't make sense.'

Logan asked: 'What about these viral videos turning up on the internet? Every time we try to control any panic or hysteria we get films of these attacks showing up. That means someone has foreknowledge of the attacks and is deliberately having them filmed and distributed in order to spread panic or for whatever reason. Can we pinpoint the source?'

Kefalas said: 'Those virals are being routed randomly via hundreds of servers around the world and, soon after people have seen them, they are programmed with a so-called "kill switch" to delete them completely. It's impossible to establish the source.'

Sir Derek Llewelyn nodded in agreement.

Logan said: 'So I've flown thousands of miles, three poor bastards have been tortured, Cley has spent a week with our intelligence chiefs, and Richard and Derek have flown from the UK for this meeting, and we end up with nothing to tell each other.'

There was an uncomfortable and embarrassed silence.

Logan went on: 'After 9/11, the President authorised the CIA to use any means necessary to destroy Al-Qaeda. The operation was code named Greystone. The CIA set up prisons known as "black sites". Private companies all over the country were recruited to help with the intelligence effort. This country is now, end to end, thick with surveillance, security cameras, license plate readers, computers, scanners, God knows what else. Many of these operations directly contravene or circumvent the Constitution and the Bill of Rights. That makes me deeply uneasy. I had been considering repealing or abolishing many of these measures, perhaps should have done so years ago. You know why I haven't?'

The others shook their heads.

'It's because the goddam terrorists are winning. They have forced us to change our way of life. This is certainly the home of the brave but I'm beginning to doubt it can ever be the land of the free again, certainly not of the unmonitored and unobserved. The American people are now the most watched people on earth, watched by the people elected to govern them.'

'I think Britain runs you close,' Harcourt said. 'We have more cameras watching our citizens than any other country.'

'Doesn't that make you uneasy, Richard?'

'Deeply, sir.'

'Damn right. It makes me uneasy. It makes me mad. But what the hell else can we do? Out there in America there is uneasiness bordering on panic. Where is Silk Fist going to strike next? It could be the ordinary Joe who lives next door who sets the bomb that kills you, or the cop on the street who takes his gun out and plugs you. I'm sure it's the same in Britain.'

Harcourt and Llewelyn nodded.

'The media are whipping this up into a frenzy, the people are frantic for an answer and what can I tell them? We don't know anything? We can't do anything to stop this? That, gentlemen, is unacceptable.'

Harcourt said tentatively: 'Isn't that why it would be a good idea to keep alive the suggestion that China is behind Silk Fist until we find out who is really responsible? It keeps the pressure off our respective governments.'

Kefalas nodded and said: 'It's good point, Mr President. It buys us some time.'

'It's immoral,' Logan said. 'There have already been so-called revenge attacks on our citizens of Chinese origin. The Chinese embassy in Delhi was attacked by a mob.'

'The same in Britain,' Llewelyn said. 'Our Chinese population are becoming worried for their lives. But at least deflecting the blame towards China keeps the focus of hatred away from us. Gives the people a scapegoat, you might say.'

Logan looked at Llewelyn and attempted to keep the distaste out of his expression. He said: 'Some guy working down the New York sewers might think he's got the dirtiest job in the world but compared to some things we have to do in politics that guy smells of roses. Okay, it's despicable but it's sensible. It buys us time. Let's neither confirm or deny the China scenario but hint that's where we believe attention should be directed. Cley, I want you to go back and tell our intelligence chiefs to redouble their efforts. And our police, and our military, whatever it takes. Richard, I would ask the same of the British government.'

'I'll certainly convey that to the Prime Minister, sir. We'll do all we can to resolve this menace.'

Logan said: 'Cley, I don't want you to infer that I'm making any criticism of what you've already done. I don't mind saying this in front of our British guests. Your help during my administration has been invaluable. We were once rivals for the Presidency. I got it and you didn't and yet you have put any resentment away and served me and the country diligently and conscientiously.'

'It was my duty, sir,' Kefalas said, with a trace of embarrassment.

'I'm halfway through my second term. In two years the people will have to elect a new President and I'm going to do my damnedest to make sure that new President is Cleytus Kefalas. You will make a fine President, possibly a great one, but if this administration doesn't resolve the Silk Fist problem then you can kiss goodbye to the Presidency and my reputation with posterity will be lower than Nixon's. But our personal ambitions are not important. What is important is for the people of the United States, and our friends and allies, to sleep secure and in the certainty that they face no danger when they go about their daily business. I want these goddamn Silk Fist bastards smashed and smashed for good.'

There was a hesitant knock on the door and Amy looked in. 'I'm sorry to interrupt, sir, but Deputy Chief Isaiah Franklin is here and wishes to speak to you urgently.'

'Okay, Amy. I think we're about finished. Our British guests are just leaving.'

Amy said: 'Sir, Chief Franklin would like to speak to the Foreign Secretary as well as you.'

Logan and Harcourt looked at each other, both mystified. Then Logan said: 'Okay, show him in.'

Franklin hesitantly entered the Oval Office.

Logan said: 'Come on in, Stack. Gentlemen, this is Deputy Chief Isaiah Franklin. He commands the Secret Service detail within the White House. What have you got for us, Stack?'

'Sir, I've just reported to Mrs Logan and she said I should come and tell you immediately.'

'Okay, Stack, I always do whatever my wife wants, immediately if possible. What's the news?'

'Linda Marquez has disappeared.'

'Disappeared? I thought she was in Florida with her folks?'

'She was, sir, or so I've just been told by Mrs Logan.'

Logan caught the hint of disapproval in Franklin's tone. 'We didn't tell you, Stack, because we figured the less people knew where Linda was the safer she would be. We should have kept you in the loop. My apologies, Stack.'

'Well, Linda gave her parents some excuse, managed to evade

her guards, and disappeared. We've located her car. It was parked in the Amtrak station in Jacksonville. She's taken the train to New York. A ticket was bought in her name.'

Logan, with a trace of impatience, said: 'This is all very interesting, Stack, but what has this got to do with the British Foreign Secretary?'

'Sir, she was accompanied by a man, the man who bought the tickets. He answers to the description of Sergeant Christopher Wyatt.'

'Wyatt?' Logan said. 'That guy we think is involved with Silk Fist. I thought we were tailing him?'

Kefalas said uncomfortably: 'Sir, I didn't tell you because I thought you had enough on your plate. The Canadians lost him and we haven't been able to find him.'

'So now he's shown up in Florida and Linda has gone off with him? Who is this guy? A cross between Houdini and the frigging Pied Piper?'

Franklin said. 'Whether Linda was coerced or threatened or went with him voluntarily we cannot be sure. Knowing Sergeant Marquez as a courageous and loyal agent, my guess is that she is somehow playing along with Wyatt in order to find out what he is up to. Sir, I believe her life could be in grave danger. I'm very worried about her. Wyatt is a trained and ruthless killer.'

Kefalas asked: 'When is the train due into New York?'

Franklin looked at his watch and said: 'Ten minutes ago, sir.'

Logan exploded. 'So Wyatt has slipped through our net again! Okay, put everything you can on this, Stack. I'll order the Feds to do the same. We have to find him. Wait a minute, though. Could we still stand back and see what Wyatt is up to? That was the original plan. Perhaps if we give Linda the rope she can hang this guy for us.'

Kefalas said: 'With respect, Mr President, we shouldn't take any chances with Linda's life. I don't believe that Wyatt has any information about Silk Fist when all our intelligence assets have failed to find anything. He's a dangerous maverick. If our guys get a chance they should take Wyatt down, no questions asked. I would recommend that if he cannot be detained then he should be eliminated as soon as he is located.'

Logan turned to Foreign Secretary Richard Harcourt. 'Richard, I must apologise for discussing the elimination of a British citizen in front of you, but you are aware of how serious the situation is.'

Harcourt said: 'I appreciate your dilemma, sir, and I would ask you not to be concerned. I agree with the Vice President. Wyatt is a highly trained and vicious maverick. If he happened to be eliminated by American officers then I assure you that His Majesty's government would not make any diplomatic waves. In fact, you'd be solving a problem for us.'

26

Dominion Building, Sugar Hill, New York City, March 17th

Linda Marquez entered the lobby of the Dominion Building at a quarter after seven in the evening. Her footsteps on the marble floor echoed around the low ceilinged space. The lobby was decorated with strings of green paper shamrocks and leprechauns.

The lobby attendant stood up from his desk within his security cubicle when he saw Linda approaching. He slid the safety glass panel aside. 'Mrs O'Brien... Mrs Marquez, this is a pleasant surprise. I mean we've missed you around here. I mean we were all very sad about your husband. Happy St Patrick's Day. I'm sorry, that might not have been...'

'It's okay, Billy.' Linda smiled reassuringly. 'It's good to see you again. How have you been?'

'Just fine, mam. Is there anything I can do...'

'No. I'm going up to the apartment. I'll take the stairs.'

'Of course, mam.'

'You've made a great job of decorating the lobby, Billy. Happy St Patrick's Day to you.' Linda pushed through double doors into the elevator and stairway area.

Billy watched the doors swing back into place. He picked up his cell phone.

Linda unlocked the door of apartment six, went in and closed the door behind her. She keyed in the security number to deactivate the alarm within the prescribed thirty seconds. She stood in the darkness. The memories came flooding in but after a few seconds she thrust them aside. Remembrance could wait, her mission could not.

Linda walked across the living area and opened the double doors that led on to the verandah. She stepped out and took a length of rope from her shoulder bag. She carefully tied one end to the cast iron railing of the verandah and threw the other end down to the ground. There was a light rain falling and the maple tree in the communal garden helped to conceal her actions from any curious neighbours on the other side.

Linda looked down and saw Wyatt pick up the rope. He tested the rope to make sure it would hold. Linda expected him to brace his legs against the wall but Wyatt thrust out his legs and hauled himself up hand over hand. He was climbing over the verandah railing within seconds.

'Impressive,' Linda said.

Wyatt was not even out of breath. 'Just like *Romeo and Juliet*. We had to do that up the side of cliffs in Wales.'

'Okay, let's get this done. Come on in.'

Wyatt followed Linda into the apartment. Linda left the verandah doors open but went around closing all the drapes. While she was in the master bedroom she opened the drawer of her nightstand and took out the small pistol she kept for home security. Making sure that Wyatt could not see, she slipped the pistol into the pocket of her jacket.

She came back into the living room and went to the door. 'Don't put the lights on until I get back.'

Wyatt nodded and Linda went out.

Billy stood up again when he saw Linda come out into the lobby. He asked: 'Is everything all right?'

'No,' Linda said, only half-pretending to be in the thrall of strong emotion. 'I thought I could go back in there, Billy, but I can't bear it.' She began walking down the lobby towards the street door.

Billy called out: 'You're leaving already?'

'Yes, I'll be back sometime but not yet.'

Linda pushed out on to the street as Billy left his cubicle and shouted: 'Wait, mam, wait!'

Linda walked quickly down the street and took the first left. She cautiously looked back to see if Billy was following. He was not.

Linda waited anxiously below her apartment verandah for several minutes before Wyatt appeared. She wound the rope around her wrists and took a firm grip. She felt herself being hauled up and, using her legs to brace against the wall, she helped as much as she could by walking up the wall. As she climbed over the verandah rail her foot caught and she tumbled to the floor before Wyatt could catch her.

'Good job I'm wearing jeans,' Linda said. 'Where the hell did you get to?'

'I was watching out the front. You were right. The cops arrived minutes after you left the building. Someone must have told them you'd already gone and they went away again.'

'I suspected as much. Billy would sell his own grandmother for an extra buck. Now we can look around in peace without him or the cops realisng we're here.'

Linda closed the drapes over the verandah door and then went over to switch on the lights.

Wyatt looked around. 'Wow, this place is beautiful, Linda.'

'One of the most desirable apartment blocks in the entire city. It was built in the early twentieth century in the art nouveau style. When Mike and I got married I persuaded the family to buy it as an investment. I usually hate trading on the family fortune but I so wanted to live here. To be married and live in New York in a place like this with Mike was my fairy tale. We were going to be so happy. We were happy. Now I'd rather live in a cave.' Linda suddenly realised she was lost in her memories and glanced at Wyatt to gauge his reaction. She expected some sarcastic comment about his poor background but she saw nothing in his expression except calm understanding. She went on: 'I'm going to move out as soon as I can. The family can sell it, rent it, do what they like. It's all over.'

Wyatt said: 'I'm truly sorry for what you've lost, Linda. I've been so wrapped up in my own problems that I can't remember if I've said it before.'

Linda nodded. 'Thanks. Now, what have we got to do? What are we looking for?'

'Anything that might suggest Mike was being drugged or brainwashed. Anything unusual or out of place. Check that any substances or drugs in the bathroom and kitchen are what they say they are on the label. I see you've got a lot of books. We'll flip through the pages for any hidden notes. Open up your old CDs and your vinyl sleeves for the same. Look behind appliances and furniture. Did Mike have a cell phone?'

'Yes. He carried it at all times. I guess he took it with him on the day... the day he died.'

Wyatt nodded. 'The police will have kept that. What about a computer or laptop?'

'Yes, there's a computer in the spare bedroom. That doubled as Mike's den unless his folks or mine stayed over. He didn't have a laptop.'

'Okay. I've brought a memory stick with me. With your permission I'll download all the files on the computer and we can analyse the information later.'

'Do you know how to do stuff like that?'

'No, but I have a very clever Indian friend who can.'

'I'll have to meet this Indian friend one day. He sounds like quite a guy.'

'He is. He saved my life once and, like you, he understands the pain of losing someone he loved deeply because of Silk Fist.'

'Who did he lose?'

'I'm sure Prem will tell you when you meet him. I suggest that you start the search by going through Mike's clothes, his pockets and so on. Feel if anything might be concealed or hidden. It will be hard for you, Linda, but it's better if you do it than me.'

'I can cope. Why don't you start with the spare bedroom? Do your thing with the computer and search that room and then we can both search the less intimate areas.'

'Sounds like a plan.' Wyatt went into the spare bedroom and switched on the computer. He downloaded all the files into the memory stick and had a quick look on the screen menus to see if there was anything obvious. There was nothing.

The computer was standing on an antique side table with two drawers on either side. The top left hand drawer was filled with bills, letters, catalogues and other domestic literature. Wyatt sifted through it but there was nothing unusual. The bottom left hand drawer was empty.

The top right hand drawer contained a watch, cuff links, a diary with no entries, and a small metal cash box. The box was locked. Wyatt shook the box. It sounded as if it might contain coins and notes but there was also a sound that suggested a larger object.

Wyatt took the box and looked into Linda's bedroom. The bed was piled with Mike's clothing. Linda was searching through it. She had her back to him. Wyatt said: 'Linda, there's a small cash box here. It's locked and I can't find a key. Do you have a key?'

Linda did not look around. Her shoulders moved as she silently wept. In a tremulous voice Linda said: 'No, I don't have a key. Lever it open or whatever.'

Wyatt took the box into the kitchen. He found an old fashioned can opener. It sheared the lid off the cash box in seconds. Inside there were a few coins and a stack of one and five dollar bills. Wyatt took out the bills. Underneath was a small brown medicine bottle containing ten capsules. The original label had been picked off and another label stuck on with clear Scotch tape. There was a single word written in pencil on the label.

Wyatt read the word and the implication struck him immediately. He stared at the word for several seconds. His stomach was churning with excitement. This had to be the connection. He looked around quickly. Linda was still in the bedroom. Wyatt put all the money back in the cash box but slipped the medicine bottle into his jacket pocket.

Wyatt left the kitchen and as he passed Linda's bedroom he said: 'Nothing in it except a few coins and notes. I'll put it back.'

'Okay.'

Wyatt sat on the bed in the spare room and thought about the small bottle in his pocket. It was too easy. Did Linda Marquez know the bottle was in there? Did she have any idea about the importance of that bottle? It had been her suggestion that he start searching in the spare bedroom. Was she setting him up to see if he would admit finding the bottle?

Yet it was possible, even probable, that he was the only person in the world, apart from the Silk Fist perpetrators, who understood that the word written on that label was of vital significance. He had to find out, for sure, whose side Linda Marquez was on. He decided to say nothing about the bottle. He would set her up in turn and gauge how she reacted. He would keep playing the game.

They spent the next two hours scouring the apartment, pulling out drawers to see if anything was hidden behind, flicking through the books for hidden notes, opening drink and food containers to check the contents, checking the few drug containers to make sure the contents were correct, dragging out appliances, taking up carpets, taking down pictures and examining the frames. Wyatt suggested slashing the stuffed furniture to feel inside but Linda vetoed that idea. Wyatt did not care, he was playing the game, convinced that he had already found what he needed to find.

'Nothing,' Linda said, as they stood in the middle of the living room. 'All this effort and upset and we find nothing.'

'There's Mike's computer files. Perhaps that will show something.'

'Perhaps you're plain wrong, Wyatt. Mike was a sweet and decent guy who'd developed a few problems. All this crap about Silk Fist. Mike had nothing to do with it.'

Wyatt understood how upsetting the experience had been for Linda and said nothing.

'Let's get out of here,' Linda said.

She went over to switch off the lights. As she did so there was a loud rap on the outer door. Wyatt put his fingers to his lips and gestured that Linda should move away from the door.

Linda whispered: 'Look through the spyhole.'

The spyhole was disguised by a moveable escutcheon. Wyatt silently pushed it one side and looked out. A man stood with his back to the door. He was wearing a hooded coat and was carrying something.

Wyatt guided Linda back into the apartment and described what he had seen.

'Let's get out,' Linda said.

'No. I want to know who he is, what he's up to. He might have a weapon or a bomb. Or we might get some useful information.'

The man knocked on the door again, this time more urgently.

'Wyatt!' Linda hissed. 'Let's just go!'

Wyatt ignored her and moved towards the door. He took a look through the spyhole then opened the door. He kicked the man in the back of the knee. Two pizza boxes went flying, the contents strewn on the carpet, as the man dropped to the floor with a cry of pain.

Wyatt grabbed the man in a headlock and said: 'Who are you?' He wrenched back the hood.

The kid was no more than eighteen and utterly terrified but putting on a show of bravado. He stammered: 'I'm Leroy. What the hell, man? What you doin'? I'm only deliverin' pizza. I forgot which number the boss told me. I didn't mean no harm, mister.'

Wyatt let him go. He took out his wallet, counted out fifty dollars and handed the notes to the kid. 'I'm sorry I assaulted you, mate. This will pay for the pizza and something for yourself.'

Leroy looked at Wyatt warily but then accepted the money. 'That's cool, man.'

Wyatt went back inside the apartment. Linda locked the door and they went out on to the verandah. Linda lowered herself down the rope and Wyatt followed.

They stood in the communal garden, in the soft rain, and looked up at the verandah. Wyatt said: 'We'll have to leave the rope there although it's an invitation to burglars.'

Linda shrugged. 'It doesn't matter. I'm never coming back here. Let the burglars take what they like. I suppose we'd better find somewhere to stay for the night.'

'Yes, but before that I've got a yen for a pizza. Leroy's pizza smelt really good and I'm starving. Can we get a pizza around here at this time of night?'

Linda laughed. 'You really don't know much about the Big Apple, do you Wyatt? You can get anything, any time of day or night.'

'I thought you said only tourists call this the Big Apple?'

'Yep, and we natives call it "the City", not New York. That's the truth.'

Wyatt thought, yes, and I'm going to wheedle some more truth out of you, Sergeant Marquez.

The agent calling himself Leroy hobbled down to the lobby and flipped open his cell phone. 'Chief, they're in there. The pizza trick worked. It was Wyatt alright. Had me down on the floor real fast. Yeah, I know he's supposed to be some dangerous killer but he seemed like an okay kind of guy. Even gave me a tip for putting myself in harm's way. That's more that you've ever done, chief. Yeah, bite me. Anyway, they're in there and there's no way they can get out except past us.'

27

Bel Air Pizza House, New York, March 17th

'I love this place,' Wyatt said. 'It's like those diners you see in old Hollywood films, all scrubbed and sparkling and with sexy waitresses wearing gingham dresses and aprons. It's like eating inside an old 1950s car, all chrome and red leather.'

'That's why it's called Bel Air,' Linda said distractedly.

'I thought Bel Air was out in California somewhere.'

'It is. This place is named after the Chevrolet Bel Air automobile from the 1950s.'

'I feel like John Travolta in *Grease* except I can't dance like him.'

'Just eat your pizza, Wyatt.'

'Gladly. This is great pizza.'

'That's why I brought us here. Best pizza in the city.'

'You're not eating much.'

'I'm not hungry.'

'Why not?'

Linda sat back and shook her head with exasperation. 'You're an insensitive bastard. We've just ransacked my home, the home I shared with the man I loved. I could see him everywhere in that apartment.' Linda looked out at a group of revellers walking by the window. 'Mike loved St Patrick's Day. He was proud of his Irish roots.'

Wyatt took another slice. 'I'm proud of my Irish roots as well. My mother is Irish.'

'You remind me of Mike in some ways, especially your dark brown eyes.'

Wyatt smiled. 'Black as a pint of Guinness.'

'Who told you that?'

'My ex-girlfriend. Her name is Stephanie.'

'Why ex-girlfriend?'

'Because, according to her, there were three of us in the relationship. Me, her and the Princess Royal.'

Linda nodded. 'I've been there. With Mike and me it was the First Lady. Three months ago my life was about as good as I always dreamed it would be. I had a job I loved, a husband I loved, a loving and wealthy family, a great apartment in the greatest city in the world. Now I'm a bereaved fugitive sitting in a diner watching a crazy guy stuff his face with pizza like he hasn't eaten for a week.'

Wyatt pushed his plate away. 'Believe me, Linda, I'm not insensitive. It's a survival instinct in the military. You eat as much as you can when you can. You'll need the energy and somewhere along the line there won't be time to eat. You make a joke when facing a bad situation, otherwise you'd weep at the stupidity. It's the only way I know how to deal with what we're going through. I'm not your enemy. I'm not the cause of your problems, but Silk Fist is.'

Linda relaxed a little and looked at Wyatt. She could not figure him out. He made her angry but he was also reassuring. She should be afraid of him, he had been trained to kill, but she sensed a gentleness and love of peace that he dare not expose to the world. His ideas bordered on lunacy and yet there was a deep core of sanity within him. She found him a strange mixture of unsettling, disturbing, and yet comforting. 'Okay, Wyatt, so where do we go from here?'

'The first thing you have to do is get back to Washington and report to your superiors. No doubt they are curious, to say the least, as to why you disappeared with me. That's an easy get out. Tell them that you hoped that I would lead you to some information about Silk Fist, and you have.'

'What to you mean? We didn't find zip?'

Wyatt said: 'Can we get some coffee?' He was curiously guilty about the lie he was going to tell and was seeking to put off the moment. He instinctively trusted Linda Marquez but he feared it was a trust built on her raven black hair, her green eyes and her almost irresistible femininity. It was dangerous to make judgements based on physical attractiveness. He was trained by special forces to understand that female terrorists employed feminine wiles to deadly effect. Linda Marquez was not a lethal terrorist but he had to be sure which side she was on. He watched her order the coffee. He desperately wanted to believe that she was on his team but he had to be certain. He could not afford to make a mistaken judgement.

Linda turned back to him and said: 'What did you mean by that, about finding information?'

Wyatt pretended to be hesitant. 'I haven't told you everything I've found out.'

'What have you found out?' Linda asked suspiciously.

'I was given a name, someone who might be involved in the Silk Fist conspiracy.'

Linda leaned forward and hissed: 'Are you serious? You've been given the name of someone involved with all this mayhem and we're sitting here eating frigging pizza? Who is it?'

'I'm not going to tell you... yet.'

'Why not? Don't you trust me?'

'I trust you. I don't trust your superiors. I certainly don't trust my superiors. They set me up as the renegade traitor. Before I give the name I want something in return.'

'What?'

'Protection. I want the American authorities to intercede with my own. I want the British authorities to admit, publicly and in no uncertain terms, that I am not involved with Silk Fist. You're close to the First Lady, which obviously means you're close to the President. You're close to Stack Franklin. He seems like an honest bloke. I need you to get me off the hook.'

Linda Marquez frowned with anger. 'Is that what all this was about in the first place, to get yourself involved with me, knowing I've got some influence in the White House, just to get yourself a pardon? What you told me about how Mike died was a pack of lies, wasn't it?'

'No, Linda. I swear that it's true about Mike. I really did think we might find some evidence in your apartment. Mike was acting strangely. He had been influenced, drugged, brainwashed somehow.'

'Okay, I'll believe you because I have to. How did you get this name?'

'You remember that the Silk Fist story was broken in the *London Sentinel*. That newspaper is owned by a Russian oligarch named Yaroslav Blokhin.'

'I've heard of him.'

'I used to work for Blokhin as a bodyguard and security adviser. Your guys can check the truth of that. Blokhin set me up as a fall guy, that's why I'm on the run, but he let slip the name of another man who is involved in Silk Fist.'

'Then we should pick up this Blokhin character and sweat him for what he knows.'

'Easier said than done, Linda. Blokhin has disappeared back to Russia. He's a very powerful man, hides himself and his family well, surrounds himself with ex-Spetsnaz bodyguards.'

'Okay, so I'll take you to the White House and you can explain…'

'Hold on, Linda. I'm not going anywhere near the White House yet. You can go in first and explain what we've both been doing. If I were you, I'd contact Mrs Logan first and tell her that you are coming in. If she knows then the President knows and that means there is less chance of a cover up if someone thinks it's a good idea to get rid of me.'

'Come on, Wyatt. What do you think we are, a bunch of Nazis? This is a law abiding society and government. We don't let the CIA bump people off. You watch too many bad films.'

'Even so, we do it my way. While you're in the White House, I will go and book into a hotel and wait. I will not tell you which hotel. When you have made the arrangements you then drive away from the White House, then you ring my cell phone. I will tell you where I am and you, and you alone, can come and get me. You tell your bosses that if there is any attempt to tail you then the deal's off and I'll disappear and take the name of the Silk Fist suspect with me.'

'You can't do that, Wyatt! People are being killed out there. People are beginning to panic, in fear of the next attack. It's your duty to give us that name.'

Wyatt shrugged. 'That's the only way I'm going to play it, Linda.'

Linda looked at Wyatt with contempt. 'Just when I was beginning to think you may not be such a bad guy after all you prove that you're a total selfish asshole.'

'Think what you like, Sergeant Marquez.'

Wyatt congratulated himself on a neat plan. He hated to dupe Linda Marquez but if she succeeded in bringing him in from the cold and interceding with his superiors in London, then he could give them the bottle he had found in Linda's apartment. He had lied about having the name of a suspect but the medicine bottle would buy him the credibility. If, for some reason, Linda did not succeed and the authorities would not make a deal then he could disappear and take his evidence to someone who would listen, in all probability to his ally in New Delhi.

Linda said reluctantly: 'Okay, Wyatt, I'll buy it, but if you double cross me or put me in danger I swear I'll have you hunted down.'

'Your people have been searching for me for several days and I'm still free. I'm not going to put you in any danger and I'll make a solemn promise to you.'

'What's that?'

'After what happened to the Princess Royal nobody else is going to die on my watch, unless I'm dead already.'

'That's less than comforting, Wyatt.'

'I'll pay for the pizza, or rather the Indian government will, and then we can find a hotel for the night.'

'Forget the hotel, we're driving to Washington.'

'Tonight? It's nearly eleven o'clock. How far is Washington?'

'Couple a hundred miles or so. We'll be there in four hours, tops. Past your bedtime, is it, Wyatt? If you have vital information about Silk Fist my people need to know about it as soon as possible. I can go in to see Marty as soon as she's gotten up.'

'Okay, I had plenty of sleep on the train last night. I thought you didn't want to be alone in a car with me?'

Linda looked around to make sure no-one was watching and then took out the Smith and Wesson revolver from her jacket pocket. 'Don't try anything.'

'Where the hell did you get that?'

'You're not the only one who can play games, Wyatt.'

Wyatt held up his hands in mock surrender.

'Come on,' Linda said. 'We've got a long drive and no time to lose.'

28

The White House, Washington, March 18th

Linda Marquez was allowed into the Presidential bedroom at five minutes before eight. She was disconcerted to find that Martina Logan had just come out of the shower and was wearing only a large bath towel.

Linda said: 'I'm sorry, Marty, I didn't realise you hadn't got dressed yet. I'll come back in a few…'

Martina Logan beckoned her further into the room. 'Come in, come in, Linda. Don't worry, the President's not here. I wanted to see you as soon as possible so I told security to bring you straight here. I'm told you've been here for over an hour. Where were you?'

'Being searched and interrogated by my Secret Service colleagues. They were making sure I wasn't armed or working for Silk Fist and out to kill you.'

'And are you?'

'Oh, Marty, you shouldn't make jokes like that. Anyway, there's two armed guards outside that door if I try anything.'

'I trust you more than anyone in the world, Linda. I know you'd never want to hurt me. I've been worried about you. Where have you been?'

'I've been with that British guy everyone is looking for, Christopher Wyatt.'

'Oh, my God, did he kidnap you or something?'

'No, he didn't force me to do anything but he had some crazy idea that Mike might have known something about this Silk Fist business.'

'Mike? You mean your husband Mike?'

'Yes. I went along with Wyatt hoping I could find out what he was up to. I couldn't contact you for fear of spooking him. We searched my New York apartment yesterday.'

'Did you find anything?'

'No. It was absurd. Mike wasn't hiding anything. After we'd finished Wyatt claimed that he knows the name of somebody involved with Silk Fist.'

'Okay, that is vital information. I'll get dressed and then we'll go see Cley Kefalas. He's co-ordinating the intelligence effort against Silk Fist. He'll bring in Stack Franklin and whoever else he needs. Joe's out of town until tomorrow but he'll want to be informed about this right away.' Martina Logan sat down on her bed and took off her bath towel.

Linda said: 'I'll leave you to get dressed, Marty.'

'Oh, stop worrying, Linda. We're all girls here. I don't mind you seeing me naked. I think I'm in pretty good shape for a woman of my age. I can see that you're wondering about our sleeping arrangements, two queen size beds instead of one double or king size.'

Linda was embarrassed to be caught. 'Marty, it's nothing to do with me.'

'Joe is stressed out, overweight, mostly tired, diabetic and with a bad back. You do the math.'

Linda sensed that Martina Logan desperately wanted to talk about her marriage but because her husband was President of the United States that was simply not possible.

Marty stood up and turned round to face Linda.

Linda could not believe what she was seeing. She said: 'Jeez, Marty, a tattoo like that, down there, on the First Lady!'

Martina Logan laughed. 'What can I say? I was a wild child back in New Mexico, Linda. I was Miss Santa Fe and thought I could do anything. This tattoo reminds me of how far I've travelled. I wish I

189

hadn't chosen such a stereotypical image but I was young and high most of the time and it was the end of the Seventies. I met Joe soon after I had this done. He was like an exotic creature from another planet. He settled me down, showed me a purpose in life, so you're the only other person who knows about this, except for my gynaecologist. I know I can rely on your discretion.'

'Of course you can. I won't breathe a word. That's why I love working for you, Marty. You're always full of surprises.'

Martina Logan laughed again. 'Come over to the closet and help me chose what to wear. Back to business. Where is Wyatt now?'

'He's in Washington. He's checking into a hotel but he wouldn't tell me which one.'

Martina Logan selected a cream suit with a red blouse. She said: 'I'm glad you came to me first but you should probably have gone to Stack Franklin with this information before me. He's your superior officer.'

'This was Wyatt's idea. He insisted that I report to you first. Wyatt wants our authorities to intercede with his own people. He claims to have this information and wants to come in from the cold. I don't think he trusts Isaiah Franklin, perhaps doesn't even trust President Logan, but he trusts you, thanks to what I've told him about you. Wyatt figured that if you were aware of the situation first then you'd make sure that he wasn't dragged off in secret to Guantanamo Bay or somewhere.'

Martina Logan buttoned her blouse. 'He's a careful guy, this Wyatt. What do you make of him having spent time with him? Is he crazy?'

'No, he's not crazy. He's clever, and certainly tough, but I think he's misguided. I'm not sure what to make of him. When he talks about his family or his ordinary life in England I find myself warming towards him. Then he'll do or say something that seems crazy or odd, like believing that Mike might have left evidence in our apartment, and I want to punch him. He pointed a gun at me but I never for an instant believed he would actually use it. There's a kindness in his eyes. I don't think he'd hurt anyone who wasn't out to hurt him. He's got that typical English way of making a joke about something serious, as if he's terrified of showing emotion, but whenever he's talked about the Princess Royal I see hurt in his eyes, more than he can express. He's deeply guilty about her death, that's why he's so eager to find out something about Silk Fist, to make up for letting her die. In another life I think I'd like him.'

Marty Logan smiled. 'You're certainly voluble on the subject of Christopher Wyatt. When we saw him in London I couldn't help noticing that he is tall, fit and good looking with dark eyes and lovely black hair. If I wasn't the wife of the President I wouldn't mind a roll in the hay with a man like that. Perhaps you do too?'

Linda felt herself colouring up. 'Stop it, Marty. I've thought no such thing. Mike was the man for me and it's going to take a long time to get over him.'

Martina Logan took Linda by the hands. 'I'm so sorry, Linda, I was only teasing you. It was a crass remark and an insensitive joke to make. Please forgive me. Come on, let's go.'

Linda Marquez followed Martina Logan out of the bedroom. Then she remembered an overheard conversation. The implications literally stopped her in her tracks.

Martina Logan turned around. 'What's the matter, Linda?'

'No, no, it's nothing, Marty.'

'Come on then, let's go bring Sergeant Wyatt in from the cold.'

Linda followed her boss out of the Presidential bedroom, past the armed guards and into the West Sitting Hall. She thought of Wyatt waiting in a hotel room somewhere out in the city.

Perhaps Wyatt wasn't so crazy after all.

29

Room 52, Parker Plaza Hotel, Washington, March 18th

Christopher Wyatt lay on the bed and stared out of the window. The sky was darkening and rain looked imminent. His mind kept turning over and over what might go wrong, what he might have omitted to consider as a potentially disastrous snag. It was now late in the afternoon. Linda had been in the White House for several hours. He was beginning to accept that Linda Marquez had betrayed him.

Wyatt's cell phone rang. He picked it up and said: 'Hello, Prem.'

'Linda's car is moving. She's driving away from the White House.'

A surge of relief. 'Okay. She should be ringing me within minutes. I realise it's the middle of the night where you are, Prem, but stay with me. Keep tracking her.'

'Of course I will. Good luck, Christopher.'

Five minutes later Wyatt's cell phone rang again. 'Hello, Chris Wyatt.'

'It's Linda. I've left the White House. I'm parked in a shopping center. I've done the deal. My people are willing to trade. Where are you?'

'Good work. I'm in Room 53 at the Parker Plaza Hotel. It's a big place that looks like huge white cubes stacked on one another. It's on Parker Street in Foggy Bottom. Repeat, Room 53.'

'Okay, I'm on the way. Wait a minute, there's a car pulled in behind me. There's four men in it.'

'Linda, lock the doors and drive away now.'

'Okay, I'm… shit, there's a truck pulled in front of me. It's blocking me. Some men are getting out!'

'Linda, go into reverse and ram the car behind.'

'It's too late. Chris! They've got sledgehammers. They're smashing the windows. I can't…'

'Linda, you've got a pistol! Use it!'

'I'm trying. They're getting in. Help me, Chris! I can't…'

Linda's cell phone went dead. Wyatt was cold with fear. He rang Prem. 'Is Linda's car moving?'

'No. What's happening?'

'Some thugs are breaking into her car. Can you give me the exact location of the car?'

'It's parked in the Metro Mart Shopping Center. Can you get to her?'

'I haven't got a car. All I can do is ring the police.'

'If she is in a parking lot there must be other people seeing what's going on.'

'I'll get back to you.'

Wyatt dialled 911.

A voice said: 'Please state the nature of your emergency?'

Wyatt said: 'We need the police. There's some men breaking into a woman's car in the Metro Mart Shopping Center. Get somebody there as quick as you can.'

'Can I have your name and address, sir?'

'No. I'm here. It's happening now. The woman works for the Secret Service. She works for the First Lady. You have to get somebody there now. Metro Mart Shopping Center.'

'Yes, sir, but I need…'

Wyatt cut the call. He rang Prem. 'Still not moving?'

'No.'

'Damn,' Wyatt said. 'I think she's been taken.'

'Be careful, Christopher, they could be leading you into a trap, whoever it is. What are you going to do?'

'Nothing more I can do, Prem. If they've taken Linda they might be coming after me next. If they're from the government they could have intercepted Linda's cell phone call and found out where I am anyway. I'm keeping my cell phone ready. Are you still set up?'

'Yes. We're ready if anything happens.'

'Are you sure it will work? We need proof.'

'If whoever comes for you is on a database we will find them in time. Trust me.'

'Thanks, Prem. All I can do now is wait here and hope they come for me and lead me back to Linda. I hope to God that I haven't caused her harm by my stupidity.'

30

Church of Christ in Glory, near Congress Heights, Washington, March 18th

Marlon moved his chair right in front of Linda Marquez. He was so close, face to face, that Linda could smell his breath.

Marlon said softly: 'You're one gutsy lady, I'll give you that. Look at you, tied to a chair, blouse ripped off, cigarette burns all over those pretty titties. Enough is enough, girl. All you have to do is tell us where this guy Wyatt is and we'll let you go. Hell, I don't care. I ain't nothin' to do with this Silk Fist shit but Wyatt knows something. Maybe he told you. Give us a name and we'll let you go. Tell us where Wyatt is and you can walk out of here. You see, these guys behind me are foreigners, and they're mean sons of bitches. Now, I'm a person of colour. I ain't black and I ain't white, I'm somewhere in the middle, just like you are, but at least we're both Americans but we don't owe nothin' to the man. These guys behind me want to use you and then kill you but I don't want that, girl. You're too damn pretty.'

'You'll kill me anyway.'

'Whoa!' Marlon said in mock surprise. 'The girl's got a tongue after all! What makes you think we're gonna kill you?'

'Because you don't care that I've seen your faces and know your names. Marlon, Liridon, Besnik, Visar, Isidor and Kushtim. You'd better kill me because if you don't I'll make you pay. My people are looking for me.'

Marlon laughed. 'No they ain't, baby. They don't know shit

about where you are. One of your own kind sold you out, girl. You don't owe them nothin'. Look around you. This used to be a church but there ain't no God left here. It might be a wooden piece of shit but it's strong. The windows are boarded up, the doors are strong, I got a man posted outside. Even if the whole US army turns up you'll be dead before they could get inside.'

Linda agreed with Marlon's tactical assessment. She had considered her options and concluded there were none. She could not move or free herself. All the pews and ecclesiastical furnishings had been removed, leaving only a few broken wooden chairs and a plain metal table upon which had been left a brass cross. The place was thick with dust and cobwebs. There was little decoration or ornament apart from a stained glass window at the far end. The walls were painted beige and there were paler areas where pictures or crosses had once hung. It was a depressing place to die and Linda had resigned herself to death. The only purpose she could achieve in death was by not betraying Wyatt and thus the name of the person involved with Silk Fist.

Marlon was saying: 'There ain't nobody coming to rescue you, lady. If you start screaming there ain't nobody going to hear you, we're stuck in the middle of a wasteland of weeds and grass and abandoned buildings, and even if they did hear you they ain't gonna do nothin'. That's the sort of neighbourhood it is. The only way you're gonna walk out of here alive is by telling me where Wyatt is.'

'Okay, Marlon,' Linda said. 'You win. I'll tell you where Wyatt is but I don't want those thugs to know. Let me whisper in your ear.'

Marlon leaned forward. Linda bit down as hard as she could on Marlon's earlobe. Marlon screamed in pain and kicked back his chair.

'You fucking bitch. Okay, string her up!'

Isidor and Besnik untied Linda from the chair but re-tied her wrists and shackled the ropes to a short chain with a hook on the end. They lifted her up bodily and attached the hook to one of the metal rafters.

'That's right, you bitch,' Marlon screamed, attempting to staunch the flow of blood from his ear. 'Now you're hung up like a piece of meat in a butcher shop. You think you've suffered before. You fucking asked for this.'

Isidor and Besnik picked up a whip-like rattan cane each. The first blow was across Linda's back. The pain was unbelievably agonising but Linda was determined not to cry out or beg for mercy. The second blow was across the back of her legs. After that Linda could not count. The blows kept on and on until she felt herself falling into unconsciousness.

The ringing of a cell phone brought her back. The blows stopped.

Marlon was saying: 'No, the bitch won't talk. Okay, okay, we'll keep her alive until we get him here.'

Marlon walked up to Linda and said: 'You're one lucky bitch, for now.' He turned to his accomplices and said: 'That was the Englishman. They've found Wyatt.'

The one named Kushtim looked at Linda Marquez. 'Do we take her down now?'

'No,' Marlon said. 'Let the bitch hang there and when Wyatt has told us what we want to know, they'll both die.'

31

Room 52, Parker Plaza Hotel, Washington, March 18th

Wyatt was on the verge of giving up hope. It was growing dark outside. If Linda's abductors had been from the US government they would surely have come for him before now.

Then he heard tapping on the door of room number 53 across the corridor. A guttural voice said: 'Room service, Mr Wyatt.'

Wyatt rang Prem and said quietly: 'Someone's outside the door of the other room.'

'Okay. We're ready, Christopher.'

Another tapping and the voice said again: 'Room service, Mr Wyatt.'

A few seconds later there was a cracking sound. Wyatt glanced out of room 52 and saw two men entering room 53. They had broken the lock with a crowbar. They were big men. One was wearing a dark suit and had a shaven head. His companion, slightly shorter, had long straggly hair and was wearing a bomber jacket and beige trousers. They were both brandishing pistols.

Wyatt said quietly: 'Prem, I'm going in. Stand by.'

Wyatt picked up his silenced Glock and went out into the corridor. He pushed open the door to room 53 and shot the taller man in the back of the knee. The man dropped his pistol and collapsed on to the carpet. His accomplice turned and stared at Wyatt with fear in his eyes, as Wyatt had hoped.

Wyatt pushed shut the door with his leg and said: 'Drop the gun and kneel down. Hands on your head. That's a good boy. Both of you. Hands on head.'

The wounded man struggled to sit up, his back supported by the bed. He said in a guttural accent: 'Who are you? You fucking cripple me. What you want with us?'

Wyatt said: 'You're such handsome lads that I want to take your picture. You might have a future in modelling. Move and I'll kill you both.' He took out his cell phone and took photographs of the two men and sent them to Prem.

Within three minutes Prem said: 'We've got them. They're Albanian gangsters. Nasty low grade muscle.'

'Albanian?' Wyatt said with surprise.

'Yes. They're on the Washington police database. Two brothers named Isidor and Kushtim Bunjaku. Isidor is the older, shaven-headed one. He is a vicious swine. Convictions for armed robbery, grievous bodily harm, drug dealing and rape. Suspected of murder but never charged. Kushtim is the younger brother, the one with long hair. Convictions for assault and petty theft but nothing like his big brother. Be careful, Christopher, the Albanian gangs are particularly vicious.'

'So am I. Okay, thanks, Prem.' Wyatt closed the cell phone. 'Isidor Bunjaku, who are you working for?'

'You cripple me, you fucker,' Isidor said. 'How you know my names?'

Wyatt repeated: 'Who are you working for?'

Isidor said: 'Fuck you, whoever you are. I die before I tell you.'

'Okay,' Wyatt said. He fired one shot into Isidor Bunjaku's forehead. The body lay sprawled against the bed, the duvet behind the head soaked with blood.

Kushtim was trembling with shock and staring at the corpse. 'You killed my brother. You killed my frigging brother.'

'Who sent you?'

'Fuck you.'

Wyatt fired one shot within an inch of Kushtim's temple. 'Why, Kushtim, you've wet yourself. This really isn't your line of work, is it? I haven't got time to waste, Kushtim. Who are you working for?'

'I don't know who. He hire us sometimes. He an Englishman, talks funny. We never see him. He pay well. I swear is true.'

Wyatt tried not to show his surprise. English?

Wyatt said: 'Where is Linda Marquez?'

'I don't know no Linda Marquez.'

'Why did you come here for me?'

'We have to take you to some old church.'

'Where? In Washington?'

'Yes.'

'Where is it? What's the address?'

'I don't know address. I know where it is.'

'Have you got a car?'

'Yes. I got car.'

'Then you'll take me there.'

'I can't. I take you there with gun and they kill me.'

Wyatt sighed. 'Kushtim, you have two choices. You take me to this church and, if you're telling the truth, I'll let you go. If you don't I'll kill you here.'

'You kill me after anyway.'

'It's a gamble you'll have to take, Kushtim. I don't like killing people, except your piece of shit brother. Take me to this church and you'll live. Don't take me and you'll die here, next to Isidor.'

'Okay, okay. I show you.'

'Good boy. You should buy some dark trousers if you're going to piss yourself on the job.'

32

Church of Christ in Glory, near Congress Heights, Washington, March 18th

Linda Marquez wanted to die. The pain from the cigarette burns, the welts from the canes and the burn of the rope chafing her wrists was too much to bear.

Linda realised she was almost delirious from the pain. Perhaps all this was Wyatt's doing. Marlon had taken his orders from someone he called the Englishman. Perhaps Wyatt had sold her out with some sort of elaborate ploy. Linda could not believe that anyone within the White House could have sold her out to these barbarians. It had to be Wyatt. He was on the way to kill her. The lying Limey bastard had led her to doom.

Besnik, a huge man with a bald pate and grey hair, the oldest of the gang, was saying: 'Isidor and Kushtim should have been back long before now. I don't like it. I think the cops got them. Perhaps the cops already surround the church.'

Marlon said sarcastically: 'Visar is outside watching. Don't you think he would have told us if we were surrounded by police?'

Besnik said: 'I say we kill the bitch and get out.'

Liridon stared at Linda lasciviously: 'Couldn't we have some fun with her before we go?'

Linda could not keep down the bile and threw up down her front.

'Oh, yuk!' exclaimed Liridon. 'The dirty bitch.'

Marlon said: 'We'll give them another five minutes then we shoot the woman and get out. Understand?'

Linda craned her neck around to look at the stained glass window at the other end of the church. The window showed Christ being received into Heaven by God, the angels and the saints. It was naïve in style but Linda found comfort in the simplicity and the message. The rays of the setting sun struck the stained glass and suffused the church with coloured light.

Despite her pain, Linda was reassured and calmed. She had once been a dutiful Catholic but had lapsed in recent years. She accepted that she was going to die. She prayed to ask God for forgiveness and to receive her soul into His blessed love.

Marlon said: 'That's it, we have to get out.' He raised his pistol and aimed at Linda.

Linda thought that the bullet had entered her brain as the stained glass shattered into thousands of multi-coloured shards. The car, roaring backwards, smashed through the wooden wall sending showers of splinters and clouds of dust flying through the church. Wyatt wrenched the steering wheel and the car swerved and screeched to a halt. Wyatt flung open the door and leapt out. He knelt and took firing position.

Marlon died first, his jaw shattered, a look of blank incomprehension in his dead eyes. Liridon was trying to take out his gun but was thrown back by two shots in the chest.

Besnik, despite his huge size, reacted fast and dived behind the metal table, pulling the table down towards him to act as a shield. He was out of Wyatt's line of fire. Fearing that Besnik would kill Linda, Wyatt ran towards Besnik and fired off a shot. The shot pierced the table top but missed Besnik. Besnik fired back simultaneously. The shot grazed Wyatt's gun arm and the Glock went flying out of his hand.

Besnik, a grin of triumph on his face, rose up to fire again. Wyatt dived to the floor and picked up the brass cross. He used his momentum to slide towards the table. Besnik fired at the same instant as Wyatt kicked the table against him. Wyatt felt the shockwave of the bullet as it zipped past his ear. Besnik was momentarily unbalanced. Wyatt leapt up and, using all his force, swiped Besnik across the temple with the heavy base of the brass cross. Besnik, with an almost comical look of surprise, dropped his pistol and collapsed on to his knees, blood seeping from his nose and his eyes.

Wyatt was aware that the church door had opened and that someone had entered. Wyatt turned. Visar had been aiming his pistol at Wyatt but had been afraid to fire for fear of hitting Besnik. Now Besnik was out of the way. Linda was hanging behind him. She wriggled up to take hold of the chain and with one monumental effort swung her legs up and kicked Visar in the back of the head. Visar, swearing angrily, stumbled forward but stayed on his feet. Distracted by rage he turned to shoot Linda. Wyatt leapt forward, grabbed Visar's gun arm and brought it down across his knee. Visar screamed in agony as his arm snapped and the pistol flew out of his hand. Wyatt took Visar in a headlock and wrenched until his neck snapped. He let the body slump to the floor and then quickly looked back to see if Besnik was stirring but he was plainly dead.

Wyatt went to Linda and supported her weight as he shook free the hook and chain. He gently lowered her to the ground. He untied the ropes securing her wrists and her feet and looked around for her blouse. It was lying on the floor, dirty and ripped. Wyatt took off his jacket and helped Linda put her arms through the sleeves. He carefully fastened the buttons.

Linda was trembling. Wyatt took her in his arms and held her until, gradually, her trembling subsided. She said: 'I've heard that God is an Englishman. Perhaps it's true.'

Wyatt gently stroked her face. 'I'm no God, Linda. Far from it. I'm the bloody idiot who nearly got you killed. I'm so, so sorry.'

'Let's get out of here. Please.'

'That's exactly what we have to do, Linda. We're both in grave danger. I don't know who to trust now, except you. Someone must have heard the gunfire. The cops could be here at any minute. Can you walk to the car?'

'Yes, I think so.'

Wyatt picked up his own pistol and also took Besnik and Visar's weapons. The trunk of the car was stoved in but, miraculously, the rear lights were still on even though the glass covers had been smashed. Wyatt closed the buckled trunk lid and managed to jam it shut with shard of wood.

Wyatt looked out of the gap where the car had smashed through. There was no-one watching. The church was on a large area of waste ground.

'It's all clear, Linda.' He opened the passenger door and helped Linda into the seat.

Linda saw the spots of blood on the arm of Wyatt's shirt. 'Are you hurt, Chris?'

'Only a graze. Nothing to worry about. I was lucky.'

Linda, exultant to be alive, determined to be brave, said: 'Nice wheels, Chris. Where did you get this piece of crap?'

'An Albanian friend leant it to me.'

'Which one? Isidor or Kushtim?'

'Kushtim. I've persuaded him to seek a new career. He certainly ran off fast enough to start it.'

'What about Isidor?'

'His career is over. Permanently.'

Wyatt started the engine and slowly drove out of the church and on to the brown wasteland. He engaged drive and as they bounced over rough ground towards the road he said: 'We have to disappear, Linda. You need to rest and recover and so do I. Somebody sold you out. I'm even more of a wanted man than I was before. We have landed ourselves in the middle of something out of our control. We're on our own, there's something I have to tell you and we have a lot of decisions to make.'

33

Gadsden Travel Lodge, near Hanover, Pennsylvania, March 20th

Linda Marquez woke when the light from the rising sun permeated the thin curtains of the motel room. The room was basic, sparsely furnished and decorated, but clean and comfortable.

She looked at Wyatt. He was sleeping on the other bed. He was fully clothed, apart from his shoes, and had covered himself with a single sheet. He was restless and murmuring in his sleep. His pistol was ready on the bedside table.

Linda threw aside the duvet and, as quietly as she could, went into the bathroom and locked the door. She lifted the cheap T-shirt she had bought at a gas station and examined her wounds in the mirror. The bruises from the beating were coming out, purple and yellow welts. The cigarette burns were painful but were healing cleanly. There were dark circles under her eyes. Now that the euphoria of being alive had abated she was dispirited and desperately tired, lost and cast out. All night she had dreamed of hanging from that rafter, of gunshots and blood and shattering stained glass.

Linda came out of the bathroom and closed the door. The latch clicked. Wyatt woke up with a start, wild eyed, and grabbed for his pistol. He saw Linda, realised where he was and put down the gun. Despite the coolness of the room there was a sheen of sweat on his forehead. He sat on the edge of the bed and ran his hands through his hair and rubbed his face in an effort to wake up and clear his senses.

'I'm sorry I woke you,' Linda said. 'You looked as if you were having a bad dream.'

'I was. I was in the army for ten years but I've killed more men in the past month than in that whole ten years. It makes me sick to my stomach.'

'I've always imagined that you'd killed more men than that.'

'No. It doesn't get any easier. In fact, the reverse.'

'If you hadn't killed those bastards yesterday then I wouldn't be here.'

Wyatt nodded and grunted. 'I was trained to do a job and sometimes it has to be done but no-one except a lunatic would enjoy it. Do you still see the Bishop of Carlisle in your dreams?'

'Yes,' Linda said. 'Every night. I'll make us coffee. Or would you prefer tea?'

'I'd love a mug of tea, but not that iced crap you Yankees like.'

'You mean hot, sweet and milky?'

Wyatt smiled. 'That's right. Heavenly! Can you do it?'

Linda laughed. 'I'll give it a shot.' She went into the tiny kitchen.

Wyatt said: 'Use two of those ridiculous little teabags with strings on.'

'Okay. Anything to eat?'

'Have we got anything?'

'No.'

'I'll stick to tea then. How did you sleep?'

'Bad dreams but better than I expected. Exhausted I guess.'

'You have every right to be. You need to see a doctor.'

'I'm doing okay. I examined myself in the mirror. I hurt and ache all over but I don't think those bastards broke anything or hurt anything vital inside me.'

Linda came out of the kitchen carrying two mugs. Wyatt had drawn back the drapes and was looking out of the window at the forested hills far away. He was edgy and restless, wary and watchful.

'Come and drink your tea and relax,' Linda suggested. She sat down at the dining table. 'I think we're safe enough for a few minutes.'

Wyatt joined her. 'That's not what I'm concerned about.'

'What then?'

'Linda, I have a confession to make.'

Linda put down her coffee mug. 'Oh, it's never good when a conversation starts with those words.'

'You're right. I lied to you, Linda. I didn't trust you, so I lied to you, and it nearly cost you your life.'

'Okay,' Linda said, more calmly than Wyatt had expected. 'What did you lie about?'

'About knowing the name of somebody involved in Silk Fist. I don't. I was testing you to see how you would react, how your bosses would react.'

'Okay, I can accept that, Chris. *I* didn't trust *you* before yesterday. But what would you have done if you had come back to the White House or some other place for interrogation.'

'I don't know.' Wyatt was intensely relieved by Linda's acceptance. He had debated whether to tell Linda about the medicine bottle but had decided not to. He justified his decision by reasoning that it would be for her own safety if she did not know about that bottle yet. Whoever was responsible for yesterday's kidnapping might try again. If Linda did not know then she she could not be forced to confess. He said: 'Linda, I'm truly sorry for endangering your life with my stupid deception.'

Linda could see that he was genuinely contrite. 'It wasn't so stupid, Chris, because it flushed out the enemy within.'

'You mean within the White House?'

'Yes. The only people outside the White House who knew about the plan beforehand, for me to come and pick you up at that hotel, was we two. Right?'

'Agreed. Well, there was Prem. He knew you were in the White House but he didn't know about our plan and I can't imagine that he could have arranged a kidnapping by Albanian thugs from his office in New Delhi.'

'Right, so it had to be someone who was aware of what I was doing in the White House.'

'Agreed again,' Wyatt said. 'How many knew?'

'In the end there were several people, from the President down. There was Marty, the Vice President, my boss Stack Franklin, four or five other senior Secret Service chiefs, the CIA, FBI, NSA, Homeland Security. Your people in London were told that you wanted to come in. Even Jonathan Schneider, the CIA chief in London was told. Anyone of them could have had the time and the contacts to arrange the kidnapping.'

Wyatt sat back. 'I hate to say it, Linda, but we're not only in grave danger but we're totally on our own.'

'I know,' Linda said with a sigh. 'I keep trying to persuade myself that if I simply go back to the White House and explain everything to Marty, she will straighten everything out. But I know I can't. So what do we do?'

Wyatt looked at his watch. 'We have one friend we can trust. It's about half past three in the afternoon in Delhi. Let's consider our possibilities and what we need and I can ring Prem to ask if he can supply us. We still have his secure cell phone and laptop. I remembered to pick them up before young Kushtim drove me to the church. We have the Glock with ten rounds left and the two Albanian revolvers with a few shots left. I have a little cash and the credit card kindly donated by the Indian government. I can't go back to the Parker Plaza hotel so I have no change of clothes and no shaving gear. You'll have to put up with me scruffy until I can find a place to buy a razor.'

'That shouldn't be difficult in America,' Linda said. 'We can't go back to my apartment, that will be crawling with Feds by now, so I also have to buy some fresh clothes. I have no cell phone, no cash or credit cards, no weapon.'

'Ideally we need a new set of wheels. Kushtim's old jalopy will be hot but I'd be reluctant to go anywhere to hire or buy a car in case our details or description have been circulated.'

Linda nodded. 'Then I'll have to hot wire a car.'

'You know how to do that? Secret Service training I suppose?'

'Nope. When I was a teenager my clever godfather showed me how to hot wire a car in case I ever needed to. My parents still don't know about that particular skill of mine.'

Wyatt chuckled. 'Sergeant Marquez, you're full of surprises. I have another confession to make.'

'What's that?'

'You make a good mug of tea. Not great, but good.'

Linda laughed. 'High praise indeed from a Limey.'

Wyatt said: 'Okay, things are looking more hopeful. We need to find somewhere to rest up, restock and regroup. I'll ring Prem to see if he can help us.'

Wyatt went to the bedside table, picked up his cell phone and rang Prem's number. The call was answered but before Wyatt could speak, Prem said jovially: 'Ranji, how nice to hear from you again! Are you still coming to visit me? Excellent! Let me check my diary and I'll get back to you in a few minutes.'

The call was ended. Wyatt had understood the message. He said to Linda: 'That sounded like bad news. Prem doesn't want to be heard speaking to me openly. I hope he'll ring back from somewhere private and secure.'

Linda said: 'I'll switch on the TV news. There might have been some new Silk Fist disaster or development.'

'Good idea. I'll go and shower while you check.'

Prem rang back as Wyatt was stepping out of the shower. He said: 'Christopher, you're becoming a dangerous man to befriend. I see you're in Pennsylvania somewhere. What is going on?'

'I'm with Linda Marquez. We're on the run. Someone within the White House or within the intelligence services betrayed her.

She was kidnapped yesterday by our Albanian friends and I had to help her out.'

'It wouldn't have been in the Parker Plaza hotel and then an old church, would it?'

'Yes.'

'I thought that must be you. There are bodies everywhere. The official line is a gangland vendetta but the authorities know it was you. They're searching for you both.'

'That's why I need your help, Prem. We don't know who we can trust. Do you have anything like a safe house around here? I need ammunition, cash, new passports and papers for Linda and me. And I...'

'Christopher, wait. I can no longer help you officially. I've been ordered to drop you. The Americans have somehow found out that we are backing you and went straight to the top. Prime Minister Mishra told my boss that we are heading towards a dangerous diplomatic split with America if we continue to support you. I can't help you with anything, officially.'

'Okay. I understand, Prem. At least I still have the credit card.'

An awkward silence.

'Prem? Has the credit card been cancelled?'

'Yes. I'm sorry. It's out of my hands. Keep in touch and I'll help you in anyway I can, unofficially.'

'Okay, Prem. I understand.'

'Listen, Christopher, I can send you some cash, perhaps some equipment if you let me know where to...'

'It's okay, Prem. I understand. You mustn't endanger yourself and your career on our behalf. I'll be in touch.'

'Christoper, wait. I can...'

Wyatt cut the call. He dressed and left the bathroom. Linda was watching the news.

'Anything happened?' Wyatt asked.

'Yes, a lone madman working in a cloud computing center in

Chicago sabotaged his workplace and lost trillions of bits of information, and a lone madman working at a hydroelectric dam in Italy opened the gates and flooded thousands of acres of the Po Valley causing a black-out that will last for days and which killed scores of innocent people. And in Washington police are looking for a man and a woman seen leaving a disused church in which four bodies were found.'

'Have they put out our description?'

Linda shook her head. 'No. They're ascribing the killings to a gangland feud. I heard you talking in the bathroom. Was that Prem?'

'Yes. I'm afraid we're really on our own, Linda. The authorities know it was us at the church. They've contacted India and Prem's been ordered to drop us. Your people are really pissed with India. The credit card's been cancelled. I've got something like twenty dollars to buy gas and food. For a start we need money, quickly.'

'Perhaps we can rob a liquor store, like Bonnie and Clyde.'

Wyatt was relieved that Linda was joking.

She said. 'My parent's could send me all the money we need.'

Wyatt shook his head. 'Too dangerous. They are undoubtedly being watched. It would lead the authorities straight to us.'

'You're right, and I wouldn't want to get my parents mixed up in this mess. I sure do miss them and they must be worried sick about me. I wish I could tell them I'm okay.'

'You can. We still have the untraceable cell phone. You can ring your folks later but don't tell them where we are.'

Linda was suddenly despondent. 'Is it time to face reality, Chris? If Prem has cut us loose then this is as far as we can go. We have to turn ourselves in. We could ask for the protection of the local police, perhaps here in Pennsylvania somewhere. We could trust them.'

'We could trust the local police, sure, but it would mean giving up the search for whoever's behind Silk Fist. There's one thing I'm now sure of, it's not China behind Silk Fist. Silk Fist is much closer to home.'

'I agree with you, but what can we do? We have no money, hardly any weapons, no back-up, no friends.'

'That's what we need more than anything,' Wyatt said. 'A friend who would believe us, who is outside and independent of the authorities, and who can supply us with anything we need.' He smiled. 'Do you know anybody in the Mafia?'

Linda did not smile in return. 'Mike might have known somebody. If I give myself up I'll ask Mike's colleagues to protect me. They'll see that I don't come to anymore harm.'

Wyatt nodded. 'If you want to turn yourself in, Linda, I'll respect your decision, but I'm going to carry on. I don't know how, I don't know where, but I have to try. And ask yourself, Linda, would the people behind all these Silk Fist atrocities worry about getting rid of someone like you, however many New York cops were protecting you? The very fact that they snatched you and were torturing you for information tells us that we are close to something.'

'I accept what you mean. I want to carry on as well, Chris, but I simply cannot see where we go from here. I'll go take a shower. Maybe the water will clear my head. It will help the burns and bruises as well.' Linda opened the bathroom door. 'How's your arm?'

Wyatt made a fist and raised and lowered his arm. 'It's fine. I was lucky.'

'Good.'

Neither moved or spoke for several moments, things to be said but neither willing to say them.

Eventually Wyatt said: 'I'll respect any decision you make, Linda, but I feel compelled to carry on, even if the odds are stacked against me and I end up making a right bloody Charlie of myself.'

Linda closed the bathroom door. 'Charlie? Yes, Charlie. It's a possibility. A long shot, but a possibility. Charlie always thought I was hot.'

'Charlie's not wrong, but who is he? Some sort of Mafia boss?'

'No. Charlie is more resourceful and useful than any two-bit Mafia hood, and the clincher is that Charlie is undoubtedly going to love you!'

34

Charlie's Night Club, Harlem, New York, March 20th

Linda Marquez and Christopher Wyatt drove into New York late in the morning. Wyatt parked the stolen Dodge in a side street several blocks away from their intended destination. Linda insisted on making a note of the license plate number.

'What are you doing that for?' Wyatt asked.

'I'm an officer sworn to uphold the law and I've committed a felony by hot-wiring this person's car and driving it away without their permission. It had to be done but I'm going to make an anonymous call to the police to tell them the vehicle is abandoned here and, when this all over, I'll make sure the citizen concerned is compensated.'

'If we're still alive,' Wyatt said. He picked up his case from the back seat and they set off.

The main streets were crowded and rain was falling heavily, driven by a fresh breeze.

Linda was wearing Wyatt's jacket. She said: 'Your coat is sodden already. I feel like a frigging bag lady, or a contestant in a wet T-shirt competition. How are you doing? Don't you feel cold wearing just a shirt?'

'I'm okay,' Wyatt said.

'At least a wet T-shirt with no bra will give Charlie a thrill and help get us through the door.'

Charlie's Night Club was located down a side street off 125th Street. Over the door was a domed portico, covered with a gold material, which extended out to cover the sidewalk. The only sign to indicate the nature of the premises was a small brass plaque with engraved black lettering that read 'Charlie's' in script lettering. It was attached to wooden double doors. Linda tried the door. It was locked. She knocked on the door. They waited for several seconds but nobody answered. Linda knocked again, louder, but still nobody answered.

'There has to be staff in there,' Linda said. 'There's a show every night except Sunday, and they serve food. There must be someone in there making preparations.'

Wyatt asked: 'What time does the club open?'

'Six tonight and stays open until early hours.'

'Perhaps we should come back at six?'

'Are you nuts?' Linda said. 'I'm soaking wet and starving with no money between us to buy a hot dog. I'm not going to sit in the park in the rain for the next six hours.'

'Then we better keep knocking until somebody gets so annoyed they'll come to get rid of us.'

'Agreed.' Linda knocked again, and kept on knocking.

'At least it's dry under this portico,' Wyatt said.

'Oh, yeah, things couldn't be better,' Linda said scornfully.

Wyatt smiled and joined in the knocking.

After five minutes the door opened. A tall heavily built man looked out. He was wearing a T-shirt with the name 'Charlie's' across the front in the same script as the plaque on the door. His biceps bulged under the T-shirt. He said: 'We're closed. We don't open until six.'

Linda said: 'I know. I need to speak to Charlie urgently. I'm a friend.' She deliberately let her jacket fall open.

The doorman looked at Linda's soaked T-shirt and then Wyatt's stubble and sodden shirt. He said: 'Charlie's not here.'

Wyatt said: 'Can you give us Charlie's address or cell phone number?'

'No. I'm not allowed to give out private details.'

Linda said: 'I'm a member of the United States Secret Service. It's vital that we talk to Charlie on a matter of national importance.'

'Oh yeah? You got a badge?'

'A badge?'

'Yeah, a badge or some form of identification because from where I'm standing you look more like a hooker or a drowned rat than a secret agent.'

'No, I haven't got any form of identification. I lost it in a shoot-out with some Commie agents. Come on, Chris, we'll have to find Charlie some other way.'

The doorman looked at Linda's wet T-shirt again and said: 'Hold on, sister. You look like the kind of broad that Charlie would go for. Step inside a minute and I'll make the call.'

'Okay,' Linda said. 'Thank you. But I'm not a "broad".'

The doorman grinned. He had one gold tooth at the back of his mouth. He opened the door.

Linda and Wyatt walked into a large foyer with a cloakroom and rest rooms on the left and two offices on the right. The foyer was decorated with chrome fittings and silver motifs. There was a thick pile black and silver carpet underfoot.

'Very 1930s,' Wyatt said. 'Who's the cabaret tonight? Fred Astaire or the Nicholas Brothers?'

The doorman said: 'You're a white posh boy who's heard of the Nicholas Brothers?'

'Sure. I've seen them on TV. They were brilliant.'

Another doorman, also well-built but wearing a suit and a tie, came through the double doors that led into the club. 'What's going on, Hank?'

'Hank?' Wyatt said. 'I've never heard of a black guy called Hank before.'

Hank said: 'My folks had a warped sense of humour.' To his colleague he said: 'Nothing to worry about, Mace. These two need to contact Charlie, urgent.' He took out his cell phone.

'Hank and Mace,' Wyatt said. 'Sounds like a double act.'

Mace glared at Wyatt.

'Only joking, mate,' Wyatt said.

They waited while Hank made the call. After several seconds he said: 'Charlie's not answering. Too early.'

Linda said: 'Can you give us the number so we can ring later?'

'No,' Mace said. 'We give you Charlie's location and we're out of a job. You better come back tonight.'

Wyatt shrugged and moved towards the door. Linda did not move. Mace stepped towards her and took her arm. Wyatt said: 'I wouldn't do that if I were you.'

Mace said: 'You think I'm scared of some candy-assed white boy with stubble on his face?'

Linda brought her shoe down hard on Mace's instep, elbowed him in the groin, and swept his legs from under him. Mace toppled sideways and crashed on to the carpet. He reached inside his jacket but Linda took out Wyatt's Glock. She handed it to Wyatt.

'I told you that was a bad idea,' Wyatt said. 'Let's all calm down.'

'Damn that felt good,' Linda said. 'I'm getting tired of being pushed around.'

The door behind them opened and a female voice said: 'What the hell is going on in my club?'

Wyatt looked around. The woman standing in the doorway was as tall as he was and she was dressed in a full-length coat made out of some sort of white fur. Her hair was braided into long cornrows. She looked to be at least seventy years old. Standing behind her was a male attendant carrying shopping bags.

Linda said: 'Hello, Charlotte. Remember me?'

'Linda? Linda O'Brien? Is that really you? Good God, girl, you look like shit. What's going on?'

'We desperately need your help, Charlie.'

'We?' Charlie said, looking at Wyatt. 'Who's this cracker scarecrow pointing a gun in my club?'

Wyatt put the Glock in his trouser pocket and said: 'I apologise profusely for my unshaven appearance. I'm afraid I was deprived of my electric razor and some other possessions by some bad guys.'

Charlie said: 'Are you English?'

Linda said: 'Charlie, this is Sergeant Christopher Wyatt of the London Metropolitan Police Royal Protection Squad. Chris, this is Miss Charlotte Windsor, the unofficial queen of Harlem.'

'Royal Protection Squad?' Charlie said. 'Do you know the royal family?'

'Yes, mam, very well. I've guarded them all.'

Linda said: 'Chris was guarding the Princess Royal when she was murdered. It was Chris who shot Dr Flaherty.'

Charlie looked at Wyatt with a mixture of confusion and adoration. 'You were with the princess when she died? You knew her well?'

'Yes, mam. I'm proud to say that she regarded me as a friend. I was devoted to her.'

Charlie said: 'But what the hell are you two doing here? Mace, get up off the floor. You and Hank go and get on with your work.'

Linda said: 'Charlie. Can we talk to you?'

Linda found herself embraced in voluminous white fur.

'Linda, honey, I was so sorry to hear about Mike. You and him were such a perfect fit, and he was such a sweet guy. You must miss him terribly.'

'Yes, I do, Charlie, but I've been so busy since he passed. Can we tell you about it?'

'Sure. Let's go up to the apartment. I'm guessing you two need somewhere to stay and rest up.'

'We do, desperately,' Linda said. 'And the less people know we're here the better.'

'Okay, I'll tell Mace and Hank to keep their traps shut. They'll do what I say. You take those bags from my man Sylvester and come on through.'

Charlotte pushed through the double doors and led them imperiously through her night club. There was a long bar on the right, a small stage at the far end and many tables, booths and rows of banquettes on different levels.

Charlotte took them through the kitchen and into a private elevator. They went up to the third floor and stepped out into a private apartment. The apartment was decorated in chrome, black and purple and hung with paintings of female subjects by the same artist. There was a long bar, a kitchen, bathroom, shower room, and a bedroom.

'Make yourselves at home,' Charlie said as she opened the door to the bedroom.

Wyatt watched in fascination as Charlie pulled off satin sheets from the king size bed to reveal a naked white girl, no more than twenty years old, underneath.

'Get dressed, honey,' Charlie said. 'You're being evicted.'

'You're kicking me out?' the girl said.

'Yep. I've got new tenants for this place.'

'You mean it's over between us.'

'Honey, it never started.'

'But where will I go?'

'I'll give you money,' Charlie said. 'Stay in a hotel for a while. You won't be wanting for accommodation very long.'

'You selfish old bitch,' the girl spat.

'That's a fact,' Charlie said, and closed the bedroom door. She turned to Linda and Wyatt. 'How long will you folks be staying?'

'A few days, perhaps,' Linda said. 'It depends on what you can do for us and how long it will take.'

'Okay. Are you two getting it on?'

'What!' Linda exclaimed indignantly. 'Are you asking if we're sleeping together? No, we are certainly not.'

'It's a possibility, you must admit. Two beautiful young people like you. If I was batting for the away team then a handsome hunk of Englishman would be just my cup of tea.'

Wyatt laughed at Charlotte's attempt at an English accent. 'I think what Linda means is that we have to keep things purely business-like, whatever we think of each other. We are up to our necks in trouble and we can't afford to complicate things further, even if we felt like it.'

Linda said: 'I lost Mike only about a month ago. He was the only man for me.'

Charlie said: 'Don't you be saying that, sister. Mike's gone but life goes on. That's the world we were born into for better or worse. You're a beautiful healthy young woman. You take your pleasure when you can and don't you go feeling guilty about it. One of you can take the bed, the other can sleep on the couch. Now, what sort of trouble are you in.'

Wyatt said: 'Linda, why don't you show Charlie what they did to you?' He turned his back and walked away to examine one of the paintings.

Linda hesitated, then took off her jacket and lifted up her T-shirt. Charlie stared at the livid purple bruises, the black cigarette burns, the red weals around Linda's wrist. At that moment the young girl came out of the bedroom carrying a bag. She looked at what was going on. 'You sick old bitch,' she murmured, and walked over to the lift.

Linda lowered her T-shirt.

Charlie said: 'God almighty, girl. Whoever did that to you must be crazy. Are they still after you?'

'Thanks to Sergeant Wyatt over there, the thugs who did this will never go after anyone again but we are still in danger.'

Charlie said: 'Are you two hungry?'

Linda and Wyatt looked at each other. 'Ravenous,' Wyatt admitted.

'I'll go down to the kitchen and order us some lunch and coffee. I've got to sort out one or two other things, then we'll talk. Help yourself from the bar.'

Charlie went down in the lift.

Wyatt said: 'I think we've earned a large brandy. Do you want to join me?'

'It's a bit early but why not. As you say, we've earned it.'

'You were right about Charlie,' Wyatt said as he poured the drinks from the optics. 'She's an amazing character. How did you get to meet her?'

'Mike got to know her through his police work. Charlie is tough and resourceful but she's not a criminal. She's been fighting for the rights of black people, and Harlem in particular, for fifty years. She's never used violence but she's untouchable. She won't tolerate hard drugs in this club. A lot of the cops were suspicious of Charlie but Mike understood what she was trying to achieve. She was like the conduit between the black community and the authorities. She's used her intelligence and diplomatic skills to achieve great things for her people. Harlem is now a thriving and vibrant part of New York, that's partly why Mike and I decided to come live here.'

Wyatt said: 'Are you sure she'll be able to get what we want? I mean, if she's not a criminal, how will she... '

'She's *not* a criminal,' Linda interrupted firmly. 'That doesn't mean she can't be underhand and ruthless in a good cause. She's had to be, many times, for the sake of her people. She knows everyone who's anyone in New York, black, white, Hispanic or any colour. She fights hard but when the battle is won she has no prejudice. Black, white or brown, if she likes you, that's all that matters and colour doesn't count. If anyone can help us, Charlie can.'

'I like her,' Wyatt said as he handed Linda her drink. 'Why is she so obsessed with the British royal family?'

'I don't know. You'd have to ask her that. Her real surname is Bruce or Brice or something but she changed it legally to Windsor, same as the royal family. Everyone's allowed their little peccadilloes.'

Wyatt looked around the apartment. 'Interesting colour scheme. Like some groovy pad from the Sixties.'

'Charlie started out as a singer back then. She was in a group, something like the Supremes, that sort of act. She had some success but soon realised there was more money and more chance of a long-term career in running the venues than doing the singing.'

The lift doors opened and Charlotte stepped out followed by two waiters bearing trays of food and a pot of coffee. They set it down on the dining table. 'Come on you two,' Charlotte said. 'Let's eat and talk.'

The waiters left and Wyatt followed Linda to the table.

'That smells good,' Wyatt said.

'Enjoy!' Charlie said. 'While we eat you can tell me what's happening and what you need from me and then Chris can tell me all about England and the royal family.'

They told Charlie everything that had happened. When they had finished eating they moved to the black leather armchairs. Wyatt poured another brandy for all of them.

'That's the damnedest story I ever heard,' Charlie said. 'So this Silk Fist shit they're talking about is nothing to do with the Chinese Commies but might involve our own government, or the British government.'

'That's why we came to you,' Linda said. 'We had nowhere else to go and you've been fighting against the bad guys for years…'

'Don't say how many, honey.'

'You have the contacts and the know-how to help us.'

'Okay. What do you need?'

Wyatt said: 'We need passports and documents to allow us to move freely in and out of the States. We need ammunition. We need a credit card and a line of credit.'

Linda said: 'We've lost everything. We need new clothes. We need money. A lot of money.'

Charlie nodded. 'What you also need, Linda, is a doctor to check your wounds.'

'I'm okay, Charlie, really.'

'That's not up for discussion, sister. I'm getting you checked out. I know a physician who's been treating gang members for years. He knows what he's doing and he knows to keep his mouth firmly shut, whatever he sees or hears.'

'Okay, I give in,' Linda said. 'Can you get what we need?'

'Money, clothes, ammo, no problem. Credit card, perhaps a couple of days. Passports and documents, perhaps four or five days, I'm not sure. That's gonna be tricky, and expensive.'

Wyatt said: 'That's what concerns us, Charlie. If you do all this for us, we don't know when we'll be able to reimburse you.'

Charlie looked at Linda and smiled. 'You see, that's why I love the English. They don't say "pay you back", they say "reimburse" you. The language of Shakespeare and Dickens. Are you an aristocrat, Chris, like a lord or something?'

'No, I'm afraid not. I'm the son of a subway train driver and a school cook. I come from a humble background.'

'You sound like an aristocrat.'

'Well, your name is Charlie but Linda tells me you don't allow cocaine in your club, and charlie's the slang name for coke, isn't it?'

'Yes, it is,'

Wyatt said: 'I daren't tell you what Charlie means in Cockney rhyming slang.'

Charlie looked puzzled so Wyatt said: 'You know Cockney rhyming slang, apples and pears means stairs, trouble and strife means wife. Charlie is derived from Charlie Hunt.'

'So it's something that rhymes with hunt?' Linda said.

Charlie laughed. She leant forward and slapped Wyatt on the knee. 'You're a wicked, wicked man, Chris Wyatt, but you're alright. I don't think Linda has worked it out yet. Regarding the money, if you track down these Silk Fist bastards who are causing all this suffering then it's money well spent, so don't you bother about that. Perhaps I'll get a knighthood from your king!'

'You're a woman, Charlie, so you can't be a knight. You'll have to be a dame.'

'I've been that for seventy years, honey! Come on, Chris, you can pay me back by telling me all you know about the royal family.'

'It'll be a pleasure,' Wyatt said, 'but why have you got such an interest in England and the royals?'

'I'll tell you a story about my granddaddy. He was born in the South and raised on a farm. He was a smart guy and a genius with anything mechanical. He was fascinated by aircraft and flying but when the war started he couldn't become a pilot because of his colour. Best he could get was in the motor pool servicing and repairing jeeps and staff cars and such like. Anyway, granddaddy had experienced little but prejudice, segregation and hatred from white people. Then his unit was stationed in England for a few months getting ready for D-Day. He said it was like a different world, like being transferred to Paradise. He and his black buddies went into pubs, were invited to parties, invited into people's houses and, instead of meeting hatred and prejudice, he met acceptance, thanks and friendship for helping you English to fight the Nazis. He couldn't believe the difference in attitude. He fell in love with England, the people, the scenery. He had a lucrative sideline repairing cars and bicycles for the local community. I think he even got it on with a couple of English girls. He was in heaven. He eventually had to come back to the States but I grew up hearing stories about England. I used to dream of being a princess. That's why I love your royal family. Such class, such breeding, especially the Princess Royal. I cried for a day when I heard she'd been murdered. I grew up dreaming of this marvellous magical land far away where black people were not hated.'

'England has changed a lot since the war, and not always for the better. Have you ever been to England?'

'No, I never have. I realise that I've probably lived an illusion about England. I didn't want to spoil my fantasy.'

Wyatt smiled. 'That's very wise.'

'Anyway, people change, countries change. My generation have had to spend most of our lives fighting prejudice. It's not over but the battle is largely won. America is a better country. Hell, we've even had a black President. No country will ever be perfect but this land has grown up a lot. And I'm a New York girl. I love this frigging town.'

Wyatt and Charlie were disturbed by light snoring. They looked at Linda.

Charlie said: 'That girl even snores pretty.'

Wyatt said: 'Linda went through hell yesterday, and it was my fault. She's wiped out, mentally and physically. I can't thank you enough for taking us in and giving us shelter.'

'You can thank me by pouring me another brandy and telling me all about the Princess Royal.'

'It'll be my pleasure,' Wyatt said.

Two days later Wyatt rang Premendra Dhawan. Wyatt timed the call so that Prem would be off duty. He timed it well. Prem was at home and could talk freely. Wyatt explained their situation and what he had in mind.

'Can you do that, Prem?'

'Yes, I can. I will have to be extremely careful. If my superiors find out what I am doing I could lose my job, perhaps even end up in prison, but if you have a lead about the scum who murdered my wife, I will do as you ask.'

'I suggest that we meet up somewhere neutral where we won't be recognised. Do you like the idea of a holiday, Prem?'

'I have some time off due to me. Where do you suggest, Christopher?'

'I hear the Seychelles is nice at this time of year.'

'The Seychelles is nice at any time of the year. About now it's perfect.'

'Good. As soon as we're prepared I'll let you know and we'll fly out and enjoy some tropical sunshine. Linda needs some rest and I've got something vitally important to tell you.'

35

Cabinet Office Briefing Room, Whitehall, London, March 30th

Jonathan Schneider said: 'Thank you for agreeing to convene this meeting at such short notice, Prime Minister.'

'Don't thank me, Jonathan. It's the only time I have free for the next week. I'm flying to Germany in two hours to sort out yet another dispute with Europe, and to discuss this damnable Silk Fist business. One of their leading industrialists has recently been murdered with all the hallmarks of a Silk Fist attack. Is your visit to do with Silk Fist?'

'Yes, sir. That's why I requested to meet you here in the Briefing Room. There is video footage that will interest you and the Home Secretary and Assistant Commissioner Sherman. Thank you all for coming.'

Home Secretary Clare Barnard said: 'I suspect that the presence of myself and Mrs Sherman is because of something to do with Sergeant Wyatt?'

Schneider said: 'Indeed so, mam.' To the Prime Minister he said: 'Sir, I've just flown back from Washington. The President asked me to report directly to you on Wyatt's actions and to express his grave concern about the possible danger to one of our Secret Service agents, Sergeant Linda Marquez.'

Sherman said: 'She is the agent who Wyatt tried to see at your embassy and who he's been in contact with in the States?'

'Yes. Sergeant Marquez, as well as being a Secret Service operative, is also the special personal assistant to the First Lady.

Strictly between us, I think President Logan is getting it in the neck from Mrs Logan for not being able to locate her, despite the President ordering all the combined resources of our intelligence services to find them.'

Montrose said, with a hint of smugness: 'Our special forces boys are well trained in avoiding capture.'

'Indeed so,' Schneider said sourly. 'We have received information that definitely implicates Wyatt as working for Silk Fist.'

Montrose said: 'I apologise for my levity, Jonathan. What have you found out about Wyatt?'

'Vice President Kefalas was once the director of the CIA and one of his former assets in Russia has confirmed Wyatt's involvement in Silk Fist.'

Sherman said: 'I can't believe it, Jonathan. I've known Wyatt for years. There has never been a hint of subterfuge or disloyalty.' A warning glare from the Prime Minister. She said: 'I suppose I could be wrong.'

Schneider said: 'Many people have been fooled by clever traitors over the years, your Kim Philby, our own Aldrich Ames and so on. Wyatt once worked for Yaroslav Blokhin, the Russian oligarch, and they recently had contact in Switzerland when Wyatt was on leave. Our asset has given us proof that Blokhin is involved and, through him, so is Wyatt.'

Clare Barnard said: 'Wyatt was involved in some sort of street fracas outside his home. Neighbours reported a man being shot and possibly killed but his body was spirited away. That was before Wyatt flew to Canada. We obtained a search warrant and searched Wyatt's house but came up with nothing suspicious.'

Schneider said: 'Apart from the fact that Blokhin owns that house and allows Wyatt to live there free of rent, council tax and even utility bills.'

Clare Barnard turned to Sherman. 'We were not aware of that, were we?'

'No, we weren't,' Sherman said, wrong-footed and uncomfortable under Barnard's scrutiny.

Schneider went on: 'Wyatt and Marquez visited her apartment in New York. We had our people watching the apartment but again they managed to evade capture. We searched the apartment but found nothing of interest except a computer. We have analysed the information on that computer and found nothing suspicious. The police are also in possession of a cell phone belonging to Marquez's husband who committed suicide. Again there was nothing remotely suspicious on there.'

Montrose said: 'So what are you saying, Jonathan? Do you believe that Linda Marquez is with Wyatt under duress and is in danger.'

'We believe so, sir. Marquez visited the First Lady at the White House with a story that Wyatt had information about Silk Fist but Marquez was abducted by Albanian gangsters as soon as she had left the White House. We believe that Wyatt may have been trying to plant false information and, when the attempt failed, hired a gang of thugs to abduct Marquez. I regret to tell you that the bodies of those gangsters were found later, one in a hotel room, four in an abandoned church in Washington.' Schneider operated the remote. 'This is CCTV footage of Wyatt leaving the Parker Plaza hotel in the company of an Albanian gangster named Kushtim Bunjaku. The body of his brother was found in a hotel room booked by Wyatt. We found some of Wyatt's belongings still in the hotel. We have analysed the ammunition used in the hotel killing and at the church. The ammo used to kill three gangsters matched Wyatt's Glock pistol, the same one he used to shoot Dr Flaherty. Wyatt obtained a car from Kushtim Bunjaku. Kushtim has disappeared, presumed dead. The car was found abandoned in Pennsylvania.'

Montrose asked: 'Why would Wyatt kill these Albanian thugs if they were helping him?'

'We presume it is to cover his tracks, get rid of the witnesses.'

Sherman shook her head but dare not make any further comment to incur the Prime Minister's wrath.

Schneider pressed the remote again. 'We found this CCTV footage of Wyatt and Marquez walking through New York. You can see that Marquez is soaked to the skin, shivering and looks downcast and exhausted. Despite an intensive search, Wyatt and Linda Marquez have disappeared again. Wyatt is a ruthless and vicious killer and we believe that Sergeant Marquez is in grave danger.'

Prime Minister Montrose pursed his lips. 'It is indeed a melancholy recital. What does the President want from us?'

'The President requests that you employ all the resources at your disposal to find him and, for the sake of his marital harmony, ensure that no harm comes to Sergeant Marquez.'

'And Wyatt?'

'It is, of course, better if he was taken alive but, if we find him and he resists, then we will use all force necessary to bring him down, hopefully with no detrimental impact on Anglo-American relations.'

'No, of course not, Jonathan. I offer you and the President my sincere regrets that one of our operatives has gone rogue. I will order all co-operation with your people and make it top priority that Wyatt is found. As for Sergeant Marquez, I dread to think what possible ordeal she might be enduring.'

36

Golden Palm Villas, Mahe, Seychelles, March 30th

Linda Marquez looked out over the Indian Ocean. The white sand was warm beneath her feet and the surf frothed around her toes with a delicious tickling sensation. The white clouds piled high above the horizon and a gentle breeze ruffled the palm fronds. Further along the beach a group of children were laughing and playing, jumping through the incoming blue rollers and shrieking with delight. Linda closed her eyes and turned her face up to the morning sun.

Wyatt noticed that Linda had stopped walking. He turned around and walked back. 'Anything wrong, Linda?'

'No,' Linda replied, without opening her eyes. 'This place is perfect. I guess I'm reluctant to start work again, to start thinking about death and destruction, violence and killing.'

'A couple of days rest in the sun has done you a world of good,' Wyatt said. 'You look... very well.'

Linda smiled. 'You've browned up nicely as well. It suits you.'

'Thank you. Come along, we're already late. Prem was expecting us at ten. It's twenty past.'

Linda threw him a mock salute. 'Don't forget you're only a sergeant, like me.'

'When you dress in a sarong like that I have to forget a lot of things. Come on, Prem has risked a lot to meet us here. We have to do our duty.'

Wyatt was tense and uncomfortable. He was about to reveal what he had found in Linda's apartment and he was unsure how she would react. They had spent many days together and arrived at a condition of wary but amiable companionship. That desirable condition might be imminently shattered by recriminations.

They walked around a long jutting crescent of sand. At the top of a low cove was a small white-painted villa with a green roof. It was surrounded by a verandah and by tropical plants, some dazzling in the colours of the morning sun.

'It looks idyllic,' Linda said. 'Why didn't we get a place like this instead of staying in a hotel?'

'Because we're spending Charlie's money and we'll have to pay it back some day.'

'Such concern for Charlie's money! I think you're in love with her.'

'I fall in love with any woman who gives me money and can drink me under the table.'

They walked up narrow steps cut into the rock, then three wooden steps leading on to the verandah.

The door opened before they knocked. Prem said: 'I saw you admiring my little shack.'

The two men shook hands.

Wyatt said: 'It's good to see you again, Prem. Let me introduce Linda Marquez of the US Secret Service. Linda, this is Prem Dhawan of the Research and Analysis Wing of Indian intelligence.'

Prem took Linda's hand and said: 'I'm delighted to meet you at last, Linda.'

'Thank you, Prem. It's a pleasure to meet you. Chris has told me a lot about you.'

'Welcome to my temporary home. Come in, come in.'

Wyatt and Linda stepped inside. The villa was light and airy, a ceiling fan gently circulating the air, the furnishings a tropical mix of cane, bamboo and dark ebony wood.

Wyatt said: 'You've done yourself proud with this place, Prem. It's charming, and well appointed by the look of it.'

'I wanted somewhere comfortable but secluded, away from prying eyes. Can I get you anything to drink before we begin?'

'I think we're good,' Linda said. 'We had a big breakfast at the hotel. I must have put on five pounds since we've been here.'

'Then why don't we make a start?' Prem said. 'Sit down at the table here. I've printed out the information and, as you can see by the wallscreen, I've also made a PowerPoint presentation.' Prem handed Linda and Wyatt a large folder each. 'These are all the details I could find about the perpetrators of the Silk Fist attacks. I accessed our own files and also hacked into the police and intelligence files in other countries.'

Linda, intrigued despite her earlier misgivings, began sifting through the reports.

Prem said: 'Linda, before we begin I wish to offer you my most profound condolences on the loss of your husband. I suspect that we are going to have to talk about him in intimate detail. I beg your forgiveness in advance.'

Linda said: 'I fully understand, Prem. Chris has told me that you lost your wife. Her name was Rhea, wasn't it?'

'Yes.'

A brief silence, then Prem said briskly. 'Christopher, you have something to tell Linda.'

Linda was suddenly alert. 'What is it?'

Wyatt said: 'I've been keeping something from you, Linda, and I did so for your own protection. I *did* find something in your apartment, something that I'm sure belonged to Mike, something that I believe is highly significant.'

Linda's tone was dangerously subdued. 'What is it?'

Wyatt took the small plastic medicine bottle from his shirt pocket. 'Do you recognise this, Linda?'

'No. What are those capsules for?'

'I don't know.'

Silence.

'Why didn't you tell me you'd found this?'

'I had to be careful. I didn't know, at that time, whether I could trust you. You might have been involved in Silk Fist, or Mike might have been, or you might have been deliberately feeding me false information. The kidnapping proved you had nothing to do with Silk Fist. Having been tortured once for information I considered it was better not to tell you about this bottle until the right time. It was for your own protection. If you didn't know about it you couldn't tell anyone, under torture or not.'

'I don't believe you,' Linda said, her calmness more intimidating than anger. 'You didn't want me to know so that I couldn't take it to my own people.'

'I swear that's not true but after what happened don't you think that was the right decision?'

'No. People are dying out there, all over the world. If those capsules have something to do with Silk Fist then we should have turned ourselves in, whatever the consequences to us personally, and let the authorities analyse the contents. That was Mike's property, not yours. You should have told me. I thought we had reached some sort of trustworthy relationship. I was wrong.'

Wyatt was floundering. 'I did it for your own protection, Linda.'

'I don't need you to be my nursemaid, Wyatt. I'll decide whether I need protection or not. Fuck you.' Linda stood up and hurried out of the door. She ran down the steps of the cove and out of sight behind the rocks.

Wyatt said to Prem: 'I've never heard her use that word before, except when I was pointing a gun at her. I didn't think she'd be this angry. I'll go and talk to her.'

'No,' Prem said. 'I'll go.'

While he was alone Wyatt tried to read the Silk Fist reports but he could not concentrate.

Twenty minutes later Prem returned to the villa without Linda.

'How is she?' Wyatt asked anxiously. 'Did you find her? Is she still mad?'

'I think she is more hurt than mad, Christopher. She wants a few more minutes to herself. Are you two sleeping together?'

Wyatt threw up his hands in exasperation. 'Why does everyone ask that question? No, Prem, we are not sleeping together. We have been too busy trying to survive and stay alive. Whatever our feelings we have to stay professional and alert. Linda is grieving deeply for her husband. I would not be such a clumsy and insensitive pig as to force my attentions on her, even if I thought Linda would welcome such attention. We're in grave danger and can't afford to become emotionally involved.'

'I'm sorry to ask such a personal question but her reaction suggests she is more fond of you than she realises herself. More than that, she trusted you and you kept something secret from her, something that belonged to her beloved husband.'

'But I explained the reasons for that!'

'And she accepts that you were right to be cautious in the beginning but you should have told her after you had accepted that she was not involved with Silk Fist. Can you imagine what that poor girl has gone through? She has lost her husband by suicide. Believe me, Christopher, to lose your life partner leaves you raw and naked to emotions that would have hardly touched you before. She's been kidnapped, tortured, watched men being killed in front of her, lost her belongings, forced to abandon her home. The one solid rock she had to cling to was Christopher Wyatt, the man who saved her life, and now she has found out that you have been deceiving her.'

Wyatt nodded. He said: 'I was wrong. I'm a soldier, Prem. I'm an ordinary bloke, not highly educated. I'm not good with feelings and emotions. I'm not good at espionage and all this subterfuge. You're an older and wiser man than me. I accept your judgement. I am actually full of admiration for Linda, the courage and dignity with which she has faced these devastating disasters is exemplary.

I'm sort of proud of her. I screwed up, Prem. I made a wrong decision. Will you go and tell her that I'm truly sorry?'

A voice at the doorway said: 'No need. I'm back now. I accept your apology, Wyatt, and thank you for what you said. But no more secrets. Do we have a deal?'

'We have a deal,' Wyatt said. 'I promise.'

'Excellent,' Prem said. 'The obvious place to start our investigation is for Christopher to explain why he thinks this bottle is so important. It may prompt a line of enquiry and save us time and effort.'

Wyatt handed the bottle to Linda. 'I found this in the top right hand drawer of the desk in your spare bedroom. It was locked inside a metal cash box. It must be Mike's. Do you agree?'

'Yes,' Linda said. 'The writing on this label looks like Mike's.'

'Writing?' Prem said. 'What does it say?'

Linda handed him the bottle. 'One word. It says H'iatus.'

'Hiatus means a pause or a gap,' Wyatt said.

'Basically, yes,' Prem said. He opened his laptop. 'Let's look at the dictionary definition. It can mean a gap or pause or opening, a missing part, or a break in a work or an action. In grammar, it means the joining of two vowels in succession. In anatomy, it means a hole or cleft in bone or any other anatomical structure. Does that mean anything to anyone?'

'No,' Wyatt said. 'I've been thinking about the meaning ever since I first found it.'

'I could have been helping,' Linda said. 'You've wasted a lot of time.'

Wyatt accepted the rebuke and did not reply.

Linda said: 'What about this accent or apostrophe, this punctuation mark after the "h"?'

'Exactly,' Prem said. 'Such a mark indicates a contraction, that two words or a full word has been abbreviated, such as the use of "what's" instead of "what is" and so on. Was Mike a punctilious man when it came to spelling, Linda?'

'Yes, he was. The correct use of spelling and grammar is vitally important when preparing police and legal reports.'

'So the inclusion of this accent mark would not have been a mistake or an accident?'

'No, I wouldn't think so.'

'And the use of such a mark indicates a hiatus in the word hiatus itself. That's clever.'

'Is it?' Wyatt said. 'I don't understand why.'

'Because you are not a cryptanalyst. Linda, was Michael taking any medication for any medical condition?'

'No, not that I'm aware of. He would not have hidden it from me even if he had been.'

Prem decided not to challenge Linda's faith in the openness of her deceased husband. He said: 'We need to have these capsules analysed for their content. Perhaps they have nothing to do with Silk Fist.'

'No,' Wyatt said. 'As soon as I read that word I realised that it was vitally important to find out what those capsules are.'

'Why do you say that?' Prem asked.

'When Dr Flaherty was dying he asked what I thought was the question "why hate us?". His throat was filling with blood and his words were garbled. I now believe that what he actually said was "hiatus". I believe that Dr Flaherty realised that these sort of capsules were the reason why he had attacked the princess and was trying to tell me.'

'Yes,' Prem said, leaning forward with excitement. 'Dr Flaherty was a chemist. Perhaps he had been taking these capsules and realised the effect they were having and analysed them before he died. Also, Flaherty said something like "mao", didn't he?'

'Yes,' Wyatt said. 'It sounded like "it was mao" or "killer mao".'

'As you will see from the forensic reports, all the victims had traces of so-called MAO inhibitors in their blood. It could be that Dr Flaherty had already established that fact.'

'That makes sense,' Wyatt said.

Linda said: 'Dr Flaherty committed an act that was directly opposed and repugnant to his real nature, as Mike did when he committed suicide in such a strange way. Chris, have you told Prem the full details of how Mike killed himself, including the silver bullet.'

'Yes, I have,' Wyatt said. 'It was important.'

'I agree,' Linda said. 'Prem must be told everything. So here we have two decent and respectable men who are suddenly behaving in a savage or strange way that is directly contrary to their normal personality.'

Prem held up the medicine bottle. 'And such a transformation can only be achieved by drugs or brainwashing. Whatever these capsules are, they must contain the answer. The problem is that all the perpetrators had traces of the same drugs in their bloodstreams but none of the drugs are capable of altering behaviour to such an extent.'

'So we could still be on the wrong track?' Wyatt asked.

'Possibly,' Prem said, 'but I've been doing my job for over twenty years. You get a feeling, an instinct, when you are on the right track. H'iatus, in the form of these capsules, is the key. Christopher, you have the memory stick from Michael's computer?'

'Yes.' Wyatt took it out of his shirt pocket and handed it to Prem.

Prem said: 'With your permission, Linda, I will analyse and investigate the contents of your computer to ascertain whether there is anything about H'iatus on there. I have brought with me several programmes specially developed by my department that can quickly carry out such analysis. Do you mind?'

'Of course not, Prem. I certainly haven't saved anything secret or embarrassing on our computer, and I don't think Mike had.'

'I assume you use email,' Prem said. 'Did you also use any social networking sites, such as Twitter and Facebook and so on?'

'No. Neither of us thought it appropriate or safe, given the nature of our respective jobs.'

'That's excellent,' Prem said. 'That will make my job easier. I suggest that you two study the reports on the Silk Fist perpetrators. You can go through them together using PowerPoint or read the separate files.'

Wyatt asked: 'Have you found any connections or clues, Prem?'

Prem smiled and waved an admonitory finger. 'One or two, but it would be better if I did not affect your judgement or evaluation. You two might find conclusions I have missed.'

'In that case,' Linda said, 'it would probably be better if Chris and I read these reports separately and then we can pool our conclusions later.'

'I agree,' Prem said. 'Right, let's get to work.'

Linda and Wyatt decided to work out on the verandah. They set up loungers on either side of the doorway.

Three hours later, Linda Marquez went back inside. Prem was working at his laptop. Scattered on the table were devices that Linda did not recognise.

Linda said: 'I've completed my analysis and found some interesting connections.'

'That's excellent,' Prem said. 'How is Christopher getting on?'

'He's fast asleep. I don't think he's made any notes. How's it going with you?'

'Puzzling, my dear. Very puzzling.'

'Why's that?'

'Before I answer that question I'd rather hear what you and Christopher have found in the reports.'

'Sergeant Wyatt seems to be more interested in taking a siesta.'

Prem chuckled. 'Christopher admits he is no scholar, but he is a man of the world with vast experience of encountering nasty, deadly and devious people. I expect his input to be valuable despite his lack of notes.'

'I wouldn't bank on it, Prem.' Wyatt stood in the doorway

rubbing the sleep from his eyes. 'I'm sorry, I must have drifted off.'

'Have you read the reports, Christopher?'

'Yes, boss.'

'Are you both ready to present your conclusions?'

'If you like,' Wyatt said, 'but most of them are pretty obvious and I'm sure you've spotted them already.'

'No, Christopher,' Prem said firmly. 'In intelligence and investigative work it is easy to overlook the blindingly obvious, to consider it of no value. I want you to tell me everything that is in your mind.'

Linda said: 'In Wyatt's case, that shouldn't take long.'

'We can't all be A grade students. I bet you were a prefect when you were at Sweet Briar.'

'We didn't have prefects but I did volunteer to be a hallway monitor and I was class president.'

'That figures.'

Prem said: 'When you two have finished sniping, perhaps you'd like to sit down and we can begin. Linda, your first conclusion please.'

Linda consulted her notes. 'In terms of criminal records or political activism, I can't find any link between the perps. Some have minor criminal convictions, two are hard line criminals, a few have some record of political activism but nothing violent or radical. The majority are American or British citizens, with a scattering of other nationalities, mainly European. They live in different areas, except the ones that live in cities like London or New York where you would expect to find a clump of them. Whatever was causing them to act as they did, I don't think that they were working in concert with each other.'

'Excellent,' Prem said. 'I agree that we can safely rule out the theory that this was some sort of action organised by the perpetrators themselves. What did you make of the testimony of their friends, family and colleagues as to their behaviour before they committed their particular atrocity? Linda, you had first-hand evidence of this with your husband Michael.'

'Yes,' Linda said. 'All the reports suggest that their behaviour and personality changed before the attacks. Some more than others, some weeks before, most days before, a few only hours before. Mainly, as with Mike, they became aggressive, sarcastic, paranoid. Some became euphoric, a few hardly seemed to change but in those instances they had exhibited violent or aggressive personality traits beforehand.'

Wyatt said: 'None of these people were insignificant in terms of the jobs they were doing. Most of them were in positions of power, authority, or with privileged access to commit acts of sabotage in important installations or industrial sites. It's as if they were handpicked for the crime they went on to commit.'

'My thoughts exactly,' Prem said. 'I'm sure that fact has not escaped the intelligence services. How are these people being compelled to commit these deeds? What are your thoughts about the autopsy and medical reports?'

Linda said: 'All the autopsies show the presence of monoamine oxidase inhibitors, or MAOIs.'

'Yes,' Prem said. 'This is an old class of drugs that were once used to treat depression but are no longer used because of possibly fatal side effects with other drugs or foodstuffs. I've no doubt that whatever is in Mike's bottle marked H'iatus, those capsules will contain a MAO inhibitor.'

Linda went on: 'The blood tests showed markedly increased levels of testosterone and the vast majority were suffering from depression, according to chemical markers in their blood.'

Prem said: 'There is still nothing to indicate why these people were suddenly compelled to commit acts of such heinous violence or destruction. They all had vastly increased levels of testosterone. So what does that tell us?'

Linda said: 'All thirty perps, except one, are male. All, except one, are white Caucasian. One black man, no Hispanics, Latins, Indians or Asians. All, except two, are in the age range early twenties to late forties.'

'What does that tell us? Why select males?'

Linda answered: 'Obviously because if you want people to commit violent and aggressive acts then males are bigger and stronger. Also, generally speaking, there are more males in positions of power and influence than females.'

'Then why no Hispanic men, or Latins, or Asians, and only one black man? All males of these ethnic groups are certainly big and strong enough to commit violent acts.'

Wyatt said: 'At the risk of being racist, is it because there are more white men in positions of power and authority?'

'In Britain and the USA that still holds true although it is changing rapidly, but these attacks were happening all over the world. Why send a South African brute to attack our Prime Minister and destroy the life of my beloved wife when there are certainly enough Indian fanatics who would have been prepared to do the job? Why approach a European working at a baby food manufacturer in Japan when the workforce was mostly Japanese?'

Wyatt suggested: 'Are white men more susceptible to drugs or brainwashing?'

'There is no evidence to that effect,' Prem said.

'Are they more prone to depression?' Linda said.

'I have looked at the statistics and it appears that black men, Hispanics and some Asians and Latins are more prone to suffer from depression than white men.'

'Do white men have higher testosterone levels?' Wyatt said.

'No. The differences in testosterone levels are more to do with diet, environment and age than race. And on the subject of age, none of these perpetrators, except the Bishop of Carlisle, was over fifty years of age, and none of them were under twenty four. If you are looking for violent young men with high testosterone levels, then the under twenty-fours would logically be a better target group.'

'But they have not usually risen to positions of power or authority,' Wyatt said.

'True, but most positions of power and authority, especially in politics and business, are held by men over fifty years of age. Why not recruit them into Silk Fist?'

Wyatt sat back in his chair and smiled. 'Prem, you're teasing us. I think you have found the answer already.'

Prem returned the smile. 'Look back at the photographs. What do all these people have in common? Even the woman.'

Wyatt shuffled through his files and said: 'None of them would win a beauty contest.'

Linda said: 'Yes, I see it now, Prem. You were right about overlooking the obvious.'

Wyatt asked: 'See what?'

Prem ignored Wyatt and said to Linda: 'I don't have a photograph of your husband because he has not been included in the Silk Fist investigation by the authorities. Was he the same?'

'Yes. He had suffered from a scalp condition that had caused some of his hair to fall out. He was desperately concerned about it.'

'What are you two talking about?' Wyatt asked irritably.

'Christopher, all these people, even the woman, are suffering from advanced hair loss.'

Wyatt shuffled quickly through the photographs. 'You think that all these people committed atrocities because they were going bald?'

Prem fleetingly looked exasperated. Linda put her hand on Wyatt's arm. 'What Prem is advancing as a theory is that these men didn't commit atrocities because they are bald but because they were taking medication to alleviate the condition, medication that somehow altered their personality. Those capsules in that H'iatus bottle could be the key to what is happening.'

Wyatt was contrite. 'Okay, I understand. I apologise, Prem. You really think that was how these poor sods were being manipulated.'

'It's a theory, but I believe a sound and viable theory. I had noted the hair loss in all the perpetrators and considered whether that could be the connection but it seemed absurd and outlandish. When you produced that H'iatus bottle the theory suddenly seemed strong. We have to find out what H'iatus means and what those capsules contain.'

Nobody spoke for several seconds. Then Wyatt said to Prem: 'If we've found these H'iatus capsules and this connection to hair loss surely the intelligence services would have found it. After all, they've got endless banks of computers, endless investigative resources, the best laboratories at their beck and call.'

'Not necessarily. What has happened with Linda and yourself is that, by coincidence, two people, separate but personally affected by the Silk Fist conspiracy, have met and shared information that is unknown to the authorities. For instance, Christopher, as soon as you saw that bottle with the word H'iatus on it, you realised it was significant because of what Dr Flaherty said. An ordinary investigator would not have made the connection. And you were in Linda's apartment because Linda had personal knowledge of the behaviour of a Silk Fist victim, her husband, and you two met up quite by chance in the line of duty.'

'But surely the homes of these perps were searched,' Wyatt persisted. 'The cops must have found more of these capsules.'

Prem said: 'Why should they consider such capsules significant, especially if the bottle was unmarked or labelled as something else? Men of a certain age, married or sexually active, are peculiarly sensitive to losing their hair. They are even more sensitive to their loved ones being aware of the fact that they are taking medication to correct that hair loss. They would perceive such a course of action as desperate, pathetic or embarrassing. They would actively seek to keep it a secret. Also, many of the perpetrators deliberately killed themselves after committing their atrocity. They were probably brainwashed into doing so and were probably brainwashed into getting rid of the H'iatus tablets once the course of treatment had ended. I don't believe for a second that these capsules actually do anything to cure baldness but it is an excellent way to deliver mind-altering medication to men who have been convinced that such a drug might work. Male pattern baldness is much more prevalent in white men. American and European men are much more prone and sensitive to hair loss than in Asian, Hispanic and black populations. That's why the white male population was targeted.'

'You believe they were specifically targeted?' Linda asked.

'Yes I do,' Prem said. 'As Christopher rightly pointed out, the perpetrators were handpicked for the specific atrocity they went on to commit.'

Linda nodded. 'I had no idea that Mike was so worried about his hair loss. I told him time and again that it would make no difference to how I felt about him but he could not accept that. Poor Mike, I would have loved him if he was as bald as a billiard ball. It made no difference to me.'

Prem said: 'When it comes to baldness there is, strangely, no end to male vanity.'

Wyatt said: 'All this is supposition, Prem. I still don't buy it. There are many other treatments for baldness, things such as hair weaves, implants, toupees.'

'A good point, Christopher. Weaves are expensive, implants are very expensive and toupees look ridiculous unless they are very well made. Perhaps H'iatus offered a less expensive solution.'

'Did you find anything on the computer?'

Prem sat back with resignation. 'I installed a program to search the world wide web for the word Hiatus or H'iatus in the context of our search. There is nothing. That is why the intelligence services cannot find any clue about who is responsible for Silk Fist. They almost certainly do not know about H'iatus. They may not have made the connection about hair loss because the perpetrators are so diverse and widespread. You remember, Christopher, how I explained that every email and cell phone call can be plucked out of the ether by modern surveillance technology?'

'Yes, I remember,' Wyatt said.

'I believe that whoever is responsible for the Silk Fist conspiracy is well aware of such capability and has scrupulously avoided the use of websites or electronic communications where possible, or hidden them so deep within the internet that they cannot be found, even if the authorities understand what they are looking for.'

'How can they hide them?' Wyatt asked.

'The best method is a piece of software known as TOR. It was developed by the US navy but has become a favourite with drug dealers, arms dealers, pornographers and paedohiles all over the world. It operates a hidden black web by routeing and re-routeing your connection to the internet through a maze of encrypted nodes around the world. That makes it virtually impossible to find the origin of a website. Fortunately, we at RAW have developed software to help search the black web. I have searched Michael's computer for evidence of H'iatus within this black web.'

'Did you find anything?' Linda asked. 'If it's really bad then let me down gently.'

'Don't worry, Linda. I found nothing incriminating except one encrypted file that needs a password to get into, and I cannot find the password. The file is named "A Police Guard".'

'Then it's surely something to do with Mike's police work,' Linda said.

'Almost certainly,' Prem agreed, 'but why hide it deep within the black TOR web?'

Linda shook her head. 'I don't know. Probably for security if Mike was dealing with dangerous criminals.'

Prem said: 'I want you to think hard, Linda, and see if we can find the password that Mike might have used. Favourite passwords are pet names, birth dates, social security numbers, and so on.'

Linda said: 'Try "kappa" first.'

Prem keyed in the word. He said: 'No. Password rejected.'

Two hours later Wyatt looked at his watch and said: 'It's gone seven, it's dark outside, I'm starving and my brain aches. We've tried hundreds of possible passwords. Shall we have a break and go to dinner?'

Prem yawned. 'We're doing no good here. We haven't even begun discussing these strange code words that the perpetrators shout before committing their acts. That will have to wait. A break would be most welcome.'

Linda stood up and said: 'Listen, shouldn't we take this information to our respective governments. This is too important to be left to us. Governments have all the resources necessary to investigate this. More innocent people might die before we find the answer, if we find the answer.'

Wyatt said: 'I've been set up as a fugitive and a murderer by my own government. I don't know who to trust. If we give this information to the wrong person, it could be lost or buried.'

Prem said to Linda: 'On the last occasion you decided to trust your government you were abducted by gangsters. I agree with Christopher. We cannot trust anyone. We must do this ourselves.'

Linda said: 'Do you trust your government, Prem? They ordered you to stop helping us.'

'Yes, for fear of upsetting your government. I'm here unofficially. I don't know whether I trust my government but I do trust my boss, Colonel Chatterjee. If I am to be given the resources we might need to solve this Silk Fist business then I might have to trust him, and him alone, with anything we find here. I have put Colonel Chatterjee's reputation on the line and I have put my career on the line. I believe H'iatus will lead us to Silk Fist but we have not found a shred of proof to connect them. If we cannot find such proof then my career is finished. Linda, I beg you not to contact your people until we can provide definite proof.'

Linda nodded. 'Okay, I'm persuaded by your arguments. Come on, let's go back to our hotel for dinner. I hope you will join us, Prem.'

'I'd be delighted.'

Linda helped Prem put on a white jacket. She said: 'Perhaps a good meal will revive our mental powers. I'm disappointed we couldn't figure out Mike's password.'

Prem opened the front door. 'Mike was wise enough not to use passwords that are obvious. For instance, I enjoyed his password to his personal police diary. It was entitled "I bonk crime".'

Linda said: 'What are you sniggering for, Wyatt?'

'Well, I don't know what "bonk" means to Americans but it has a different meaning in English slang.'

'Take your mind out of the bedroom, Wyatt. "I bonk crime" is simply an anagram of Mick O'Brien. Mike was fond of using appropriate anagrams as passwords… shit, how could I be so stupid?'

Linda went back to the table and grabbed a pen and a notepad. She wrote down "A Police Guard" and began working. After three minutes she held up the notepad in triumph. 'This, gentlemen, is an anagram of "A Police Guard".'

Prem closed the front door and went back to read what Linda had written. He said: 'Linda, you are brilliant.'

Linda nodded. 'Brilliant, but too slow.'

Prem switched on the laptop. 'It simply has to be right.'

Wyatt said: 'I'm still hungry. Shall I ring for pizza?'

37

Office of the Prime Minister, Secretariat Building, New Delhi, March 30th

Prime Minister Arnesh Mishra poured a glass of whisky from a crystal decanter. 'Would you like a drink, Ashok?'

Colonel Chatterjee was wary and uneasy. 'No, thank you, sir. I don't drink alcohol.'

'I'm aware of your abstemious habits,' Mishra said, with a tone of disappointment. 'I meant fruit juice or coffee?'

'No, thank you.'

'I allow myself one drink at the end of the day. Two if the day has been difficult. Never any more than two. Today has been a one drink day.' Mishra sat down at his desk. 'It was close to becoming a two drink day. What do you think of the refurbishment?'

Colonel Chatterjee made a show of looking around. 'Well and tastefully done, sir. I'm also happy to find that security is much improved. It is now extremely difficult to get in to see you, even for me.'

Mishra smiled. 'Do I detect a veiled rebuke?'

'By no means, sir. I did not mean to imply any criticism. This is how it should be after such a tragic event as the Du Preez bombing and in the midst of this Silk Fist business.'

Mishra sipped his whisky. 'Plaster and brickwork and wood and curtains are easily replaceable. My principal secretary cannot be replaced and my heart aches every day. Rhea Dhawan was an exceptional woman.'

'Indeed she was, sir.' Colonel Chatterjee decided to say no more until he understood the reason for this late summons.

As if on cue, Mishra said: 'Thank you for coming to see me so late in the day, Ashok. I had a visit from the American ambassador earlier today. A charming woman but with a hint of steel. I believe she used to be a film actress.'

'I believe so, yes, sir.'

'So American to choose a film star as an ambassador.'

'As they once chose a film star as their President.'

'He was more of a supporting actor than a star,' Mishra said. 'The ambassador brought me a note from President Logan together with a personal message for my ears only.'

'Yes, sir.'

'The President is deeply concerned about the welfare and whereabouts of his wife's special assistant, this Sergeant Marquez woman. She was last seen in the company of Sergeant Christopher Wyatt and now both of them have disappeared. The Americans do not know whether Marquez was taken under duress of whether she is with him voluntarily. The Americans were angry that India was covertly assisting this man Wyatt at the behest of Premendra Dhawan. They have since found further evidence of the extent of that assistance in Washington, together with several dead bodies.'

'I see, sir. I can assure you that such assistance has now ceased, as you ordered.'

'Really, Ashok?' Prime Minister Mishra examined his crystal glass as if entranced by the play of light reflecting off the facets. Then he asked: 'Where is Premendra Dhawan?'

Chatterjee was relieved to be asked a straightforward question. 'He is on leave for a week, sir.'

'That surprises me. He was so keen to investigate Silk Fist and find the culprits responsible for the murder of his wife, his wife who died just outside that outer door over there, that I'm surprised to learn that he has taken time off from his investigations. Where has he gone?'

'Egypt, sir. He is touring the ancient sites. It's something he has always wanted to do.'

'Are you sure that's where he is?'

Chatterjee was genuinely puzzled. 'I'm certain, sir. I gave him a lift to the airport and saw him off. The aircraft he boarded was definitely a flight to Cairo. I saw the hotel reservation as well.'

'He certainly arrived in Cairo but he didn't stay long. CIA surveillance in Cairo saw him disembark but he never checked into the hotel and now he has also disappeared.'

'The CIA are watching Dhawan?'

'Not specifically. The Americans have eyes everywhere, in every part of the world. Where is he, Ashok?'

'If Prem is not in Egypt then I don't know where he is, sir.'

'You definitely ordered him to withdraw the covert assistance that he was giving to Wyatt?'

'Yes. He had my full approval for that assistance at first but, as you ordered me, so I ordered him to back off.'

'The Americans don't trust us, Ashok. They think we're up to some sort of dirty work. President Logan is spitting blood. He has warned me that if Dhawan, meaning India, is in any way assisting this renegade Wyatt then the diplomatic consequences will be dire. We cannot afford to upset America, especially while Silk Fist is going on. We need their arms, their intelligence, their finance. Logan suspects that Wyatt may be duping Dhawan and, perhaps, Marquez. If you know what Dhawan is up to and where he is, then tell me, Ashok, or the consequences could be severe, for both of you.'

Chatterjee leaned forward for emphasis. 'Sir, I swear I don't know what Prem is doing or where he is.'

Prime Minister Mishra sat back and considered Chatterjee's response. He asked: 'How far do you trust Dhawan?'

'I would trust him with my life.'

'Is he loyal?'

'If you are asking whether he is loyal to India then, yes, he is totally loyal.'

'My fear is that Dhawan is so obsessed with avenging his wife's death that this Wyatt character can manipulate him into giving away vital intelligence.'

'Prem is a shrewd and intelligent man, sir. He is more than a match for a rogue squaddie, as the British call their soldiers. If Prem is in contact with Wyatt then it is because he genuinely believes he can find information about Silk Fist.'

Prime Minister Mishra finished his whisky and said: 'If Premendra Dhawan and then Rhea Dhawan had not caused Du Preez to slow down and be shot by my bodyguards then it is almost certain he would have reached this inner office and I would now be dead, so I am prepared to give Premendra Dhawan a great deal of the benefit of my doubt, but there has to be a limit to my gratitude for the sake of India. We go back a long way, Ashok. You trust Dhawan, even though he has pulled the wool over your eyes, and I'm going to trust you. But be warned that if Dhawan's actions in anyway endanger the security of India or compromise our search for the Silk Fist culprits then the consequences for him, and you, Colonel, will be severe and, as far as your careers are concerned, terminal.'

38

Golden Palm Villas, Mahe, Seychelles, March 30th

Premendra Dhawan opened his laptop and located the file entitled "A Police Guard". As Wyatt and Linda sat and watched, he tapped in the password anagram that Linda had discovered: "Alopecia Drug". A website flashed up.

Prem said: 'We're in. There it is, H'iatus.'

The website was headed with the word H'iatus. It was simple and basic in design, not much more than a letter to the recipient.

Prem read aloud: *'Hair loss and baldness affects many men. It can affect your sexual confidence, which in turns affects your ability to perform in the bedroom, which can then lead to depression and anxiety. THERE IS A PROVEN SOLUTION TO ALL THREE CONDITIONS. H'iatus is guaranteed to restore hair growth, improve testosterone levels, and alleviate depression and anxiety, all in one simple treatment. Your worry about hair loss, impotence and depression has led you to research the problem on the internet. Our legitimate phishing software has found your urgent requests for help. Sounds phishy to you? You are right to be cautious.'*

Wyatt asked: 'What does phishing mean?'

Prem said: 'Phishing is searching for and stealing confidential or useful information from a website or email. In this case it gives a good indication as to why this H'iatus site is so hard to find. Whoever is running this, as it states above, has found likely customers before they are aware of anything like H'iatus.'

'Come on, scroll down and carry on, Prem,' Linda said impatiently.

'You are asking yourself that if H'iatus is such an effective product why is

it not freely available over the counter at your drug store or pharmacy or available on prescription from your doctor? The answer is that H'iatus has not been approved by the drug regulation authorities in North America, Europe and most other parts of the world, and is thus deemed illegal to be sold or prescribed by a clinician. H'iatus has to be administered after a medical check-up and under the supervision of a qualified physician, but don't worry because we supply a personal physician to care for you while H'iatus is being taken. This means that H'iatus does not come cheaply. It is expensive to make and expensive to administer, but it is guaranteed to be 100% effective and 100% safe if administered within our strict medical guidelines. How much does it cost? Depending on each individual case, the travel and time expended by one of our team of qualified physicians, we have to charge from $2,000 to $5,000 (£1,000 to £2,500 sterling, €1,500 to €3,000). These are approximations and can be less, may be more. Is it that much to pay for a full head of hair, total confidence in your sexual ability and that sheer joy of living that comes with both?'

Prem said: 'There is the answer to your earlier question, Christopher. This supposed H'iatus treatment is much cheaper than a hair weave or transplant.'

'WHAT IS H'IATUS AND WHERE DOES IT COME FROM? Many years ago, scientists in eastern Europe discovered that male pattern baldness is caused by a high level of the substance known as Prostaglandin (PGD2). While studying PGD2 they also discovered that it can not only be suppressed but reversed by a combination of drugs, testosterone (which restores and enhances sexual performance) and monoamine oxidase inhibitors (MAOIs) (which treat depression). This most fortuitous discovery, along with another active ingredient that we must keep secret, led to the formulation of the wonder drug H'iatus. A short course of tablets will restore your full head of hair within weeks, your sexual potency and your enjoyment of life. You will understand that because H'iatus is illegal in most countries we cannot tell you who we are or where we are. If you would like our medical experts to assess your suitablity to be prescribed H'iatus, complete the series of questions below. Email it back to us and you will be contacted again.'

Linda said: 'What questions are they asking?'

'Look here… name, address, contact details, height, weight, nationality, previous medical history, married or single, sexual orientation, other drugs being taken, all questions to perhaps disguise the vital question, occupation.'

Linda asked: 'Can you trace where that email address is located, Prem?'

'I'll certainly try but I have no doubt that it will lead me a merry dance through several cut-offs. Whoever set up this website is certainly skilled enough to ensure that their original location is untraceable.'

Wyatt said: 'So Silk Fist can select possible targets who have access to important people or installations or whatever, and the victims actually pay Silk Fist to do it. Clever!'

'That would seem to be the case,' Prem agreed, 'but there is still no actual evidence here that directly links to Silk Fist. Linda, I'd like to ask you a personal question.'

'I can guess what you are going to ask, Prem. Mike's change in personality began about a month or three weeks before he died. He didn't seem to be depressed, although he was hyperactive, restless and critical. You are wondering about our sex life. Mike showed no signs of impotence, although our sex life became frenzied and urgent, which was not pleasant for me. There was no sign that his hair growth was being restored.'

'Thank you, Linda. That must have been difficult for you. The advertisement admits that testosterone and MAO inhibitors are contained in these capsules. I would guess that this so-called active ingredient probably has nothing to do with hair loss or baldness but is the chemical trigger for altering behaviour in connection with the other two drugs. This advertisement cleverly plays on the fears and vanities of sexually active men who are attempting to retain their youthful vigour and identifies them as possible perpetrators. Thus if the response to this advertisement shows that a man has a quite ordinary job, then it may not be acted upon, but if the response indicates that the man has a significant job in relation to business, industry and politics, with access to important people or functions, then they are singled out for the Silk Fist treatment.'

'That makes sense,' Wyatt said, 'but you searched the internet for references to this H'iatus stuff and you couldn't find any except this one. Why is that?'

'That is an excellent question, Christopher. Linda's husband was a policeman. Although he was tempted into using this product he was also well aware that it was illegal and very suspicious. He hid the truth from Linda but he buried this advertisement deep within the black web, protected by a password. I believe that Michael O'Brien is helping us from the grave.'

Linda suddenly stood up and went out on to the verandah.

Prem went to the door and said: 'I'm so sorry, Linda. I phrased that clumsily.'

'It's okay, Prem. It's not you. I miss Mike so much and what we are doing here is all so strange. You two carry on. I'll be okay in a few minutes.'

Wyatt looked at Linda. She did not appear to be weeping but her body was tense. Wyatt experienced an unexpected surge of sympathy and affection for her. Prem was right about the traumatic extent of Linda's loss and her brutal exclusion from her familiar world. Her courage and dignity was wholly admirable.

Wyatt turned back to Prem as he sat down. 'Why couldn't you find this advert when you searched the internet?'

'Because it's now been taken off the internet by whoever put it there, or possibly the advertisement was programmed to self-destruct at some time after the recipient read it and responded.'

'Is that possible?'

'Oh, yes. A simple piece of programming. This is why the intelligence services cannot find a single clue through electronic eavesdropping. Firstly, they have no idea that H'iatus has anything to do with Silk Fist and, even if they did, a transitory advertisement that deletes itself would be fiendishly hard to find. I believe that Michael became aware that this was a significant piece of evidence and took steps to preserve it deep within the dark net.'

'So you think that Mike deliberately saved this advertisement in a secure location?'

'Yes. Michael probably became aware of the affect that this H'iatus drug was having upon him, perhaps in the early stages, before the drug entirely took control.'

'Dr Flaherty was doing the same,' Wyatt said. 'He was dying and he tried to tell me about H'iatus when I thought he was saying "why hate us".'

'Yes, and Dr Flaherty was a chemist. He became aware that H'iatus was having a strange affect on him and may have analysed the contents before his personality was completely lost, that's why he was talking about MAO.'

'Yes,' Wyatt said. 'I assumed he meant something about Maoists but he was trying to tell me about these MAO inhibitors.'

Linda said. 'Perhaps there's something else.'

The two men had not noticed that Linda had come back in.

Linda stood behind them and pointed at the laptop screen. 'Have you noticed the background?'

Wyatt said: 'It's faint but it looks like an eagle or some sort of bird of prey.'

'It is an eagle,' Linda said. 'It's an American eagle, the symbol of America, known as the white eagle or, more popularly…'

'The bald eagle,' Prem said.

Linda said: 'I was wondering why the name H'iatus was chosen for this drug. Nothing to do with hair loss except in a vague sense. The apostrophe in the word indicates that a complete word has been contracted or abbreviated. If you look up the Latin name for the bald eagle I think we'll find what the full word is.'

Prem tapped the request into the search engine. He read: 'The

American white eagle, or bald eagle, has the Latin zoological name *Haliaeetus leucocephalus*. There are two species, the northern and southern, both of the genus Haliaeetus. So H'iatus is a contraction of Haliaeetus. Linda, you are inspired.'

Wyatt said: 'That's ingenious but I don't understand. Is this Silk Fist or some organisation calling itself Bald Eagle or something?'

'I don't know,' Linda admitted. 'Dr Flaherty was brought up to speak Irish Gaelic and only later learnt English. Prem, if you look up the Irish name for the bald eagle, you will see what I'm talking about.'

Prem tapped into a search engine translation service. He said: 'The Irish name for the bald eagle is "iolar maol". Is that what Dr Wyatt was trying to tell you, Christopher?'

'I don't know. It sounded like "it was Mao" but I couldn't understand.'

Linda said: 'When Dr Flaherty was close to death his mind might have reverted to his original Irish language and he was trying to tell you something you could not understand. He was trying to expiate his crime by pointing you to the real culprit, this drug called H'iatus.'

There was a silence for several seconds. Then Wyatt said: 'Where does this get us? It gets us no further towards discovering who is behind Silk Fist. This H'iatus drug may not be anything to do with Silk Fist. Even if it is, why give us clues like putting a picture of a bald eagle in the background of that website? Was it a joke?'

Prem said: 'I have no doubt that H'iatus is the work of Silk Fist and that it is undoubtedly the method by which they are delivering some mind-altering drug to the unfortunate victims. What the bald eagle reference is all about, I don't know. It would be useful to find out what these H'iatus capsules actually contain.'

Linda said: 'You two will disagree again but we have to take this to our respective governments. They will be able to analyse these capsules and warn people who might be taking H'iatus to stop and inform the authorities what they are doing and seek treatment.'

Wyatt said: 'I agree that we ought to let people have this information but I'm not sure who to trust in my government or yours, Linda. Let's give this information directly to the media, then it can't be buried by the powers that be. What do you think, Prem?'

'I would make two points. By going directly to the media we might unleash a panic or some sort of firestorm of Silk Fist activity over and above what has already been going on. The second point is that we may already be too late.'

'What do you mean?' Wyatt asked.

'The H'iatus advertisement has been removed from the internet. Whoever has planned and perpetrated these Silk Fist attacks is clever enough to realise that such a scheme cannot go on for long without being detected. Perhaps all the victims have been selected and already infected with this drug.'

'And perhaps they haven't,' Linda objected. 'We have to make this public knowledge. People are dying out there.'

Wyatt said: 'You're right, Linda, and even if we have found Silk Fist, we haven't answered the big question and that is why they are launching these attacks? I can't think of any reason that makes sense. Can you?'

'No,' Prem said.

Linda shook her head.

Wyatt went on: 'We three have discovered all this when our governments have failed completely. I suggest that, before we tell them what we have found, we have H'iatus analysed to identify what drug is being used. Prem, could your people in India do that?'

'I'm sure we have the facilities but such analysis is not in my expertise, so I'm not sure. Linda is correct, this is much too important to keep to ourselves.'

Linda said: 'Prem could take some of the capsules to his people while we take the rest and have them analysed. It would be a sort of double blind test.'

'That's an excellent idea,' Prem said. 'Having lied and duped my boss, a man I deeply respect, I can take this evidence and these capsules back to him and hopefully save my career. But, much more importantly, Linda is right. We have to act swiftly before many other people die.'

Wyatt said: 'Linda, would you agree that we keep this information to ourselves until we can find out what is in these H'iatus capsules?'

'Reluctantly, yes. But we mustn't delay too long.'

'The problem is,' Wyatt said, 'I have no idea where we could take our capsules to be analysed, somewhere trustworthy and confidential.'

'I do,' Linda said. 'I've enjoyed the sunshine here in the Seychelles. I could do with some more. Time for a visit to my clever godfather.'

39

Gold Coast, Queensland, Australia, April 3rd

'This is it,' Linda pointed. 'This road on the right.'

Wyatt turned the car on to a deeply rutted track. 'Hardly a road,' he muttered as his head bounced off the roof.

They bumped along the track until another narrow road intersected. Off to the left was a cherry red Chevrolet Corvette parked above a chalet built on the beach.

'That's Uncle Nathan's Chevvy,' Linda said. 'That must be his villa.'

'Hardly a villa,' Wyatt muttered. 'I thought you said he was your godfather, not your uncle.'

'I've always called him uncle. He's about the sweetest guy you could hope to meet.'

Wyatt parked the hire car behind the Chevvy and they got out.

Linda looked around and said: 'This is fabulous.'

The air temperature was in the mid-seventies with a cooling breeze off the sea. The bright yellow beach of the Gold Coast stretched as far as they could see in both directions. Far in the distance was the ultra-modern skyline of Surfers Paradise. The white-topped breakers crashed gently on to the sands below them and huge banks of scudding white clouds moved majestically across the horizon.

'This sure beats Hackney Marshes,' Wyatt said.

'What's Hackney Marshes?'

'It doesn't matter. Let's go and meet Uncle Nathan.'

The red shingled roof of the chalet was below them. They

walked down wooden steps set into a steep sandbank thickly overgrown with marram grass. There was a side door to the chalet but Linda carried on walking around to the front.

Professor Nathan Travers was sitting on the verandah drinking a cup of coffee. He was medium height and, Wyatt estimated, about sixty years old. He was wearing shorts and a gaudy Hawaiian shirt. He was heavily sun-tanned, a tan set off by a circle of snow white hair around his bald dome. He had a beaky nose and a weak chin. His eyes lit up with joy when he saw Linda. He stood up. Wyatt watched as the two of them embraced.

Linda said: 'It's wonderful to see you again, Uncle Nat.'

'It's been too long, Linda. What is it, about ten years since I left the States? I was always hoping that you'd come and see me one day.'

'Well, here I am. First thing I want to do is thank you for the letter you wrote me after Mike died. It was a great comfort.'

'I'm glad it helped. I was desperately upset for you and for Mike's family.'

Linda turned to Wyatt. 'Uncle Nat, this is the colleague I told you about. I didn't want to say too much over the cell phone. This is Sergeant Chris Wyatt of the Metropolitan Police in London. Chris, this is my beloved godfather, Professor Nathan Travers.'

The two men shook hands. Wyatt said: 'It's a pleasure to meet you, sir.'

'Please call me Nat. Linda tells me you're not a bad bloke for a Pommy, and that's good enough for me.'

Wyatt laughed. 'That's quite a compliment coming from Sergeant Marquez. I'm flattered.'

Nathan Travers looked at his visitors. His expression became serious. 'Now, you two, a visit from a sergeant in the United States Secret Service, even if she is my beloved goddaughter, accompanied by a sergeant from the British Metropolitan Police leads me to believe that this is more than a social visit. As you requested, Linda,

I haven't told anyone that you were coming here. What's going on?'

'Uncle Nat, we desperately need your help.'

'Then you'll get it. Shall we go inside? Would you like something to drink? Chris, I'd offer you tea but I'm an ex-patriot Yankee. I only drink coffee.'

'Coffee will be fine, Nat.'

They stepped into the chalet through an open glazed sliding door that took up the entire front of the chalet.

'I had this installed so that I always had a view of the Coral Sea,' Travers explained.

The interior of the villa was plain and minimal and neatly kept. Colourful watercolour paintings of marine subjects covered almost every inch of wall space. There was a small kitchen off the living area and Travers went in to make the coffee.

Wyatt looked around. 'Linda told me you were an artist, Nat. I take it these are your works?'

'Yes. Do you like them?'

'Linda would tell you that I'm not a cultured man but I love your use of colour. They're vibrant and intense with a great sense of movement, especially the fish and the sharks.'

'Thanks. Sounds like your cultural senses are perfectly tuned.'

Linda said: 'He's simply trying to impress you, Uncle Nat. He'd never heard of Picasso until the French named a car after him.'

Wyatt laughed. 'That's not true. I thought the French called it a Rembrandt.'

Travers came out of the kitchen carrying a tray. He put down mugs on the coffee table followed by a plate of savoury pastries. He said: 'Try one, Chris. I'm a great cook.'

'Cook, artist, scientist. Is there no end to your talents, Nat?'

'Unfortunately, yes.' Travers put the tray on the floor and sat down in an armchair. 'Now, despite your excellent manners and Linda's evident pleasure in seeing me again, I can sense that you two are champing at the bit. What can I do for you?'

Linda said: 'You must be curious as to why I asked you not to tell anyone that we were coming here, Uncle Nat, not even my parents. I would also ask you to keep the reason for our visit strictly to yourself. It's not that I don't trust you, I trust you completely, but it's for your own safety.'

'Okay,' Nathan said. 'I'm now fully intrigued. What do you want me to do?'

Wyatt took out the bottle of H'iatus capsules from the inside pocket of his jacket and handed them to Travers. 'We're asking you to analyse these capsules to establish their chemical contents.'

Travers unscrewed the top and looked inside. He said: 'Chris, I couldn't help noticing when you opened your jacket that you're carrying a firearm. Linda, are you carrying a weapon?'

'Yes. We apologise for bringing firearms into your home.'

'I'm not upset that you're carrying weapons but I am upset by the fact that you think you need to. I take it you are involved in dangerous business.'

'Very dangerous,' Wyatt said.

'Are you going to tell me what it is?'

Linda said: 'Best if you don't know, for the time being.'

'Why not take these capsules to experts in your respective countries? You both work in intelligence or the police. Why come to me?'

Linda said: 'Because I trust you completely.'

'Meaning you don't trust your own authorities?'

'No, we don't trust them. And, as a scientist, you are the best.'

'No need for flattery, Linda. I'll do as you ask. I'll take them into the lab tomorrow. Today we can have some fun.'

Linda said: 'This is very urgent, Uncle Nat.'

'You mean you're asking me to go into work today, on the weekend?'

Linda smiled. 'If you wouldn't mind, Uncle Nat.'

Travers said to Wyatt: 'She could always wrap me around her

little finger with that smile.' He stood up and went to a side table to pick up a bunch of keys.

Wyatt said: 'Please don't show those capsules to anyone else.'

Travers nodded. 'I get the picture. I'll be the only one working in the lab. This may take a few hours. Make yourself at home and take as much food and drink as you want.'

Travers went out of the side door and a few seconds later they heard the roar of the Corvette engine starting and then fading into the distance.

Wyatt said: 'He's an interesting man. You said he was a friend of the family. How did that happen?'

'I must have been about seven or eight years old when the family orange groves became infected with citrus canker. Uncle Nathan was working for the state of Florida as a scientific expert in agriculture and the environment. He was sent to advise us on methods to protect our orange trees and his expertise saved the family business. He and my father liked each other so much that they remained friends. Uncle Nathan took a shine to me and we also became friends. I suppose he sees me as the daughter he never had. He taught me so much about plants, nature, the world around us. It was fascinating. The Marquez family became a sort of surrogate family. Eventually he became my godfather. He's a brilliant man and I love him dearly.'

'Has he ever been married?'

'No. He's an intensely private man. I've never known him to be involved with anyone, male or female. I suspect his real home, his real love, is diving in the ocean with his beloved fishes. Underneath all that brilliance, and all that kindness, I sense a great loneliness.'

Wyatt nodded. 'Why did he leave the States?'

'I'm not entirely sure. He was attracted by the sound of a sunny beach named Surfers Paradise but we have plenty of sunny beaches in the States. Nathan loves America and Americans but had serious reservations about our government. He has never explained exactly why. He decided to emigrate and make a fresh start here in Australia. With his expertise he was welcomed with open arms by the Queensland agricultural and industrial community. He set up his own research laboratory and in his spare times dives and paints the marine life.'

Wyatt stood up and went to look out at the ocean frothing on to the warm sand. 'I envy him this little stretch of paradise. It would be so easy to disappear and let the world go to hell.'

'We can't, Chris. We might be the only hope for the world, or at least for a lot of innocent victims.'

'You're right.' Wyatt was silent. Then he said: 'Linda, how would you like to take a walk along the beach to Surfers Paradise? I'm intrigued by the look of it. It looks like some celestial city on the horizon. If Nathan is going to be away for a few hours we could have lunch and visit the attractions. We could have some fun for a change.'

Linda stood up and said: 'I like the way you're thinking, big man. We'll leave a note for Uncle Nathan. I think we deserve a little fun.'

Wyatt and Linda arrived back at the chalet late in the afternoon. Nathan Travers had not returned.

'What an amazing town,' Linda said as she slid open the glass door. 'I really enjoyed the atmosphere.'

Wyatt said: 'Any place that employs beautiful girls in golden bikinis as meter maids gets my vote.'

'Yeah, I noticed you getting a good eyeful.'

'Don't pretend you didn't notice those life guard guys. Some of them had six-packs on their six-packs.'

Linda chuckled. 'I may have taken a peek. Are you hungry?'

'No. Are you?'

'A little,' Linda admitted.

Wyatt feigned astonishment. 'After the lunch you had! I thought you'd entered some sort of eating contest.'

'I couldn't resist. That seafood was great. I'll make myself a sandwich.'

Linda went into the kitchen. Wyatt turned on the television and found a news channel.

'Anything happening?' Linda asked when she came back from the kitchen.

'Back to reality,' Wyatt grunted. 'A series of explosions along the Trans-Alaska oil pipeline. Millions of barrels of oil lost, cost millions to clean-up, not to mention the environmental damage. The guy who did it took himself out in the final explosion. All the hallmarks of Silk Fist.'

'Anymore on what happened at the Elysee Palace yesterday?'

'Yes. The guy who crashed his car through the gates has died in hospital. The French security team shot him. The car was packed with explosives but it didn't explode. He was a respected surgeon at a Paris hospital.'

'Did they show a picture?'

'Yes. Claude Montain, forty years old.'

'Bald? Thinning hair?'

'Yep. He was heard to shout "bureau" or "burro" or something like that as he drove in. Definitely Silk Fist.'

'Let's hope that Uncle Nat can do his stuff and we can put a stop to this quickly.'

The sun went down and Nathan Travers had still not returned. Linda and Wyatt were becoming concerned.

Wyatt asked: 'Have you got his cell phone number?'

Linda shook her head. 'He doesn't use one. Doesn't believe in them.'

'Where's his laboratory?'

'Two or three miles down the Gold Coast Highway and then inland a mile or so at a town called Rayleigh.'

'I think we should go and look for him.'

As they were preparing to leave they heard the throb of the Corvette engine.

'That's a relief,' Linda said.

A few moments later Nathan Travers entered through the side door. Wyatt and Linda stood up expectantly as he came into the living area.

All trace of avuncular hospitality had vanished from Travers's demeanour. He said: 'You two have a lot of explaining to do.'

'What is it, Uncle Nathan? What are those capsules?'

'Something I hoped I would never find again. Something I hoped had been buried forever and one of the reasons I left America.'

Travers walked over to the window and looked out at the moon shining on the phosphorescent sea. He turned and said: 'If certain people become aware that you are in possession of those capsules then you are in grave danger. Is that why you are carrying guns?'

'Yes,' Wyatt said. 'Have you brought the capsules back with you?'

'No. I had to use them all to verify my findings. I'm glad they've all been destroyed. Are there any more?'

Wyatt said: 'Yes. A certain friend of ours has taken some for independent verification. Tell us what they are, Professor Travers.'

The roar of an outboard motor somewhere out at sea broke the tense silence. Travers pulled a sheet of paper from the pocket of his shirt. 'I noted down the active ingredients in code. If anyone else sees this list then these words will mean nothing. I'll explain it to you and then I recommend that you find the nearest police station and ask for protection.'

Wyatt said: 'We've looked after ourselves this far.'

'Then you've been lucky. You've been carrying something that...'

Travers last words were lost in a cry of agony as machine gun bullets tore through the glass wall behind him. Several ragged red blotches appeared on his chest as a waterfall of glass cascaded to the floor. Travers pitched forward. Wyatt and Linda threw themselves to the floor. They heard the sound of an outboard motor revving up again. Linda drew her pistol and crawled towards the body of her beloved godfather.

Wyatt ducked up and switched off the lights before diving through the empty space where glass had been. A rubber dinghy manned by two men was pulling away from the beach. Wyatt drew his pistol and fired twice but the dinghy was already out of range and hidden by darkness.

Wyatt looked around. A group of people having a barbecue along the beach were staring in amazement. Other figures were running towards him from the opposite direction.

Wyatt ducked back into the chalet. Linda was holding the body of Nathan Travers in her arms. She was covered in his blood and Wyatt saw that she had gashed her legs on broken glass. She was weeping uncontrollably. Wyatt carefully picked up the piece of paper that Travers had been about to give them. He said: 'We have to go, Linda. We have to go now. The police will be here within minutes and then we won't be able to finish what we've started.'

'No, no, I have to stay,' Linda wept. 'I have to stay with him.'

Wyatt said: 'I'm sorry to do this, Linda.' He took her under the arms and pulled her to her feet. Travers body flopped back on to the blood soaked glass.

'Let me go, you bastard,' Linda shouted.

Wyatt dragged her away. It took all his strength to prevent her from pulling away and going back to the body of Travers. He held her tightly in his arms and said: 'Linda, listen to me. Nathan is dead. Nothing you can do can help him now. We have to escape to carry on the fight. We have to leave now!'

Linda looked up at him. She was trembling with shock but she nodded in agreement.

'Good.' Wyatt took her by the hand and led her out through the side door.

They ran up the steps and climbed into the hire car. Wyatt started the engine, slammed it into gear and pulled out past the Corvette. The wailing sound of sirens filled the night air behind them. Wyatt accelerated along the bumpy track, turned left on to another track and soon came out on to the Gold Coast highway. He slowed down to obey the speed limits.

'Where are we going?' Linda asked.

'I've no idea,' Wyatt said. 'As far as way as possible for a start. You're injured. We need to treat you.'

'I'm all right, just a few nicks.'

'You're badly hurt, Linda. Here, in case one of us doesn't make it, read what it says on this piece of paper Nathan prepared.' Wyatt took it out of his pocket and handed it to Linda.

Linda read it and said: 'This makes no sense to me.'

'That doesn't matter. Memorise the words.'

'Okay, I've done that. Who were they, Chris? Did you see them?'

'No. They were gone before I could do anything. It was a well planned professional hit.'

'Were they after us or Nathan?'

'They were after Nathan. They didn't care that we were there.'

Linda said: 'I'm sorry I called you a bastard.'

'Forget it. I'm not the bastard in this case.'

'What do you mean?'

'Think about it. Only three people knew we were coming here and where to find Professor Travers. One was me, and I know it wasn't me. One was you, and I know you wouldn't have done or said anything to endanger your godfather. And the third was…'

'Premendra.'

'Exactly. That bastard must have set us up. There is no other possibility.'

'But we wouldn't have got nearly this far without his help. He saved your life in London. It doesn't make sense.'

'Can you think of how else those killers knew that Travers was there and that we were going to visit him?'

'No,' Linda admitted.

'Exactly. There are three things we have to do now. First, find a place to rest up, recover and treat your wounds. Then we have to decipher Nathan's note. We don't have any capsules left. The note is the only evidence we have.'

'What's the third thing?'

'The third thing is that I'm going to find Premendra Dhawan.'

40

Pelican Beach Motel, Coffs Harbour, New South Wales, Australia, April 4th

Wyatt gave the pre-arranged sequence of knocks on the chalet door. He unlocked the door and called: 'Linda, it's me.'

'Okay,' Linda called back. 'Everything is okay.'

Wyatt picked up his two shopping bags and carried them into the living room. Linda was sitting in an armchair with her legs up on a dining chair. She had wrapped towels around her legs. The towels were spotted with blood. She looked beaten, hollow-eyed and desperately tired. She put down her pistol and said: 'It's way past midnight. Where the hell have you been?'

Wyatt braced for an uneasy conversation. 'It took a while to find what we need. There aren't many stores open at this time of night.' Wyatt put the shopping bags on the dining table and took out the contents. 'I've bought some food, drinks, and I found a drug store open for bandages and iodine. I can treat your cuts.'

'They've stopped bleeding now.'

'I'll clean them up and bandage them anyway.'

'Where did you leave the car?'

'At the bus station. If anyone took the license plate number or can give the police a description of the car it might buy us some time if the police think we've hopped on a bus and got away.'

Linda grunted. 'You're an optimist.'

'How are you feeling now?'

'I'm okay physically but every time I close my eyes I see Uncle Nathan's body lying on the floor.'

'The police will have taken his body by now. He'll be treated respectfully. He's at peace now.'

'You're a big comfort,' Linda said bitterly. 'I should have stayed with him instead of letting you drive me like a maniac to this place.'

'We had to get away, Linda. We have to stay free.'

'Why this place?'

'Because it was on the way and there's an airport nearby and because this motel was open for business. You have to admit it's luxury accommodation, better than your average motel.'

'Well, that's okay then. My beloved godfather has been riddled with bullets but I have a comfortable armchair. And it's more of Charlie's money we'll have to pay back some day.'

'Don't worry about that now. As soon as you recover we can get on a flight and get away.'

'And go where, Chris?'

'I don't know,' Wyatt admitted. 'Unwrap those towels and let me treat your cuts. We'll think of something.'

Linda unwrapped the towels from her legs and threw them on the floor. 'We'll think of something, will we? I'm sick to my stomach with all this. I've lost my husband, I've lost my Uncle Nathan, I've lost my career, I've lost my life. Here we are hiding out in another frigging motel half a world away from home.'

Wyatt said: 'You're in shock and everything seems black. It's entirely understandable under the circumstances but I'm not going to let myself be drawn into your black mood.' He knelt down and examined Linda's wounds. 'These are bad cuts. I'm going to see if there are any pieces of glass left in the flesh before I bandage you. I'm going to stroke your legs. Don't read anything into it.'

Wyatt gently took Linda's right leg and turned it to and fro to check for shards of glass below the skin.

'Where did you study medicine, Doctor Wyatt?'

'You're right leg is clean. We were trained in the army to treat basic combat wounds.'

273

'Is that how you see all this, as if we were in combat?'

Wyatt examined Linda's left leg. 'That's clean as well. I'll treat the cuts with iodine and bandage them. I think we are in combat, Linda, as much as if we were on the battlefield.'

'And who are we fighting, Chris? Who is this enemy we can't find? As soon as we think we're getting somewhere, somebody else dies. I should never have allowed you to drag me into all this. When will it be our turn to die?'

Wyatt did not reply until he had finished bandaging. 'We can't give up, Linda. We have to be like Robert the Bruce watching his spider or Alfred the Great hiding in the marshes from the Danes. It looked hopeless for both of them but they battled through and won in the end and saved their country.'

Linda's tone was contemptuous. 'Oh, for Christ's sake, spare me your twee homilies from British history.'

Wyatt stood up. 'All right, let's try American history. Washington at Valley Forge or the defenders of the Alamo. They didn't give in. Although given your ethnic background perhaps the Alamo is not the right example.'

'That's it, throw in a bit of racism.'

'It's not racism. I'm trying to keep things light.'

'There were as many Mexicans fighting for the independence of Texas as there were fighting for General Santa Anna.'

Okay, okay. There were twelve Englishmen, four Scotsmen and nine Paddies defending the Alamo as well. All I'm saying is they didn't give up and neither must we.'

'At least they all had an enemy they could see. Where do we go? The only clue we have left is a piece of paper stained with Uncle Nathan's blood and with words we don't understand.'

'We understand two of them. We have to figure what the rest of them mean. If necessary I'll fly to Delhi and get back the rest of the capsules from that treacherous bastard Premendra Dhawan.'

Linda said defiantly: 'It wasn't Prem.'

'What makes you say that? He was the only other person who could have told the killers where to find Nathan.' Wyatt picked up the blood stained towels but then stopped. 'Wait a minute, you didn't tell anyone else where we were going behind my back, did you?'

'No, I didn't,' Linda retorted angrily. 'You're the one who keeps secrets and deceives people. I'm saying that Prem did not betray us either.'

Wyatt fought down growing anger and foreboding. 'What makes you so sure?'

'If Prem had betrayed us why didn't he order those assassins to kill us as well? He could have gotten rid of all of us at the same time.'

'Perhaps he's become fond of us. Perhaps he couldn't stand the thought of ordering our death. More likely we are useful patsies leading him to the killers of his wife and he wanted us kept alive. I still ask you the question why you're so sure that Prem did not betray us?'

'I talked to Prem about his wife, his sons, his life. He told me things he wouldn't tell you.'

Wyatt failed to keep a sneer out of his tone. 'So what is this? Some touchy feely female intuition with no basis in fact or reason?'

'It wasn't Prem.'

Wyatt looked at the secure cell phone on the dining table. 'If he rings us we won't answer.'

'I've already answered,' Linda said. Her expression dared Wyatt to argue.

Wyatt took a deep breath. 'You mean Prem rang and you answered?'

'Yes.'

'So now he can pinpoint exactly where we are from our transmission signal. That was bloody stupid, Linda. Do you want more killers breaking down the door?'

'You're not my commanding officer, Wyatt. I make my own decisions.'

'And there was I thinking we were partners, a team. Thanks for putting me straight.'

'I'm telling you, Prem did not betray us.'

'Well, what did you say to him?'

'Before he could tell me what was in the H'iatus capsules I told him that Uncle Nathan had been murdered.'

'How did he react?'

'He was genuinely shocked.'

'In his line of work he has to be good at subterfuge and deception. Perhaps he's a good actor.'

'I told him that Uncle Nathan had given us a piece of paper with clues to the formula for the H'iatus drug but we couldn't understand them.'

Wyatt flung the towels across the room. 'Jesus Christ, Linda! Have you lost your bloody mind? That guarantees that his thugs will be breaking down our door soon!'

Linda remained icily calm. 'Prem told me that his scientists have isolated the active ingredients in those capsules but it's like nothing they've ever seen before and they don't know what it is?'

'Well, this is just perfect! What a bloody shambles! Did you tell him that I suspect him of betraying us?'

'Yes. He sounded distraught to be accused.'

'So that's another Oscar winning performance to fool the naïve Sergeant Marquez.'

'Fuck you, Wyatt. It wasn't Prem.'

Wyatt picked up the cell phone. 'As you've already given away our location, I'll ring Mr Premendra Dhawan myself.'

Prem answered on the first ring. 'Christopher, is that you? Listen, I…'

'No, you listen, Prem. Did you betray us? Did you tell anyone where we were going today?'

'No, Christopher, I swear I didn't.'

'Then how did a pair of trained killers know exactly where and when to sail up the beach and kill Professor Travers in cold blood right at the opportune moment?'

'I don't know, Christopher, but I swear again that it was not my doing.'

'Well, here's what's going to happen, Prem. Linda was badly injured and can't travel for a couple of days but I advise you not to send any more of your assassins because we are armed and ready this time. Then I'm coming to Delhi to get back the rest of those capsules. If you want to live you better make sure I get them.'

'Christopher, they've been handed over to Indian government scientists. I can't get them back.'

'Think of something, Prem. Get me those capsules or take the consequences. Now, fuck off and don't ring us again.' Wyatt threw the cell phone back on the table.

Linda looked at him with revulsion. 'Every time I think I'm beginning to like you, you do something brutal or stupid like that. Prem did not betray us.'

'I hope you're right, Linda, or else you might need some of my stupid brutality again.'

'And you could do with some of Prem's intelligence and humanity.'

Wyatt went to the window and opened the curtains to look out at the sea and the night sky.

Linda said: 'You're making yourself a good target.'

'So be it,' Wyatt replied. He was overwhelmed with fatigue and took several deep breaths to subdue his anger. Then he said: 'It seems like a lifetime ago but earlier today, when we were in Surfers Paradise, that was good, wasn't it? We had a good time. We liked each other, didn't we? We sort of connected, didn't we?'

'Yes, we did, Chris. It was good. It was normal again. We had fun.'

'I understand how you feel about what we're doing, Linda. You've suffered too much. I'm sorry I lost my temper. I'm not going to Delhi. I couldn't harm Prem even if he did betray us. While we're stuck here, let's make a genuine effort to decipher those clues that Uncle Nathan left us. If we can't then we'll go our separate ways, report back to our respective governments with what we've found out, and let whatever happens happen. Is that a deal?'

Linda nodded. 'That sounds reasonable. It's a deal.'

'Good. Well, I think I'll turn in. I'm exhausted.'

'Me too.'

'Which bedroom do you want?'

'Either one. It doesn't matter to me. Thanks for taking care of my legs.'

Wyatt smiled. 'They're legs worth taking care of. Try to get some sleep. We have a lot of thinking to do tomorrow.'

'I'll try.'

An hour later Wyatt was still awake and staring at the ceiling of his darkened bedroom. He could hear Linda Marquez weeping softly.

The next morning Linda Marquez and Chris Wyatt were making efforts to be polite and considerate.

Wyatt called out from the kitchen: 'How do you like your eggs, Linda? Sunny side up?'

Linda was looking out of the window at the ocean. She turned and said: 'No, over easy, please.'

'I've no idea what that means so scrambled it is. Any ideas yet?'

Linda was stung by guilt and retreated from the window to look again at the cryptic bloodstained note that Nathan Travers had bequeathed. 'No, not yet. I can't make any sense of these words.'

'Grub's up! Or chow, whatever you like to call it.'

'I'm not really hungry, Chris. You eat mine.'

Wyatt looked out of the kitchen. 'Come and eat something, Sergeant Marquez. That's an order.'

'I don't think I can.'

'You have to keep your strength up. Remember what Napoleon said: *An army marches on it's stomach.*'

'We don't have the Grand Army with us, Chris. There's only the two of us and I think we've met our Waterloo.'

'Come on, come and eat. You haven't lived until you've tried Wyatt's special scrambled eggs on toast.'

Linda conceded defeat and went into the kitchen. She sat down at the breakfast table. 'You're a big bully, Wyatt, just like Bonaparte.' She stuck her arm out straight. 'Vive l'Emperor!'

'I think you're confusing Napoleon with Adolf Hitler. How did you sleep?'

'Fitfully. You?'

'Not very well. How are your wounds?'

'They feel much better.'

'I'd suggest taking off the bandages then after your shower leave them open to the air for the day. Your legs will heal a lot quicker.'

'Okay. You're keeping up a brave face, Chris, but I suspect you feel like I do.'

'How's that?'

'I want to go home. I want to see my family, be normal again. Go on, admit it, you feel the same. These eggs are good, by the way.'

'Thanks. You're right. I'm trying to stay positive but the odds against us are almost impossible. If only Nathan could have told us what those words mean before he... well, you know.'

'I'll stick to our deal. We'll try to decipher those words but if we can't then its game over.'

'That was the deal,' Wyatt agreed. 'Looks like a lovely day out there in Oz. Perhaps we could go for a walk along the beach later.'

'Too dangerous,' Linda said.

'Also I told the proprietor that we were newly married and he wouldn't be seeing much of us outside.'

Wyatt was relieved when Linda laughed. 'So he thinks we're in here ripping each other's clothes off.'

'Gave the old boy a cheap thrill. It was an act of charity. Aussies don't have much to live for except feeling superior to the English.'

After breakfast they took their coffee out into the living room and worked at the dining table. Wyatt took a sip of coffee and picked up the note.

TEST

MAO

ULTRA ?

NAO<u>M</u>I ?

DELTA ?

<u>K</u>APUT ?

'So we agree that "TEST" must refer to testosterone and "MAO" to these monoamine oxi… thingies.'

'Yes,' Linda said. 'The H'iatus website confirmed that they are constituent parts.'

'What can we say about these other four words? Remember what Prem taught us and don't be afraid to state the blindingly obvious.'

'Okay. They are all five letter words and Uncle Nathan wrote a question mark after each one. That suggests a range of alternatives and he was looking for the right one. And why did he underline the letters M and K?'

'MK is the abbreviation for a computer game called Mortal Kombat.'

'That adequately describes our predicament,' Linda said.

'It's also the abbreviation for Milton Keynes.'

'Who's he?'

'Not he. It's a new town in England that you can easily get lost in.'

'What about KM? Stands for kilometer, of course.'

'M is the Latin numeral meaning one thousand. Could Nathan have been indicating one thousand of something, perhaps one thousand kilometres?'

Linda shook her head. 'That doesn't seem to make any sense. None of these words look or sound like the names of drugs or chemicals. Let's go through them one by one. Ultra, that means beyond or to the highest degree.'

'It was also the code name for the intelligence that the British gleaned from the German Enigma decoding machines during the Second World War.'

'Okay, that's good. That suggests something cryptic, covert, hidden. Anything else?'

'Ultravox had a hit during the Eighties with *Vienna*.'

'I doubt whether Midge Ure is trying to destroy the world. Come on, be serious. Could it mean that a certain chemical has been treated by ultraviolet light?'

'Or by ultrasound?'

'Good, good,' Linda said. 'That's scientific. That sounds like a possibility. What about Naomi?'

'Um, girl's name. Wasn't she in the Bible?'

'Yes, I believe she was. Perhaps her life or deeds will give us a clue. It's a pity we haven't got the internet.'

'We have,' Wyatt said. 'Prem's secure mobile phone is linked to the internet.'

'But you said he could trace our position if we use it.'

Wyatt shrugged. 'He's traced us already if he wants to. Let's take the risk. We have to solve this conundrum.'

Linda picked up the cell phone and switched on. 'Here we are. Naomi was the mother-in-law of Ruth. Ah, her name means "sweet" but she later called herself "bitter". That could suggest a substance that starts sweet but ends up tasting bitter. I wonder what that could be?'

'I've no idea,' Wyatt said. 'What about Delta? A letter of the Greek alphabet. River delta? Delta Airlines? How about Delta Force, American special forces. Perhaps they used or tested some sort of drug?'

'Oh, rats! There's literally millions of definitions under "delta".'

'Alright, let's go on to "kaput". That means dead, beaten, moribund. That certainly suggests Silk Fist.'

'Moribund?' Linda smiled. 'You do know some big words for a common squaddie. Again, there are millions of references for "kaput".'

'Perhaps we're looking at this in the wrong way?' Wyatt suggested. 'Perhaps these five letter words are anagrams or a word puzzle of some kind that will reveal the name of a drug.'

'Okay, let's get some paper and play around with them. It's worth a try.'

By two in the afternoon Linda's eyes were drooping and Wyatt was staring out of the window. He said: 'I can't think of another damn thing.'

'Nor can I,' Linda muttered, trying to stay alert.

'Then, reluctantly, I admit defeat. We're at the end of the road, Linda. The only thing we can do is go back to duty, present this list and our findings to our superiors and let much more clever people than us sort it out.'

'Agreed. How do we do it? Who do we trust?'

'We've talked about this possibility before. We go to our families first so they'll know we're back, and then all our friends and colleagues. We inform our local police that we have vital information regarding Silk Fist and we may be in danger. We give it to the media. We lodge something for safekeeping in a bank vault and tell our bosses that if anything happens to us, if we disappear or end up dead, the media, the police, our legal representatives and our family will be crawling all over them asking questions.'

'That sounds feasible,' Linda said. 'Can we rest up here for another day or two? I suddenly feel so tired.'

'Yes, of course. When you feel ready we'll get a bus down to Sydney. I can get a flight to London and you can get a flight back to the States. Would you like any lunch?'

'No. I think I'll go take a nap. I'm zonked out.'

'Okay. I'll take the first watch. If Prem or anyone else has sent their assassins then they have to get through that door and past my trusty old Glock first.'

'Okay, Chris. Thanks.' Linda stood up. 'I'll say one thing for you.'

'Only one? What's that?'

'I feel safe when you're around. I'm sorry I called you a stupid brute last night.'

Wyatt said: 'As our Australian friends say, no worries. Go and get some sleep.'

41

Pelican Beach Motel, Coffs Harbour, New South Wales, Australia, April 7th

Linda came out of her room with her few belongings packed into plastic shopping bags. 'That's everything. I'm ready.'

Wyatt turned to look at her. 'The rest has done you a power of good. You look much better.'

'You've looked after me well. How do you feel?'

'Despondent and defeated. I don't like losing. I'm not used to it.'

'I understand what you mean. We did so much. We've lost so much. We came so far and lost out in the final stretch. We have to swallow our pride and move on.'

Wyatt nodded without enthusiasm.

A knock on the door.

Wyatt said: 'That'll be the taxi.' He took out his pistol and kept the security chain on while he opened the door. He cautiously looked out.

Premedra Dhawan was holding a pistol by the barrel, not the butt. He said: 'If you think I betrayed you then take my gun and shoot me. Or use that Glock you are hiding behind the door. I have lost the love of my life to these Silk Fist bastards. I want them brought to justice more than you do, Christopher. If you cut me out from what you have found then please shoot me now. I will have nothing left to live for.'

Wyatt hesitated but Linda said: 'Let him in, Chris.'

Wyatt said: 'This could be a trap.'

Prem said: 'There is no trap except in your mind, Christopher.'

'Who betrayed us, Prem, if it wasn't you. Who ordered Professor Travers to be killed?'

'I'm not sure but surely it must be Silk Fist. You are right to be suspicious and cautious but what would I have gained by having Professor Travers killed?'

'You could be working for Silk Fist. You're the only one who could have betrayed us.'

'Then shoot me, Christopher, now.'

Linda said: 'Enough of this macho shit. Let him in, Chris.'

Wyatt stood aside and said: 'On your head be it, Linda.'

Linda detached the security chain and opened the door. 'Come in, Prem. Come and sit down. You must have had a long journey. Can I get you something to drink?'

'A glass of water would be most welcome, Linda. Put that damn gun away, Christopher, and let's talk like men and not gangsters. Have you deciphered the note that Professor Travers gave you?'

Wyatt did not answer. An uneasy silence.

Linda came out of the kitchen and handed Prem a glass of iced water. She said: 'No, Prem. We're completely baffled.' She took out the unbloodstained copy from her jacket pocket and gave it to Prem. 'We're reasonably sure that "TEST" refers to testosterone and "MAO" to Mao inhibitors, but we cannot make anything of these other words. Can you?'

Prem said: 'I would be a poor cryptanalyst and an even poorer intelligence agent if I didn't immediately recognise what these words refer to.'

'You understand what they mean?' Wyatt said with astonishment.

'Yes, I do. And if you had trusted me we would not have wasted three days. This explains so much about the origin of this H'iatus drug.'

Linda sat down at the table and said: 'Then please tell us, Prem.'

'All four names are the code names for secret and highly illegal research experiments carried out by the CIA. Project MKUltra was a research experiment about mind control. The experiments began in the 1950s and were officially discontinued in, I think, the 1970s. I emphasise officially discontinued. MKUltra involved the surreptitious use of drugs and other chemicals to manipulate people's minds and alter their behaviour and mental states. The research was undertaken mainly at hospitals, prisons and pharmaceutical companies. Project MKUltra became public knowledge during the 1970s. The director of the CIA ordered all MKUltra files destroyed but there is strong evidence to suggest that Project MKUltra continued for many years afterwards.'

Linda said: 'So all this leads back to our good old CIA?'

'I'm afraid so. Do you know if Professor Travers worked for the CIA or was in any way involved in MKUltra?'

'He never told us but it would be a good bet and would explain why Uncle Nat was so disgusted with his former life. What about these other code names?'

'MKDelta was another CIA program associated with Ultra. Again it was a experiment involving the surreptitious use of LSD and other biochemicals to alter the behaviour of unwitting guinea pigs, both American and foreign. Again it was highly illegal but reportedly very effective. There is even less known about MKNaomi. It lasted from the 1950s through to the 1970s. I believe it was the successor to the other two and concentrated on agents that could either incapacitate or kill a test subject or radically alter their personality, as we are seeing with the Silk Fist perpetrators.'

Wyatt said: 'No wonder we couldn't find any references on the internet by looking up these words.'

'You needed to put the MK in front of them. That's why Professor Travers underlined those letters. Everything I have told you is freely available on the internet, except MKKaput.'

'What do you think that is?' Wyatt asked.

'I suspect that it is the culmination of all these years of experimentation as we are seeing with Silk Fist.'

Wyatt asked: 'Are you saying that the CIA are behind all these attacks?'

'No, most certainly not,' Prem replied. 'That would be catastrophically stupid. It must be someone who has detailed knowledge of the drugs and chemicals used in these experiments.'

'Someone like Uncle Nathan,' Linda said mournfully.

'I'm afraid so.'

Wyatt said: 'It also explains why someone within the American and British establishments is so anxious to shut us up, even to the extent of having us killed.'

Linda said: 'This knowledge makes it impossible for us to go back to our respective authorities and tell them what we have found. If we do that it might get covered up despite whatever precautions we take.'

'Or worse, get us killed,' Wyatt said.

Prem said: 'It would be useful if we could find someone else who worked on these secret projects, especially MKKaput.'

'How do we find them if it was all so secret?' Wyatt asked. 'Could your people find out, Prem?'

'No. You may wonder why I know so much about these projects off the top of my head. We tried, for may years, to find out what the CIA had been up to. We tried hacking and bribery and interception and even threats but we came up empty handed. We were worried about the brainwashing and mind control techniques being developed by the Chinese. We couldn't find anything.'

'Then we're stumped again,' Wyatt said.

'I fear that is so.'

'Not necessarily,' Linda said. 'There is someone who might be able to find some names.'

'Who's that?' Wyatt asked.

'Our friend Charlie.' Linda looked at her watch. 'It's about midnight in New York. Charlie will be hitting her stride. I'll give her a ring.'

'Wait a minute,' Wyatt protested. 'How will Charlie be able to find this information?'

'She has contacts everywhere, senators, congressmen, policemen, CIA agents, and most of them owe her a favour.'

'Okay,' Wyatt said. 'Give it a try.'

42

Pelican Beach Motel, Coffs Harbour, New South Wales,
Australia, April 9th

Charlie rang back two days later. Wyatt and Prem had spent the morning in an internet cafe researching the background to the CIA mind control experiments and had returned to the motel minutes before.

Linda picked up the cell phone. 'Hi, Charlie. What have you got for us?'

'Besides an enormous bill for your holiday in the sun, I've got you, and me, a shitload of trouble.'

'How do you mean, Charlie?'

'I mean the reaction of some of my contacts when I mentioned this MKUltra and MKKaput business. It's like they had stuck their fingers in a light socket. I hope this information is as important as you say it is.'

'It is, Charlie, believe me.'

'Then I'll send you a text with the names you wanted, those that are still alive.'

'Still alive?'

'Yep. I came up with twelve names. Three died years ago from proven natural causes. Five of them have been found dead in so-called accidental or suspicious circumstances within the past year. That leaves four. I could only find the whereabouts of one of them as you'll see from the text. You be careful, girl.'

'I will, Charlie.'

'At least you still got that gorgeous hunk of Englishman to protect you. Are you two getting it on yet?'

'Oh, stop it, Charlie.'

'I'll take that as a yes or else you're way too slow. Give him a kiss from me.'

'I will. Thanks Charlie.'

The text message arrived a few seconds later. One of the names given as still alive was Professor Nathan Travers.

'So Uncle Nathan did work for the CIA,' Linda said. 'And he's not the first one to have been murdered over the past few years.'

'Okay, that let's you off the hook, Prem,' Wyatt said. 'I apologise for my suspicions.'

'You were right to be suspicious. It's all forgotten. Where do we go from here?'

Linda said: 'It looks like we're taking a trip to Alaska.'

43

Charlie's Night Club, New York City, April 10th

Charlotte Windsor was holding court at the bar. She was perched on her favourite padded stool with her back to the wall so that she could keep an eye on everything happening in her club. She enjoyed the greetings and the compliments and the flattery from her regular patrons. She could imagine that she was a member of the royal family.

It had been two hours since she had spoken to Linda Marquez. Charlie was worried about her. Charlie had not told Linda how difficult it had been to obtain the information about MKUltra personnel. She had been obliged to call in many favours.

Now Charlie watched as six uniformed policemen entered the club. They were accompanied by one man in plain clothes. Five of the policemen discreetly fanned out around the sides of the club. A uniformed police lieutenant and the man in plain clothes walked directly towards her. The singer and the band fell silent as the patrons watched. The atmosphere was tense and resentful.

Charlie said: 'Good evening, boys. Always happy to see the police in my club. And the Feds, of course. What can we get you to drink?'

The man in plain clothes said: 'Charlotte Windsor?'

'That's me.'

'I'm Special Agent John Curtin.'

'Special agent of what.'

'You don't need to know.'

'Then I don't need to talk to you.'

'I'm afraid you'll have to. This is Lieutenant Lemoine.'

Charlie said: 'I know. Lemony and me are old friends. Except I haven't seen you in here since you got your promotion, Lemony.'

Captain Lemoine looked away in embarrassment. 'How are you doing, Charlie? I wish you would have come out to the foyer like we asked.'

'I've got nothing to hide from my people. I want them to see exactly what you are doing. What *can* I do for you folks?'

Curtin said: 'You can tell us the whereabouts of Linda Marquez.'

'Marquez?' Charlie said. 'I don't know her.'

'What about an Englishman named Christopher Wyatt?'

'Nope. Never heard of him.'

'We have information that two people answering their description were recently staying in the apartment upstairs.'

'Well, Special Agent Curtin, you've been misinformed. There's been nobody living up there except me and an occasional girlfriend of mine.'

It was Curtin's turn to look embarrassed.

Charlie said: 'Hey, Lemony, you still seeing that little dancer I hooked you up with?'

Lemoine's face turned red. 'Come on, Charlie, that was years ago.'

'And your wife never found out? Perhaps it's time she did.'

Lieutenant Lemoine said: 'There's nothing I can do, Charlie. This situation is way above my pay grade. I'm just the messenger boy to vouch for the credentials of Special Agent Curtin here. We've gotta take you in, Charlie.'

'What the hell for?'

'I don't know,' Lemoine said. 'Something about endangering national security. You've been talking to people you shouldn't have been talking to about subjects you shouldn't know about and you've been talking on a cell phone and texting Wyatt and Marquez. Some government people higher up the food chain, like Curtin here, want to ask you about it. They'll tell you what laws you've broken.'

Charlie laughed. 'Okay, Lemony, relax. I'm not going to make any trouble. You better read me my rights.'

Curtin said: 'We're not arresting you, Charlie. We simply want…'

'Only my friends call me Charlie, Special Agent Curtin. You can address me as Miss Windsor.'

'Very well, Miss Windsor. We simply want you to come with us and answer some questions at this stage. It may be necessary to take you into custody later, depending on the answers we receive.'

'Don't try to bully me, Curtin. Folks have been trying that all my life and it hasn't worked yet.'

A round of applause from patrons near enough to hear what was going on.

Lemoine said: 'Please, Charlie, let's go before there's any trouble.'

Charlie stepped down off the stool. 'I'll alert all my attorneys. And make sure I get a comfortable cell. Last time I was in jail I was poor and broke and it was more comfortable than where I was living at the time. I'm used to my home comforts now.'

Lemoine said: 'Thanks, Charlie. I'm real sorry about this.'

Curtin gave Lemoine a sharp look.

Charlie said loudly: 'Good night people. New York's Finest have requested the pleasure of my company. The next round is on me.'

The patrons of Charlie's night club cheered without enthusiasm as their beloved hostess was escorted out into the cold New York night.

44

Barrow Lake, Glacier National Park, Alaska, April 16th

Their breath vaporised into wisps of white in the icy morning air.

Linda said: 'Chris, couldn't you have hired a motorboat instead of this goddamn canoe?'

'You're doing fine, Linda. Make sure that the paddle blade is fully submerged and that you take it out of the water before it hits the side of the canoe. Rotate your body to get power into the stroke, don't just use your arms.'

'I'm at the front. Should I be steering?'

'No, you leave the steering to me.'

'What makes you such an expert?'

'Ten years in the Royal Marines and the Special Boat Service.'

'Oh, yes, I forgot. This is hard work. I'm getting hot already. I wish I hadn't put on this heavy coat.'

'Keep the coat on, it's colder than it seems. Besides, you look great in red tartan. Best looking lumberjack I ever saw.'

'Thanks… I think. I have to admit that this scenery and this weather is literally breathtaking. Huge blue sky, jagged snowcapped mountains, dense green forests, morning sun sparkling off steel grey water. This really is back to nature.'

'Yes,' Wyatt agreed. 'Let's stop paddling for a moment.'

Linda took the blade out of the water.

'Can you hear it?' Wyatt asked.

'Hear what?'

'Nothing. Nothing accept that majestic hush you get in wild places like this.'

They floated in silence.

'Yes,' Linda said. 'It's awesome. Magnificent. It almost wraps itself around you like a cloak of silent solitude.'

'That's a beautiful description, very poetic. And an approaching motorboat would be heard miles away. Okay, start paddling.'

Linda asked: 'If this guy Jaso is involved with Silk Fist, wouldn't he have lookouts or sentries on his private little island.'

'Possibly. At least this silent approach early in the morning gives us a chance of surprise. He could be involved in Silk Fist or, as they said in town, he's simply a frail old man looking for some peace and quiet before he dies.'

'We don't even know if he's on his island. What if he isn't?'

'Then we take a look around his house.'

'Oh, that's great,' Linda exclaimed. 'Let's add illegal breaking and entering to our catalogue of crimes.'

'If we want our lives and our careers back we have to find something. Thanks to Prem and Charlie we've been given a second chance. I don't intend to waste it.'

'Okay, I accept your argument.' Linda pointed at the island. 'That looks like a landing stage over on the right there, in that little inlet below the cliff.'

'Yes. I can see the steps up the side of the cliff. Hold on, I'm going to reverse sweep to change course.'

The canoe tilted.

'Okay, Linda, keep paddling as before.'

The canoe picked up speed and five minutes later they were drawing the canoe up on to a small shale beach below a grey crag.

Wyatt said: 'I'll make double sure the canoe is securely stowed and tied. If we lose the canoe we're really screwed.'

'Haven't you heard of cell phones. All we'd have to do is…'

A shotgun roared and splinters of rock rained down on to their heads. They scrambled behind a boulder and peered up at the crag. A man stood at the top. He was pointing a double-barrelled shotgun.

Linda shouted: 'Mr Jaso! We apologise for invading your privacy. We need to talk to you.'

There was no reply. The man lifted the shotgun to his shoulder and fired the second barrel. Linda and Wyatt ducked as shards of rock pattered around them.

Linda said: 'I don't think he means to hurt us. He's trying to frighten us off.'

Wyatt reached into his coat and took out his pistol.

'What are you doing?' Linda said. 'You can't shoot him.'

'I'm not going to shoot him. I'm going to make him duck down so he can't see me while I run across the cove. I can scramble up that cliff behind him and disarm him from behind. After I fire, you keep him distracted by talking.'

Wyatt fired one shot into the top of the crag. Dirt and grit flew upwards. The man staggered back and Wyatt ran across to the other side of the cove. He clambered over the rocks until he disappeared from Linda's view.

'Mr Jaso!' Linda shouted. 'We are not here to cause you harm. We are not the police. You may have information that can save lives!'

There was no reply.

Wyatt said: 'Mr Jaso, I have a pistol pointed at your back. Put down the shotgun and you will not be harmed.'

Jaso started with surprise and then threw down the shotgun in disgust. He turned around. Wyatt was shocked by Jaso's appearance. He was completely bald, his face was lined, gaunt and the colour of parchment. He was inches taller than Wyatt but there was hardly any flesh on his bones and his clothes hung off loosely. His pale blue eyes burned with resentment and when he spoke he hissed through yellow teeth, his breath coming in rasping fits and starts. He said:

'Who are you? How dare you invade my property?' Jaso was seized by a fit of raw coughing.

Wyatt shouted: 'You can come on up now, Linda!' To Jaso he said: 'I apologise for intruding but it is vital that my colleague and I talk to you.'

'About what?'

Wyatt nodded at the log bungalow built in a clearing. 'We'll talk about that inside.'

'Fuck you, whoever you are. That's my home and you're not welcome in it.'

Linda appeared at the top of the steps.

Wyatt said: 'Linda, would you please pick up Mr Jaso's shotgun. He's kindly invited us inside for a talk.'

An expression of pure hatred crossed Jaso's face. 'Fuck you. You can shoot me if you like but you are not...' He bent double in a painful fit of wheezing and coughing. His legs buckled and he fell to the ground.

Wyatt put away his pistol and knelt down beside Jaso.

'Oxygen,' Jaso croaked. 'Must have oxygen.'

Wyatt gently slid his arms under the old man and lifted him up. Wyatt was shocked by how light and frail Jaso was. He carried Jaso to the door of the cabin. Linda opened the door and Wyatt carried Jaso inside. Wyatt carefully lowered Jaso into an armchair.

Linda stood the shotgun in the corner of the room. Linda found the oxygen tank and wheeled it over to where Jaso was sitting.

Wyatt said: 'Do you know how to work that thing?'

'Yes.' Linda slipped the mask over Jaso's nose and mouth and turned on the oxygen.

Within seconds Jaso regained some colour and some control over his breathing.

Linda said: 'Rest easy, Mr Jaso. Don't stress yourself. We mean you no harm.'

Jaso relaxed and closed his eyes.

Linda said: 'Why is it so hot in here?' She took off her lumberjack coat.

Wyatt took out his pistol and went off to search the cabin. He came back and said: 'There's nobody else here.' He took off his pea coat. They sat and waited for Jaso to recover.

'This is a lovely cabin,' Linda said. 'Beautifully furnished, very comfortable.'

'Yes, and he's certainly not cut off from the outside world. There was a satellite dish outside and there's enough equipment over there to open an electrical shop.'

Jaso opened his eyes and said: 'What did you expect to find? Some old fart living like Daniel Boone and eating bear meat? I'll ask you again, who are you?'

Wyatt said: 'My name is Chris Wyatt and this is Linda Marquez. We are not cops.'

'Not cops? You've got cop written all over you, both of you. Even if you are, why should I care whether you're cops or not. I've done nothing wrong. I've nothing to hide.'

Linda said: 'It's not what you've done, it's what you might be able to tell us. It's a matter of national security. I'm with the United States Secret Service and Sergeant Wyatt is with the Metropolitan Police in London.'

Jaso said: 'I thought you sounded like a Limey, Wyatt. So what does a spic bitch and a Limey want with me.'

Linda saw the anger in Wyatt's expression and said: 'It's okay, Chris, I'm used to ignorant insults like that.'

Jaso said: 'This is my home. I do and say what I like in here. If you don't want to be insulted then don't force your way into my home. Have you got any identification?'

'No,' Linda said. 'I lost my shield.'

'What about you, Limey? Got your pointy helmet and your truncheon?'

'No, but I have full authorisation from a Mr Glock.' Wyatt pointed at his gun.

'Mr Jaso,' Linda said calmly, 'we're here to ask you about Project MKUltra.'

'I've never heard of it.'

'Project MKUltra,' Wyatt repeated, 'and it's follow-up projects, Naomi, Delta and Kaput. We know you were involved.'

'You don't know anything,' Jaso said. 'I don't know what you're talking about. Get out of my home before I call the police. The real police.'

Linda said: 'If you don't talk to us then you won't have to call the police because we'll do it for you. You can either confide in us or have all the intelligence services in the world crawling over you.'

'If you think I know something, why don't you get them here and be done with it.'

Linda looked at Wyatt. He nodded to go ahead. Linda said: 'We're on the run ourselves. We're both being hunted as fugitives by our own people.'

Jaso's expression softened and his eyes lit up with interest. 'Well, why didn't you say so? Shall we have a drink? Over there in that cabinet. I'll have a very large Jack Daniels. Would you like to do the honours, Mr Wyatt?'

Linda and Wyatt refused the offer but Wyatt poured a drink for Jaso. Jaso accepted the glass with trembling hands.

Linda said: 'Should you be drinking alcohol, especially this early in the day?'

'Not according to my doctors, but screw them.'

'What's wrong with you?' Wyatt asked.

'Chronic asthma and small cell lung cancer.'

'Shouldn't you be in hospital or nearer civilisation?'

'I like the air out here. It eases my lungs. I want to die in peace without people arriving to interrogate me. The irritating thing is that I've never smoked in my life and my doctors tell me that non-smokers are more likely to get lung cancer and asthma combined than smokers. So much for morality and clean living.' Jaso looked at Wyatt. 'I guess you were a soldier before you were a policeman.'

'What makes you think that?'

'You're smartly turned out, blunt and straight to the point, and the way you took me by surprise by climbing up the cliff shows that you're not some out-of-condition desk jockey. What were you in?'

'Royal Marines and the Special Boat Service.'

Jaso grunted. 'Then I'm lucky you came here without harmful intentions. What about you Miss Marquez? You said you were in the Secret Service?'

'Yes. I was the special assistant to Mrs Martina Logan. Not anymore, I guess.'

Jaso chuckled as well as his tortured lungs would allow. He had to take several draughts of oxygen. Eventually he managed to say: 'The First Lady! That's priceless! Well, you're the best-looking Secret Service agent I've ever seen. How did you two hook up?'

Linda said: 'Sergeant Wyatt was guarding the Princess Royal when she was assassinated…'

'You're the one who shot Flaherty?'

'Yes. My superiors came to suspect that I was either incompetent or involved in the assassination plot.'

Linda said: 'My husband committed suicide some weeks ago. Chris realised that there were connections between the two events and we decided to join forces. Both Dr Flaherty and my husband had lost control of their own personality and behaviour.'

Jaso nodded. 'Then I guess you're here to ask me about Silk Fist.'

Wyatt and Linda looked at each other with excitement. Wyatt said to Jaso: 'Is there a connection between Project MKUltra and Silk Fist?'

'As soon as details of those crimes became public knowledge I realised exactly how they were being perpetrated.'

Linda said vehemently: 'Why didn't you do something or say something?'

'Because I don't care. The world and all the people in it can go to hell. I want my life to end here peacefully, not being interrogated by your CIA friends. Whatever happens I'll be dead soon.'

Wyatt said: 'You might be dead sooner than you think.' He took out the list of Project MKUltra scientists and handed it to Jaso. 'Here is a list of your former colleagues. There you are, right at the top, Dr Anthony Jaso.'

'What do these crosses next to these names mean?'

'It means they have been murdered within the last few months.'

Linda said: 'Professor Nathan Travers was murdered a few days ago. We were actually with him when it happened.'

'Really? What did the faggot have to say about all this?'

Linda said: 'The "faggot" was my godfather and the kindest man I've ever known. Whatever he told us is none of your business. We want to hear it from you.'

Jaso sighed and took a sip of whisky. 'I've been involved in unimaginable wickedness that makes me sick to my stomach. You've found me and I'll talk to you two because I find myself liking you. You've got guts and determination.'

Wyatt said. 'Tell us about Project MKUltra.'

Jaso collected his thoughts. 'I was recruited by the CIA after I left Harvard back in the late Fifties. I was a brilliant chemist and researcher. Ultra was already ongoing when I joined and I quickly rose to command the team. This was the era of the Cold War. You must have seen films like *The Manchurian Candidate*. We were concerned about possible brainwashing techniques being developed by Russia and China. Our brief was to develop such techniques for American use.'

'To what end?' Linda asked.

'Primarily for espionage purposes. We were hoping to control enemy diplomats within America and politicians and persons of influence within enemy, and even friendly, countries. We had limited success with that approach, purely for practical reasons, but we found that we could control people's motives and actions to an astonishing degree using the right cocktail of drugs.'

'Which drugs worked the best?' Wyatt asked.

'We tested hundreds. Amphetamine, morphine, mescaline, heroin, LSD, barbiturate, cocaine, as well as other recreational drugs, alcohol, marijuana. The so-called truth drug sodium pentothal was very effective, as was temazepam. We tried fertilizers, weedkillers, rat poison, even different foodstuffs. We must have tried every substance known to man.'

'Testosterone?' Wyatt asked. 'Was that one of them?'

'Yes, for use with male subjects. We found that soldiers going into combat could be made utterly courageous, highly aggressive and with no fear of dying. If we could have administered to every soldier, the United States would have had the greatest army in the history of the world. It was fascinating stuff.'

'I wish we could share your fascination,' Linda said. 'What about inhibitors?'

'Congratulations,' Jaso said. 'Travers must have told you. The old MAOI type was one of the key drugs in helping to cross over what is known as the blood/brain barrier, but it was highly dangerous and often fatal. We lost many subjects over the years.'

'How many, Dr Jaso?'

Jaso shrugged. 'Hundreds. Perhaps thousands.'

'Who were the subjects?'

'A few volunteers but mainly prisoners, mental patients, captured enemy soldiers, even clandestine testing in foreign countries. You may recall the so-called Reverend Jim Jones and the mass suicide of hundreds of people, including women and children, in Guyana. That was probably our greatest triumph of mind control, to make women poison their own children and then commit suicide.'

'That was the CIA?' Linda asked in disbelief.

'No. They would not have gone that far. That was an experiment by a small cadre of scientists in Project MKDelta. Your godfather Travers found out what we were doing and tried to stop us. We threatened to expose him as a faggot and he backed off.'

'Uncle Nathan was not a "faggot", Linda said. 'Even if he had been it makes no difference. He was a fine honest man.'

Jaso shook his head at the extent of Linda's naïvety. 'Being a faggot was illegal and a certain career killer back then. Your fine honest Professor Travers didn't have the guts and he backed off.'

'Any other of your triumphs you'd like to share with us?' Wyatt asked before Linda could respond.

'Sure,' Jaso said. 'Before I joined Ultra the crazy bastards had poisoned an entire French village named Pont-Saint-Esprit. They sprayed the place with aerosol LSD. It caused mass hysteria, over thirty villagers committed to mental hospitals, several deaths. It's all on the internet now. I had the sense to tone things down, bring some subtlety to the whole operation.'

'I'm sure we should be grateful for that,' Wyatt said.

'You can be as sarcastic as you like but we changed history.'

'In what way do you mean?'

'Several ways. Jack Ruby, the guy who shot Lee Harvey Oswald, he was one of ours. Several foreign enemies or troublemakers were gotten rid of, as well as several criminals within the States who we couldn't touch any other way, Mafia bosses and so on. Marilyn Monroe was one of ours. She was threatening to spill the beans on her affairs with both the Kennedys. We "persuaded" her to take an overdose. James Earl Ray was another. I handled that one myself. He was a helpless patsy. Martin Luther King was becoming a nuisance to certain people so I ordered Ray to hit King. Ray couldn't even remember doing it. Mark Chapman was the same. That long-haired Limey freak John Lennon was a nuisance to the US government by singing about peace and influencing millions of American youngsters. The government couldn't lock him up or deport him without being seen as fascist bullies so what better way than implant a sucker like Chapman with a hatred so deep that he got rid of Lennon for us.'

Wyatt said: 'You must be very proud, you piece of shit. Let's get to the point. We know that the drug being used by Silk Fist contains testosterone and MAO inhibitor. What is the active ingredient?'

'I don't know.'

'You can tell us or you can tell other people who won't be as gentle and courteous as we are.'

'Listen, I swear I don't know. We had great success while I was involved but I left before this Project MKKaput began. The way Silk Fist are using their drug shows that it's much more effective and sophisticated than anything we ever found. I guess they've found the Holy Grail, a drug that works so well that they can fine tune its use with anyone. How are they delivering the drug to these victims?'

Linda said: 'Can't you tell us that, Dr Jaso?'

'No, I can't imagine.'

'Does the word Hiatus mean anything to you in connection with such a drug?'

Jaso shook his head. 'No.'

'What about Bald Eagle?'

'Bald Eagle? What has that got to do with anything?'

Linda said: 'Have you any idea why Silk Fist are doing what they are doing? It doesn't make sense. They can't bring down a country or effect any real change by what they're doing. It's a crazy wrecking and killing spree with no obvious purpose.'

'I have no idea.'

Wyatt picked up his pistol and pointed it. He said: 'I'll make you a deal, Jaso. You tell us about the active ingredients in Hiatus and I won't shoot you.'

'No, you wouldn't!' Jaso sneered. 'I can see it in your face. Sure, you can kill in the heat of combat or in self-defence, but shoot a sick old man in cold blood? No, you wouldn't do it. Sergeant Marquez wouldn't let you.'

'People are dying out there every day because of the work you and your sick criminal friends did.' Wyatt put the barrel of the pistol against Jaso's temple. 'Don't gamble on what I would or wouldn't do.'

'Go ahead, Wyatt. Blow my brains out in front of your pal. I'm sure that would endear her to you.'

Linda said: 'I'll offer you another deal, Dr Jaso. Tell us what the active drug is called and we will not inform the authorities of your knowledge about Silk Fist until we have completed our own investigations.'

Jaso said: 'You'll have to pull the trigger, Wyatt, because I truly don't know, but I can point you to someone on your list who did work on Kaput and who has the facilities to make such a drug.'

Wyatt threw his pistol back on top of his pea coat. 'Who is it?'

'A guy called Francois Walden. We called him Frankie. He's down on your list as Frank Thoreau. That's the pseudonym he used, for obvious reasons, while working in America. His mother was French, his father an American, so he had dual nationality. He grew up in France but came to work on Delta while I was there and he stayed on after I left. He's an arrogant little prick but a very good practical chemist. The last I heard he was living near Paris and running his own company making some sort of products, hairspray or some such crap. Go and talk to him.'

'Do you have his address or phone number or anything?' Linda asked.

'No. I haven't seen him in years.'

'What's the name of his company?' Wyatt asked.

Jaso shrugged. 'I've no idea. You're pretending to be cops, you do a bit of detective work.'

'Okay, Jaso, we'll go and look for this Walden bloke but if you're telling us porky pies then I'll be back to see you and then you'll fully realise what I'm capable of.'

'Porky pies? What the hell does that mean?'

Linda said: 'I believe it's Cockney rhyming slang meaning "lies".'

Wyatt stood up.

Jaso said: 'Wyatt, you can look at me like I'm something a dog left on the sidewalk but how many men have you killed?'

'Too many. Unlike you I didn't find it fascinating.'

'You think you've got me taped, don't you. You think I'm a nasty psychopath with no feeling or remorse for what I've done, but you're wrong. It haunts every minute of my day. My family moved from Cuba before Castro took over. I worked for the CIA but they never really trusted me because of my ethnic background. When I started I truly thought I was doing good work for my adopted country. It was the CIA who twisted the research and they got rid of me as soon as they could. I had given them the best part of my life and they threw me out. Then I lost my wife to cancer, my only daughter was killed in a road accident, now I'm losing everything else to cancer, including my faith in God and my hair with that goddamn chemotherapy. I probably won't see next year and that's all right, but don't stand there sneering at me, Sergeant Wyatt, and thinking you understand me. You're a killer for your country as I am for mine.'

Linda stood up and said: 'We'll leave you in peace now, Dr Jaso.'

Jaso said: 'My apologies for my juvenile insult earlier, Miss Marquez. You are a beautiful woman. Would you do me one last kindness?'

'What's that?'

'Fetch me my shotgun and put it by my side. There are cartridges in that drawer over there. If the bad guys are out to get me, as you say they are, I want to be able to defend myself. They'll kill me but it will give me immense satisfaction to blow the faces off a couple of them before they do.'

Linda fetched the shotgun and a box of cartridges. She reloaded the shotgun and leant it against Jaso's armchair.

Wyatt waited in the doorway, pistol in hand, until Linda had finished.

'Don't worry,' Jaso said. 'I won't pursue you and fire at you again. I haven't the strength. Have a nice life.'

Wyatt and Linda walked down the steps to the landing beach. Wyatt unhitched the canoe and they pushed off into the bay. A light breeze had sprung up and was ruffling the waters but it was at their backs and they sped away from Jaso's island.

'What did you make of him?' Wyatt asked. 'Do you think he's involved with Silk Fist?'

'No, it's highly unlikely. The poor guy can hardly get out of the chair.'

'What did he mean when he said it was obvious why this Walden bloke changed his name to Thoreau while working in the States?'

Linda smiled and shook her head. 'Have you never heard of David Henry Thoreau?'

'No. What is he? A baseball player or something?'

'No, he was an old guy who would have loved it where we are now. It's not important.'

'Okay, so I'm thick. Do you believe that Jaso doesn't know what the Silk Fist drug is?'

'I'm not sure.'

'What are we going to do? Tell the authorities about him?'

'Damn straight we are. He has vital information and we don't know what questions to ask. We have to hand him over to the experts.'

A single shot boomed across the water and sent the wildfowl screeching and flapping into the sky. The sound reverberated around the lake. Linda and Wyatt stopped paddling.

'Jeez,' Linda said. 'Do you think he's killed himself?'

Wyatt nodded. 'Yes. I think he'd had enough.'

'Shall we go back? We ought to go back.'

'No, Linda. If he's swallowed the barrel there's nothing we can do to help him, and it's a sight that I wouldn't want to see. He realised that we would have to tell the authorities about what he knows. I don't think he could face the interrogation. We've lost another piece of evidence. Other people must have heard that shot. We can't afford to become entangled here. We have to stay free, Linda. We have to find this guy Walden.'

45

Savigny-sur-Orge, near Paris, France, April 27th

Francois Walden locked the doors of FW Produits de Beautè with an unusual feeling of relief. It had been a long day and all his employees had gone home at least an hour before.

It was a mild and clear evening in the peaceful suburban town. His factory was situated in a special zone of light industrial units. The zone was not pretty, neither was it ugly. There were far worse places in the world and Walden was content. He was also hungry, his wife was an excellent cook, and he looked forward with relish to dinner with his family.

As Walden opened his car door he noticed two people walking down the road towards him. Apart from idly wondering why they were both wearing overcoats on such a pleasant evening, Walden thought nothing of it. He was surprised when the two people, instead of walking past him, stopped either side of him.

The woman smiled. Walden noticed, with his professional eye, that she had captivating green eyes and a beautifully smooth light olive complexion. She said: 'Monsieur Walden, je vous remercie d'avoir acceptÈ de nous faire visiter votre usine.'

The man was at least six inches taller than Walden. His hair was black and the stare from his deep brown eyes was disturbing. Walden experienced a frisson of fear but the man smiled broadly and said in English: 'I want you to smile for the benefit of your security cameras, Mr Walden.' The man had an overcoat draped over his shoulders. Underneath the coat, hidden from the cameras, he was holding a pistol.

Walden said: 'Je ne comprends pas l'anglais.'

Linda said: 'You understand English perfectly, Mr Walden. You worked in the United States for many years.'

Despite his apprehension, Walden was annoyed enough to say: 'What is this? A robbery? I keep no cash in my factory.'

Wyatt said: 'I told you to smile. I don't want to hurt you, Mr Walden, but I will if you don't do as I say. Now smile and we'll go and unlock the door.'

Walden looked from one to the other. 'Are you two crazy?'

Wyatt said: 'Smile now or I *will* shoot you.'

Walden half-smiled for the cameras, took out his keys and walked back to the main door. He said: 'I have to switch off the alarm system as soon as I get inside.'

'Very well,' Wyatt said. 'Don't try anything heroic. We only want to talk to you and look around your factory.'

Walden shrugged. He unlocked the main door and ushered the two intruders inside. A red light on the alarm system control box was flashing. Walden punched in a code and the light went out. They were standing in a small reception area. Walden said: 'Do you want me to switch on the lights?'

Linda said: 'Yes, please, so we can enjoy the tour.'

Walden said: 'Perhaps if you simply tell me why you want to look around my factory then I can tell you what you want to know?'

Wyatt could tell that Walden was very frightened although he was attempting to be brave. He was a tubby man with a straggly moustache and beard. His hair was thin on top.

Wyatt said: 'I see your Hiatus drug doesn't work for you.'

If Walden had been affected by the use of the word Hiatus he hid it well. 'I don't make drugs. I make high-class cosmetics for the best boutiques in Paris and other cities.'

Linda said: 'So Hiatus is a profitable little sideline.'

'I have no idea what you two are talking about.' Walden tried to look at Wyatt but flinched under the gaze of those midnight eyes.

Wyatt said: 'Let's take a look around.'

Walden pushed through the protective rubber doors into the factory area. He said: 'On the left are offices, my office, my assistant manager's office, accounts and administration, washrooms and so on. The rest of this area is our distribution centre where the products are packed, labelled and sent out. All my products are made and packed by hand. They are expensive but they are the best.'

Linda said to Wyatt: 'I'll go take a look around the offices. You keep an eye on Monsieur Walden.'

While Linda was searching the offices, Wyatt said to Walden: 'Doctor Jaso sends his regards.'

'Jaso? I don't know who you mean.'

'Yes, you do. You worked with Jaso on Project MKDelta and then MKKaput. Professor Nathan Travers would have sent his regards but he's in a mortuary somewhere in Australia.'

This time Walden could not hide his reaction. 'That was years ago. I swear all that shit is behind me. I'm a legitimate businessman now. If Jaso is telling you that I'm involved in anything shady then tell him to go to hell.'

'I'd like to, Mr Walden, but Jaso has already gone to hell.'

'What do you mean?'

'I mean Anthony Jaso committed suicide a few days ago. Most of the scientists who worked with you on MKUltra have been killed. Jaso, Professor Travers, Hutton, MacReady, Yokichi, all dead. You will be next on the list if you don't co-operate with us.'

Walden was now visibly trembling. 'Who are you two? Police, CIA, what?'

Wyatt said: 'You could call us police. We try to uphold the law. At the moment we're concerned citizens who are fed up with scum like you turning our world into a charnel house.'

'What are you talking about? What have I done?'

'Silk Fist, that's what you've done.'

Walden was sweating. 'If you know about MKUltra then I

understand why you have come to investigate me but I have nothing to do with Silk Fist. All that CIA stuff was years ago. I moved back to France years ago. All I do now is manufacture cosmetics.'

Linda came out of Walden's office and said: 'There are locked drawers and a locked safe in here. Please come in and open them, Mr Walden.'

Walden did as he was asked. They started with the filing cabinet drawers. Linda spent several minutes leafing through sales orders and accounts. Then Walden opened the safe. There was a stack of banknotes and a small pistol inside, together with more papers.

Wyatt said: 'You told us you don't keep cash on the premises. You're a little fibber, Mr Walden.'

'It's for emergencies,' Walden protested. 'The gun as well. For emergencies. Take the money, and the gun if you like.'

Linda said: 'We are not here to steal, Mr Walden, but we do want answers, very quickly.'

'What about stuff on the computer?' Wyatt asked.

'That would take too long,' Linda said. 'I'm sure if Mr Walden has any incriminating information about Hiatus it will be well protected by passwords and firewalls.'

Wyatt held up his pistol. 'I have a very good device for ascertaining passwords from recalcitrant businessmen.'

'Even so, it would be easier to find where Monsieur Walden is actually manufacturing Hiatus.'

'A fair point,' Wyatt said. 'Let's continue the tour.'

Walden led them across the despatch area and along a short corridor. 'Through these doors is the manufacturing zone. Look around at what you like but please be careful, this is a clean room.'

Wyatt and Linda followed him through. The clean room was lit with a harsh white glare that reflected off chrome, glass and plastic. Linda searched but could find nothing.

Wyatt asked Walden: 'What's next?'

'My research laboratory. I don't need to do much research

because I buy the formula for most of my products and tweak them.'

'Clever,' Wyatt said. 'Let's take a look.'

'It's a secure area,' Walden said as he led them out into the corridor. 'I have to unlock the door with a security code. Only myself and my assistant manager are allowed through here.'

'How convenient,' Wyatt said.

They went into the small laboratory and again Linda searched without success. She said to Wyatt: 'I don't know. It looks legitimate but I'm not sure what all these chemicals and potions are for. We need an expert.'

At the far end of the laboratory was a row of three doors.

'What are they?' Linda asked.

'Storage cupboards,' Walden said. 'Here, come and look.' He opened the first door. The cupboard contained brooms, cleaning equipment and vacuum cleaners. The second cupboard was a storeroom for packaging materials. The third door was locked. Walden said: 'This is where I keep dangerous chemicals or fluids.'

'Let's see it,' Wyatt ordered.

Walden unlocked the door. Inside there were floor to ceiling racks on either side stacked with carboys, tins, bottles and jars of various sizes.

Linda went inside to look at the labels and contents. After several minues she said: 'I'm not sure. It all seems legitimate.'

Wyatt said: 'Mr Walden, it seems odd to keep packaging materials needed in the despatch department here in a locked and secure lab.'

'It's a security measure. Staff will steal anything if given the chance.'

'What if you are not here to open the door if such material is needed by your workers.'

'Then my assistant manager will be here.'

Linda and Wyatt stood and stared into the third cupboard as if an answer might magically materialise.

A voice behind them ordered: 'Placez vos mains sur votre títe.'

Linda and Wyatt turned to see two men wearing ski masks and pointing submachine guns.

Wyatt asked Linda: 'What did he say?'

'He said put your hands on your head.'

Walden, now cockily certain, said: 'Give me your pistol, Mr Whoever-you-are.'

Wyatt handed over his pistol and put his hands on his head.

Walden said to Linda: 'What about you, Miss Nosey Fucker? Are you armed?'

'No,' Linda said.

'Nevertheless, it will be my pleasure to search you.'

Walden checked Linda's overcoat pockets, then put his hands inside her overcoat and slowly ran his hands all over her body. His breathing was laboured and his bald pate beaded with perspiration.

Walden turned to the gunmen and said in French: 'You two took your time.'

There was no response from the gunmen. Walden turned back to Wyatt and Linda. 'Big mistake, you interfering fuckers. It will cost you your lives.'

Wyatt said: 'How will you explain two bodies and bloodstains all over the wall?'

'These men will kill you with the minimum mess. I can clean up the lab and outside I have several barrels full of sulphuric acid. I'm afraid they will be your last resting place. Within a day all trace of your existence will have dissolved.'

Wyatt said: 'It takes longer than a day, Walden.'

'Not if you add water and a certain other chemical in the right proportion. You forget that I am a brilliant research chemist. You two are failed detectives.' He turned to the gunmen to issue an order.

Wyatt whispered: 'Any ideas, Linda, because I'm fresh out.'

To Wyatt's surprise Linda said loudly: 'Monsieur Walden, after you have killed us I've no doubt that you will miss your wife Monique.'

Walden turned back warily. 'What are you saying?'

'You're wife, Monique. She enjoys her part time job at the old peoples' centre. You two seem happy together, and your children are enchanting. The two girls, Valerie and Eugenie, and your little boy Raphael. Such a charming little house on the Rue Delambre. Number sixteen, isn't it?'

'Are you threatening my family?'

'Yes. Do you really think that we'd come here alone, without any back-up or insurance? If we don't return by midnight then loyal Monique, pretty little Valerie and Eugenie and little Raphael will all die. I'm sure Raphael will be very brave when the knife is being drawn across his throat.'

'You're bluffing,' Walden said, without conviction.

'Not at all. Thanks to your stupidity in summoning those two apes with machine guns, you have proved that you're involved with Silk Fist. We were about to leave empty handed. We are forced to be as ruthless in stopping Silk Fist maniacs as you are in committing these crimes, so if we die, Monique, Valerie, Eugenie and Raphael will also die.' Linda pronounced the four names slowly and with emphasis.

Walden hesitated for several moments. Then he turned to the two gunmen and said in French: 'You can go. I have made a mistake. You will be paid a bonus for your trouble.'

The two thugs backed away out into the corridor and disappeared.

Wyatt asked: 'Are they Silk Fist?'

'No,' Walden said. 'They are local muscle on retainer for situations like this. But you win. I love my wife and family. I would rather die myself than let you harm them. I'm afraid I am going to be sick.'

Wyatt said: 'My pistol, if you please, before you heave your guts up.'

Walden handed back the Glock and rushed over to one of the small aluminium sinks.

As Walden was noisily retching, Wyatt said quietly: 'That was brilliant, Linda. How did you know about his family?'

'I talked to someone at that old peoples' centre when we were searching for Walden. We had a long gossipy conversation. The Waldens are a well-liked family. You enjoyed my performance?'

'Enjoyed? You scared the shit out of me. You even had me believing you were an insane psycopath. Now we know that Walden is involved with Silk Fist we have to find some proof.'

'I was about to say, before those two gangsters rudely interrupted us, that this factory is shorter on the inside than it is on the outside.'

'What do you mean?'

'When we walked past the factory, that road sign outside looked to be situated about two thirds along the length of this unit but here we are seemingly at the end of the unit.'

Wyatt said with admiration: 'You're on fire tonight, Linda. I'm bloody glad you're here.'

Walden staggered back. His face was chalk white and all the fight had gone out of him.

Wyatt said: 'Now we'll go through to where you make Hiatus.'

Walden did not even argue. He stepped into the secure chemical cupboard and opened a hidden door built flush into the far wall.

They went through into a small windowless laboratory. This time there was no doubt. There were several bottles and packages containing tablets identical in shape and colour to those found in Linda's apartment.

Wyatt picked up two bottles and put them in his jacket pocket. 'We'll take these for analysis. Question one, Walden, if you want your family to live. Apart from testosterone and MAO inhibitor, what is the active ingredient of the Hiatus drug?'

'Hiatus is a precise cocktail of testosterone, MAO inhibitor, scopolamine, temazepam and sodium thiopental.'

Wyatt said: 'Write down the formula for making Hiatus.

Precisely, please. If you lie or try to deceive us you understand what the consequences will be.'

Walden said: 'Can I sit down?'

'Go ahead.'

Walden drew out a laboratory stool and sat down. He took a ballpoint pen from his jacket pocket and found a yellow notepad in a desk drawer. He wrote down the formula and handed it to Linda.

Linda looked at it and said: 'Is this what Doctor Jaso referred to as the Holy Grail of Project MKKaput?'

'Yes. By administering that drug we found we could make anyone do anything, even destroy their own life.'

Wyatt said: 'Who is behind Silk Fist?'

'I don't know. I was involved with Delta and Kaput but I got out years ago. I wanted to get right away from the States so I came here and started this business. I thought I'd got out completely but about a year ago someone came to see me and said that I had to start manufacturing this Hiatus drug in quantity. I refused but he did as you did and threatened my family. Now I'm caught between you two, and whoever you represent, and Silk Fist. Whatever I do now, my family dies.'

'Not if you co-operate with us,' Linda said. 'Believe it or not we're the good guys and we've got a bigger army than Silk Fist. You deal squarely with us and we'll protect you and your family. Who is this man who came to see you?'

'I swear I don't know. He knew all about Delta and Ultra but he wasn't one of the old scientists. I agreed to start making Hiatus but I never dreamt they would use it to kill so many people.'

'Who are "they", Walden? Give us names?'

'You'll have to shoot me because I don't know.'

Linda asked: 'What happens to Hiatus after its manufactured? Where do you deliver it?'

'I don't. Hiatus is made in capsule or intravenous injection form and has to be made carefully. The proportion of the ingredients of the cocktail have to be very precise or else the drug is not as effective.

I can't make much at one time. A courier arrives every two weeks and takes the latest batch. I don't know where he takes it.'

Linda said: 'Does the courier come here to the factory?'

'No, that wouldn't be safe. I meet him in the Davout.'

'What's that?'

'The public park.'

'When is this courier due next?'

'In three days, on Sunday.'

Wyatt said to Linda: 'Let's talk tactics.'

They led Walden back out into the laboratory and locked him in the broom cupboard, then moved out of earshot.

Wyatt said: 'We could either go straight to our superiors with what we've found or try to follow it up ourselves.'

Linda said: 'I think we should tell Prem exactly what we've found out about this place in case anything happens to us but we should try to follow this courier ourselves. If the SWAT teams come in heavy handed then Silk Fist may close down and disappear before we can find out who they are and why they've been committing these atrocities. Also, if Silk Fist has threatened Walden's family we might endanger them by making the wrong move. We've caught Walden in a situation where he will do anything we say for fear of losing his family, so he'll keep quiet.'

'Then we wait for this courier and see where he leads us?'

'I think that's the best option,' Linda said. 'If the courier leads us nowhere then we hand Walden over to the authorities.'

'Agreed,' Wyatt said.

They went back into the laboratory and unlocked the broom cupboard.

Walden asked: 'What are you going to do to me?'

Linda said: 'Why, nothing, Mr Walden. Except this.' She punched Walden in the belly with all her force. Walden's face turned purple and he fell on to his hands and knees. Linda said: 'That's for feeling me up, you sweaty little pervert.'

Wyatt said to Walden: 'You will carry on with your normal life exactly as before but remember that if you betray us to Silk Fist or anyone else, then you and your family will die. If you co-operate fully then we will do our utmost to protect your family. Do we have a deal?'

Walden was trying to regain his breath. 'Yes. I'll go along with whatever you want.'

'Then you are going to meet this courier as usual on Sunday. We'll see where he leads us.'

46

La place Davout, Savigny-sur-Orge, near Paris, France,
May 1st

Linda watched impatiently as Wyatt strolled back to the car. The park was crowded with picnickers and children playing games around the huge skeleton globe, all celebrating May Day and enjoying the sunshine. Wyatt stopped for a kickabout with a group of young boys. Linda beeped the car horn.

Eventually Wyatt climbed into the passenger seat and said: 'All set.'

Linda said: 'About time, if you've quite finished playing soccer. He's moving off now.'

'Okay, I'll check that the trackers are working then we've no need to get too close.' Wyatt opened the laptop. 'By the way, the name of that game is football, not soccer. What did you think of my dribbling?'

'Of your *what*?'

'My dribbling. My footwork. I showed those kids a thing or two.'

'Very impressive… not.' Linda engaged gear and drove slowly down Rue du Mail. The courier's car was a nondescript dark blue Renault.

Wyatt said: 'The tracker in the handle of the case is working. Also the one on his car. We've got him bagged up.'

'Umm, don't count your chickens yet.'

'He's turned on to the D167 Charles de Gaulle. Let's pray that he's heading for the A6 autoroute to Paris and not heading for Orly airport. If he's catching a flight we're done for.'

'Walden was positive that the courier had never mentioned flying,' Linda said.

'Doesn't mean that he doesn't fly. I'm still not sure we can trust Walden.'

'I think we have him sufficiently terrified to have told us the truth.'

'After your queen bitch act I'd agree with you. Good, he's turning on to the D25 Henri Dunant. He must be heading for the main route into Paris.'

Linda turned on to the D25 after letting four cars get between their car and the courier. 'I can still see him. He's obeying all the speed limits. There are the signs to the A6.'

They travelled without speaking while Linda negotiated the tricky entry ramp. Then Wyatt said: 'Looks like Paris. That's the way he's heading.'

Linda turned on to the main carriageway and joined the stream of Sunday traffic heading for the capital. She asked: 'What did this guy look like?'

'He's white, in his forties, an inch or two shorter than me, clean shaven, brown hair cut neatly and fairly short, dressed casually in a beige zip-up, jeans, and those green and white Dunlop tennis shoes.'

'Handy if he has to run for it.'

They passed Chilly-Mazarin. Wyatt said: 'At this rate we'll be in Paris well within the hour. It's only about ten miles to the centre.'

Linda said: 'It'll be good to see Paris again. There's no other city like it for a mixture of culture and romance.' She indicated the smooth three-lane ribbon of road in front of them. 'The French do things with panache. Even this road is called the Autoroute du Soleil.'

'What does that mean?'

'The Highway to the Sun.'

'Very poetic. How long did you study in Paris?'

'About six months, when I was seventeen. Me and a few other

Sweet Briar girls. We had a ball but we were carefully chaperoned.'

'That's a pity.'

Linda smiled fondly at her memories. 'We still managed to sneak out a few times.'

Wyatt said: 'Orly Airport coming up on the right. Damn, he's indicating a turn.'

'Which way? Not right to the airport?'

'No, he's turned the other way, on to the A86.'

'That's out towards Versailles if I remember right.'

'Looks like that's where he's heading... no, he's turning again, right on to the D920. Towards Bourg-la-Reine.'

'Bourg-la-Reine? Why's he going there?'

They followed the courier through the tree-lined suburbs of the town. The Renault entered the town square and parked at the side of the road. Linda slowed down and parked on the other side of the square.

Wyatt said: 'He's getting out. He's taking the goods with him. The bag tracker is still okay. He's going into that hotel.'

Linda said: 'I'll turn around and find a parking space from where we can watch the entrance.'

Linda drove a circuit of the square and found a parking space that provided a clear view of the hotel entrance. She said: 'We're lucky it's a Sunday with not too many vehicles cluttering up the square.'

Wyatt looked at his watch. 'It's two thirty. He might be meeting someone in the hotel. It's too late for lunch.'

Linda chuckled. 'We're in France now, Wyatt, not England. Should we go in?'

'I don't know. We don't want to alert him or frighten him off.'

'Perhaps he's spotted us tailing him? He might slip out the back way.'

'You're right,' Wyatt said. 'I'll go take a look.'

Five minutes later Wyatt came back to the car and got in. 'There is a back entrance but it's protected by locked gates that only open from the inside. Unless he's got an accomplice in the hotel he can't get out that way.'

'He could climb out of a window, especially if he discovers the trackers.'

'I planted the tracker well underneath his car and he hasn't looked there. The tracker in the bag handle is well hidden. Unless he takes the handle apart he can't know it's there.'

Linda said: 'I think I should go in. I speak the language. I can look around, perhaps find out where he is, if he's booked a room or whatever.'

'Okay, but don't spook him.'

'Trust me,' Linda said as she got out of the car.

Linda walked across the square and went in to the hotel.

Wyatt waited anxiously, forcing himself to restrain his impatience.

Linda came out again after ten minutes. She got back in the car and said: 'This hotel is renowned for its cuisine. He's in the restaurant eating lunch. The bag was on the floor by his side. He's reading a newspaper and there is no-one else with him. He looked completely relaxed. I don't think he knows we're on to him.'

'So what do we do?'

'All we can do is stake him out until he makes his next move, even if we have to stay here all night.'

Ninety minutes later Wyatt said impatiently: 'While our quarry is inside stuffing his face I'm out here starving. How about you?'

'I could eat something.'

'I noticed a boulangerie around the corner as we were coming in. I could nip out and get us something.'

Linda said: 'You're in France now, on a Sunday afternoon and on May Day. It won't be open.'

'There must be somewhere to provide succour for the weary traveller. I'll take a quick look to see if anything is open.'

Wyatt opened the car door. At that moment a man walked out of the hotel. He was wearing a green anorak, hood raised, and carrying an ordinary plastic shopping bag. He turned to his left and then hurried around the corner away from the town square.

Linda said: 'That was him! That was the courier! I caught a glimpse of his green and white Dunlops.'

'Are you sure? The tracker says he's still in the hotel.'

Linda waved her hand impatiently. 'No, that was him. Go after him.'

'He'll have to come back for his car.'

'Jeez, Chris, go after the guy! We might lose him. If I'm wrong then we've lost nothing. If I'm right then you have to follow him.'

Wyatt got out and ran across the town square. He turned down the road that the courier had taken and spotted the green anorak far ahead. Wyatt took out his cell phone and rang Linda. 'He's heading for the railway station. I'll keep following and try to find out where he's going.'

'Okay.'

'Linda, how do I ask for a ticket in French.'

'Just say "billet simple à Paris", that means single ticket to Paris, or wherever he's going, "s'il vous plaît".'

'Okay, that's easy for you to say.'

Wyatt followed the courier into the station. The courier presented a railcard and was allowed straight through on to the platform. Wyatt went to the ticket window, bought a ticket to Paris and, not waiting for the change, went through on to the long curving platform. He moved as far away from the courier as possible and half-concealed himself behind a square column. He rang Linda. 'I'm on the platform. He's heading for Paris. I'll confirm when we're both on the train.'

'Why doesn't he carry on by car? Perhaps he's spotted our tail?'

'I'm not sure. Perhaps he's doing standard procedure to shake off any possible tail. There are big things at stake with what he's carrying. We'll keep in touch and you can drive to meet me.'

Five minutes later the RER B train to Paris pulled in. Wyatt boarded the same carriage as the courier and took a seat at the opposite end. The carriage was full enough to distract from his presence. The train pulled out. Wyatt rang Linda and said airily: 'Hello, darling. I'm on the train. Should be in Paris to meet you on time.'

Wyatt tried to relax as the train sped through the suburbs of Paris. At each of eight stops Wyatt carefully watched the courier for any sudden movement. The train had pulled into the heart of the city before the courier made his move. He abruptly stood up and walked out of the carriage. Wyatt followed. After they had left the station and were out on the street, Wyatt rang Linda. 'We're off the train, in the middle of Paris.'

'Whereabouts are you?'

'We got off at a station called St Michel-Notre Dame. There's Notre Dame cathedral in front of me and away to my right.'

'Then you're at the Île de la Cité.'

'The courier is turning the other way towards an old bridge. It's a famous bridge, I've seen pictures of it.'

'That's the Pont Neuf.'

'He's walking fast. Where are you?'

'I'm a couple of miles away. The traffic is heavy.'

'He's crossing the Pont Neuf. I'm well in touch. I don't think he's seen me. There's plenty of people milling about to hide me.'

Wyatt had to walk faster to keep in touch as the grey waters of the Seine and a river boat decorated with flowers passed under the ancient bridge.

He said to Linda: 'Now we're heading along Rue de Pont Neuf.'

'Okay, the traffic is moving fairly well. I'm coming in from the east along Quai de Bercy.'

'Looks like he's heading for something called Les Halles. I can see a big building off to the left with rows of columns like some Greek temple.'

'That's probably the Bourse. Listen, Chris, if he's trying to shake you off then Les Halles is the best place in Paris to do it. It's a sunken rabbit warren of shops and underground platforms. You have to stay with him.'

'I see what you mean, I'm already looking down at it. This place is amazing. It looks like a cascade of glass and steel with a huge drum stuck in the middle.'

'I know!' Linda shouted. 'Don't stand there gawping, get after the guy. I'll be there in ten minutes.'

Wyatt followed the courier down to the underground railway station. The courier flashed his railcard and was immediately allowed through. Wyatt thought about jumping the manned turnstiles but realised that he would be detained and that would be the best way to lose the courier.

Wyatt accepted he had already been blocked and outsmarted. He had to spend several minutes buying a ticket. He ran down to the platform to find it packed with travellers pushing forward as a train rumbled into the station. Wyatt shoved his way through, ignoring the obscenities and frantically looking around. He glimpsed a flash of green at the opposite end of the platform.

Wyatt barged his way through the throng and ran up a flight of steps, across the concourse, and up more steps and out into the street. He could not see the green anorak. He ran up and down the pavement but could not spot the courier.

In desperation he shinned up a lamp post to get some height. There were hundreds of people walking in every direction. Some looked up at him and made comments.

Then Wyatt noticed something green in a waste bin attached to a lamp post down the street. He leapt down and ran to the bin. He pulled out the green anorak. He searched the garment for labels or any possible clues but it was cheap and mass-produced and provided nothing. He stuffed it back in the bin.

With a heavy heart Wyatt took out his cell phone and rang Linda. 'I've lost him.'

'Damn. I'm just turning into Les Halles. Where are you?'

Wyatt looked around. 'I've no idea.'

'Okay, can you see the Bourse?'

'Yes.'

'I'll park and I'll meet you somewhere outside the Bourse.'

Wyatt trudged along the street and leaned on the cast iron railing that surrounded the Bourse. He had been outwitted and felt inadequate and overwhelmed with failure.

Linda arrived ten minutes later.

Wyatt could hardly look her in the face, He said: 'I'm so sorry, Linda. He outfoxed me. You were right. He disappeared into that warren of underground stations and I couldn't follow him.'

Linda said: 'Well, don't beat yourself up, Chris. We gave it our best shot. At least we've found Walden and the Hiatus factory. This is the end of the line for us. We'll have to hand the evidence over to our bosses and they'll have to run with it.'

'Which means that whoever is controlling Silk Fist will close up shop and disappear. Walden was making the drug but he's small potatoes. We've missed the big fish. The courier has probably handed over that parcel by now. It must be a handover because he can't post it on a Sunday, even if the post offices were open. It's gone five o'clock.'

Wyatt was astonished to see Linda break into a wide smile. He asked: 'What's so funny?'

'Chris, we have one more chance. There is only one post office in the whole of Europe that is open every day, all day, and all year, and it's the Central Post Office in Paris.' She pointed and took Wyatt's hand. 'There it is down the street. Come on. It's a long shot but worth a try.'

As they ran down the Rue du Louvre towards the post office, Wyatt said: 'If this comes off I swear I'll buy you dinner at the best restaurant we can find.'

There were only a few people being served in the Central Post Office and Linda went to an available window being serviced by a male teller. She gave him her most winning smile through the plexiglass screen. 'Good afternoon, sir. I'm sorry to be a nuisance but my husband brought a parcel in for posting not so long ago. He put the wrong address on it. Would it be possible for me to retrieve the parcel and correct the address?'

The teller said: 'I regret, madame, but we cannot give the parcel back to you.'

'Oh, no, no. You could correct the address for me. It's a distinctive parcel. Strong brown paper and sealed with Scotch tape in a tartan pattern. Yes, I can see it on the shelf behind you.'

The teller looked around, slid off his stool and took down the parcel. He came back and displayed the address through the security glass. Linda committed it to memory. She said: 'Oh, I owe my husband an apology. That is the correct address after all. I'm sorry to have troubled you.'

'Not at all, madame.'

Linda went to an empty counter and wrote down the address on a slip of paper.

Wyatt was pacing up and down the pavement when Linda came out. She said: 'Bingo!' and handed the slip of paper to Wyatt. She noted the expression on Wyatt's face. 'Does that address mean something to you, Chris?'

'Yes, it does. I wish it didn't, but it does.'

Linda smiled. 'Nevertheless, you owe me dinner, and we haven't eaten since this morning. I've got a yen for caviar and lobster.'

Wyatt looked at the address again. 'And I've lost my appetite.'

47

Block C, Bevin Estate, Newham, London, May 4th

Linda said: 'This stairway stinks. We should have taken the elevator.'

Wyatt said: 'Believe me, the lift would have smelled a lot worse.'

'It's hard to believe that people have to live in such harsh concrete squalor.'

'That's why I advised you to dress in jeans or something you wouldn't mind burning afterwards. And this is one of the better sink estates.'

'*What* estates?'

'In Britain these grim council-owned tower blocks are called sink estates. When you can't sink any lower you end up living here. This is it, sixth floor.'

Wyatt pushed through a swing door that was covered with graffiti. On the other side was a long concrete balcony with eight doorways, all painted in different colours in a half-hearted attempt to provide character and individuality.

The balcony was protected by a high red brick balustrade domed with concrete. Linda stood on tip-toe and looked down at the cracked weed strewn paths, the struggling brown grass and the litter blowing through the rusted swings of the childrens' play area below. A chilly wind whipped into her face.

Wyatt said: 'This place would destroy Charlie's dream of fairy tale England.'

'You've got that right. It's a long way from the sweet-smelling orange groves of Florida. Let's get this done and get out of here.'

Wyatt led the way to a paint-peeling light blue door in the middle of the row. 'This is it.'

There was no door knocker so Wyatt rapped on the wood with his knuckles. They waited for several seconds but there was no answer and no sign of movement behind the small frosted glass door pane. Wyatt knocked again. Still there was no response.

Wyatt hunched down and pressed open the letterbox. He peered through the gap and then made a face. 'Judging by the smell there's somebody in there smoking weed. They've never heard of disinfectant and cleaning products either. I can hear someone whispering. He's in there.'

Wyatt knocked again. Still there was no answer. He took out his pistol and said: 'I think we should go in.'

Linda nodded and took out her gun. 'What if the neighbours hear us going in?'

'They'll lock their own front doors and mind their own business. It's what they do in places like this.'

They looked around to check that they were unobserved.

Linda said: 'Looks all clear.'

Wyatt stepped back to the balustrade and then launched himself shoulder-first at the door. The cheap wooden door gave way and Wyatt nearly fell over as he crashed into the hallway. Linda moved in and covered him while he steadied himself. They could hear urgent whispered conversation from the living room on the right. Wyatt kicked open the door.

A man and a woman, both in their forties, were attempting to dress themselves as quickly as they could. The coffee table in front of the sofa was covered with beer bottles, a whisky bottle, and empty pizza boxes. The widescreen television was on mute. A porn movie was showing.

Wyatt said: 'Party's over, Jimmy.'

'Who the fuck are you?' Jimmy said. It was an attempt at bravado but Jimmy was badly frightened. He shakily tried to pull a cheap T-shirt over his naked beer belly torso.

The woman was dressing nonchalantly, unconcerned that she was being watched.

Wyatt asked her: 'Who are you?'

The woman, voluptuous, hard-faced, with too much make-up and dyed black hair, stared back at Wyatt and then said: 'I'm Jimmy's part-time professional girlfriend. If you've come to kill him, let me get out of the way first, after he's paid me.'

Jimmy looked at her incredulously. 'You fucking bitch!'

'That's exactly what you're paying for. What did you expect, that I'd fall in love with you? Give me my fifty quid.'

'You fuck off.'

Wyatt said: 'Give her the money. I want her out of here.'

Jimmy made a sound of disgust, took out a wallet from his jeans pocket and gave the woman fifty pounds. She picked up her bag and put the money inside. She said: 'Bye, Jimmy.' She looked at Wyatt with glazed weed-shot eyes as she shoved past him. She said: 'If you ever want to try your other weapon, give me a call.'

The woman left the room. Wyatt glanced out to make sure she had left and closed the damaged front door. 'Nice girl, Jimmy,' he said. 'Classy.'

Linda switched off the television.

'Who are you?' Jimmy asked, the fight seeping out of him.

Wyatt said: 'We're the parcel police. This place is a tip but you seem to have plenty of money, for televisions, whores, marijuana, booze, pizza, all in the afternoon. The dole money must have increased since I was out of the country.'

'What do you mean "parcel police"?'

Linda said: 'We're looking for a parcel, about the size of a large box of wash powder, if you know what that is. It's wrapped in thick brown paper and sealed with tartan Scotch tape. It was posted from France on Sunday.'

'Are you the police? Have you got a warrant?'

Wyatt said: 'As it happens, I am with the Metropolitan police.' He indicated his Glock pistol. 'This is my warrant.'

'If you are with the Met police I'll get you sacked for this.'

'Give us the parcel, Jimmy.'

'Get stuffed.'

Wyatt said: 'Cover him, Linda, while I search the place.'

Jimmy looked at Linda: 'You wouldn't shoot me. You don't look the type.'

Wyatt said: 'I wouldn't bank on that, Jimmy. The Bishop of Carlisle made that mistake. He's dead.'

Wyatt started with the sideboard and found the parcel in the bottom drawer. 'That was easy! What happens to these parcels, Jimmy.'

'I'm not telling you anything.'

'Okay, then let me take a guess.' Wyatt whispered in his ear.

Jimmy slumped down on the sofa and took a swig of whisky straight from the bottle.

Wyatt picked up a cell phone from the coffee table. 'Is this your mobile, Jimmy?'

Jimmy nodded.

'Then if you want to keep your squalid little lifestyle, make the call.'

Two hours later they heard the damaged front door being pushed open. A voice called: 'Jimmy! What happened to the front door? Are you okay?'

Wyatt nodded to indicate that Jimmy should reply. He shouted back: 'I'm okay. I'm in the living room.'

The visitor came through into the living room to find Linda Marquez holding a gun at Jimmy's head.

The visitor, shaken, said lamely: 'What's going on?'

Wyatt pushed the door closed and stepped out. 'She's with me, boss.'

Assistant Commissioner Sangita Sherman turned around and gasped. 'Chris! What are you doing here?'

Wyatt said: 'A better question would be what are *you* doing here, boss?'

'I'm here to check on Jimmy. He's a friend of the family and rang me to say that someone had broken into his flat.'

'Then why have you arrived out of uniform and without back-up?' Wyatt shook his head. 'Let's cut out the bullshit. I have a brother but I don't refer to him as a "friend of the family". I never thought I'd say this about you, boss, but it was stupid and careless to walk in here without knowing what had happened. Still more stupid to get mixed-up in what you've got mixed-up with. Why don't you sit down, if you can find a clean armchair. You remember Sergeant Linda Marquez of the US Secret Service, don't you?'

Sherman sat down. 'Yes. How are you?'

'Apart from losing my husband, my godfather, my job and damn nearly my life, thanks to people like you, I'm fine, thank you.'

Sherman said: 'What are you talking about?'

Wyatt picked up the parcel. 'What's in here, boss?'

'I don't know. It's probably drugs.'

'It certainly is drugs. How did you get involved with Silk Fist?'

Sherman's eyes widened in surprise. 'Silk Fist? Are you insane, Chris? I have nothing to do with Silk Fist!'

'Then why are you receiving parcels from Silk Fist operatives by using your little brother here as a cut-out?'

'How did you find out Jimmy was my brother?'

'Jamil Karson Desai. A distinctive name, not easily forgotten. As Sun Tzu wisely advises in *The Art of War* you should know as much as possible about your enemy but I've found that it can be just as useful to know as much as possible about the people who have power over you. I was intrigued after I found out that you and your family had been expelled from Uganda during the Seventies, along with hundreds of other decent Asian families. I discovered that

Jimmy was your little brother but that somehow you had failed to mention his existence during your rapid rise through the Metropolitan police. I can understand why. It's not something that would look good on your CV, a useless, drug-addicted wastrel scumbag as a brother.'

'Hey!' Jimmy protested. 'I'm sitting right here!'

Sherman said: 'So why didn't you give me away?'

'Because I like you. You're a damn good copper and you always supported me. I could well understand why you wanted to keep little Jimmy a secret.'

'I don't think you understand at all,' Sherman said with unexpected vehemence. 'The family lost everything when we were expelled from Uganda. People react in different ways. Jamil was very young and he was traumatised. He never recovered. You can easily call him a wastrel scumbag but you don't understand what it was like.'

'So how come you battled your way to the top?'

'As I said, different people react in different ways. After suffering under Idi Amin's regime I appreciated the importance of the law. I'm proud of what I achieved, I'm proud of my career, but something else has been more important to me.'

'What's that?'

'Money, Chris. Lots of it. Until you've been penniless you can't understand.' Sherman looked at Linda. 'When you've always been rich, like Miss Agent of the Year over there, you can afford to look down your nose at us, like she's doing right now. I love Jamil, I've supported him all these years because he deserved it. He'd lost everything else. How he lives his life is his affair. We've had to endure racism from every quarter.'

Linda said angrily: 'Before you try to take any more of the moral high ground, Assistant Commissioner, we've been working with another agent. He is from India. His wife was torn to pieces in front of his eyes because of the shit contained in that parcel. I know all about racism. You can justify your life any way you want, you can think what you like about me, but I'd never sink so low as to cause the deaths of innocent people by taking money from Silk Fist.'

'What do you keep mentioning Silk Fist?' Sherman asked wearily. 'I've had nothing to do with Silk Fist.'

Wyatt considered Sherman's reply and said to Linda: 'I can tell when Mrs Sherman is lying. I believe she's been duped by Silk Fist.'

Sherman said: 'Tell me what you think is in that parcel.'

Wyatt looked at Linda.

Linda said: 'Okay. I trust your judgment, Chris. If you want to tell her exactly what crap she's landed herself in then go ahead.'

Wyatt explained what they had discovered about Silk Fist and about the contents of the parcel.

When he had finished, Sherman said with resignation: 'If all that is true, I'm finished.'

Linda said: 'It's true, Assistant Commissioner. You better believe it.'

Jimmy asked: 'What am I going to do if sis loses her job?'

Wyatt said: 'You could try a little scheme that most of us use to earn money. It's spelt w-o-r-k.' He turned to Sherman. 'Many more people are going to die unless you tell us everything. But first, when we were at St Paul's Cathedral for the Princess Royal's funeral that day, why did you call me away from my assigned station?'

'I was paid to do it. Paid well. I didn't ask why. I couldn't see much harm or danger in it.'

'Who paid you?'

'I don't know. The money was sent through the post. I accepted it and didn't ask questions.'

Linda said: 'Where do these parcels go, Mrs Sherman?'

'Some were collected from me by various couriers. Who they were or who sent the couriers I don't know. Most parcels went to America in the diplomatic bag.'

'You had access to the diplomatic bag?' Wyatt said incredulously.

'Yes. It was a safe way of getting the parcels to the States. Diplomatic luggage is immune from search by the American authorities. I thought it was probably drugs in those parcels, the usual drugs like heroin or cocaine. I didn't know is was this Hiatus stuff you talked about.'

Linda asked: 'How did you get access to this diplomatic bag?'

Sherman looked at her brother uncomfortably. 'I persuaded the Foreign Secretary to give me access.'

'That old lecher Richard Harcourt?' Wyatt said. 'How did you persuade him?'

'I think we can all guess,' Linda said. 'Is he involved in Silk Fist?'

'No. I approached him first. He wasn't concerned about what was in the parcels as long as I did what he asked.'

'Bloody hell, sis,' Jimmy said.

'Don't be so shocked, Jamil. Your lifestyle and our survival comes at a cost. You've been protected for too long.'

'Who were the parcels sent to in the States?' Linda asked.

'I don't know.'

Wyatt said: 'You're not giving us much here, boss. We want names. Who persuaded you to get involved with all this?'

Sherman did not reply.

'You have to tell us,' Linda said.

'No,' Sherman said. 'I will not tell you. I am not going to betray a friend I once loved dearly.'

Linda raised her pistol but Wyatt shook his head.

Wyatt said: 'Boss, many people have died because of your actions. Your career in the Metropolitan police is over. If you refuse to give us the name of this "dear friend" then we'll hand you over to the British and American authorities. Another extraordinary rendition and a spot of light waterboarding in a CIA black house will soon persuade you to give the name. Your life and career will be utterly wrecked. I believe that you were duped and didn't know you were working for Silk Fist. If you give us the name now, and co-operate with us, we'll leave you in place to carry on as Assistant Commissioner for the time being.'

'Why would you do that?' Sherman asked suspiciously.

'Because I want my name cleared with the British authorities and Linda wants her name cleared with her people. You give us the name and I swear we'll help you get out of this mess with some sort of reputation intact. Probably the only job you'll be able to get is on the checkout at Tesco and your only home will be dump like this, but even this dump is better than Guantanamo Bay.'

'So what are you saying? If I give you this name you will let me stay as Assistant Commissioner and say nothing?'

'For the time being. Your power and influence might be useful to us. The crap will hit the fan one day soon and you'll have to go, but you are more use to us as Assistant Commissioner than you would be banged up in a cell. Do we have a deal?'

Sherman nodded. 'I have no choice. You're one of the few people in the world I do trust. You've always backed me up and you're loyal and honest. Okay, I was recruited by a man I first met at university in Oxford. I was in love with him and still am, but he was ambitious, shrewd and wanted the world. He's damn nearly got it.'

'Who is it, boss?'

'Philip Mountfitchet.'

Wyatt almost laughed. 'You mean Lord Mountfitchet, the Billionaire Baron?'

'Yes. I don't see what is so funny.'

'Why would he have anything to do with Silk Fist? According to the papers he's got it all anyway. Why would he risk everything for tawdry acts of terrorism, which is basically what Silk Fist is all about?'

'I have no idea,' Sherman said. 'He was already rich when I first met him. His family are rich, distantly related to the royal family, and Philip started investing when he was still at Eton. He founded

Nobar Holdings. He has a genius for business, investment and playing the markets.'

Linda said: 'No doubt his wealth was part of the attraction for you.'

'He was tall, handsome, fair-haired, aristocratic, rich and charming. What woman wouldn't be interested in a package like that?'

Linda said: 'It must have been painful for you to watch him going out with a string of glamorous women before he married that beautiful Swedish countess. So blonde, so Nordic, so unlike yourself.'

'You really are a bitch,' Sherman spat.

'No, I'm a policewoman, like you, but I haven't sold out my integrity, my country and my fellow human beings.'

Sherman said: 'Whatever you think about me, you won't pin anything on Philip. If he is involved in Silk Fist then he's been duped, like me. He is scrupulously honest and a genius and some people can't accept that.'

Wyatt said: 'Where can I find this genius?'

'He lives on a yacht. He moves around a lot, London, New York, Monaco, Bermuda.'

'Do you know where he is at the moment?'

'No, but I can find out.'

Wyatt picked up the parcel. 'It's time that the Billionaire Baron had a personal delivery from me. I'll need your authority to get this through customs, boss.'

'If I do, will you promise not to harm him?'

'It's up to Mountfitchet whether he gets himself harmed or not, and you're in no position to make bargains. What do you think, Linda?'

'You should go and pay your respects to this exalted aristocrat. It's time I mended fences on my side of the pond.'

'Will you give me time for a talk with Lord Mountfitchet?'

'Of course, but we can't keep all this to ourselves any longer. We can now prove that we are innocent of any involvement in Silk Fist. The Indian authorities have the formula for Hiatus and Prem will vouch for what we have been doing. We need back-up and lots of it. I think I should go in and talk to the President.'

Jimmy picked up the bottle of whisky and took another slug. 'I was having a great afternoon and now I'm in the middle of some world conspiracy. Which President are you talking about?'

Linda replied: 'The President of the United States, Jimmy.'

'You know him?'

'I work for his wife. I see the President on most days that I'm working.'

Jimmy took another swig. 'Hell's bells.'

Sherman said: 'Say nothing to anyone about all this, Jamil. Can I trust you?'

'You're joking, sis? Of course I'll keep quiet. You're my only income and I don't want any more goons like him breaking down my front door.'

'Good decision,' Wyatt said. 'Boss, what's the name of Mountfitchet's yacht.'

'It's called *Golden Boy.*'

'Of course it is,' Wyatt said. 'Of course it is.'

48

Number One Lounge, South Terminal,
London Gatwick Airport, May 6th

Wyatt looked out of the window and watched an Airbus 320 roar into the sky. He turned back to stir his coffee and said: 'I hate airports.'

'Why?' Linda asked.

'Too many partings, too many separations. I'm still worried that we're missing something, Linda.'

'Such as what?' Linda said, with a trace of irritation. 'We've been over this several times.'

'I'm still worried about what might happen to you back in the States.'

'Listen, I called my folks last night. I'm flying into Orlando and they're picking me up. I'm still travelling under a false name. Nobody will know that I'm back until I'm ready for them to know. My folks have arranged a local attorney, as well as one in Washington, to take my statement independently. I'm going to tell all my friends and family, as well as Mike's old police colleagues in New York that I'm back before I check in at the White House. Prem is flying over to meet me and represent the Indian government when I present my case to Stack Franklin and then probably the President. Whoever it was can't harm me like they tried to harm me before.'

'That will neutralise any underhand threat from the legal authorities, but Silk Fist is an utterly ruthless set-up. I'm worried about what they might do when they find out you're back with damaging information. I won't be there to watch your back.'

'What about you? You think I won't be worried about you? I won't be there to watch *your* back, tough guy, when you confront this billionaire bonking baron character.'

Wyatt laughed. 'That sums him up neatly. Sangita Sherman is an attractive woman but who would have guessed that she was one of Baron Mountfitchet's old conquests?'

Linda's expression registered distaste. 'I don't like that woman. Can you trust her?'

'Well, so far she's kept her part of the bargain. I'm flying to Nassau in two days and she's promised to have all the official paperwork ready so I can get the parcel through customs. It's lucky that the Bahamas is a friendly country within the Commonwealth.'

'I think what you plan is too dangerous, although you haven't really told me what you *do* plan.'

'That's because I don't know until I get there and do a reconnaissance.'

Linda was thoughtful. 'Perhaps you should come to Washington with me and, together with Prem, we can present our findings.'

'Why don't *you* come to Nassau with *me*? We have to be sure that Mountfitchet is really involved with Silk Fist. Sherman could be lying to us. I want to be sure about Mountfitchet, and possibly find some evidence, before the authorities descend upon him.'

'Okay, but don't forget, call me as soon as you've got the goods on this dodgy aristocrat.'

Wyatt smiled. 'I love to way you Yanks pronounce "aristocrat" by putting the emphasis on the "ris" bit.'

'How should it be pronounced? Like a bleedin' Cockney barrow boy, guvnor?'

Wyatt laughed at Linda's attempt at the accent. 'I'm not a Cockney. You have to be born within the sound of Bow bells for that, and north London is too far away. The next few days are going to seem really strange.'

'In what way?'

'In not having you around.'

Linda made a face of mock amazement. 'Wow, are you saying you're going to miss me, Sergeant Wyatt?'

Wyatt nodded. 'Yes. We got off to a bad start, didn't we?'

'A very bad start. I thought you were obsessed and crazy.'

'And I thought you were the original ice maiden. Now we've been living in each other's pockets for the past few weeks.'

'It's been quite a roller coaster,' Linda said. 'We've made a good team.'

'We have,' Wyatt agreed. 'I've sort of got used to having you around, now that I've got to appreciate your good points.'

'Which are?'

Wyatt shifted uncomfortably. 'Come on, I'm not going to spell it out. I've said too much.'

Linda teased him. 'An unexpected show of sentiment from a British guy! It's no good squirming, Wyatt. You've dug the hole and you can't stop now. What are my good points?'

'It's not like you to fish for compliments, Sergeant Marquez. Alright, you're not like any other woman I've ever known.'

'How many Hispanic women have you known?'

'No, it's nothing to do with race. You're very attractive but when I look at you that's not what I see.'

'So you see my ugly side!?'

'You have no ugly side, either physically or spiritually. During the past few weeks I've had to forget that you're a beautiful woman and simply regard you as a comrade-in-arms. I'd have never got through it otherwise. I've seen your courage and your dignity, the way you've held yourself together after what happened to Mike and to your godfather. I've seen your intelligence and insight. You're a lot brighter than I am, and much better educated. I'm a shallow bloke. I've never thought deeply about relationships but it's like you're the complete woman, a whole person, someone who has fitted into my life like a key in a lock and made me open up and see and feel things I've never been aware of before. It's a strange experience. I'm not putting this very well.'

'You're doing okay, Wyatt. More than okay. I'm not sure I understand but what you've said is very sweet.'

'Please don't think I'm coming on to you or anything tacky. I respect your feelings for Mike too much to take crude advantage.'

Linda nodded. 'I've realised that from the start and I appreciate it, more than I can say. It's been a crazy few weeks, rushing around the world trying to stay alive, but in a strange way it's helped me get over Mike more quickly. I've learned that you're not an oddball, far from it. I love your good manners, your considerate nature, even that self-deprecating humour you Brits love so much. You're a decent and honourable man and I've felt safe with you. There's nobody in the world I'd trust more. And you're not the only one who's had to forget that we're members of opposite sexes. I've seen you with your shirt off. You're hot!'

Wyatt laughed. 'I enjoyed checking your legs for splinters of glass. I tried not to show it.'

The public address system announced boarding for the Orlando flight.

There was an awkward silence.

Wyatt stood up. 'I'll walk you to the gate.'

'No,' Linda said. 'Let's say our goodbyes here. I don't want to board the plane with tears running down my face.'

'Okay, well, have a good flight.' Wyatt kissed Linda on the cheek. They embraced awkwardly. Then Linda kissed him on the lips and they held each other tightly. Linda broke away, grabbed the handle of her carry case and quickly walked away. She did not look back.

Wyatt was suffused with a tenderness and a bitter sense of regret he had never experienced before. He had lied to Linda once again. He could not tell her what he planned to do in Nassau. It could mean that he would not see her again for a long time, perhaps never.

He sat down and sipped his coffee. It was cold. Wyatt did not notice. He had never felt more alone.

49

Nassau, Bahamas, May 11th

Wyatt perched up a tree on the fringe of Saunders Beach. He was hidden more by darkness than by the sparse foliage. This was the only vantage point from which he had an unobstucted, albeit precarious, view of the superyacht *Golden Boy* moored out in the central channel.

Wyatt studied the *Golden Boy* through night glasses for an hour before he was satisfied that conditions were right. Some sort of party was being held. The forward end of the yacht was strung with lanterns. Laughter and the mellow sounds of a Goombay steel band floated across the still water. The tender had been making regular runs carrying guests from the dock in Nassau.

Golden Boy was one of the largest privately-owned yachts in the world and too large to be berthed in Nassau Yacht Haven. Wyatt had observed *Golden Boy* on the previous night. That night the crew had stood a regular watch but tonight they were busy attending to party guests. Wyatt reasoned that he would not get a better opportunity.

He climbed down from the tree, concealed himself between his hire car and a clump of bushes, put on his hooded wetsuit and goggles, strapped on his backpack, padded across the deserted beach and waded out into the sea.

Wyatt swam with easy rhythmic strokes towards *Golden Boy*. The sea was calm, the night was warm but cloudy. There was only faint moonlight, which helped conceal his movement, but the stars shone brilliantly wherever the clouds parted.

Wyatt swam obliquely, slightly away from the yacht, and swam around to the port side, hidden from the shore, before cautiously looking up. The party was being held in the open on the helicopter pad at the bow of the yacht. *Golden Boy* was built with three decks above the waterline. The crew were moving about on all three decks but Wyatt could not see anyone on permanent watch.

Wyatt was pleased to see that his task was much easier because the stern of the vessel included a narrow landing ledge. Wyatt ducked under the water and swam until the white stern of the *Golden Boy* loomed through the moonlit water.

Wyatt hauled himself up on to the landing dock. He took off the backpack, stepped out of his wetsuit, and took out a towel. He dried off and put on shoes, socks, shirt, tie and a white tropical suit. He had not brought a weapon. Mountfitchet would not risk murder or assault with so many guests aboard his yacht.

Wyatt looked up at the stern rising above him. It was perpendicular to the water with no rake whatsoever. There were not enough handholds to allow him to climb noiselessly so he would have to risk the grappling hook. It was made of carbon fibre and padded with foam to reduce noise. Wyatt threw the hook up and missed. He tried another six times, expecting to be discovered each time, before the hook caught the stern rail. He waited for several seconds to gauge if anyone had noticed. There was no reaction so he hauled himself up and peered over on to the deck. It was deserted. Wyatt climbed up on to the deck and threw the grappling hook into the sea. He smoothed his hair and his suit with his hands and strolled nonchalantly towards the bow.

Halfway along the deck Wyatt stopped to peer into the *grand salon*. It was fitted out with polished wood panelling, antique furniture, shining brass, deep pile carpets and crystal chandeliers. Wyatt had expected no less.

A voice said: 'Everything all right, sir?'

Wyatt turned to find a crew member carrying a tray of canapes. Wyatt said: 'I was admiring Lord Mountfitchet's living quarters. Very impressive.'

'I'm sure Lord Mountfitchet will be happy to show you around his yacht if you ask him. Perhaps best if you rejoin the party now, sir.'

'Yes, of course.'

The crew member waited for Wyatt to move and followed him towards the bow. The party area was discreetly roped off. Wyatt stepped over the rope and looked around. The helipad was thronged with guests. There were long tables, loaded with food and drink, set up on either side of the deck. The Goombay steel band was playing at the prow. They were playing softly, the mellow sound complimenting the warm night air. Scarlet jacketed waiters carrying trays of food and drinks moved among the guests. Wyatt accepted a glass of champagne.

A strikingly beautiful blonde wearing a long black and silver gown noticed Wyatt standing alone and walked towards him. She looked to be mid-thirties but when she came closer and held out her hand Wyatt could see that she was older. She said, in good English with a trace of Scandinavian accent: 'I'm so sorry, I must have missed greeting you, although I don't usually miss handsome men. I'm Helga Mountfitchet.'

Wyatt smiled and took her hand. 'From such a beautiful woman that is a compliment indeed. What's the occasion?'

Lady Mountfitchet looked puzzled. 'Didn't you read your invitation? It's my husband's birthday. I hope you brought him a present. He might be richer than God but he loves presents.'

Wyatt said, still with a smile: 'Your husband took my present yesterday but he hasn't thanked me yet.'

'Oh dear, that's a mysterious sort of statement. I'll take you over so he can remedy the oversight.'

Wyatt followed Lady Mountfitchet to the other side of the helipad where her husband was talking to another couple.

Helga Mountfitchet tapped her husband lightly on the shoulder and said: 'Excuse me, darling. I'm sorry to interrupt. Can I borrow you for a moment?'

Mountfitchet looked round. His thick blonde hair had not thinned with age and he possessed the bearing and confident ease that was the product of aristocratic rank, a lifetime of wealth and an Eton and Oxford education.

His wife said: 'Philip, may I introduce... oh dear, I don't know your name.'

'Wyatt. Christopher Wyatt. May I wish you a happy birthday, Lord Mountfitchet.'

'Thank you,' Mountfichet replied, not offering his hand. 'Christopher Wyatt? I don't remember your name being on the invitation list.'

'My name was not on your invitation list. It's a lovely evening so I swam out. Can I talk to you in private?'

'I'm trying to enjoy my birthday party.'

Lady Mountfitchet said: 'Christopher says he has already given you a present but you haven't thanked him yet.'

'Is that so? What was this present?'

Wyatt said: 'It's something you might prefer to talk about in private.'

Mountfitchet turned to his wife and said: 'Darling, could you find Anton and ask him to come and see me by the aft locker?'

Helga Mountfichet said diplomatically: 'Certainly, I'll go and find him. This sounds like boring business so I'll leave you two boys to have your private talk. Don't be long, darling, we have many other guests wanting to wish you happy birthday.'

Mountfitchet said: 'Come with me, Mr Wyatt.'

Wyatt followed Mountfitchet back past the *grand salon* and into a narrow cross passage near the aft of the yacht. The passage was in darkness and hidden from view.

Mountfitchet said: 'Make this quick. What do you want with me?'

Wyatt said: 'I sent you a message a couple of days ago saying that I had brought you a parcel special delivery from Sangita Desai, your old Oxford friend. I gave you my hotel and room number. I was sent a message in return saying that you had no idea what I was talking about and you were not interested in any parcel. Imagine my surprise when I later found that my hotel room had been broken into and the parcel was gone. You were the only person who knew about that parcel so I guess you were more interested than you indicated.'

Mountfitchet did not react. He said: 'I'm sorry to hear that you've been the victim of a hotel robbery. They are not uncommon here, as in most parts of the world, but I had nothing to do with it. The tender will take you back to the shore, Mr Wyatt. I request that you to peacefully accompany Anton off my yacht.'

Wyatt had sensed a presence behind him. He said: 'What if I don't wish to leave peacefully?'

'Then Anton will return you to the sea. You can swim home, although it might be difficult with two broken arms.' Mountfitchet nodded.

Wyatt was clamped in two powerful arms. He could smell Anton's canape and champagne breath close behind. Wyatt dipped his head forward and then jerked back to crash it into Anton's nose. Anton grunted and partially released his embrace. Wyatt relaxed all his muscles and dropped down using his own dead weight and then sprang up to drive the palm of his hand into Anton's already bloody nose. Anton, confused and angry, scrabbled to grab Wyatt but Wyatt evaded the huge man's slow movements and kicked him in the groin. Anton bellowed in pain. Wyatt punched him under the rib cage. Anton sank to his knees and deposited the consumption of the night's party all over the shining teak deck of *Golden Boy*.

Wyatt turned back to Mountfitchet. 'This is a beautiful yacht, Philip. I would hate to think that you swap all this beauty and luxury for an eight foot square cell in Pentonville prison. The inmates would love a blonde bitch like you. I have information that could make that happen. I really think we ought to talk in private.'

Wyatt had to give credit, Mountfitchet was still unfazed. He sighed and said: 'Very well. Come this way.' To Anton he hissed: 'Get yourself cleaned up and get off my yacht. Useless bastard.'

Mountfitchet led Wyatt back towards the foredeck and through a doorway leading into the main foyer. They walked upstairs to the second deck and went into a cabin furnished like a den, with a desk and a computer but also with a library of books, armchairs, a bar, and a pool table.

Mountfitchet said: 'Would you object if I make sure that you are not wired and that you don't carry a weapon?'

'Not at all, Philip. Sensible precautions.'

Mountfitchet searched Wyatt's suit and patted him down. 'Okay, Christopher. Why don't you sit down opposite me at the desk here?'

'Certainly.'

Mountfitchet sat down, opened a desk drawer, took out a small pistol and laid it on the desk. 'That's in case you try anything. I also have an alarm here that would summon the crew.'

'Again, sensible precautions, unlike the general security on this yacht. With the quality of bodyguards such as Anton, if I meant you harm you would be dead by now. I swam out and climbed aboard without a soul noticing.'

'Why did you do that?'

'Because it's the only way I can get to talk to you.'

'What do you want to talk to me about?'

'Your involvement with the Silk Fist conspiracy.'

Mountfitchet considered his reply and then said: 'Christopher, I am an investor and speculator, not a criminal. Every investigation into my affairs, whether conducted by American, British or European authorities has concluded that I am completely honest and what I do is legitimate and legal. I am very good at what I do. I do not have to resort to terrorism.'

'I could possibly accept that if it wasn't for the parcel you stole. I set you up to prove that you were involved in Silk Fist. You could not allow a batch of Hiatus to remain unrecovered, so let's not waste time with bullshit, Philip. You are involved with Silk Fist and I have the evidence.'

'I have no inkling of what you mean by Hiatus, or whatever you said. What do you propose to do with this imaginary evidence? Attempt to ruin my reputation over something I have no involvement with?'

'No, Philip. I want to work for you.'

Mountfitchet reacted for the first time. 'Well, that's a surprise. Why do you want to work for me?'

'Do you need to ask? I want a little piece of what you have on this yacht and in your homes in Kensington, Manhattan, Monte Carlo.'

'What service could you provide to warrant me giving you a little piece of all this?'

'For a start, your personal security. It is abysmal, as typified by employing a useless lunk such as Anton. I could have murdered you with the utmost ease. I've been a soldier in the Special Boat Service, I've been a personal security expert and I've worked for the Royal Protection Squad. I am the best at what I do. Ask your friend Sangita Desai. And what have I got out of it? A lousy monthly salary and a measly pension when I'm too old to fight, all for the privilege of standing on the outside and watching the royals stuffing themselves with goodies while I shiver in the cold. I'm sick and tired of crumbs, Philip. I want some of the gravy.'

Mountfitchet nodded. 'You make a good case, Christopher, especially about security on *Golden Boy*. I will have to address that issue immediately.'

'I can start tomorrow.'

Mountfitchet smiled. 'Would you like a drink, Christopher? It is my birthday after all.'

'No thanks. Not while I'm still negotiating. You go ahead.'

Mountfitchet stood up and went over to the bar. He poured a

glass of whisky and spooned in ice cubes. 'You're an interesting man, Christopher. You have played your hand well. You have secured evidence that I am involved with Silk Fist. Indeed I am, but not in a way you would understand. I've decided to believe you. It would be better to have a man like you on our side rather than against us. You have given us considerable trouble. I did speak to Sangita Desai about you. She rang to warn me that you and that American woman had unearthed our operation in France. She also told me that you were the best officer she had but you had become disaffected and bitter. I'm aware of how you despatched those stupid Albanian thugs in Washington because I arranged for them to kidnap that troublesome bitch Marquez. Impressive credentials.'

'I like Mrs Sherman,' Wyatt said. 'If you employ me I'll keep my mouth shut and there will be no reason for her to lose her rank. Nobody knows about her involvement except me and Sergeant Marquez.'

'Hasn't Marquez reported to her people yet?'

'No. I persuaded her to wait until I had talked to you.'

'I understand that Marquez is a most attractive woman. You've been with her for several weeks now. Perhaps you have become… friendly. What if something fatal was to happen to Marquez? How would you react?'

Wyatt shrugged. 'She means nothing to me. She's a stupid spic being used by the establishment, all *God Bless America* and saluting the flag. I don't care about that crap. I want cash.'

Mountfitchet nodded. 'Why should I trust you, Christopher? Why this sudden change of heart?'

'You might be aware that I was the Princess Royal's protection officer when she was assassinated. There was nothing anyone could have done to prevent that but I was blamed. The royal family dropped me after years of loyal service.'

'Actually, I'm related to the royal family.'

'Well, I'm sorry to disrespect your relatives but that's what happened. I've been turned into a fugitive and suspected of being involved in Silk Fist so I might as well join Silk Fist. Was Silk Fist your doing? It would need a lot of money to set up?'

'No, it was not my idea, but I have benefitted greatly.'

'In what way? What is the point of Silk Fist? Nobody can understand the purpose of all these killings and all the destruction.'

'Let me make one thing clear, Christopher. I don't like all these questions. You can become a member of the team but most of the team have no idea they are working for Silk Fist. I still wonder whether I can trust you. It's a shame you cannot provide references.'

'You rich people move in the same circles. Do you know Yaroslav Blokhin?'

'As a matter of fact, I do.'

'I worked for Yuri. I was aware that he was involved in some dodgy buisnesses but that was no concern of mine. I saved the lives of his family, I never betrayed him and I served him well and faithfully. You ask him.'

'An excellent idea. I think I will.' Mountfitchet lifted the desk telephone and said: 'Will you ask Mr Blokhin to join me in my day cabin?'

Wyatt was gripped with apprehension about the implications of this unexpected development. He said: 'Blokhin's here on *Golden Boy*?'

'Yes. He's a special guest.'

'I didn't see him at the party.'

'No. If you worked for Yaroslav you'll know that he doesn't enjoy the small talk at parties.'

When Blokhin entered the day cabin his face registered amazement to see Wyatt. His bodyguards, Oleg and Vladimir, followed him in and stared at Wyatt with undiluted hatred.

Wyatt said: 'Hello, boys. It's a long way from Switzerland.'

Blokhin remained standing near the doorway. 'What are you doing here, Christopher?'

'Relax, Yuri. I come in peace. I'm not going to start anything. Philip needs you to vouch for me.'

Mountfitchet said: 'Yes, it's perfectly safe, Yuri. Ask your attack dogs to wait outside. We need to talk in private.'

Oleg and Vladimir left the cabin and closed the door. Blokhin was still wary. He moved into the cabin but kept the pool table between himself and Wyatt.

Mountfitchet said: 'Christopher has offered his services to Silk Fist.'

'You have?' Blokhin said. 'Whatever happened to King and Country?'

'As I was explaining to Philip, where has that got me? The most I have ever received for the work I do is from your generosity. I can only afford to live in Islington because you provide me with free accommodation and pay all the bills. I want to extend that sort of arrangement by working for Philip. I have one question, Yuri.'

'What is that?'

'Why did you set me up after our talk in Switzerland? We talked as friends and a couple of days later my name was plastered all over your newspapers and television channels. My people branded me as a traitor.'

It was Mountfitchet who answered the question. 'We wanted Silk Fist to become public knowledge.'

'Why?'

'We wanted to implant panic and uncertainly around the world. Also, we needed a dupe, a fall guy, to take attention away from us. You were the perfect candidate. Yuri did not like the idea but he had to go along with it.'

Blokhin said: 'I'm so sorry, Christopher.'

'Never mind, Yuri. We're on the same side now, hopefully.'

'I certainly hope so because I've seen what happens when someone gets on the wrong side of you.' Blokhin moved forward and offered his hand.

Wyatt stood up and shook hands. 'It's good to see you again, Yuri.'

Mountfitchet said: 'So, Yuri, would you recommend Christopher as my chief security adviser and personal bodyguard?'

'Wholeheartedly, Philip. You could not make a better choice.'

Mountfitchet held out his hand for Wyatt to shake. 'Then welcome aboard officially, Christopher. I think we can find something a little better than your Metropolitan police salary.'

Wyatt replied, as casually as he could manage: 'Thank you, Philip. I'd like to accept that drink now.'

50

Sheridan Hotel, Washington DC, May 14th

Linda Marquez said: 'Prem, it's good to see you again. Please come in.'

'Thank you, Linda.' Prem walked in to Linda's suite and looked around. 'This is a much grander room than I can afford. The Indian government are being stingy about expenses.'

'You're welcome to seek refuge in this one anytime, Prem. You look tired.'

'I am. I've had a long journey, in more ways than one. You, however, look radiant. It's lovely to see you in a dress. Much more becoming than denim or a black Secret Service suit.'

Linda laughed. 'Thank you, Prem. I'm much more relaxed now that we're about to get our governments fully involved. All this running and hiding has seemed endless. Put down your briefcase and sit down. Can I get you anything? Drink, food?'

'It's only the middle of the afternoon but a gin and tonic would be most welcome.'

'I'll join you, Prem. I want to celebrate.'

'What are you celebrating?' Prem asked as Linda prepared the drinks at the mini bar.

'As soon as Chris arrives we can hand the whole Silk Fist file over to the proper authorities and get back to leading a normal life.'

Prem grunted. 'I wish I could share your optimism, Linda.'

Linda handed Prem his gin and tonic and sat down. 'Why do you say that, Prem?'

'Perhaps I'm becoming old and cynical but it seems there always has to be a battle to persuade the powers-that-be to do what is right rather than what is convenient or empowering to them.'

'In what way? What's happened at your end?'

'My own government is swathed in self-interest and secrecy as, I have no doubt, are the British and American governments. My so-called superiors were intrigued by this Hiatus drug. It was analysed by our top chemists and some of our leaders were in favour of keeping the formula and its effects secret for use by India. I am relieved to say that my commanding officer, Colonel Chatterjee, is a man of honour and would not countenance such behaviour. He threatened to resign, as did I, if I were not allowed to fly here and support you and Christopher when you presented the evidence to your people. It was naïve in the extreme to think that India could suppress such knowledge. Hiatus is the most insidious and devilish drug ever created by mankind, apart from alcohol. Our scientists found that the active ingredients are absorbed into the brain and act directly on parts of the brain such as the hippocampus and amygdala. These active ingredients are then absorbed by the brain and bloodstream and disappear. The testosterone and MAO inhibitors could not be so absorbed but that hardly matters. I fear that such knowledge will now be used by my own government even when Hiatus becomes known throughout the world.'

Linda nodded soberly. 'I appreciate your concerns, Prem. I lost my husband and you lost your wife to this evil stuff. I would like to think it could be destroyed forever so that no-one else has to suffer as we have.'

'Well, nobody has achieved more than you and Christopher to rid the world of this evil. Have you heard from Christopher?'

'Yes. He rang me this morning to find out where we are staying. He should be here at any minute.'

'I have to say that it was foolish bravado to attempt to get aboard Mountfitchet's yacht.'

'I agree. If I had been aware of what he was planning I would have tried to talk him out of it, but you know Chris, always restless for action.'

'Did he say if he had found anything useful?'

'Yes, he said he had found vital information.'

'That is exciting news. We have discovered how Silk Fist are controlling the minds of their unfortunate victims but we still do not know for what purpose or who is behind this conspiracy. Did Christopher say what he had found?'

'No, but he was very excitable. I tried to calm him down but he was overwhelmed with that drive and enthusiasm I've gotten used to.'

Prem chuckled. 'Why, Linda, your face lights up when you talk about Christopher. You haven't fallen for him, have you?'

Linda looked away with embarrassment. 'I'm not sure, Prem. Chris and I have practically been living together for three months. Nothing untoward has happened, you understand. It seems disrespectful to Mike's memory but I'm surprised to find that I miss Chris. I miss him a lot.'

'That's entirely natural and nothing to feel uncomfortable about. It's called propinquity. When we are in close proximity to someone for a long period then we are prone to become even more close to them, perhaps even fall in love with them, especially if we liked them to begin with. Many, many relationships begin in a work environment. That's how I fell in love with Rhea. We were at university together, taking the same classes, and we were drawn to each other until we were inseparable.'

To deflect from her own feelings, Linda asked: 'How are your sons coping with the loss, Prem?'

'Like men, I am proud to say. They have carried on with their lives, they are doing their duty, but a light has gone out of their eyes. I also notice the same whenever I look in the mirror.'

'Perhaps the light will return one day, when the bad memories are driven out by the good.'

'I hope you are right, Linda.'

There was a loud knock on the door.

Linda took a pistol out of her bag and went to the door. 'Who is it?'

'Chris.'

Linda opened the door. She made to kiss him welcome but Wyatt, distracted, ignored her and looked right past her. Linda stepped back and said: 'Come in, Chris. Prem is here.'

Linda closed the door. Prem stood up. Wyatt entered hesitantly, reluctantly.

Prem said: 'Are you all right, Christopher? You are trembling.'

'What? No, it's the long journey. I haven't been sleeping well.'

Prem said: 'Well, I'm glad to see you back in one piece. It was not wise to get aboard Mountfitchet's yacht.'

Wyatt stared at him. 'What are you talking about? What the fuck do you know about special operations? All you ever did was sit in a cockpit and play with your bloody computers.'

Linda put the gun back in her bag and said hastily: 'Can I get you a drink, Chris? We're having a gin and tonic.'

'No, I don't want a drink.' His tone was harsh, irritable.

Linda said: 'Sit down, Chris. Can I take your jacket?'

'No. I'll keep standing.

Linda glanced at Prem, expressions sharing their concern.

Wyatt said: 'What are you two looking at?'

Prem said: 'We were wondering if you found out anything on Mountfitchet's yacht. How did it go?'

Wyatt said off-handedly: 'Mountfitchet's clean. He doesn't know anything about Silk Fist.'

Linda said: 'But when you rang this morning you told me you had found vital information?'

'Did I? What about?'

'We were hoping it was something about Silk Fist.'

Wyatt took a step back. 'Why should I tell you anything? You're always asking me questions, you nosy bitch.'

Prem said: 'Steady on, Christopher. Why don't you relax and have a drink?'

'Why don't you keep out of this, you bastard. You're always trying to drive a wedge between us. They told me you would.'

'Who told you, Christopher?'

Linda put a hand on Prem's arm. 'This is how Mike behaved. This is not Chris talking. This is Hiatus.'

Wyatt said: 'What did you say?'

'I said you've been drugged with Hiatus.'

Wyatt took another step back and said: 'Yes, Hiatus that's it!' He shouted: 'Hiatus' at the top of his voice. He reached inside his jacket, took out his Glock pistol and pointed it at Linda. 'I have to kill you, Marquez.'

Prem said: 'Listen, Christopher, you have been dosed with Hiatus. Remember how you and Linda have been fighting against Hiatus. You do not want to harm Linda.'

'Stay out of this,' Wyatt said angrily. 'I don't want to harm Linda but I have to kill her. Then I have to kill you and myself.'

Prem made a move but Wyatt turned the pistol on him. Prem saw that Linda was standing stock still but did not look afraid.

Prem said: 'Christopher, remember your training with the Special Boat Service. You were trained to withstand torture and brainwashing and interrogation. You know full well it would be wrong to harm Linda. You must think, Christopher. You must fight what is going on in your own mind. The Princess Royal died because of this evil drug. You have been infected with the same drug. Be a man and fight it!'

Wyatt stared wild-eyed at Prem. He turned the gun back on Linda.

Linda said calmly: 'Shoot me if you have to, Chris, but remember everything we've been through together.'

Wyatt said: 'I remember, but I still have to kill you. The princess was evil. You are evil.' The pistol trembled in Wyatt's hand.

Linda said: 'I am not evil, Chris. Hiatus is the evil.'

'Hiatus? Evil? Yes, but I still have to shoot you. I have to shoot you. But I can't, Linda. I can't. I love you. I love you so much.'

Wyatt lowered the gun. He said: 'If I cannot kill you then I have to kill myself.' He suddenly raised the gun to his temple.

Prem shouted: 'No!' and launched himself at Wyatt. The pistol roared as Wyatt staggered backwards. The shot bored a hole in the ceiling. Linda leapt forward and grabbed Wyatt's gun arm with both hands. She brought the arm down and twisted to use all her strength to sweep Wyatt off his feet. Wyatt tumbled to the floor and the pistol went spinning out of his reach.

As if in a trance, Wyatt said: 'I've failed. I've failed.'

'No,' Prem said. 'You have beaten it, Christopher. You have won.'

Linda picked up the Glock as Wyatt struggled to his feet. He swayed slightly, glassy-eyed as if drunk, and then said: 'I don't know what... help me.' His eyes closed and, before Prem or Linda could catch him, pitched forward and lay unconscious on the carpet.

Linda knelt down beside Wyatt and took his pulse. 'It's very weak, Prem.'

'He could be having an adverse reaction to the MAO inhibitor. We have to get expert medical help immediately or else he might not make it.'

51

St Simeon Memorial Hospital, Washington DC, May 16th

Premendra Dhawan looked up from his magazine and was surprised to see Linda Marquez enter the room. He said, with a trace of unmeant irritation: 'What are you doing back here, Linda? It's only ten o'clock. I told you to stay away for the rest of the evening and get a good night's sleep.'

'Good advice which I choose to ignore, Prem. Since you rung to tell me that Chris had been released from intensive care into this private room I had to come back.' Linda held up a small case. 'I've packed a few things, for Chris as well as me, and I'm going to stay with him for however long it takes. Chris might need a friendly and reassuring face when he wakes up. How is he?'

Prem said: 'He is less restless but is still fighting something inside him.'

Linda looked down at Wyatt's pale features. His lips were moving soundlessly and his eyelids twitched as his body jerked in brief spasms. He was hooked up to a saline drip and two machines monitoring his vital life signs. Linda stroked Wyatt's black hair and said: 'I couldn't sleep. I feel so helpless.'

'We all feel like that when someone we care about is sick. I did as you suggested and rang our scientists in Delhi to ask if they had any ideas about how to treat Christopher and remove that evil drug from his system. They thought that adrenaline in large doses might help but the doctors here were already doing that. Christopher is stable but weak. There is a fear that the adrenaline, together with his very high blood pressure and testosterone levels, might have triggered a cerebral problem. The doctors have stabilised him. We can only pray that he comes out of this with his mind intact.'

Linda did not trust herself to speak.

Prem went on: 'The police came here asking about the shot fired in the hotel. They asked many questions.'

'What did you tell them?'

'The truth. They looked at me as if I was a crazy foreigner. I rang Delhi and I think they have straightened things out but the police may want to speak to you sometime.'

'They already have. They were waiting in my hotel room. I told them the truth, as you did. I don't care what they think or what happens about that. All I care about is that Chris comes out of this unharmed. I'm going to stay with him here for as long as it takes.'

Prem stood up, took Linda's arm and guided her out of the room. He said quietly: 'Physically, Christopher is in perfect condition. The doctors think he is unconscious because of what is called a dissociative fugue state. It could last hours, it could last weeks, or even months.'

'Then I will stay here for hours, weeks or months.'

'Linda, there is a serious danger that Christopher may be a mental vegetable when he recovers. He may even…'

'Enough, Prem. Please.'

'I'm sorry, Linda. You have to know the truth.'

'Yes, of course. My apologies, Prem. I'll sit with him now. You go and get something to eat and rest. I'll ring you if there are any developments.'

'Very well, Linda. I can see you are too determined to dissuade. I'll be back as soon as I can.'

Linda went back into the room. She sat down and took Wyatt's hand. 'Come on, you big lunk. Enough of this lazing around. Time you came back to me.' She picked up the magazine and started reading aloud.

Linda was still reading aloud, in between involuntary naps, at six thirty the next morning.

A voice at the door said: 'Excuse me, what are you doing here? Are you a relative?'

Linda looked up. The speaker was a young doctor, hesitant, unsure, not long out of medical school.

'No,' Linda replied. 'I'm a close friend.'

'This patient ought to rest. He's been through a drug-induced traumatic event. He should be allowed to rest.'

Linda said, with weary patience: 'I'm aware of exactly what he's been through and the last thing he needs is rest. He needs human contact to bring him back.'

'I disagree. I'll have to ask you to leave now, Miss…'

'Sergeant Linda Marquez of the United States Secret Service.'

'Can I see your identity, please?'

'I've been out in the field. I haven't got my badge. Ring the White House if you don't believe me.'

'I might just do that.'

'Bite me.'

Linda picked up the magazine and carried on reading aloud.

One hour later the elevator doors opened and Deputy Chief Isaiah Franklin stepped out followed by a swarm of Secret Service agents. He gave instructions to the agents and then asked Linda to step out of the room.

Franklin said: 'Jeez, Linda, I'm mighty glad to see you're alive. I won't ask where you've been and what you've been up to. Some doctor from this hospital rang to confirm your identity and the alarm bells went off all over the place. The President wants to see you, now.'

'Sir, you can leave agents outside this room to protect me and the man in that bed but, for the time being, he needs me more than the President does.'

'But it's the *President*, Linda.'

'Tell him he'll have to wait.'

Stack Franklin grinned and shook his head in disbelief. 'He'll be pissed with you, sergeant. Is that Wyatt?'

'Yes.'

'Is it true that you've found out who's running this Silk Fist business?'

'We've found out a lot. How did you know that?'

'Some guy from Indian intelligence got through to the President and explained a lot of things.'

'Was it Premendra Dhawan?'

'No, I think his name is Chatterjee. Yes, Colonel Chatterjee. If he's right, this is a real doozy, Linda.'

'Thanks, chief. If you'll excuse me I have to get back to Sergeant Wyatt.'

Thirty minutes later the young doctor entered the room. He was carrying two cups of coffee. He handed one to Linda. 'Peace offereing, sergeant.'

'Gratefully accepted, doc.'

'We have to be careful, especially since this Silk Fist business started.'

'I understand completely. You did the right thing to check on me and I apologise for my rudeness. The man you're treating here has done more than anyone to stop Silk Fist.'

The doctor looked at Wyatt with curiosity. 'I gathered something like that from all the Secret Service agents camped outside his room.' He took Wyatt's pulse, listened to his heart, raised his eyelids and shone a torch at his eyes. 'There's an improvement, he's stronger, and a definite reaction there. You're doing a great job, sergeant. Your treatment is working. Carry on reading to him.'

It was nine o'clock when Linda was woken by a Secret Service agent.

The magazine had slipped on to the floor. 'Oh, God,' Linda said. 'I must have nodded off.'

'I'm sorry to wake you, mam, but this man says he is with Indian intelligence and that he knows you.'

Prem Dhawan was at the door flanked by two agents.

'Yes, yes,' Linda said. 'Let him in. Good morning, Prem.'

Prem came in and said ruefully: 'I'm sorry I didn't get back last night. I was exhausted. I fell off to sleep and didn't wake up until early this morning. How is he?'

'A little bit of improvement, according to the doctor, but he's still out.'

'At least he's well guarded now.'

'Was that you're doing?'

'I rang Colonel Chatterjee and he rang your President. The cat is well and truly out of the bag now. We couldn't go on doing this alone after what happened.'

A voice asked: 'After what happened?'

They looked around at Wyatt. His eyes were open.

'Chris!' Linda said. 'You're awake.'

'Of course I'm awake. Where am I?'

'You're in hospital, in Washington.'

'Have I been shot?'

'No. You've been sort of ill.'

'Ill? How?'

Prem said: 'Christopher, do you know the name of the President of the United States?'

Wyatt frowned. 'Of course I do.'

'Would you like to tell me his name?'

'Georgia Joe Logan.'

'What about the British Prime Minister?'

'What is this, Prem, an episode of *Jeopardy*? It's that idiot Murdo Montrose.'

Prem looked at Linda and smiled. 'His mind seems intact.'

'Will you two please stop grinning like Cheshire cats and tell me what happened to me?'

Prem said: 'What do you remember about getting aboard Mountfitchet's yacht?'

'Let me think… I swam out to the *Golden Boy*. I clambered up the stern and joined the birthday party. Mountfichet tried to have me thrown off but then took me to his day cabin. I bluffed him into believing that I wanted to work for Silk Fist. We had a drink and… that's strange, I can't remember what happened after that. Then I was dreaming. I wanted to drift away and let go but someone kept reading to me out of some bloody stupid magazine and asking me to come back. It sounded like Linda. In the end I wanted to come back to tell her to pack it in… then I woke up here. What happened?'

Linda said: 'Rest easy, Chris. I want the doctors to have a look at you before we answer your questions. Prem, let's talk.'

They stepped out of the room. Linda went to the nurses' station and asked them to inform the doctors that Wyatt had woken up. She came back and said to Prem: 'I think we'll have to tell him what happened. We have to find out if he is still affected by the Hiatus. He'll get more agitated if we don't tell him the truth.'

Prem and Linda waited outside Wyatt's room while three doctors, all eager to be involved in such an unusual case, had examined Wyatt thoroughly. They pronounced him fit enough to be questioned.

Prem and Linda went back into the room.

Prem looked at Wyatt and said: 'Hiatus.'

Wyatt replied: 'What about it?'

'How do you feel after I've said that word? Do you feel aggressive or angry or murderous?'

'No. I… oh, God! Is that what they did to me?'

'I'm afraid so, Christopher.'

'What did I try to do?'

'That can wait,' Linda said. 'We got to you in time. We want to make sure you're back to your old self.'

Two hours later a Secret Service agent came to the door and said: 'Excuse me, Sergeant Marquez, but Mr Wyatt's uncle Yuri is here and wishes to visit him.'

Wyatt said: 'Uncle Yuri? Oh, yes, Uncle Yuri. Is he alone?'

'Yes, sir.'

'Have you searched him?'

'Thoroughly, sir. He's not packing.'

'Okay, let him in.'

Linda said: 'Wait a minute. Let me talk to Mr Wyatt before you let him in.' She turned to Wyatt. 'Who is this Uncle Yuri? It wouldn't be Yaroslav Blokhin, would it?'

'Yes. I don't know how he knows I'm in here but I'd like to see him. He's probably brought me some vodka.'

Linda said: 'Agent Chandler, give me your weapon.'

'I'm sorry, mam, but I don't think…'

'Give me your goddamn weapon. Then you can let Uncle Yuri come in. I'm not taking any chances.'

Yaroslav Blokhin was accompanied down the corridor and stood nervously at the doorway. His portly frame was well disguised by a beautifully cut Savile Row suit. He carried a brown paper bag.

Linda asked: 'What's in the bag?'

'Some grapes, for Christopher,' Blokhin said. 'I understand this is the traditional gift for hospital patients in the West.'

Linda said: 'Agent Chandler, take those grapes far away and bin them.'

'Come in, Uncle Yuri,' Wyatt beckoned.

Blokhin said: 'Are you not angry with me?'

'Angry? Well, I wasn't pleased with the way your newspapers branded me a renegade traitor but that's all water under the bridge now.'

'I mean about more recent events. The day before yesterday?'

Linda said: 'Chris cannot remember.'

'Remember what? What is everyone talking about?'

Blokhin said: 'May I speak to Christopher alone?'

'You may not,' Linda said. 'Anything you have to say you can say in front of Mr Dhawan and I. And be warned that I am armed and I will kill you if you try anything.'

Blokhin held up his hands. 'I have come to apologise to Christopher. And to say goodbye. I am not here to harm him.'

Wyatt said: 'Yuri, come and sit down. I trust Linda and Prem completely. Now, I'd like you all to explain to me what has been going on.'

Linda looked at Prem. 'Do you think Chris is strong enough yet?'

Prem said: 'Christopher seems completely back to normal, that is waspish and restless, apart from the memory loss caused by the Hiatus. I think it will be safe to tell him what happened.'

After Prem had finished Wyatt sank back on his pillows and said: 'So not only did I fail to find any evidence about Silk Fist, I was duped by Mountfitchet and ended up trying to kill Linda.'

Prem said: 'That about sums it up. This has, at least, proved that Mountfitchet is involved in Silk Fist but we have no proof that would stand up in a court of law.'

Wyatt was looking at Linda. 'Did I truly want to kill you?'

Linda took his hand. 'No, Chris, *you* didn't want to kill me. It was the Hiatus wanting you to kill me. If Prem hadn't been there, well…'

Prem said: 'Can you remember how you felt when under the influence of Hiatus?'

'It's like a Jekyll and Hyde feeling. One part of my mind was clear with a total certainty about what I had to do. The other part was in a fog, a tiny voice inside saying this is wrong, but an overwhelming urge to kill at all costs. And hatred. I remember feeling hatred, vicious cruel hatred. Did I say anything to you two that was untoward?'

'No, of course not,' Prem said hastily.

Blokhin said: 'Hiatus allows some sort of brainwashing technique that makes a suggestion that cannot be resisted. This suggestion is implanted very quickly, unlike earlier brainwashing techniques. The drug completely disables those parts of the brain responsible for restraint, morality, judgement and so on. The victim can go on leading an ostensibly normal life while in the grip of this cruel killing hatred. As far as I know, Christopher is the only person who has ever been able to successfully resist this implanted urge.'

Linda said: 'You clearly know a lot about Silk Fist and about Hiatus, Mr Blokhin. You have a lot of questions to answer.'

'That is why I came here today, to make amends. Believe me or believe me not, as you wish, but my visit to the *Golden Boy* was going to be the end of my involvement with Silk Fist. I've been a greedy fool. When I saw Christopher sitting in Mountfitchet's day cabin I was horrified. I realised then that Silk Fist was finished.'

Wyatt said: 'I don't know why you say that, Yuri. I was the one who ended up drugged by Mountfitchet.'

'I have learned from personal experience the sort of man you are. Even if they had killed you, you inspire the sort of loyalty and respect I see in these good friends here. They would not rest until you had been avenged and Silk Fist torn down. I could tell right away that your offer to work for Mountfitchet was a ruse. I had offered you unlimited rewards to come back and work for me but you had refused out of desire to do your duty towards your country and humanity. You would not, could not, prostitute yourself to a devious snake like that man.'

Linda said: 'So that was your plan, to offer to work for Mountfitchet?'

'Yes,' Wyatt said with a trace of embarrassment. 'I didn't tell you because I was sure you wouldn't agree.'

'What did you hope to achieve?'

'I thought that if I could be admitted to the inner workings of Silk Fist I could bring them down from inside.'

Linda could no longer contain her temper. 'Wyatt, you're a frigging idiot. I'm sick to death of you keeping things from me. If you weren't lying down I'd slug you.'

Blokhin said: 'It was a good idea but it takes a snake to recognise a snake. Mountfitchet saw your offer as a ruse. He wanted to kill you. I persuaded him to give you Hiatus instead. It was all I could think of to save your life and get you off that yacht without getting myself in danger. You walked off the yacht and on to the tender in full view of dozens of witnesses. I should hasten to add that it was not my idea to select Miss Marquez as the target. That was Mountfitchet's idea.'

'We believe you, Blokhin,' Linda said aggressively. 'You've got a frigging nerve coming here today. I should have you arrested right now.'

'Before you take too much of the moral high ground, Sergeant Marquez, ask yourself how I knew that Christopher was in this hospital?'

'I guess you had him followed or you put a tracker on him?'

'No, I didn't know where he was until somebody from this hospital rang the White House earlier today.'

Linda asked: 'Are you saying you have an informant in the White House?'

'I'm saying no more. Christopher saved the life of my wife and child. It is a debt I can never repay except perhaps by giving you all the information I have about Silk Fist. In return I want to walk out of here and return to Russia. There I will disappear to enjoy my wealth and the rest of my life far away from this tangled web of murder and deceit. I will do my utmost to help bring down Silk Fist from there. If I am arrested today I have made arrangements to be released that will cause a bloodbath. Do we have a deal?'

Linda said: 'We don't like being threatened and we don't make deals with criminals, Blokhin.'

'Nonsense. You do it all the time. What is it called? "Copping a plea" in return for a lighter sentence.'

Linda said to Wyatt: 'Do you believe him? Would you trust him?'

'Yes, I would. Yuri is tough and hard. He is clever but he is not as clever as he thinks and can be used by more clever men. He has a native Russian cunning that can be twisted by more sophisticated men such as Mountfitchet. But Yuri is basically straight and honest. Why else would he come here today?'

Blokhin shook his head and said: 'You can be brutal, Christopher, with your tongue as well as your fists. Ask me anything you like about Silk Fist. One chance then I am gone forever or locked up in silence.'

Prem said: 'I think we should accept the offer.'

Linda sat back with resignation. 'Okay, go ahead.'

Prem asked: 'Who is controlling Silk Fist? Is it Mountfitchet?'

Yuri chuckled. 'No. Mountfitchet is another pawn. An important pawn but a pawn nevertheless.'

Prem said: 'Who *is* controlling Silk Fist?'

'I truly don't know. Mountfitchet is the highest level I dealt with.'

Prem said: 'What is your involvment in Silk Fist?'

'I provided initial funding and personnel.'

'Personnel of what kind?'

'Mainly as security, ex-Spetsnaz special forces men. Some computer specialists, many medical staff to administer the Hiatus.'

Wyatt said: 'What the hell is the purpose of Silk Fist?'

'For me it was greed, greed for more money and, especially, more power and influence. I have been paid truly astonishing amounts to be a part of it but I was duped. There is a purpose that I don't know about. Whoever controls Silk Fist is planning something big. I don't know what it is, I swear, but I have heard whispers.'

Linda said: 'You're not giving us much here, Mr Blokhin. If you want to get out of here, you had better come up with something better than "I don't know" or "I'm not sure".'

Blokhin fixed Linda with an icy stare. 'Miss Marquez, you do not understand how much I have risked to come here today.'

'And you don't understand, Mr Blokhin, how much pain you have caused to me because of the death of my husband or to Mr Dhawan for the death of his wife, along with hundreds of other innocent victims. You are culpable, and I don't like making deals with greedy scum like you.'

'I ask you to believe, Miss Marquez, that I was not aware of the true extent of the death and destruction that would be unleashed by Silk Fist. I am trying to make amends in the only way I can. If you will allow me to walk out of here and return to Russia, I will give you information that will allow you to destroy Silk Fist. Can we make a deal?'

Prem said: 'If Mr Blokhin is making a genuine offer then I would agree. It is more important to end Silk Fist than seek vengeance against one sadly misguided man.'

Wyatt said: 'I would trust Yuri to keep his end of the bargain and do all he can to destroy Silk Fist within Russia.'

Linda said: 'Okay, I'll go along with it. Give us the information, Mr Blokhin.'

'Firstly, I have already instructed my lawyers to set up a trust fund with the initial capital of one hundred million dollars to help the victims of Silk Fist. Secondly, for Christopher, I have instructed my lawyers to transfer ownership of the house in Islington to your name.'

'Yuri, there is no need to…'

'It is done, my friend. Don't thank me because now you will have to pay the bills and the iniquitous council tax. The house will never be of any use to me. I will never be able to return to my beloved London, or indeed New York. I will miss them both, the shops, the theatre, the museums, particularly the restaurants. I will be stuck in a dacha in the wilds of Russia guarded by grunting ex-Spetsnaz, but at least I will be with my wife and family.'

Linda said: 'The information please, Mr Blokhin.'

'It is no coincidence that Mountfitchet spends so much time on his yacht in the Bahamas. The nerve centre of Silk Fist is situated on one of the small islands of the Bahamas. I don't know which one. I was taken there in total secrecy once. It's a privately-owned island and the only building is a large house or mansion. Such a location is eminently convenient for visiting the States or Europe or South America. Your drones and spy planes and satellites, Miss Marquez, should easily be able to establish which island it is but it is well-guarded and well-protected with weaponry and electronic surveillance devices, so be very careful. That is all I have to say.' Blokhin stood up. 'Christopher, may I shake your hand.'

'No, Yuri, there is too much blood on yours.'

'A pity. Goodbye, Christopher.'

Blokhin walked out of the room.

Linda said: 'I don't trust him.'

Prem said: 'At least we now have something firm to take to the President tomorrow. If you will excuse me, I will have to report back to Delhi.'

Wyatt pushed back the bed covers and made to get out.

Linda said: 'Where do you think you're going?'

'We have a lot to do before tomorrow.'

'I have a lot to do, you're staying here to rest.'

'I feel fine now. Who's going to stop me?'

'Me, for a start, and then those four Secret Service agents stationed outside.'

'You make a good case, Sergeant Marquez.'

52

Situation Room, White House, Washington DC,
May 17th

President Joe Logan led Wyatt, Prem and Linda into the White House Situation Room. Already waiting was Vice President Cley Kefalas together with two other men. All three stood up when the President entered.

Logan said: 'Please sit down, gentlemen.'

Wyatt said: 'This place is very similar in size and layout to the COBRA briefing room in London. Did we copy you or did you copy us?'

Logan smiled. 'I guess there have to be certain similarities in places like this. It's totally secure, bomb proof, and with all these screens and equipment I can run the entire country from in here. Sometimes I come down, lock myself in and watch a movie to get away from Marty.'

Nobody was certain whether to smile or not.

Logan looked at the assembled faces and said: 'I'm kidding, guys.'

His comment was met with relieved half-smiles.

Logan indicated the chairs grouped around the table. 'Let's sit down. Gentlemen, this is Sergeant Linda Marquez of the Secret Service, Sergeant Christopher Wyatt of the Metropolitan Police in London, and Premendra Dhawan of the Research and Analysis Wing of Indian intelligence. These are the people who unearthed Silk Fist without our help when all our investigative systems failed. I'm not sure whether to give them a medal or lock them up for hiding from us.'

Vice President Kefalas grinned and said: 'I'm embarrassed that all our resources could not find out what you three found out. Your report this morning was the damnedest thing I ever read. Well done.'

Logan said: 'This meeting is small and ultra secure. We don't want anymore leaks before we're ready to take down Silk Fist. These two in civilian clothes are the military officers who are planning the assault on Silk Fist headquarters. I requested that they dress in civvies to minimise drawing attention to what we are planning. First, this is Lieutenant General Bob Briscoe, commanding officer of the army Special Operations Command.'

Briscoe nodded in acknowledgement. He was a big man, almost fleshy, with jowls than made him look like a bulldog. He had thinning sandy hair with freckles on his head. He looked uncomfortable in suit and tie but there was no mistaking his air of command and the steely intelligence in his eyes.

Logan went on: 'This is Captain Bill Knighton. He will command in the field and lead the SEAL assault teams.'

Knighton was a lean black man of average height and, despite being in his early forties, a trace of grey in his hair. His speech and actions were quick, almost nervy. His eyes darted everywhere, not missing anything. He said: 'Sergeant Wyatt, the Vice President told me that you were in the Special Boat Service.'

'Yes, sir, that's right.'

'Pity you'll have to sit this one out.'

Wyatt nodded but said nothing.

Logan said: 'We seven are the only ones who know about the planned raid on Silk Fist headquarters. I have deliberately not involved the CIA, FBI or NSA, nor any services of a foreign country, including Great Britain. Surprise will be paramount to the success of this mission. Captain Knighton's men have been training but they are not yet aware of the purpose of their mission. They will not be told until they are on their way to the target. Bob, would you like to tell us what you've found out about Silk Fist headquarters.'

'Yes, sir.' Briscoe stood up and went to a large screen at the far end of the Situation Room. He picked up a laser pointer and a map of the Bahama islands appeared on the screen.

'Silk Fist headquarters is located on a small island called Starfish Cay. As you can see from the map, Starfish Cay is situated to the north of Grand Bahama. If we go in close you can see why the island is so named. It's roughly shaped like a starfish with those five arms sticking out. It's located some seventy miles off the coast of Florida and a three hour flight from New York. There are regular flights to the Bahamas from London, so it's ideally situated for travelling between the two countries if, as we suspect, Silk Fist is a mainly Anglo-American operation. Grand Bahama is a world centre for yachting so if Silk Fist are using communications by sea, such as Lord Mountfitchet's *Golden Boy* yacht, they would not be noticed in amongst all the other sea traffic.'

Linda asked: 'Does Mountfitchet own that island, or live there?'

'No. Starfish Cay is a privately owned island, registered in the name of a company called Zeta Bail (UK) Limited. Mountfitchet's Nobar Holdings does own that company but Zeta Bail is one among dozens of companies they own and Mountfitchet is not recorded as a resident.'

Linda picked up a pen and White House notepad. 'Could you spell the name of that company?'

Briscoe spelt it out.

Prem asked: 'Does that name mean anything to you, Linda?'

'Perhaps. Let me think about it.'

With a trace of irritation at being interrupted, Briscoe went on: 'The only significant building on Starfish Cay is a large and sprawling two-storey house strongly constructed from stone and brick. The satellite and the drone shows that it must have several rooms, probably about twenty. We have been unable to locate the architect's plans. Here is the photograph. It's further protected by that overhanging roof. It's built about two hundred yards off the southern beach. Inland is dense with tropical trees and shrubbery but the drone picked up evidence of radar and anti-aircraft defences. There is a fleet of fast speedboats, ostensibly for the amusement of the guests, but they patrol regularly. There are two or three out at all times. Also, there are these umbrella type thatched constructions. They look like shelters for sunbathers but they could be disguising all sorts of nasties such as missile launchers or machine guns. There are at least twenty or thirty men on the island but we didn't see any women.'

Logan said: 'So these guys are ready for trouble?'

'Yes, sir, definitely.'

Wyatt said: 'If Blokhin was telling the truth then they are certainly ex-Spetsnaz special forces personnel, which means big trouble.'

Kefalas said: 'Okay, so let's lob a Tomahawk cruise missile right into the middle and blow the bastards to smithereens. Game over.'

Prem said: 'That's a tempting and easy solution but it would be useful to seize as much information as we can about Silk Fist, not only to help the poor souls who have been affected but also because Blokhin hinted that Silk Fist were planning something really big.'

Kefalas said: 'I take your point but we will be risking the lives of our boys by staging some sort of raid. If you go in by sea, even in fast attack boats, they'll be able to destroy the evidence and have time to stage fierce resistance. Same if you parachute in. Not only will they have time to destroy the evidence, they'll be able to shoot you out of the sky.'

Wyatt said: 'There's only one way of taking them completely by surprise and that's a HALO drop. We'll be on top of them and taking them out before they even know we exist.'

Captain Knighton nodded and said: 'That's exactly what we're preparing at this moment, a HALO drop combined with a perfectly timed back-up assault by fast boats and choppers.'

Linda asked: 'What does HALO drop mean?'

Wyatt said: 'HALO stands for High Altitude, Low Opening parachute jump. We can jump from thousands of feet up, preferably at night, way above any radar or human spotters they may have, glide in, open our chutes at the last moment and we'll be on them before they know it. We'll take them completely by surprise.'

Logan said: 'Captain Knighton, please explain your attack plan in more detail.'

Knighton stood up and joined Briscoe at the screen. 'There will be two SEAL teams. One will land at these beaches to the north. Their objective will be to move inland and eliminate any surface-to-air missile capability or anti-aircraft weapons before the choppers fly in. The other team will land at the southern beach and will secure the house and contents before they can be destroyed. Thus we also catch the defenders in a pincer. There will be a fire fight but the operation will be co-ordinated with a combined assault by sea and with helicopters. They can come in almost simultaneously, thus the enemy will be way outnumbered as soon as possible. There will inevitably be casualties but we hope to keep them as light as possible.'

Wyatt said: 'When is the raid being carried out?'

President Logan said: 'Tomorrow night or early morning of the next day. It has to be done as soon as possible. Yaroslav Blokhin has disappeared into Russia. I'm not best pleased with the deal you three made with Blokhin but I accept we wouldn't have learned anything if you hadn't done so. Mountfitchet must be aware that his attempt to kill Linda and Prem by dosing Wyatt with Hiatus has failed. We'll ask the British or Bahamian authorities, wherever he may be, to pick him up as soon as the raid starts. We don't want Silk Fist to get an inkling of our actions beforehand. As soon as the raid starts I'm going to tell the world about Silk Fist so that anyone who is in possession of the drug can hand it in or destroy it or stop using it or whatever. So, when we all leave this Situation Room I want mouths firmly shut. I'm not even going to tell the First Lady. If anyone spills the beans about this they'll end up in Guantanamo wearing an orange suit. That's a promise.'

Prem asked: 'Mr President, have the Bahamian government been informed of this assault. After all, we'll be taking military action in a foreign country.'

'No, no-one has been told, or will be told beforehand. I'll take any international diplomatic flak for authorising the raid. After all, Starfish Cay is privately owned and no Bahamian citizens will be harmed. Bob, and Captain Knighton, I authorise you to go ahead. You can have any equipment or back-up you need from anywhere. If you run into any obstruction or objection, let me know and I'll boot them out of the way. Okay, let's move.'

The men made to stand up but Linda said: 'Mr President, may I ask about Charlotte Windsor. Has she been released from custody yet?'

'She was released yesterday and I called her myself to apologise for her treatment. She's quite a girl. She was more worried about you and Sergeant Wyatt than she was about herself.'

'Can I also ask about this man Francois Walden?'

'What about him?'

'Sir, we found it necessary to threaten the life of his wife and family to extricate ourselves from a bad situation but he told us that Silk Fist had already threatened to kill them for real if he betrayed them. I would hate to think that Walden's family would suffer because of his actions.'

Wyatt said: 'I agree with Linda, sir. Walden is a creepy piece of shit but his family are completely innocent. If, by any chance, Silk Fist did find out that Walden had co-operated with us then they might take it out on his wife and kids.'

Logan nodded and said: 'It's a good point and I accept your concern. We want that factory intact as well. The President of France owes me a favor. I will request, as soon as we're finished here, that his special forces boys, in total secrecy, move in to protect Walden's home, family and factory.'

Logan stood up but Wyatt said: 'Mr President, I'd like your permission to go in with the HALO team.'

Logan sighed and sat down again. Before he could reply, Knighton, who had remained standing, said: 'That's out of the question, Sergeant Wyatt. I will not endanger this operation, or my men, by taking along amateurs to get in the way. It's far too dangerous.'

'With respect, captain, I'm not an amateur. I've been trained for HALO drops.'

Linda grabbed Wyatt's arm and said: 'Chris, are you crazy? You've done enough to destroy Silk Fist, more than any of us. Leave it to the experts.'

'I am an expert. I've learned more about Silk Fist than anybody. I could be useful.'

Knighton said: 'As I understand, you've recently been hospitalised after a traumatic event. That could leave you more vulnerable to hypoxia.'

'I'm well aware of the risks. Mr President, I appeal to you again. Give me permission to go with the HALO team. It would be good for Anglo-American relations to have one British participant.'

Logan looked at Wyatt while he considered the request. 'It's true you have more knowledge of Silk Fist than anybody else and it would be a good diplomatic move to have a Brit on board. Captain Knighton, if I give permission for Wyatt to go, could he be prepared in time.'

'Theoretically, yes sir, but I still say…'

'Sergeant Wyatt, do you genuinely feel physically able to do this?'

'Yes, sir. Get me checked out by the doctors if you don't believe me.'

Knighton said emphatically: 'I'll certainly be doing that.'

The President nodded. 'Very well, Sergeant Wyatt, you can go with them. That's an order, Captain Knighton.'

Knighton could hardly contain his fury. 'I will, of course, obey your order, sir, but I'd like it on record that I protest most strongly about taking Wyatt. If the mission is compromised or any of my men harmed because of his involvement then I will shoot him myself.'

Linda said angrily: 'Dammit, Chris, you're a stubborn son of a bitch. You've risked your life several times already. Why not sit this one out?'

'I've never been one for sitting things out, Linda.'

'Well, if you're taking part in the raid then so am I. Mr President, I want permission to go in with one of the choppers.'

Logan looked at Linda with something like amusement. 'Hey, this is not a day trip to Coney Island.'

'I'm a serving officer in the Secret Service, sir. If this British officer is allowed to go, then so should I be.'

Wyatt said: 'Bloody hell, Linda, you're exasperating at times. Just because I volunteer doesn't mean you have to.'

Logan said: 'Bob, what do you think?'

Briscoe said: 'We could put Sergeant Marquez in one of the later back-up choppers. That should be safe enough.'

Prem said: 'If Linda takes part then I request to go with her.'

Logan sighed wearily: 'Bob, will that be all right?'

'Yes, sir. There'll be room.'

Logan said: 'Perhaps I should invite my Aunt Florence from down in Macon. Okay, now we've decided on the passenger list, can we please get this show on the road.'

They stood up. Logan held Linda back as the others filed out of the room. He said: 'Marty's back and she'd like to see you now we've finished here. She's up in our living quarters.'

'Do you know what she wants to see me about, sir?'

'I've no idea but she seems... edgy.'

53

Presidential Quarters, White House, Washington DC, May 17th

For the second before the butler announced that she was there, Linda caught a poignant impression of how privileged and yet how lonely the life of the First Lady could be.

Martina Logan was eating lunch alone in the dining room. The television news was on but with the volume turned off. The First Lady's favourite composer, Brahms, was playing softly in the background. She looked sad and distracted.

The butler coughed discreetly and said: 'Excuse me, mam, Sergeant Marquez is here.'

Martina Logan's face lit up with unfeigned pleasure as she stood up and embraced Linda. 'It's so good to see you again, Linda. I've been so worried about you. I feared that something bad had happened. Is it true that you and that guy Wyatt have found out what Silk Fist is all about?'

'We've found out a lot, yes.'

'So Wyatt wasn't a renegade traitor after all.'

'No, he's not. He's a loyal servant of his country and a good friend of America.'

'That's good news. Come and sit down and have a cup of coffee with me. Tell me what's been going on.'

'I can't stay long, mam. I have to report… well, I've been given an assignment.'

'What's all this "mam" business. I'm Marty, remember. What's your assignment?'

'I'm sorry, Marty, but I can't tell you.'

Martina Logan looked surprised. 'Can't tell me?'

'No. I'm sorry.'

'Who ordered you not to tell me?'

'The President himself.'

'He surely didn't include me in that order.'

Linda did not reply.

Martina Logan said: 'You mean he did include me?'

'I'm afraid so.'

'Is this something to do with Silk Fist.'

'I can't tell you.'

'Well, never mind.' Martina Logan poured coffee. 'Tell me what you've been up to these past few weeks.'

'I'm sorry, Marty, but the President has ordered me not to say anything about that either.'

Martina Logan looked at her personal assistant with a mixture of puzzlement and concern. 'Are you okay, Linda? You seem tense and edgy.'

'The past few weeks have been a strain.'

'Of course, it must have been. It'll be good to get you back in harness. I've really missed your sound advice, not to mention your company and friendship. You'll need a vacation, of course, but when do you think you'll be coming back to work?'

Linda looked down at her hands. 'I don't know, Marty. Lot's of things have changed in the past few weeks. Lots of things I was certain about don't seem so certain anymore. I'll need time to think, depending what happens in the next few days.'

'You're not thinking of leaving the Secret Service, are you?'

'No. I love my job. I think I make a useful contribution.'

'Indeed you do. Are you thinking of leaving me?'

'I haven't made any decision yet, Marty. I'll have to see what…'

'Look at me, Linda. Something's changed between us. I was genuinely delighted to see you walk through that door a few minutes ago, but you looked at me warily. There's a barrier between us that wasn't there before, even allowing for all that you've been through this year. I regard you as a true friend, not just someone who happens to work for me. Won't you tell me what's wrong?'

Linda took a deep breath. 'Marty, I do love working for you and I, in turn, regard you as a true friend, but you have put me in an impossible situation.'

'Have I? In what way do you mean?'

'Your husband is the President of the United States, which means he is my commander-in-chief. I owe him my total allegiance.' Linda glanced out of the doorway to make sure the butler was not hovering to overhear. Then she leaned forward and said quietly: 'Marty, I know you're having an affair with Cley Kefalas.'

Linda expected a denial but Martina Logan did not react for a few moments. Then she said: 'How did you find out?'

'The looks, the body language. I suspected. After all, not only am I a woman but I've been trained to look for such signs. I couldn't be certain until I overheard the Vice President call you Speedy when we were on that flight back from London. It seemed a curious pet name. It wasn't until I saw you dressing and noticed the small tattoo of Speedy Gonzales that my suspicions were confirmed. That tattoo is on a part of your body that the Vice President has no business knowing about.'

'That tattoo was a stupid adolescent prank. I could have simply told Cley about it.'

'Are you denying that you two are having an affair?'

'No. How long have you suspected?'

'Since earlier this year, about when all this Silk Fist stuff erupted. Marty, if you were an ordinary woman then your personal life would be entirely your own business. I even understand why you're having an affair, but you're the First Lady and the President is my commander-in-chief. What the hell am I supposed to do?'

'An affair is hardly a matter of national security.'

'It is when it involves the First Lady and the Vice President. Why are you doing this?'

'Why do you think?'

'It's not up to me. I…'

'No, come on, Linda. I'm being open with you. You tell me. I've been the First Lady now for nigh on six years. That's the First Lady, Linda, not the First Woman. Sometimes, a lady is not what I want to be. I still love Joe but you've seen what the job has done to him. The worry, the strain, the eating and the drinking to help him survive the stress. I'm proud of him, of what he has achieved, but he's become overweight and over-tired, old before his time. He hasn't shown any interest in me as a woman for a long time. I like sex, Linda, and I'm still in good shape. Cley is a widower and a charming and good-looking man. He showed his interest and I welcomed it. There, I guess I've answered my own question.'

'I guess you have. I understand all that, Marty, and I can't say I blame you but it leaves me in an awkward dilemma. My duty should be to tell the President.'

'Are you going to do that, Linda?'

'No, Marty, not for the time being at least. In the next few days there are things that are going to happen that will need the President's full attention. I don't intend to distract him.'

'Then after that?'

'It's up to you, Marty. Are you going to carry on with the affair?'

'Would you stay with me if I stopped it?'

'Yes. I've always wanted to serve out the last two years of the administration and stay with you in the White House. Are you going to end it?'

Martina Logan said: 'I don't know whether I can. My feelings for Cley are very strong. We became even closer after that business in London when we were both injured. I'm not sure what I'm going to do.'

'Then neither do I, Marty. Neither do I.'

Linda left the presidential quarters and took the lift down to the first floor. She smiled to herself about thinking of it as a lift, in Wyatt's British terminology, instead of an elevator like a good American girl.

Wyatt... she could hit him for volunteering to take part in some insanely dangerous military action. She had already lost a loved one this year. The thought of losing Wyatt as well...

Linda stepped out but then stopped as the lift doors closed behind her. She took out the note she had written down in the Situation Room. Thoughts and words had made a connection in her mind. There had to be a connection.

She walked along to the Press Corps office and went in. There were five reporters working in the office, two of whom were aware that she was the First Lady's personal assistant.

One veteran reporter looked up and said: 'Wow, this is an unexpected privilege! Hey, Linda, where's the President today? What's going on? There's a lot of activity but nobody is telling us anything.'

Linda said: 'Sorry, guys, I'm just a humble secretary. All I do is type memos and make the coffee.'

The reporter laughed. 'Humble secretary? I wish I knew half of what you know goes on around here, I'd have made editor years ago.'

Linda smiled. 'My lips are sealed, boys. Can I use one of your screens?'

'Help yourself. I promise I won't peek. Not until you've gone anyway.'

Linda sat down at the nearest PC and typed her request into an internet translation service.

Ten minutes later, having deleted the record of the information she had accessed, Linda hurried into President Logan's outer office and asked to see him on a matter of national urgency.

Five minutes later she was shown into the Oval Office. The door closed behind her.

Logan was sitting behind the Resolute desk. He said: 'Hello, Linda. What can I do for you?'

'Sir, I've found out who is behind Silk Fist.'

54

C-130 Hercules Transport Aircraft, above Grand Bahama, May 19th

T he jumpmaster ordered: 'Five minutes to drop zone. Form lines!'

Wyatt stood up. He was last in the starboard drop queue. Captain Knighton had informed him, in no uncertain terms, that he and his men were not waiting for Wyatt. Wyatt was completely on his own and, if he screwed up, Wyatt would be at the end of the line and could not interfere with the mission.

The jumpmaster ordered: 'Switch on your oxygen.'

The red lights, necessary to adjust the eye to the darkness outside, cast an eerie glow inside the cavernous aircraft. It was three o'clock in the morning.

The jumpmaster said: 'You will be exiting at 25,000 feet. Wind speed is low, five mph. The ground temperature is 63 degrees. There is minimal cloud and ground level is clear. Your HGRPs are set to open at 3,500 feet. The descent to this altitude will take two minutes. After that control of the HGRP is in your hands. Any questions?'

There were no questions.

The physiology technician approached Wyatt and asked: 'Sergeant Wyatt, how do you feel?'

'Fine,' Wyatt lied. He was more nervous that on similar previous missions and was taking a big risk so soon after suffering the effects of Hiatus.

The PT said: 'If you have any doubts or any problems, state them now. Do not endanger yourself or this mission.'

'I'm fine. Peter Piper picked a peck of pickled pepper. How's that?'

'I haven't any idea what that means but you seem okay. Good luck.'

The jumpmaster was going through his check list as the rear loading bay door lowered to reveal wispy clouds and, thousands of feet below, the lights of Grand Bahama Island. Starfish Cay was not yet visible. Wyatt was relieved that conditions were almost perfect for a night jump. He had not done this in a long time.

Captain Knighton, first in the starboard queue, turned and said through his radio mic: 'As soon as we jump the fast assault craft will be called up into position and when the island is secured the helicopters will be called in. Our job is to neutralise all resistance and all dangers within that house and surroundings before they arrive. Good luck, men.'

The jumpmaster said: 'Thirty seconds to HARP. Double check oxygen!'

Each SEAL team member, twelve in the port queue and twelve in the starboard, was wearing a black helmet, anti-biological warfare breathing apparatus combined with oxygen supply, parachute on the back, weapons packs on the front, gloves, jump suits and boots. The only colours allowed were the small Stars and Stripes and regimental badges on helmets and jump suit. Wyatt thought that his companions looked like alien monsters, as he must look.

The jumpmaster was counting down. 'Five, four, three, two, one… go.' The launch light changed from red to green and Captain Knighton stepped off the loading platform. His men followed him and Wyatt shuffled along until he too stood on the edge of the world. With only a momentary hesitation he took a deep draught of oxygen and hurled himself into the void.

Wyatt was horrified to find himself tumbling head over heels but after a few seconds he managed to right himself and adopted the freefall position with arms and legs splayed out and slightly bent.

He was rusty and was glad that his mistake could not be observed by the others below him.

The cold at this altitude, even in the mild Bahamas, was intense. The curvature of the Earth, gilded by an eerie green-gold glow, was visible at the edge of the horizon. Off to the east, invisible to any radar over the horizon on Starfish Cay, was the aircraft carrier from where the Seahawk helicopters would take off. Off to the west a much smaller warship had launched six fast assault craft. Wyatt could see their white wakes but the black rubber craft were invisible as they sped towards their objective.

Below him the SEAL teams looked like sinister black insects as they fell to earth. Wyatt's heart was pounding but with exhilaration rather than fear. He had almost forgotten how liberating and life-enhancing it was to be plummeting unfettered towards a dangerous enemy.

He was now falling at over 120 miles per hour. The wind resistance made it difficult to turn his head or adjust his limbs. The roar was deafening despite the protection of the helmet. Wyatt could hear his own rasping breathing, lungs sucking in oxygen so that the decompression would not ravage his bloodstream like a deep sea diver with the bends.

Starfish Cay was now visible like a black spider set against the phosphorescent green sea. There were no signs of activity or alarm but they were not quite close enough to be certain they had not been seen.

Wyatt suddenly found it difficult to breathe. His limbs began to tremble and his heart rate shot up. It was difficult to think and there was a blackness around the edges of his vision. Wyatt recognised the first stages of hypoxia. He began talking to himself to ward off the unconsciousness that swirled around his vision and his mind. He battled to stay alert and ward off panic and then, to his intense relief, he saw Knighton's High Glide Ratio Parachute open at the 3,500 feet mark.

Their target, Silk Fist headquarters, was now clearly visible, stark against the white sands and the jade green sea. All SEAL team parachutes had opened and then Wyatt felt the reassuring tug as his own flying wing blossomed above him. His breathing and pulse steadied and he regained full alertness.

Wyatt saw that Knighton had landed near the house but had somehow stumbled. He had managed to release his parachute but was having difficulty standing up. Two of his men landed and tried to help but Knighton angrily urged them forward to assault the house.

Wyatt was desperately trying to control his descent using the adjusting strings either side. He was out of practice and was swaying alarmingly and swerving left and right. He dreaded the humiliation of crashing into the trees or into the house.

The SEAL team had surrounded the house. Knighton had painfully got to his feet and was hobbling towards his men. The SEALs had deployed grenade launchers to lob gas and stun grenades straight through the windows of the house. Some of the inmates were returning fire with machine guns. The beach had become a blinding and deafening cacophony of machine gun fire and exploding grenades. On the other side of the island there were enormous puffballs of orange explosions and the rattle of machine guns as the second SEAL team took out the anti-aircraft missile installations.

Back at the house some of the defenders were already reeling out of the front door, choked and stunned by the grenades and dispirited by the unexpected ferocity of the assault. They threw down their weapons, unwilling to die for a lost cause, and the SEALs moved forward to secure the house.

Wyatt swayed towards the beach. A defender ran out from the protection of the tropical undergrowth. He was shirtless, wild-eyed and dishevelled but he was brandishing a handgun. He aimed the pistol at Knighton's back. Wyatt shouted a warning through his mic but Knighton could not hear through the deafening din of the assault. Wyatt did not have time to take out a weapon. He was directly above the gunman. He thumped the parachute release and fell straight down from thirty feet. He landed on top of the gunman and they crashed into the soft sand. The gunman, shocked and winded, dropped his pistol. He began shouting obscenities in Russian.

Wyatt stood up and tried to grab the gunman but was hampered by the weapons pack strapped to his front. The gunman wriggled away and picked up his pistol. Wyatt reached for the combat knife sheathed in his boot. He hurled it at the gunman. The knife pierced his left shoulder but did not disable him. The gunman roared with pain and fired two shots. Wyatt was knocked backwards by the impact. Then the gunman's chest was torn and pockmarked with red blotches as machine gun bullets ripped through him. He collapsed face down in the white sand.

Knighton hobbled towards Wyatt and said: 'Are you okay?'

Wyatt said: 'I'm okay, thanks to Kevlar and a full weapons pack. Good shooting, boss.'

Knighton helped Wyatt to his feet. Wyatt unstrapped the weapons pack and took out a lightweight Hechler and Koch submachine gun. It had been dented by a bullet but was operable. Wyatt supported Knighton as they walked towards the house.

Suddenly there were two explosions further down the coast. Bright orange fireballs lit up the night sky. The six fast assault craft roared up on to the sand. The Marine units jumped out and fanned out to form a defensive perimeter. There was the thwump of helicopter rotor blades in the distance.

One of the SEALs came out of the house and reported to Knighton that the downstairs was secured.

Wyatt asked: 'Any sign of Silk Fist equipment yet?'

'No. The downstairs area is fixed up as a barracks with sleeping quarters, kitchens and bathrooms and so on. We're about to secure the upstairs area.'

Knighton said: 'You go in with them, Wyatt. That's what you're here for.'

Wyatt went inside. Swirling smoke and gas filled the house. The SEALs were leading or carrying out ten wounded defenders in various states of unconsciousness or choking on tear gas. Wyatt followed the SEAL team as they started up a central staircase.

Upstairs and off to the right were several rooms that proved to be empty. To the left a short corridor led to a locked metal door.

Wyatt said: 'That's where Silk Fist will be, behind that door.'

The SEAL team leader said: 'Whoever is in there will almost certainly be unconscious from the gas but we have to be careful. We'll blow the door and go in.'

Wyatt wanted to ask them not to cause too much damage but decided to stay silent.

The SEAL leader called up a colleague who produced a round object that looked like a small landmine. He attached it to the metal door and set the timer. The leader ordered everyone to go back around the corner and into the shelter of the stairway. Within seconds there was a ground-shaking explosion and a pall of grey smoke billowed out. The SEALs leapt around the corner, lobbed two stun grenades into the room beyond and then went in.

Only moments later the team leader came out and said: 'Room secure. One occupant, unconscious. Wyatt, you'd better come and look at this.'

Wyatt went in. Through the gradually clearing smoke he saw that he was in a large room equipped with filing cabinets, computers, laptops, radio receivers and other equipment he did not recognise. Two large metal waste bins were filled with charred paper that had been crushed down to fine dust. The filing cabinet drawers were open and empty. The computer and laptop hard drives had been taken out and hacked and hammered out of shape and beyond any chance of retrieval.

The SEAL leader said: 'Looks like this guy was destroying this stuff long before we arrived. He's even wearing an oxygen mask against the gas but the stun grenades knocked him out. Do you recognise him?'

Wyatt walked over to where the man was slumped forward unconscious on a desk. Wyatt pulled him back by his shirt collar and then let go again with a start. 'Bloody hell!' he exclaimed.

'You know who he is?'

'I certainly do,' Wyatt said. 'Whatever else you do, make sure he stays alive.'

'Those are our orders, and to seize anything and everything we find in here. I'll call in the medics and the tech boys as soon as the choppers land.'

Wyatt was suddenly overwhelmed with strain and fatigue. He said: 'I'm going outside for fresh air. There's nothing more I can do here.'

Wyatt went downstairs, walked out to the beach and took off his helmet and oxygen mask. He took several deep breaths of clean night air and immediately felt invigorated.

Helicopters with powerful searchlights beaming down were criss-crossing the island. The SEALs and their Marine comrades were swarming all over Starfish Cay, making secure and searching for any remaining personnel and equipment.

Captain Knighton noticed Wyatt and hobbled over. He said: 'Six of theirs killed or wounded. On our side three wounded, one serious, but no-one killed. Trust me to wrench my goddamn ankle on landing.'

Wyatt smiled. 'Perhaps you're getting past it, like me. You were right, captain, I should not have joined in. I narrowly avoided being a liability tonight.'

'No, you did good tonight. Thanks for saving my ass out on the beach.'

'Thanks for saving mine. If that bloke had got a shot at my face I'd have been a gonner. Congratulations, captain. This was a most impressive operation.'

Knighton nodded and limped off to supervise the clear-up.

Wyatt saw Linda and Prem walking towards him from the secure helicopter landing area down the beach. He waved in greeting. Prem waved back. Linda did not.

As they walked nearer Prem said: 'Thank goodness you are safe, Christopher.'

'Thanks, Prem. Nothing so invigorating as diving out into nothingness from 25,000 feet.' Wyatt turned to Linda. 'Wow, you look good even in helmet and combat fatigues.'

'Thanks,' Linda said curtly.

'Are you still angry with me? I'm still in one piece.'

'More luck than sense. It was a stupid macho move to join in with all this. Did you find anything inside?'

'Yes. Blokhin was right. This is where Silk Fist operates. I'll bet you a hundred dollars you'll never guess who we found inside.'

Linda said: 'I'll take that bet.' She whispered in Wyatt's ear.

Wyatt exclaimed: 'How the hell did you know that?'

'I'll tell you later. Make sure you have the hundred bucks ready and I won't take a cheque. Come on, Prem. Now that macho man here has got his rocks off for the evening let's go see what we've got in here.'

55

Langley Oaks Hospital, Washington DC, May 24th

Linda Marquez and Christopher Wyatt were escorted into a private room on the top floor of the hospital.

The man they had come to interview was fully clothed and sitting in a wheelchair by the window. He was looking out at a leaden grey sky and down at the screen of armed soldiers guarding the outside approaches to the hospital.

Dr Anthony Jaso turned his wheelchair to greet his visitors. He appeared even more gaunt and wasted. He was deathly pale, the last wisps of hair burned from his skull, his teeth yellow, a lanky and emaciated living cadaver. In a frail voice, struggling for breath, he said: 'Ah, the sergeants two. How nice to see you again. You must have been surprised to find me alive on Starfish Cay.'

Wyatt said: 'No surprise to Sergeant Marquez, Jaso. She worked out the hidden clue in the name of your company.'

'How clever of you, Linda!'

'My friends and other civilised human beings call me Linda. You may call me Sergeant Marquez.'

'Ouch,' Jaso said. 'All this hatred and security for a living corpse like me. Armed guards inside and out, a special room in a special hospital normally reserved for the great and good of the CIA, all the medical equipment necessary to keep me alive, and my bed neatly made by a caring nurse. I'm very grateful to the authorities. Won't you please sit down? I arranged for a pair of comfortable armchairs to be brought in. I suspect this will be a long session.'

Wyatt and Linda reluctantly sat down.

Wyatt said: 'Why us, Jaso? Why did you refuse to talk to anyone else except we two?'

'Because I like you. You were kind to me on my little island on Barrow Lake, despite your attempts to intimidate me. I could see in your eyes, both of you, that you suffer from the fatal flaws of compassion and morality. Also I'm intrigued. I understand that you two were mainly instrumental in bringing my empire crashing down upon my head.'

Linda and Wyatt made no reply.

'Such modesty!' Jaso said. 'I fooled everybody. I duped all the so-called intelligence services… except you two. You told me you were fugitives, that you had evaded the machinations of your superiors as well. No doubt you've been prepared for this meeting by teams of government officials and intelligence service chiefs, but rather than being interrogated by robotic agents in suits, I chose to talk to you two, my worthy adversaries.'

Wyatt said: 'If it was up to me, Jaso, I'd simply pump you full or sodium pentathol. Or, better still, wire your testicles to the mains.'

'I'm sure the government spooks would have done the same but the doctors would not allow it, bless their hearts. America is a strange country, governed by politicians who are prepared to invade and kill thousands out of belief in the American way of life, with those governed displaying such humanity, kindness and respect for the law that I wonder why they tolerate the excesses of their rulers. But just as the British deify their only too human royal family, we Americans deify our only too human Presidents. Such treatment as you suggest, Sergeant Wyatt, would inevitably have finished me off and then you would learn nothing about Silk Fist. I thought that a pleasant chat with you two would be much more acceptable as one of the last things I ever do. Can't we talk without unpleasantness?'

Linda said: 'The husband I loved is dead because of you. So are the loved ones of hundreds of others. If you want pleasantness then find someone else to confess to.'

'I understand your pain, Linda. No, don't say anything. As I told you, I lost my wife to cancer and my daughter to a road accident. I understand the pain of loss. I've been told that this room is not wired and that this conversation is not being recorded. That, of course, is arrant nonsense. It certainly is being recorded and I'm sure that your superior officers wish you to ask pertinent questions in order to learn more about Silk Fist. Bitter as you are, they do not want a simple bout of name calling. I am inordinately proud of what I achieved with Silk Fist. In criminal terms, I am on the same level as Napoleon and the great Alexander were in military terms. I want a record of what I achieved. I want it known. Shall we proceed on that basis?'

Wyatt said: 'Okay, let's get this over with so we can get away from you as soon as possible. Who tipped you off about our raid on Starfish Cay so that you had time to destroy all the evidence?'

'No-one "tipped me off". After I was informed about your escapade aboard Mountfichet's yacht, that you had defeated the effects of Hiatus and that Blokhin had disappeared into Russia, I suspected that he had betrayed me and that you would be paying me a visit. I decided to pre-empt you and destroy the evidence first.'

'I don't believe you,' Wyatt said.

Jaso shrugged. 'As you wish. I would like to ask Linda how she worked out my involvement from the name of my company. Well, technically it was Mountfichet's company but I gave him the name. I didn't think anyone would solve the conundrum. How did you do it, Linda? And remember, the President himself will probably hear this recording, so do your duty.'

Linda used all her self-control to answer. 'It was not difficult for anyone with a knowledge of the Basque language. My heritage is northern Spanish and...'

'Hence those lovely green eyes,' Jaso said. 'A feature more common in northern Spain than almost anywhere else. Go on.'

'I've studied Spanish and other languages and took a special interest in Basque. When I heard the name of your company, Zeta Bail (UK) Limited, it sounded like many companies registered in the United Kingdom with the UK part in parentheses. But I also realised that "zeta" is a Basque word meaning "silk". Bail and UK are an anagram of the Basque word "ukabil" meaning "fist". I researched your background, discovered you were of Basque heritage, and that your surname can mean "sorghum" but can also mean "lift". Thus "lift a Silk Fist". There was too much there for it simply to be a coincidence.'

'Bravo, as we Spaniards say! Ingenious!'

Linda said: 'I don't need your plaudits, Jaso.'

Wyatt said: 'Why did you point us towards Frankie Walden when we talked to you at Barrow Lake? That doesn't make any sense. You could have said nothing and denied knowledge of anything.'

'You underestimate your own effectiveness, Sergeant Wyatt. You are a large, fit and intimidating man. You could break me in two with your bare hands and when you held a pistol to my head I was not completely sure you would not use it, despite my bravado, and I was not ready to die at that moment. The good people who live around Barrow Lake think I am a harmless invalid and warned me that you were looking for me. I made sure to be at home when you visited my island but, even so, I was badly shaken when you two unexpectedly arrived by canoe. I wanted to get rid of you. I estimated that if I subtly pointed you towards Walden, who was coming to the end of his usefulness anyway, you would leave me alone. Walden didn't know that I was the creator of Silk Fist. I used him as a sacrificial lamb to turn attention away from me. I gambled that even if you found Walden you would never find out where the Hiatus was being delivered. Walden didn't know. Once again I underestimated you two.'

Wyatt said: 'The simplest solution would have been to have us murdered. After all, we were on the run. The authorities didn't know where we were. We would have simply vanished.'

'I decided it was not worth the effort to look for you. I had better ways of thwarting you.'

'Would you care to explain those "better ways"?' Linda said.

Jaso smiled. 'No, I would not.'

Wyatt said: 'What was the point of firing your shotgun after we had left? Was it simply to persuade us that you had committed suicide?'

'Yes, of course. In the hope that you would leave me alone and not report me to the authorities.'

'What if we had returned to see if you needed help?'

'Then I would have blasted you both to kingdom come with a little booby trap that I have installed in the cabin. Explosives are another field of expertise for me.'

Wyatt said: 'Jaso, you really are a vile piece of shit. Let's cut to the chase. What was the point of Silk Fist?'

Jaso grinned, a terrible death's head. 'At first, money. Pure and simple.'

'Money?' Linda said. 'You caused all this death and destruction simply to make money.'

'There was nothing simple about it, Linda. Tell me, what does money bring?'

Linda and Wyatt did not answer.

'Power and influence,' Jaso said. 'The more money, the more power. It began simply as money but the more I made the more power I attained. You would be surprised to learn how little it takes to bribe a senator or a Member of Parliament or a chief executive or even a judge or top policeman. It assuaged my bitterness over the loss of my wife and daughter. In the end, after I received my own death sentence through cancer, it became an entertaining game to see how far I could go, how far I could evade surveillance in the most surveilled countries in the world, the United States and the United Kingdom, in which George Orwell's nightmare scenario of government intrusion into our lives long ago became fact.'

'Okay,' Linda said. 'It started out as money. Why?'

'I had been working for the CIA on Project MKUltra and its descendants. After we made some astonishing breakthroughs towards development of the drug now known as Hiatus, the CIA decided to dispense with my services. They had never trusted me, the fact that my family had come from Cuba, my Basque heritage, my arrogant certainty, who knows? I had never made much money. Here I was, a brilliant chemist, unemployed, nearly penniless and bereaved. The iron entered my soul. I decided I wanted to make lots of money and, as fate would have it, I stumbled on the greatest non-lethal crime, certainly the greatest confidence trick, in the history of the world, and all literally hidden behind the decorous marble halls of the American and British banking systems, a catastrophic abomination and failure of the system of which governments took advantage. They are still frantic to suppress all public knowledge of such criminal corruption. It began with dead peasants' insurance.'

'With *what*?' Wyatt said.

'The correct term is "stranger originated life insurance". I made the discovery that you could take out insurance policies on another person's life, even if they have nothing to do with you. A certain huge American retail company had taken out dead peasants' insurance on all it's employees so that whenever any one of them died the company received a payout, often running into hundreds of thousands of dollars. The entire life insurance market was being corrupted by a huge hidden industry that was betting on other people's lives. This developed into the perfect scam with the introduction of so-called "viaticals". People who were suffering from Aids could take out life insurance policies that agreed to look after their needs until they died, after which a lump sum would be paid out. The catch for investors was that the longer the patient lived the less money the investor received. I invested in several Aids victims and used drugs in various forms to hurry them along to their graves. I literally made a killing!'

'And this was legal?' Linda said.

'Yes, perfectly legal, apart from my lethal interventions. Insurance scams were merely the start. They had provided me with a grub stake to become involved in the greatest scam in history, the derivatives market or, to be specific, the secret over-the-counter derivatives market that operated not only without government regulation but, in the beginning, without government knowledge. I had made so much money that I invested it with the most shrewd and clever speculator that I could find.'

'Lord Philip Mountfichet?' Wyatt said.

'Yes! The man is a genius and, up until this time, he was completely honest. He was in at the start of this brilliant so-called "black box" market. American and British regulators had no idea that it was going on. You had to be invited and vetted before you could join in. OTC derivatives were basically companies insuring other companies against their investments failing. There was no record keeping and no reporting. Deals were made in private between individuals. It was literally an entirely unregulated market. There was no need for transparency, no requirement for capital reserves. Fraud and manipulation were rife. All records were kept on pieces of paper locked in filing cabinets all over New York and London. This market soon became worth $27 trillion dollars. Let me emphasise that figure. Not millions, not billions, but *trillions*. This entirely secret and unregulated market was worth more that most countries, almost worth more than the entire United States. This money was being invested in legitimate hedge funds and currency speculation and so on. All the major banks were riding the boom. The entire national economy was riding the boom. Then, in 1998, the US government made things even easier by repealing the so-called Glass-Steagall Act.'

'What was that?' Wyatt asked.

It was Linda who answered his question. 'The Glass-Steagall Act was introduced during the 1930s, after the Wall Street Crash, to prevent banks from taking deposits from customers and then using them to gamble on the stock markets.'

'Absolutely right,' Jaso said. 'Following the repeal of this act the politicians were using the profits from the subsequent boom to get themselves re-elected by handing out financial bribes to the electorate. Gradually the financial authorities became aware of the size of the OTC derivatives market, notably a shrewd lawyer who was the head of the Commodity Futures Trading Commission. She went to see the head of the Federal Reserve Bank, who was then an avid and revered free marketeer whose judgement was thought to be nigh on infallible. When it was suggested to him that the OTC derivatives market should be regulated, his answer was met with frank amazement. He actually stated that he didn't believe fraud should be regulated and that market forces would balance everything out. The head of the CFTC persisted but the financial lobby is the most powerful lobby in Washington and Congress blocked her attempts to regulate these so-called "dark markets" and forced her out of her job. By 2007, the OTC derivatives market was worth nearly $600 *trillion* dollars. I myself had made billions in profits. Communism was dead, capitalism had triumphed!'

Wyatt said: 'That's absurd. It's a fantasy, a fairy tale.'

'On the contrary,' Jaso said. 'All the facts are available on the internet. Check them if you think I peddle fantasy.'

'We didn't come here for a history lesson, Jaso. What has all this got to do with Silk Fist?'

'I can see that you don't share my fascination with this shoddy period in American and British history, so I'll move on swiftly. You remember the outcome of this crazy boom. In 2008 came the sub-prime mortgage catastrophe. One bank collapsed and many others followed and had to be rescued by national governments. The whole financial integrity of the world was balanced on a knife edge. Our boom time of rich pickings had come to an end, but we wanted to carry on. We wanted more.'

Linda said: 'When you say "we", who do you mean?'

'Myself, Mountfitchet, Wyatt's friend Yaroslav Blokhin. He had become involved. We had entered the realm of the super-rich. Did you know that the wealth invested offshore by the likes of us are worth more than the American and Japanese GDPs combined? Or that over ten trillion dollars in assets are owned by about 90,000 people, a tiny elite who pay no taxes and are immune from national governments. We are truly the only free people left in the world.'

Wyatt said: 'Those guards patrolling outside don't seem to confirm your freedom.'

'That is thanks to you and Sergeant Marquez. You have ruined it for us. Two tiny and insignificant low-grade operatives such as you. How much do you two earn?'

Linda said: 'Get on with your story, Jaso. When are you getting to Silk Fist?'

Jaso sighed. 'Do you know what all super-rich people have in common?'

'They are murderous shitbags like you?'

'No, Sergeant Wyatt, they are greedy. However much money they possess they want more. The accumulation of money becomes their purpose in life. In the course of garnering their wealth they have lost their souls or any idea of how to actually enjoy life despite the lavishness of their life styles. When you can have anything you want, nothing has any meaning. Myself, Mountfitchet, Blokhin, we are all worth billions of dollars and yet we have lost what we really care about. We want more. Do you know what factor influences investments and stock markets more than any other?'

Wyatt and Linda did not reply.

'Emotions and empathy, that's what drives stock markets. An irrational herd instinct if you like. It's what John Maynard Keynes called "animal spirits". The stock market booms of the 1920s and 2000s were driven by a frantic herd instinct that these booms would never end and that if you didn't start riding the boom you would get left behind. Only a few shrewd investors could resist this lure. But the only reason that stock markets are driven by such emotions is because we cannot see into the future. Imagine that you went to the race track and knew for sure which horses would win every race. You could stake your life savings on every race and leave the track several times richer than when you entered. Then you could do the same the next day and the next day *ad infinitum*. Silk Fist was a way of seeing into the future because we were creating the future. I was unique because I bestrode two worlds, the ultra secret world of CIA mind experiments and the world of betting through hedge funds, currency and commodity markets. I had discovered a method of forcing people to perpetrate horrendous crimes that would affect the stock markets. Take the Princess Royal, for example. The very fact that the heir to the British throne was murdered affected the British stock market and, by knowing it was going to happen, we made several million pounds profit.'

Wyatt said: 'So you caused the death of a young woman for the sake of piling a few million pounds on top of the millions you had already made?'

'Yes. I can see in your face, Sergeant Wyatt, that you would love to kill me. This time I believe you are capable.'

Linda said: 'So you induced people like my husband to respond to your Hiatus advertisements on the website and answer the questionnaire?'

'Yes, and thus we could select likely victims from the nature of those answers. A garbage man in Milwaukee or a shop assistant in Manchester were of no interest to us, but top businessmen, famous people, politicians, policemen, workers in vital major industries, even bishops, were of considerable interest because they were in a position to radically affect society, and thus the stock or commodity or currency markets. After the initial response via the internet, everything was done by personal courier or by the old fashioned postal system, that's why the authorities, with all their electronic surveillance equipment, could find nothing about Silk Fist. We despatched a medically trained agent to personally deal with each prospect. Such agents could earn literally a hundred times their annual eastern European or Russian salary just for one visit. That, and the threat of death, ensured complete silence and obedience. They would administer the initial dose of Hiatus to gauge the reaction. The results were amazingly successful. Most subjects responded well, a few died after the first dose because of an adverse reaction but that was collateral damage. These men were too embarrassed to tell friends and family that they were undergoing treatment for hair loss, impotence and depression, and they were paying us to administer this quack treatment! Most went on, after indoctrination, to commit acts they would not dream of committing in their normal state, such as you, Wyatt, attempting to shoot Miss Marquez. No need to look so contemptuous, Wyatt. Most of our medically trained personnel were recruited from Russia and its former satellites by your friend Blokhin who owns the house you live in. Besides, as far as I can tell, you were the only victim to successfully resist the brainwashing affects of Hiatus. You are to be congratulated.'

Wyatt said: 'I'm still baffled by your motives, Jaso. You, and your accomplices, were already rich beyond reason. Silk Fist must have meant an enormous amount of work, expense and effort on your part. What was the point?'

Jaso nodded slowly. 'You make a perceptive point, Sergeant Wyatt. I am super-rich but I can live in only one room at a time, eat only one meal at a time, travel in one expensive car at a time, watch the same sunset, enjoy the same things that poor people enjoy. In the end such immense wealth is an illusion. We were more powerful, financially, than national governments but what could we do with such power? Silk Fist was a challenge, an experiment to see how far I could push the boundaries, how far I could manipulate society and my fellow men. To be blunt, it became something to do, a hobby, while on the long road towards the grave.'

'And you deemed it necessary to take hundreds of innocent people with you?' Linda said.

'It came with the package. Regrettable, but necessary. Also, there is one other thing you should know.'

'What's that?' Wyatt said.

'I started the Silk Fist conspiracy but I will not be the one to end it.'

'What do you mean?' Linda said.

'I mean that Silk Fist has been taken over by forces outside my control. You think that by capturing me then Silk Fist is finished.' Jaso smiled in triumph. 'The finale is yet to be played out and there is nothing you can do to stop it.'

'What finale, Jaso?' Wyatt said.

'You will see.'

'Then why tell us?'

'Because I want you two, and the whole world, to fully understand how I outsmarted you.' Jaso collapsed into a fit of coughing and wheezing. He moved his wheelchair forward to reach the oxygen mask. When he had recovered his breath, he said: 'It was kind of the authorities to allow me to keep my personalised wheelchair.'

'Screw the wheelchair,' Wyatt said. 'What finale are you talking about?'

'You've come this far, sergeants. It's up to you to go the full distance.' Jaso leaned forward. 'Remember, all solutions are contained in the head.'

'Enough riddles,' Linda said. 'What is going to happen?'

'You will witness a demonstration sooner than you think.'

'A demonstration of what?'

'You two make such a lovely and effective couple, although I guess you've had your clashes. When you work together, like two rivers meeting, you are literally unstoppable.' Jaso laughed, a laugh that turned into the hacking cough of a braying jackal.

Wyatt stood up and said to Linda: 'I've had enough of this maniac. He's playing with us now. We won't get any more out of him.'

Jaso said: 'You're a man of action, Wyatt, but Sergeant Marquez is fascinated by language and meaning. I can read in her eyes that she is already considering what I've said.'

Linda also stood up. 'You're wrong, Jaso. I'm with Chris, I've had all I can stomach of your psychopathic gloating. We'll leave you to the experts. They won't be nearly as gentle as we have been.'

Wyatt opened the door.

Jaso grinned, a terrible rictus grin of malice and triumph. He said: 'Goodbye to you both.'

Wyatt held the door open for Linda to leave first. He closed the door behind him and said: 'Did you believe what he said about...'

An ear-splitting explosion flung open the door. The blood-smeared door crashed against the wall and the violent shock wave punched Wyatt in the back. It shoved him, with Linda caught in front, across the corridor and smashed them against the far wall. They were enveloped in billowing white smoke. Wyatt's vision and reason was lost in a kaleidoscope of red and orange pulses. He collapsed against Linda, his body weight dragging her down. Linda, gasping for breath and stunned by the impact of hitting her head against the wall, heard the faraway jangle of emergency alarms as blackness descended.

56

Langley Oaks Hospital, Washington DC, May 26th

Premendra Dhawan went into Christopher Wyatt's room to find Linda Marquez sitting by the side of his bed.

Linda said: 'Hi, Prem. It's good to see you again. We haven't seen you since our adventure on Starfish Cay. Where have you been?'

'I'll come to that in a moment. I wanted to visit as soon as I heard what Jaso had done to you but I was ordered to stay at my post. I'm reassured to find you so well protected. I was thoroughly searched and vetted before they would even let me come up to this floor. How are you recovering, Christopher?'

'This grand tour of Washington hospitals is becoming wearisome but I'm recovering well. Pull up a chair and sit down, Prem.'

Prem said: 'I'm relieved that you are not hooked up to any bleeping machines although you're face is not pretty.'

Linda said: 'Chris had concussion, severe bruising and lacerations on his face. He never was a handsome brute, even less so now, but if he hadn't shielded me from the explosion then I would have been seriously injured, if not dead.'

'On the contrary,' Wyatt said. 'If I had been slammed straight into the wall instead of Linda's body then my injuries would be much more severe. Sergeant Wyatt makes a most attractive and well upholstered cushion.'

Linda smiled: 'Not so much of the well upholstered, Sergeant Wyatt.'

'It was lucky that my face slammed into the wall and not Linda's face.'

'I feel sorry for the wall,' Linda said. 'I was shocked, concussed and stone deaf for a day but no permanent damage.'

Prem said. 'Do you think Jaso meant to kill you?'

Wyatt shook his head. 'I'm not sure but I don't think so. If he had wanted us dead then he would have detonated the explosion while we were still in the room. Jaso wanted us to survive. It may have been a warning or a demonstration of his so-called cleverness. Jaso faced interrogation about Silk Fist. He he didn't have long to live and wanted to confess, in some strange bragging way, before he died.'

'How did Jaso smuggle explosives past all the security devices?'

Linda answered: 'The experts say that the explosives were contained in the hollow metal frame of his wheelchair. They had allowed him to keep his own wheelchair because it had been especially adapted for his needs.'

'But wasn't it checked or searched?'

'No-one had thought to scan it for explosives. It was a pretty mess in that room and it's difficult to say exactly how Jaso had concealed the explosives. At least the explosion did not destroy the recording of our talk with Jaso. Your copy of the transcript is on its way.'

'I have to fly back to Delhi tomorrow. Would you mind going over what Jaso said, for my benefit?'

Linda said: 'Better still, you can read my copy of the transcript.' She took a folder out of her bag and handed it to Prem.

Wyatt and Linda waited in silence while Prem read the transcript. When Prem had finished he put the folder down on Wyatt's bed but said nothing.

Linda asked: 'What are you thinking, Prem?'

Prem sighed. 'I am thinking why my Rhea had to die simply for these people to make more money. Her life was so much more worthwhile than these crazy, greedy, evil bastards.'

Wyatt said: 'It's not over yet, Prem. Blokhin told us that Silk Fist was planning something really big and Jaso hinted at the same thing. Let's hope that the experts can find some evidence from the stuff seized at Starfish Cay.'

'Ah,' Prem said disconsolately. 'I have been working at CIA headquarters for the past two days by lending them my expertise, such as it is, to their DOCEX experts examining the Starfish Cay evidence. That is why I haven't had time to visit before.'

Wyatt asked: 'What are DOCEX experts, or whatever you said?'

'DOCEX stands for Document Exploitation, in other words the retrieval and analysis of any documents, files, hard drives, whatever. I was selected, as your friend, to bring you the bad news. I'm afraid that Jaso has outwitted us again.'

'In what way?' Linda asked.

'Jaso had taken out the hard drives from his computers and laptops and damaged them sufficiently to prevent us retrieving information from them. All the paperwork was burnt and the ashes crushed to fine powder.'

Linda said: 'Didn't your experts find *anything*?'

'Nothing, apart from one piece of half-burnt paper. It had somehow slipped down in the gap between two desks.' Prem took a folded sheet of paper out of his jacket pocket and handed it to Linda. 'That is a photocopy.'

Linda looked at the paper. 'The names and addresses of six guys. I assume they are using Hiatus.' She handed the paper to Wyatt.

Prem said: 'The CIA are investigating them at this moment. Following President Logan's national and worldwide television broadcasts there has been a steady stream of information from Silk Fist buyers or users but nothing that would give any clue as to what this planned big event will be.'

'It could be anything,' Wyatt said. 'Linda and I have been talking about possible targets but it simply could be anything.'

Linda said: 'I'm convinced it's the G20 meeting at Tortola in four days time.'

Prem said: 'Why do you think that?'

'It's the obvious target. Remember what Jaso said about gambling on the stock markets and the currency markets. If a single American President is assassinated or a single British Prime Minister or a single Indian Prime Minister, the nation mourns but the world soon carries on as normal, but a cataclysmic event such as the assassination of several heads of state and their most important ministers would affect the markets more than any other event barring a huge natural disaster. I think Silk Fist plan to eliminate them all, possibly by planting an atomic bomb or something on Beef Island.'

Wyatt said: 'It would be the perfect target for Silk Fist but the location of the G20 meeting has only been publicly announced within the past few days. That leaves very little time for Silk Fist to plan an attack or plant a bomb. The security at the G20 meetings is always very rigorous because of mass protests by anti-Capitalist protesters, but because of Silk Fist it will be ultra-rigorous this time.'

Prem said: 'My prime minister is going and I can assure you that the security procedures on that island are the most detailed and thorough going I have ever known.'

Linda said firmly: 'Even so, I think I'm right. Even our combined intelligence services cannot cover all possible Silk Fist targets. The G20 conference is the obvious target, the biggest single immediate target, and Silk Fist will have to act quickly. It makes sense to concentrate on that.'

Wyatt nodded. 'Perhaps you're right.'

They talked for another half hour and then Prem stood up. 'I have to go. I have to return to my duties in Delhi but I will keep in touch. Christopher, I'm relieved to find you recovering so swiftly.'

'Nurse Marquez is looking after me well.'

Linda also stood up. 'I have to go as well. Prem, will you walk me to my car?'

'What?' Wyatt said. 'Leaving so soon, Linda? Can't you stay a bit longer?'

Linda stroked Wyatt's hair and kissed him on the forehead. 'You need to rest and recover. Get some sleep. I'll be back later.'

Prem and Linda walked across the hospital parking lot.

Prem said: 'One of the things that always fascinates me about America is the number and quality of your cars. In India the cars are kept and repaired and made to run for thirty or forty years but here every automobile is new and shiny and beautiful, especially on a bright sunny day like this with the light reflecting off all the chrome and the glass.'

Linda smiled. 'You sound almost poetic on the subject, Prem. Perhaps we Americans worship our vehicles too much. We don't care to walk too far.'

'And yet I note that you have parked your car right at the end of the lot, well away from the hospital security cameras and any possible microphone surveillance devices.'

'I've learned to be cautious over the past few months. You think I parked here deliberately?'

It was Prem's turn to smile. 'Linda, I possess only half the normal allocation of arms but I have my wits in full measure. I take it you have something you want to talk about in privacy. Do you think the authorities have us under surveillance as well?'

'Given that we have been at the centre of the Silk Fist conspiracy for months, it would be strange if they were not watching us.'

Prem nodded. 'I agree. What do you wish to talk about?'

Linda said: 'In a few minutes we will say goodbye, two friends leaving each other. I will kiss you on the cheek and slip a piece of paper into your jacket pocket. Written on that piece of paper are two telephone numbers, one a land line, the other a cell phone number. I'm asking you to use your expertise to monitor those two numbers for the next few days, or until Silk Fist is killed off. You're the only person I trust to do this, Prem. You're the only person I can turn to.'

'So you do have suspicions about someone?'

'Suspicions, yes. Hard evidence, no.'

'Does Christopher know about this?'

'No, Prem, and I would request that he never knows, despite what any outcome might be. You're aware that I've developed a deep affection for Chris but this goes beyond the personal. Chris can be impulsive, too hasty to act without sufficient thought. I would trust Chris with my life, my parent's life and the life of my children, if I had any, but I also have my duty to my country and my oath as a Secret Service agent. What I'm asking of you is dangerous, Prem.'

'Am I allowed to know the name of this person I will be monitoring.'

'Yes, of course.' Linda leaned forward. Prem felt the piece of paper being slipped into his jacket pocket. Linda kissed his cheek and whispered the name.

Prem could not hide his dismay. He said: 'If your suspicions are correct, Linda, then I pray to the great preserver god Shiva to protect us both.'

57

Oval Office, White House, Washington DC, May 29th

It was late in the evening by the time Wyatt and Linda, accompanied by Stack Franklin, were admitted to the Oval Office. President Josiah Logan and Vice President Cley Kefalas were standing in front of the Resolute Desk in deep conversation. Several secretaries and aides were bustling in and out of the Oval Office while several more people waited outside hoping for a minute of the President's time.

Logan noticed the new entrants and walked over. He said: 'Hi, Stack. Linda, Chris, it's good to see you again. I apologise for keeping you waiting and for not being able to fit you in sooner but it's been extra busy what with that crisis down in Panama and having to prepare for the G20 conference. I hope you two are fully recovered from your ordeal?'

Wyatt said: 'Yes, sir. I'm still a little bruised but I feel fine.'

Linda said: 'I was deaf for about a day but no permanent damage. It was lucky we were in a hospital when it happened.'

Logan said: 'I can only spare you a few minutes but I asked Stack to bring you here tonight because I have some good news for you. The sole piece of paper recovered from Starfish Cay revealed the names of six victims of the Hiatus drug. The CIA rounded them all up and investigated their background. One of them works for a soft drink manufacturing company. This company had been given the contract to install a soft drinks vending machine at the G20 venue on Beef Island. The machine was installed inside the main conference room and was found to be packed with explosives. If that had gone off while the heads of government were in conference it would have left the richest and most powerful countries in the world without their leaders, so we've foiled Jaso's big finale.' Logan waited for a reaction from Wyatt and Linda. He said: 'What's the matter? You two don't look very pleased with the news.'

Wyatt said: 'Sir, don't you think that was all a bit too easy?'

'What do you mean?'

'Jaso managed to destroy all the hard drives and every piece of paper except the one that oh so conveniently slid down between two desks and led to the discovery of the vending machine bomb. It's as if Jaso wanted us to find that one sheet.'

Kefalas stepped forward and said: 'Mr President, forgive me for interrupting, but allow me explain to these two. The vending machine bomb, according to our experts, was a highly sophisticated device that would have taken months to design and build. If you're thinking that it was merely a decoy then we have considered that possibility carefully. Our explosives experts are, and have been for days, searching every inch, quite literally, of Beef Island for further threats.'

Wyatt repeated: 'It's too easy.'

President Logan attempted to contain his exasperation. 'Sometimes we get lucky in life, Chris. Maybe that one piece of paper was sheer luck. Perhaps Jaso was not the all-encompassing evil genius you think he was. I can understand your concern but I assure you that everything humanly possible is being done to keep us safe on Beef Island. Linda, what do you think?'

'I agree with Chris, sir, that's why we've been trying to see you before you left. If ever the term evil genius should be applied to anyone, it should be applied to Dr Anthony Jaso. It's difficult to explain unless you've talked to the man and looked in his eyes, as Chris and I have. The whole ethos of the Silk Fist conspiracy would find a triumphant culmination in the assassination of so many heads of state at the G20. Sir, I urgently beg you to cancel the summit.'

Logan almost snorted in derision. 'That's impossible, Linda, and you know it. Even if it was entirely up to me, which it isn't, it's too late to cancel and reschedule. I'm flying down to Tortola in a few hours time. Every other head of state has arranged his or her schedule to accommodate the G20 meeting. Besides, we can't be seen to be cravenly giving in to threats and terrorism. That would be political suicide.'

Wyatt said: 'You might find it will be suicide for real.'

Logan looked at Wyatt and this time did not try to conceal his irritation. He said: 'Prime Minister Montrose warned me that you could be a blunt man. You've done great service, Chris, but don't presume to question my judgement or my courage or my authority.'

'Sir, I don't question any such things. From what I've seen of you I like you and respect you, but long serving heads of state get so used to having their arses kissed by people climbing up the ladder that they often lose sight of reality.'

Stack Franklin said: 'Whoa, hold on, Chris. You can't talk to the President like that.'

Logan turned to Kefalas and said: 'Can you believe this guy? He's talking to me like this, here in the Oval Office!'

Wyatt said: 'Sir, your mandate, as voted for by the American people, is to govern this country. I took part in no such vote and being a British subject I owe you no allegiance or respect other than what I choose to give you, man to man. Believe me, I do respect you but I've been a serving soldier, and so has the Vice President, and I hope he will confirm that sometimes soldiers have to save politicians from the folly of their own actions, that's why I urge you to consider cancelling the G20 conference.'

Cley Kefalas was looking down at the floor to conceal his grin. 'You certainly are blunt, Chris, and at the risk of incurring the displeasure of my boss, I agree that the military has to extricate their political masters from bad calls, but the President is correct on this one, it's impossible to cancel the G20. The President has to go.'

Logan said: 'Okay, Chris, you've said your piece. Now I'll have to wind this up.'

Wyatt said: 'One more question, sir. How was this vending machine bomb going to be detonated?'

'By the guy we arrested,' Logan replied. 'He would have been called in to service the machine and punched in a special code to detonate the explosives.'

'A suicide mission?' Linda said.

'I guess so, but weren't most of these Silk Fists attacks suicide missions?'

'Yes, they were,' Linda said. 'So this man was brainwashed by Hiatus?'

Kefalas said: 'The drug was found in his apartment.'

Linda said: 'When was the vending machine installed?'

Logan said: 'What the hell does that matter?'

'Please, sir, indulge me.'

'It was installed last year, in late December.'

'And when did the venue for the G20 meeting become public knowledge?'

'Not until several weeks later. Tortola is in the British Virgin Islands and is a British overseas dependency. I'd received a personal phone call from Prime Minister Montrose suggesting the venue in September last year but I didn't tell anyone, except Marty, until it was confirmed by the Brits in about December. What are you getting at?'

Linda said: 'I'm saying that if Silk Fist took months preparing this bomb they must have known the venue well in advance. Someone must have given Jaso that information.'

Now President Logan was genuinely annoyed. 'Linda, be careful! You're not suggesting that Marty gave it away?'

'No, no, of course not, sir. But somebody must have given it away or been careless.'

Stack Franklin said: 'If I may correct you, Mr President, I was told of the venue as soon as it was confirmed. I sent a team down to Tortola to report on the security situation but they *didn't* know that it was to be the G20 venue.'

Logan nodded. 'You're right, Stack. As I recall, Jonathan Schneider, our CIA man in London, was also in the loop. He was under orders from me not to tell his own boss.'

Linda cut through the momentary silence by saying: 'Sir, I respectfully request that Chris and I be allowed to attend the G20 conference.'

'What for, sergeant?' Logan asked irritably.

'Sir, Chris and have learned, by hard experience, more about Silk Fist and their methods than anyone. We might be able to see something or somebody that others miss.'

'But dammit Linda, the island is crawling with military, agents, diplomats, scientists, experts and counter-intelligence operatives. What could you do that they can't?'

'With respect, sir, Chris and I have already demonstrated what we could do about Silk Fist when all other government departments failed.'

Logan threw up his hands. 'God almighty, I'm supposed to be the leader of the free world and here I am standing in the Oval Office being bullied by a Brit and by a sergeant in my own Secret Service! Request denied!'

There was an awkward silence. Then Wyatt said: 'By coincidence, Mr President, I am owed leave and I am going to spend my holiday in the British Virgin Islands, on the island of Tortola.'

Linda said: 'I'm also owed leave, sir, and I too am going to take my vacation in Tortola.'

Logan turned on her and said: 'What if I refuse you permission to take your leave?'

'Then I resign from the service with immediate effect.'

Cley Kefalas had been looking highly entertained by the exchanges. He said: 'Mr President, I respectfully suggest that Chris and Linda have a good point. They do know more about Silk Fist that anyone else and they are simply trying to protect you and the interests of their respective countries. Perhaps they should be allowed to go?'

Logan said: 'Well, if even the Vice President is ganging up on me then I'd better capitulate. Sergeant Marquez, have you ever flown in Air Force One?'

'No, sir. I once cadged a lift in Marine One.'

'What about you, Chris? Would you like a ride in the President's personal jumbo jet?'

'I'd enjoy that very much, sir.'

'Good. At least I can be certain I won't be travelling with a kiss ass. You can wait for me here in the White House. We leave in six hours, and if Jaso found some cunning way to shoot Air Force One out of the sky then remember, you two, that it was your decision to get in harm's way.'

58

*Apartment 12, Prasannata Building, Chanakyapuri,
Delhi, May 29th*

P remendra Dhawan was exhausted. For the past two days he
and his team had worked almost without cease preparing for
the Prime Minister's trip to the G20 conference, ensuring
that every security measure possible had been put into place.

Now Prem lay on his bed, the bed he had shared for so many
years with his beloved Rhea, but sleep would not come. It was an
oppressively hot night and Prem had left the ceiling fan turning,
even though the low swishing noise made it more difficult to get to
sleep. Slanting moon shadows gave the bedroom an unusually
sinister quality. Prem was deeply concerned about the Prime
Minister's safety, for the safety of Christopher Wyatt and for the
future of Linda Marquez. He had, with the greatest difficulty,
achieved what she had asked. If the subject ever discovered the
discreet and untraceable surveillance then Linda Marquez and
himself would be in the gravest trouble.

Prem agreed with Wyatt and Linda's estimation of Dr Anthony
Jaso. Jaso had enjoyed and revelled in his devious cleverness and
Prem was convinced that he had prepared a deadly trap that they
had somehow missed, despite the subtle clues Jaso had offered.
Prem had thought endlessly about the transcript of Jaso's
conversation with Wyatt and Linda but he could not decipher or
glean any clues.

Prem drifted away. Now he was with Rhea again. They were
young, soon after their marriage, a time when Prem had both arms

with which to hold his beloved wife. They were visiting the holy site of Prayag in Allahabad.

According to the scripture, at the end of each aeon, a great deluge covers the Earth but Prayag remains intact and becomes the home of the great Lord Vishnu.

Rhea was laughing and telling Prem of her desire to start a family and why this place was perfect because Prayag is the most fertile place in the world. They were looking out at the flowing waters. Rhea was saying: 'Listen to me, husband, Prayag is where the River Jumna meets the sacred River Ganges. You must think about this.'

Prem awoke with a start and sat up. The dream had been so vivid. Perspiration was running down his back. He was now wide awake. He threw off the thin cotton sheet and leapt out of bed. He padded out to his office and took out the transcript of the Jaso conversation.

Yes, there it was. It had to be. His beloved Rhea had given him the solution but it was devilish, merciless and unstoppable, unless he could act swiftly.

59

Air Force One, May 30th

Linda Marquez awoke with a start when someone shook her shoulder. It took her a bewildered second before she remembered that she was travelling in Air Force One.

The steward said: 'I'm sorry to wake you, mam, but the President wants you and Sergeant Wyatt to join him in his quarters for breakfast. Give yourselves ten minutes to freshen up and then come forward.'

Wyatt had woken up. 'What's going on?' he asked.

'The President wants to see us,' Linda replied.

Wyatt yawned and looked out of the window. A fighter plane was cruising a few hundred metres off the port wing. The sun was rising and the sea below was bathed in a magical pink light. Wyatt said: 'This is the way to travel.' He turned to Linda. 'Did you sleep okay?'

Linda nodded. 'I was way down.' She looked at her watch. 'I've been out for three hours. I wonder why the President wants to see us?'

The chief steward ushered Chris and Linda into the President's private quarters.

Thinking the President was not there, Wyatt said: 'This looks like a hotel room except we're on an aeroplane. Weird.'

The President looked out of the bathroom. He was dressed but tieless and was shaving with an electric razor. He called out: 'Welcome to the Logan hotel. Come in and make yourselves at home, guys. I'll be finished in a minute.'

Wyatt looked out of the windows. There were two more fighter planes escorting Air Force One on ether side.

'I'm being well looked after,' President Logan said as he came out of the bathroom. 'Somewhere above us is the AWACs plane watching out for any sort of threat from air, land and sea. You guys are still worried about the danger from Silk Fist so I wanted you to see what is being done to neutralise any such threat. We'll be landing at Beef Island in about forty minutes. There are a couple of things I want to tell you.'

The steward entered the cabin bearing a tray covered with breakfast dishes, cups and a pot of coffee. He arranged the items on the dining table and then withdrew.

Logan said: 'Sit down and help yourselves to whatever you like. Don't stand on ceremony. The first session of the G20 conference gets under way this afternoon and I won't have much chance to enjoy my food, and I do enjoy my food, so let's dig in.' Logan ladled scrambled eggs on to his plate.

Wyatt pointed at a dish and asked: 'What are those?'

Linda said: 'They're called hash browns. Try one. They're delicious.'

Wyatt picked up a hash brown and took a bite. 'Umm, that is good.'

Logan said: 'Eat as many as you like.'

Wyatt said: 'It's good of you to treat us like this, Mr President, especially after I was so blunt earlier.'

'Hell, after everything that you two have done to free us from the threat of Jaso and his Silk Fist pals, the least I can do is treat you to breakfast. I'm not concerned about blunt speaking, Chris. As you rightly pointed out I'm not used to it. The ancient Roman emperors, when they celebrated a triumph, used to have some guy with them in the chariot whispering "remember you are mortal" in their ear. It was a good system. You're my guy in the chariot.'

Wyatt laughed. 'A position I accept with honour.'

Logan went on: 'Before we land I wanted to update you. Yaroslav Blokhin, as we know, is in Russia but Lord Philip Mountfitchet has disappeared. His yacht, his homes, his companies have been seized or searched but so far there is no trace of him. Foreign Secretary Richard Harcourt, has resigned in order "to spend more time with his family". Everybody in the Westminster village will assume he's been caught *in flagrante delicto* yet again, which in a way he has. He allowed Assistant Commissioner Sherman to use the diplomatic bag in return for her sexual favours but the Prime Minister accepts that Harcourt had no idea he was helping Silk Fist. Sherman herself, and her brother, have been arrested and are still being questioned.'

Wyatt shook his head. 'That news gives me no satisfaction. She was a damn good copper but her experiences at the hands of that maniac Idi Amin in Uganda had scarred her outlook and made her greedy for money. I don't believe she realised what sort of evil she was getting involved with.'

Linda looked at Wyatt and shook her head with exasperation. 'Chris has a soft spot, or a blind spot, when it comes to his old boss.'

'That's true,' Wyatt admitted.

Logan said: 'I asked Murdo if you would be in line for Sherman's job but the Prime Minister tells me you've turned down promotions before.'

'That's also true, sir. I couldn't be a pen pusher. I like to be at the sharp end. I'm not interested in empire building.'

President Logan chuckled. 'That's where you differ from a sordid politician like me. We want power on any basis and we'll push as many pens as we can to achieve it.'

'Well, that's all right as long as you use the power wisely and with justice when you've achieved it.'

'I try, Chris, but as somebody once said, politics is the art of the possible. Sometimes you have to make compromises you don't like, or even bend the law if it's truly for the public good. Talking of bending the law, your friend Charlotte Windsor has been bending it pretty sharply recently.'

'That was certainly for the public good,' Linda said.

'I agree,' Logan nodded. 'The intelligence services gave her a real hard time after she was arrested but she protected you and never told them a thing. The expenses that you two incurred in her name are going to be reimbursed by the US Treasury. I'm also thinking of giving her an award, not only for her help with Silk Fist but also for her service to her community.'

Wyatt said: 'That's good to hear. Nobody deserves an award more than Charlie.'

The chief steward entered and said: 'Excuse me, Mr President, but we'll be landing in a few minutes. I've been asked to tell you that your aides are gathered in the conference room.'

Logan sighed and finished his cup of coffee. 'Oh, well, back to duty. Come with me to the conference room. Bob Briscoe will be making his security report as soon as we land. Let's go and strap ourselves in.'

Wyatt and Linda followed President Logan to the conference room in the mid-section of Air Force One. The assembled aides and advisers stood up as the President entered.

'Sit down, sit down,' Logan said. 'Make yourselves comfortable and strap yourselves in. I've invited Sergeant Marquez and Sergeant Wyatt to join us for the security briefing.'

The President took his place at the head of the table while Wyatt and Linda found a pair of seats and strapped themselves in.

Air Force One banked and Logan said: 'Chris, Linda, if you're still worried about security, look out of the starboard window now.'

The island of Tortola was several thousand feet below them. The long narrow island was studded with white villas amongst the profuse tropical greenery and edged with shining white beaches. The marina at Road Town was filled with yachts. The sea was now pale blue and jade green in the growing dawn light. All around Beef

Island, on the eastern side of the island, and for miles in every direction, was a flotilla of warships, large and small, looking like a swarm of dark water-borne insects.

Logan said: 'Half the US Navy and the Royal Navy are on patrol down there. Nothing can threaten us by sea.'

A voice came over the public address system. 'This is the captain. Please fasten all seat belts. We'll be landing in five minutes.'

Logan fastened his seat belt and said: 'He's the only guy on the plane who outranks me, but only until we get on the ground.'

The giant airliner made another shallow banking manoeuvre and gradually lost height as it approached. The US Air Force fighter aircraft peeled off as soon as Air Force One touched down. A fleet of armoured personnel carriers, armoured cars, fire trucks and ambulances were now speeding along either side. Air Force One made a smooth landing and slowly taxied to its allotted position.

President Logan said: 'Okay, we all stay here until the perimeter is secured and then Bob Briscoe will come aboard and make his report before we go anywhere.'

They watched as armed troops fanned out all around Air Force One until it was completely surrounded by an unbroken screen of firepower.

Ten minutes later Lieutenant General Bob Briscoe entered the conference room. He was accompanied by a female civilian.

Briscoe said: 'Good morning, Mr President. This is Dr Erica Ericson of the National Security Agency. Dr Ericson is leading the explosives search team. Her input has been invaluable.'

Logan said: 'Welcome, Bob, and welcome Dr Ericson. Please make your report.'

A map of Tortola and Beef Island appeared on the wall screen. Briscoe said: 'The G20 meeting is being held in the so-called Alhambra, the main conference hall of the resort and business complex known as Spanish Head. The estate is situated at the southern tip of Beef Island, at Spanish Head, and comprises the conference and entertainment complex, a hotel and forty villas. The heads of state and their senior aides are being housed in the villas while the ancillary staff are housed in the hotel. The complex is owned by a British businessman named Brian Ransome. He offered the complex to the British government as a possible venue for a G20 conference at no cost.'

Wyatt put his hand up and asked: 'When did Ransome offer the complex to the British government?'

'It was several years ago when his resort first opened. Long before Silk Fist. He was after the free publicity, as he usually is.'

Muted chuckles around the table.

Linda asked: 'Is Ransome, or any other staff, aware that the tight security is mainly because of Silk Fist?'

Briscoe said: 'Not specifically. We have only told people on a need to know basis. Ransome reads the news like everybody else, he can probably guess, but he hasn't been told the extent of our precautions. Ransome has been thoroughly vetted by British intelligence as well as our own. He is completely clean and honest, something of a media celebrity as you know, with no links to any known Silk Fist operatives.'

President Logan asked: 'Is Ransome here on the island?'

'Yes, sir.'

'Good. That's extra insurance. Carry on, Bob.'

'Spanish Head, in geographical terms, is easy to secure and defend. In the air we have the AWACs plane, drones and a satellite watching the air space for hundreds of miles around Beef Island. It's surrounded by the sea on three sides and we've got the biggest fleet since D-Day guarding the approaches. The resort is well away from the rest of the population so we were able to throw a security cordon along the land approach, which has the double advantage of excluding all those goddamn anti-capitalist protesters. We've been here a fortnight and in that time no-one and nothing could move in or out of the area without being searched, checked and vetted.

Everything within the security perimeter, every building, every villa, every room, space, nook and cranny has been thoroughly searched on a daily basis. We've had sniffer dogs, ultrasound, geophysical equipment to look underground, and Dr Ericson and her team have been checking for explosive devices. She will make her report on that when I've said my piece. The main problem we have faced is vetting the people. All the ancillary staff, the cooks, waiters, and so on are subject to discipline and have been thoroughly checked. They were not the problem. The problem has been with the heads of state and their staff. Many of them objected strongly to being searched and tested for signs of this Hiatus drug, but I did not allow any of them, even the presidents and prime ministers, to avoid it. Mr President, I am going to be the subject of many diplomatic complaints after this.'

President Logan said: 'Don't worry, Bob, I'll carry the can for you. You've done exactly the right thing. I understand that everyone entering the perimeter has been issued with a special security pass that also tracks their movements and can even monitor their conversations and the atmosphere around them if need be. Is that so?'

'Yes, indeed, sir. I have also introduced a system whereby any armed troops in the area are constantly checking each other. I expect everyone, including you, Mr President, to be the subject of full body searches. Don't worry, folks, it's done using the sort of X-ray scanner you get at airports.'

Logan looked around the table and said: 'Everyone on this plane who is going to the security area will subject themselves to vetting and checking without complaint, including myself. That's an order.'

Briscoe said: 'While the heads of state are gathered together in the conference hall, there will be a screen of troops and armoured cars outside the building, and carefully selected troops guarding inside and watching all participants for sudden odd behaviour as caused by the Hiatus drug. They have been ordered to shoot to kill if necessary. That's it. Any questions?'

President Logan said: 'The security precautions sound watertight, Bob. My guests, Sergeant Marquez and Sergeant Wyatt over there, have had painful first hand experience of what Dr Jaso could do with explosives and they are still worried about my safety, and that of all the other heads of state. Dr Ericson, can you reassure us on that threat?'

Dr Ericson was a thin, pale woman who wore her light brown hair in an old-fashioned bun. Linda wrote a note and slid it across to Wyatt. It read: 'She looks like my old schoolmarm.'

When Dr Ericson spoke her voice was husky but firm and certain in tone. 'Mr President, there has been talk of some sort of atomic or nuclear device being hidden within the complex. The detection of such devices is now surprisingly easy, however carefully they may be concealed, because of the radiation they produce, even if they are buried deep underground, hidden behind rock or whatever. We have searched every inch of ground, underground, every villa and every building with devices on land and with specially adapted drones. I can swear, with total certainty, that there are no atomic or nuclear devices on or near Beef Island and Tortola.'

'Well, that's a relief,' Logan said with a smile.

Dr Ericson did not smile back. 'A much bigger problem is the possibility of hidden conventional explosives. Since the Montreal Convention of 1991 all commercial explosives have been made with a detection taggant so that the explosive can be detected by a trained sniffer dog or mechanical and electronic detectors. The explosive concealed within the drinks vending machine at Spanish Head was old Semtex made before the Montreal Convention.'

Wyatt asked: 'Dr Ericson, were you involved in examining how Dr Jaso had hidden explosives inside his wheelchair?'

'Yes I was. He used old pre-taggant Semtex packed into the metal tubes making up the frame of the wheelchair. The Semtex was triggered by a hidden switch on the panel that controlled the motion of the wheelchair. Quite ingenious.'

Linda said: 'That's what concerns us, Dr Ericson. We've had first hand evidence of how ingeniously evil Dr Jaso could be. Is there any way that he could have concealed any more explosives within the Spanish Head conference hall or nearby?'

'I was coming to that,' Dr Ericson said. 'Obviously, when the vending machine was installed, no-one was looking for explosives inside it. We now have a technique that makes it impossible to conceal any explosive from our search. I won't bore you with the details of how we do it.'

Wyatt said: 'I rather wish you would bore us, if the President doesn't mind.'

Logan said: 'No, I'm intrigued myself. Do tell us, Dr Ericson.'

'Well, the standard technique uses a well-known phenomenon in physics known as Raman scattering, named after the great Indian physicist. To simplify, photons usually bounce off a material in the same form, same colour, same energy. A photon is an elementary particle of light or electromagnetic radiation. Very rarely a photon will bounce off a material in a different form or colour. This effect can be calibrated and detected by using powerful telescopes and lasers. We can detect a material, in this case an explosive, hidden behind rock or bricks or metal or anything you like. We have been over every inch of Spanish Head, particularly in and around the conference hall, and there are no traces of explosives. There are no hidden explosives within the security area and, if they are hidden outside, there is not a conventional explosive in the world powerful enough to affect the security area.'

Logan said: 'And you assure us that this technique is completely foolproof?'

'For all intents and purposes, yes, sir.'

'That's ambivalent,' Logan said with uncharacteristic sharpness. 'I'll ask the question again. Is there any known way that your detectors can be foiled?'

'Yes, but the chance is so small that it is statistically insignificant.'

'Please tell us, Dr Ericson.'

'The only known flaw in the detection technique is caused by fluorescence, which is a phenomenon similar to Raman scattering. There is a minute chance that a liquid explosive hidden within flourescent material could go undetected but we have allowed for that eventuality and checked for flourescence everywhere and, where found, we have checked meticulously by actually drilling or dismantling where such flourescence has been detected. There is no possible way that a lethal quantity of explosive could be hidden within the conference centre or ancillary buildings. I assure you again that there are no explosives or explosive devices within the security area, and certainly not within the conference area. I would stake my life on it.'

60

Beef Island, Tortola, May 30th

Chris Wyatt and Linda Marquez stood at the edge of Spanish Head and looked out over the Caribbean Sea. Armed guards were stationed on the narrow beach and cove far below. A Royal Navy minesweeper, equipped with a helicopter, was anchored a half mile offshore. The serenity was occasionally broken by the whirr of helicopter blades, the hum of a drone or the engines of an incoming aircraft.

All around them, built on undulating slopes dense with greenery, were luxury villas. Each villa had its own garden, patio and roof garden and each one was carefully positioned to provide the clearest views of the ocean.

On the narrow winding roads connecting the villas, armed soldiers in jeeps patrolled ceaselessly. During their walkabout, Linda and Wyatt had been asked for their security passes five times.

'It helps,' Wyatt had commented to Linda, 'that you are back in your regulation Secret Service suit with a glittering blue and gold Secret Service badge on your belt. It impresses the troops. It certainly impresses me.'

Now Wyatt surveyed the far horizon, the edge of the blue sea almost indistinguishable from the blue sky. He said: 'This place is like paradise. I couldn't afford a holiday here on my salary.'

'Yes, it's nice,' Linda said distractedly.

Wyatt looked at her. 'Of course, you come from Florida. You're used to this kind of warmth and scenery.'

'Umm, no it's not that. I was thinking of something else.'

'Thinking of what?'

Linda crossed her arms and moved away. 'It doesn't matter.'

'Linda, I'm aware that you're probably working on something that you can't tell me about. I'm okay with that. You're a serving officer in the Secret Service. You have to put your duty first, but please tell me you're not keeping anything back about Silk Fist.'

'No, I'm not. Well, not directly. I'm still convinced that something is going to happen, something that Jaso planned and cannot be stopped. Do you remember what he said when we interviewed him?'

'Which part?'

'He said something like we'd got this far and it was up to us to finish it. He said something about all solutions being contained in the head. I was thinking that he meant something else but here we are standing on a head. Is that what he meant?'

'Yes, a Spanish Head,' Wyatt said enthusiastically. 'It could mean something. Jaso was of Spanish descent.'

'No, he was a Basque. The Basque region might be part of Spain but the Basques don't consider themselves Spanish. They are fiercely proud, courageous and clever, like Jaso but without the evil part. That piece of paper from the Starfish Cay raid and the explosives planted in the soda machine was too easy, too obvious. Jaso is taunting us from the grave.'

'I agree, Linda, but what can we do? That expert, that Dr Ericson, was certain that there are no explosive devices in the security area. She has all the expertise at her disposal. Look at all this firepower all around us. What more can we do?'

Linda shrugged. 'You're right. There's nothing we can do. We're at Jaso's mercy.'

'You said you were thinking that Jaso meant something else about the head. What were you thinking of?'

Linda wanted to tell Wyatt but accepted that she could not. She said: 'It was nothing.' She looked at her watch. 'It's half past one.

The meeting starts at two. Let's walk back to the conference hall and watch the heads of state arriving. We might be able to spot something.'

Chris sighed and turned away from the warmth of the sun and the hazy silken sea. 'You're right, Sergeant Marquez. Let's go.'

Linda and Wyatt were obliged to show their security passes and walk through the body scanner before they were allowed into the foyer of the conference centre.

Linda looked around. 'Wow, this is amazing. I love this place. It must appeal to my Spanish heritage.'

The foyer was crowded except for a cordoned off reception area where the heads of state were arriving to be greeted by Prime Minister Murdo Montrose, the official host of the G20 conference.

Montrose had noticed Wyatt and Linda entering and when he had finished greeting the President of France, he beckoned them over. Montrose and Wyatt had not met since arriving

'Ah, Sergeant Wyatt, there you are. How are you?' The Prime Minister's tone was apologetic, almost bashful.

'I'm fine, sir, thank you. You remember Sergeant Marquez of the United States Secret Service.'

Montrose shook hands with Linda. 'President Logan speaks of you in glowing terms, Sergeant Marquez, as he does you, Wyatt. In time I will add my thanks on behalf of the United Kingdom, but in the meantime I have a conference to host. Let me to introduce you to Brian Ransome, the chap who built and loaned us this amazing venue.' Montrose turned and beckoned to a slim casually dressed man with long fair hair and a full beard. Wyatt recognised Ransome from the media coverage of his business exploits and publicity stunts. Ransome looked incredibly youthful for a man in his mid-forties.

Montrose said: 'Brian, these are the two officers I was telling you about, Sergeant Wyatt and Sergeant Marquez.'

Brian Ransome smiled and offered his hand. 'It's an honour to meet you both.'

Linda said: 'I love the architecture, Mr Ransome.'

'Please call me Brian. I'm glad you like it. I had to build the hotel in a modern style to stay sensibly within costs but with this theatre and conference centre I decided to go with my heart. I love the palaces of Seville and Granada and, as this complex is called Spanish Head, I decided to go mad and build my Alhambra exactly how I wanted it, hence all these colonnades and multi-coloured tiles and those wonderful horseshoe arches.'

Montrose said: 'Excuse me. Duty calls.' He moved away to greet the Prime Minister of Canada.

Linda said to Ransome: 'My ancestors came from Spain. I've never had the chance to visit Seville or Granada but I hope to get there one day.'

Ransome said eagerly: 'Linda, you simply must! Nothing in the world can match the cool elegance of the Alhambra and I've tried to replicate that ambiance here. What do you think of my creation, Sergeant Wyatt?'

'It reminds me of the flashy cinemas in north London when I was a kid. Too florid for my taste.'

Linda nudged Wyatt in the ribs. 'Please forgive him, Brian. Chris is a common soldier with a taste for simple hardship and no aesthetic sense.'

Brian Ransome laughed. 'At least he's honest. Usually I can see the true reaction in people's expressions but they're too polite to say so. Are you two on duty?'

'Not exactly,' Linda said.

'Would you like to join me upstairs and watch the opening of the conference. My private offices are up there and there's a balcony from where we'll be able to see everything. There are a couple of marksmen up there but they won't intrude.'

Linda said: 'I'd love to watch from there.'

'Come along then.'

Brian Ransome led his two guests through the throng drifting into the main conference hall. In the corner of the foyer a door, padded with red leather, was guarded by a US Marine. The Marine had been introduced to Ransome but still insisted on checking all their security passes before he allowed them through.

Ransome led his guests up a wide spiral staircase until they emerged on to a balcony that extended all the way along one side of the conference hall. The balcony was embellished with slender Moorish colonnades tiled in red and white.

The two marksmen checked their security passes again and then moved away, one at each end of the balcony to provide cover for the entire conference hall. They remained watchful.

Ransome led Wyatt and Linda to the best vantage point. Below them was a huge circular table signed with places for each head of state. Behind each placement was a desk and seating for the aides and advisers. The flags of the attending nations were hung all around the walls. The hall was lighted by six enormous gold and crystal chandeliers.

It was a few minutes before two o'clock. Most of the world leaders had arrived and most of the seats had been taken.

Linda looked down and said: 'This is spectacular. This is a fabulous venue, Brian.'

'Thanks. We also put on stage shows and concerts in here. We've had most of the big names in world entertainment. That's part of our luxury holiday package. Our guests demand the best and are used to the best so we have to compete with Las Vegas and Sun City and so on.'

Wyatt said: 'How much are you charging to hold the G20 here?'

'Not a penny, Chris. It's very good publicity.' Ransome grinned with self-satisfaction but then said: 'Mind you, it cost me a fortune to renovate the place.'

'Doesn't look like it needed renovating,' Linda said.

'It was getting a bit shabby in places and I decided that, with all the cameras and publicity, I wanted the old place to look its best. Most of it simply needed a good clean, especially after all these security people had been in here checking for bombs or whatever. It was a nightmare.'

'They do tend to be very thorough,' Wyatt said.

'Thorough doesn't begin to describe it. I'd had a new wooden floor put in. That cost me a packet. They came in with some sort of detection devices, lasers and so on. They drilled holes in my new floor! They filled them in neatly but they scuffed the floor badly.' Ransome pointed up. 'I had this ceiling retiled with these beautiful tiles decorated in the Moorish style. You can see them well from up here. Do you like them?'

Linda and Wyatt looked up. The tiles were about thirty centimetres square and vividly decorated.

'They're lovely,' Linda said.

'They wanted to drill holes all over the ceiling but I put my foot down and they limited themselves to a few tiles at the sides where the damage would be out of sight.'

Wyatt said: 'They must have cost a lot more than the wooden floor?'

'Oddly enough, they didn't. A chap came to see me one day and offered to replace the existing tiles with these at cost price. He had found out I was renovating the place and wanted publicity for his tiling business. He brought me these samples and I fell in love with them. They're ceramic and quite thick for ceiling tiles. I was a bit worried that they might be too heavy but this chap assured me they would be okay.'

Below them, Prime Minister Montrose was making the opening speech.

Linda asked: 'When did this guy volunteer to do all this for you?'

'It was at the beginning of this year. He offered to do it immediately after Christmas and get it done before we started getting busy with the spring and summer seasons.'

Wyatt asked: 'What was he like, this bloke?'

'His name's Powell, Harry Powell. Scottish, I think. Travelled from Glasgow to offer his services. I can't imagine how he found out I was renovating this place. He's a big chap, well-built, shoulders like a bull, well over six feet tall, a few inches taller than you, Chris. He's a good worker, always tidied up, left the place clean. Strange sort of bloke though. It was if he was in a trance most of the time. He used to talk to himself. But he fell in love with Beef Island and Spanish Head in particular. He booked one of the best villas, number eighteen up on the hill past the helicopter pad, and he's been living here permanently ever since he finished the ceiling. With all his money you would have thought he could afford a proper toupee. He had the worst syrup I've ever seen in my life.'

Linda asked: 'What the hell's a syrup?'

Wyatt looked at Linda and said: 'It's Cockney rhyming slang. Syrup of fig, meaning wig.'

Linda said: 'So this guy is bald? Jeez, Chris, could it be?'

Wyatt said: 'Yes, it could. Brian, quickly, did you ever look closely at these tiles. I mean look at what they are made of?'

'Only once,' Ransome said, aware of the sudden tension. 'Powell usually tidied up but he missed a broken tile once. I had a look at it. The tile was almost sparkly inside, with some sort of material sandwiched in between that had been coated with flourescent paint. And some sort of liquid had dribbled out of the middle. I suppose the liquid was to save weight. I didn't…'

Wyatt was already making for the stairs. He said: 'Linda, Brian, get everyone out of the conference hall, now!'

'Where are you going?' Ransome shouted as Wyatt pushed open the balcony door.

'Villa Eighteen,' Wyatt shouted back as he bounded down the spiral stairway.

Wyatt swung open the leather door and pushed through the people waiting in the foyer. He burst out of the front door, saw that there were no jeeps, turned left and started running. The Marine guards tried to grab him and then shouted for him to stop. They raised their M15 carbines. Wyatt shouted back: 'Follow me, don't frigging shoot me.'

Wyatt was running up a gentle slope, legs pumping as fast as he could move them. The sun was full and he was already sweating. The Glock pistol in his unbuttoned jacket bounced against his chest. He was running with lung-bursting intensity. Any second he expected to hear a massive explosion behind him. The helicopter pad was a quarter mile away and Villa Eighteen was a quarter mile beyond that. The road was getting steeper. He heard Jeep engines starting. He forced his legs to move faster and ignored the burning sensation in lungs and muscles. He remembered his training, run until you die and then run faster. He passed the concrete circle painted with a huge letter 'H'. He passed Villa Sixteen and turned right up an increasingly steep road. Sweat running down his back, his whole body crying out to stop but Wyatt pushed himself on and on and on. He passed Villa Seventeen. He could see Villa Eighteen at the crest of the hill. He could hear Jeeps moving closer. One last lung-tearing effort, breath ragged, legs weighted with lead. Faster, you lazy bastard, faster. Almost there.

Wyatt ran into the small garden, leapt up four steps and launched himself shoulder-first against the front door. The door burst open. A small lobby with another door in front. He crashed into it, shoulder first, with all his force.

Powell was sitting at a table with a radio transmitter in front of him. He looked up in astonishment as Wyatt burst in. Powell stood up and reached towards the transmitter. Wyatt hurled himself forward and swept the transmitter away from Powell's reach with his left hand as he crashed into the table. The edge of the table caught Powell in the groin. Powell toppled backwards but managed to right himself and launched himself in the opposite direction to get to the transmitter. He was bellowing with fury.

Wyatt, no time to pull out the Glock, leapt up on to the table and threw himself at Powell. He grabbed Powell around the waist and tried to force him backwards but Powell was too strong. Powell grunted and punched Wyatt repeatedly in the side of the head. Wyatt was dizzy from the blows. Weakened by the run, Wyatt could not hold on and Powell broke away from his grip. Wyatt tried to ram his palm into Powell's nose but Powell turned away in time. Powell roared an obscenity and shoved Wyatt violently in the chest. Wyatt flew backwards and crashed into a glass cabinet. Excruciating pain as he fell on to shattered glass. Wyatt's strength had gone. Powell was on top of him, face distorted with rage, eyes popping and spitting obscenities. He straddled Wyatt and gripped him around the neck with hard calloused hands. Wyatt brought his knee up into Powell's groin but with no power and no effect. Wyatt was losing consciousness. It was all over. His strength and stamina had been drained by the run. He thought of Linda and all they had been through, all he wanted to say. He could not breathe, he was falling away, a red curtain descending over his eyes, then blackness.

The crack of a pistol far away in Wyatt's consciousness. Suddenly Powell's grip released and Wyatt sucked in ragged lungfuls of air. His vision cleared. Powell was looking up, an expression of surprise as blood spouted from his arm. His face contorted with murderous rage as he hauled himself to his feet. Wyatt turned his head. Linda Marquez held her aim steady as Powell stumbled around the table towards her. She fired again. Still he came on. Linda stood firm and fired three more shots into his chest. Powell staggered and moaned and then dropped at her feet.

Two Marines entered the room. Linda ordered: 'Get the medics here, now!'

Wyatt managed to croak: 'Linda!' Linda went to him, knelt down beside him and stroked his face.

Wyatt found it was agony to talk. 'Linda, transmitter on the floor over by the window. Secure it. Don't let anyone touch it until the experts see it. Is everyone out of the conference room?'

'Yes, they're all safe. How are you doing, sergeant?'

'All the better for seeing you, sergeant. You have the loveliest smile. I need to see a doctor. Several doctors. I guess that bastard Jaso wasn't as clever as he thought he was.'

Wyatt tried to get up and then passed out.

61

Villa Five, Spanish Head, Beef Island, Tortola, May 30th

Christopher Wyatt discharged himself from the hospital in Road Town after a thorough medical check. The doctors, and Linda Marquez, had urged him to stay overnight for observation but Wyatt adamantly refused.

Linda drove him back to Spanish Head in a borrowed US army jeep. The jeep was returned to the military and they walked the short distance to the hotel.

Linda said: 'Apologies for the bumpy ride. Those jeeps are not very well sprung. How do you feel now?'

'I feel wonderful, Linda. We've stopped Jaso's last devious plot, it's a beautiful Caribbean evening, I'm in the company of a beautiful woman, and we can begin to get our lives back to normality.'

Linda smiled but made no reply.

Wyatt looked at her and asked: 'What's the matter? Do you think there is still a threat?'

'No, no, not here, but Silk Fist is still out there somewhere, perhaps planning another atrocity.'

'It's in the hands of the authorities now, Linda. We've done our bit. More than our bit.'

Linda stopped and looked out to sea. 'I never want to have to shoot anyone ever again.'

'You saved my life because you did.'

'It had to be done but Powell was probably a normal guy leading a normal life until the Hiatus got hold of him. It's all such a tragic and unnecessary waste.'

'Your compassion does you credit, Linda. Are you hungry?'

'I could eat a little. How about you?'

'My throat still aches like hell. Whatever I eat it will have to be soft and mushy.'

'Perhap's the hotel has Gerber's on the menu.'

'What's Gerber's?'

'I'll tell you later.'

They showed their security passes and were admitted to the hotel lobby. Stack Franklin was waiting for them.

'Hi, chief,' Linda said. 'Are you waiting for us?'

'Yes I am. Or, rather, the President is waiting for you.'

Wyatt sighed and said: 'No more trouble is there, Stack? I don't think I could stand another beating.'

Franklin smiled. 'Don't worry, Chris. This is purely a social event at the President's villa. There's plenty to eat and drink. I've been ordered to escort you.'

President Logan's steward showed them into a small private garden. The garden was strung with necklaces of paper lanterns. A buffet table, loaded with food and drink, had been set out. The garden was secluded, surrounded by bushes and armed guards on the other side and stationed all around the villa. The evening air was warm and fragrantly scented by tropical flowers.

There were several other heads of state in attendance but President Logan was standing talking to two men. One of them was Prime Minister Murdo Montrose. Logan greeted the new arrivals by clapping Wyatt on the back. Wyatt winced in pain.

'I'm so sorry,' Logan said.

Stack Franklin said: 'If you don't need me anymore, Mr President, there are a few things I have to check out.'

Logan said: 'You go ahead, Stack.' He turned to Wyatt and Linda. 'Let me make the introductions. You know Prime Minister Montrose, of course, but let me introduce the Prime Minister of

India, Mr Arnesh Mishra. Arnesh, this is Sergeant Christopher Wyatt and Sergeant Linda Marquez.'

Mishra said: 'So these are the famous team of Wyatt and Marquez. After what Premendra Dhawan said about you I was beginning to believe that you were mythical creatures, such is the exciting nature of your exploits.'

Wyatt said: 'I'm not sure about exciting, sir, but they've certainly been painful.'

'Yes, of course,' Mishra said sympathetically. 'I'm relieved that you were not more seriously injured. If they have released you from hospital then I should make the not so intelligent guess that your injuries are not life threatening.'

'No, sir, I was lucky. No broken bones but plenty of bruises, especially around the throat where Powell tried to throttle me, so forgive my croaky voice. Powell would have succeeded if it hadn't have been for Linda's timely intervention.'

Prime Minister Montrose said: 'Sergeant Wyatt, we swapped harsh words back in England. I didn't trust you, I didn't like you and I thought you were wrong but it was me who was wrong. For perhaps the first time in my life I am delighted to be wrong. You saved all our lives earlier. I'm immensely grateful.'

'Linda and I happened to be in the right place at the right time. Anyone would have done the same.'

'I doubt that,' Mishra said. 'Premendra Dhawan told me a lot about you. Dhawan didn't want me to come to this conference. He warned me of the danger in no uncertain terms but I could not be seen to stay away in cowardly fashion when all the other heads of state were arriving. I have to say he was so insistent that he was on the edge of being impertinent.'

Linda said: 'Prem is a good and honourable man who cares deeply about you and your country.'

Logan said: 'Can I get you two a drink or something to eat?'

Wyatt said: 'A cold beer would go down perfectly on such a lovely evening.'

Linda said: 'I'd love a white wine, sir.'

The President's steward moved away to fetch the drinks.

Wyatt asked: 'Has Dr Ericson had a chance to examine those ceiling tiles yet?'

Logan chuckled. 'Indeed she has. I couldn't stop her. The poor woman was so upset and embarrassed that she and her team had not found the explosives. She offered her resignation but I refused.'

Linda said: 'I'm pleased to hear that, sir. I wouldn't want another life ruined because of Dr Anthony Jaso. He was a devious and clever man. He fooled many people for many years.'

'Indeed he did,' Logan nodded. 'Every tile contained a small quantity of a liquid explosive called Astralite protected by a sandwich of flourescent material that completely bamboozled Dr Ericson's lasers and detecting equipment. Her team had drilled into some of the tiles but, after Brian Ransome's vigorous objections, had confined the search to the edges of the ceiling where the damage would not be noticeable but those tiles were completely ordinary. Jaso must have calculated that would be the case. It was the tiles in the centre of the ceiling that contained the explosive. Also, the filling contained metallic filaments that would respond to an electrical charge detonated by the radio transmitter device that Chris knocked away from Powell's hand. Fiendishly clever and if it had gone off then all of us sitting underneath would have been history. I cannot bear to think of the damage, what with those glass chandeliers hanging over her heads.' The President shuddered.

The steward returned with drinks for Wyatt and Linda.

President Logan raised his glass of bourbon and said: 'I'd like to propose a toast to Chris and Linda for their exemplary service and for saving the skins of all we politicians. Well done, guys.'

Linda said: 'One last question, sir. How did Powell escape detection with all these intense security checks going on?'

'We're not sure, Linda. The best guess is that Powell had an accomplice who was using Powell's name and identity for when the agents arrived, an accomplice who was completely free of this Hiatus drug and with impeccable credentials. But we're not sure yet. Anyway, our host, Prime Minister Montrose, with commendable calmness, moved everyone into the hotel and the conference went ahead as scheduled. It was a bit cramped but it did the job. There's another all-day session tomorrow and then we go our separate ways. I have to say that everyone behaved with…'

The President's speech was interrupted by shouting and arguing from away down the road. Seconds later a jeep screeched to a halt outside the garden and Stack Franklin climbed out of the driving seat. Without ceremony he shoved through the chest-high bushes protecting the garden and said: 'Mr President, you and the two Prime Ministers must come with me now.'

'Why?' Logan said, visibly irritated.

'Sir, USS *Pensacola* reports that a BrahMos cruise missile has been launched and is on a trajectory towards Beef Island.'

'It's aimed at us?'

'Yes, sir. If you could…'

'Nuke or FAE?'

'Unknown, sir. Please get in the…'

'Can't the navy bring it down?'

'They've tried, sir. We have ten minutes to get you away.'

'Hold on, Stack. Can't anything…'

Franklin shouted: 'As head of your security I order you to get in the jeep now or I'll damn well carry you in. And you two Prime Ministers. You must move… now!'

Wyatt and Linda watched in astonishment as Stack Franklin virtually pushed the three statesmen through the foliage and helped them clamber into the jeep. Stack Franklin looked back at Wyatt and Linda with a despairing glance and shook his head. He climbed into the jeep. It roared off with a squeal of tyres.

Linda turned to Wyatt and asked: 'What the hell just happened? I didn't understand anything that was said.'

Wyatt sagged inside as if all his strength and hope had drained away. 'I'm sorry, Linda, but it means that Jaso has beaten us after all.'

'How? What was Stack talking about? I don't understand?'

Wyatt tried to keep the sickening despair out of his voice. 'Linda, a BrahMos is a supersonic cruise missile. If Beef Island is the target then, in less than ten minutes time, we've had it.'

Linda was stunned and floundering. 'I don't… why should we? It's not possible.'

'The President asked if it was nuke or FAE. If the missile has a nuclear warhead then we are all going to die, including everyone on Tortola. If it's an FAE warhead then the President may escape in time but you and I and everyone else on Beef Island are still going to die.'

'What do you mean by FAE?'

'It stands for fuel air explosion. It's vastly more powerful than any conventional explosive, almost as bad as a small atomic bomb but without the radiation.'

'Well, can't we run or take shelter somewhere?'

'In either case, Linda, it's pointless. There is no escape, even if we could find the deepest underground cavern, in the time available. A fuel air explosion, directly above us, will destroy everything on the island and even if the blast doesn't kill us then the aftermath literally sucks the air away from everything, including our lungs, wherever we may be hidden.'

'Can't it be shot down or something?'

'The BrahMos travels at two thousand miles per hour and they are guidable. It can out-run and out-turn any defence.'

'Then we're going to die?'

Wyatt nodded. He could not look at Linda. He could hardly trust himself to speak. 'I'm going to take my beer and walk up that slope and watch my last sunset. I'm happy that I'm spending it with you. Will you take my hand?'

Linda took Wyatt's hand. They pushed through the gap in the

hedge left by President Logan's rapid departure and began walking up the lane towards the edge of Spanish Head.

Linda said: 'Before we go, I want to ask you something.'

'Okay.'

'When we were in that hotel room in Washington, when you were about to shoot me because of the Hiatus, you couldn't do it. Do you remember why?'

'No, I don't,' Wyatt said. 'My mind was so messed up I don't remember anything about that.'

'You said you couldn't shoot me because you loved me so much.'

They stopped at the top of the hill. The sea below was perfectly still, as if it was holding its breath. The sunset was a giant red ball in the west and the stars were coming out in the clear sky.

'Is that what I said? That I love you so much?'

'Yes, Chris. I guess it was the drug because you haven't said it since.'

'That's because I didn't think you'd want to hear it, for Mike's sake.'

'Then you do love me?'

'With all my heart, Linda. I've loved you since our time in Surfers Paradise.'

Linda nodded. 'I love you. I never thought I would, or even could, love again so soon. I'd rather have the five minutes we have left with you than spend a lifetime with any other man.'

Wyatt threw his glass down on to the beach. It burst into a thousand splinters on the rocks. He took Linda into his arms. They kissed with the passion of knowing it would be the last time and then held each other tightly.

Wyatt looked out towards the sunset and saw a tiny black dot low in the livid red sky. He could see the white wake on the sea caused by the air being pushed aside at supersonic speed. The cruise missile was moving directly towards them.

Linda had closed her eyes. She looked at peace. Wyatt held her even more tightly. He had protected Linda from so much, as she had protected him. Now there was nothing they could do to protect each other, yet Wyatt was intensely happy and fulfilled. He was ready to die.

Wyatt could not be sure but the cruise missile seemed to be deviating from its direct course. It wobbled and veered and passed over them with an ear-splitting sonic boom before turning out to sea.

Linda, her voice muffled by Wyatt's shoulder, said: 'Are we still alive?'

'Yes. If it's an FAE we're safe. If it's a nuke…'

Hope began to seep in. Wyatt, feeling Linda in his arms, now desperately wanted to live.

Miles out at sea the purple night burst into a flash of blinding white heat that filled the sky and then turned into an orange rain pouring down until the waters beneath boiled and thrashed in an agony of scalding heat.

Wyatt said: 'Linda, keep your mouth and nose as tightly closed as you can!' He pulled her down, covered her body with his own and clamped his hand over her mouth. The shock wave streamed over them with an agonising blast of heat like a red-hot evil hand trying to rip the air out of their lungs. Then it was gone and the peaceful evening light returned.

Wyatt found himself laughing, almost hysterical with relief. 'We're alive, Linda. We're safe. It was fuel air explosive, not a nuke. Even Jaso couldn't get his sticky little hands on a nuke.'

Linda opened her eyes and ran her fingers through Wyatt's hair. 'I've often wondered what it would be like to have you on top of me.'

Wyatt kissed her and said: 'You'd better get used to it.'

'I can't wait.'

'I love you so much, Linda. I never thought I'd ever be laying in the warm grass with you, our whole lifetime in front of us. I suppose

I have to thank Jaso for something. Without him I would never have met you.'

'He's not the only one you have to thank for getting us together.'

'Isn't he? Who else do you mean?'

'All in good time. For now, I have to…'

Wyatt's cell phone was ringing. He took it out of his jacket pocket. 'Hello, Chris Wyatt.'

'Christopher!' Prem said. 'You're alive!'

'Not only am I alive but I've never been so happy in my life.'

'Why is that, Christopher?'

'I'm laying in the grass on top of Sergeant Marquez.'

'Oh, I'm sorry. Shall I ring back?'

Linda giggled and said: 'Hello, Prem!'

Wyatt said: 'We're laying in the grass because someone launched a cruise missile at our heads.'

'I know.'

'It missed and exploded out at sea.'

'That's what I hoped would happen.'

'You mean you had something to do with all this, Prem?'

'Yes, Christopher, but you must thank my darling wife Rhea and the great lord Vishnu.'

'That's too mystical for my prosaic mind, Prem, but I'll thank anyone you say for getting us out of this one. How did you do that?'

'I'll explain later. I'm relieved that you two, and everyone else, are safe. Please ask Linda to ring me as soon as she can.'

Wyatt said: 'Did you hear that? Prem wants you to call him. Perhaps we had better get back?'

Linda put her arms around him tightly. 'Not so fast, Sergeant Wyatt. You're not going anywhere.' She pulled him down and kissed him passionately.

Wyatt felt his jacket being slipped off his shoulders, then his shirt buttons being undone. Wyatt said: 'I'm pretty beaten up, Linda.'

'Don't worry, sergeant. I'll be gentle with you.'

62

Air Force One Conference Room, June 2nd

Christopher Wyatt thought, with a frisson of guilt, that he should be listening to the conversation between President Logan and his aides and advisers but, for some reason, he could not concentrate. He glanced out of the window. The fighter escort was in place and, glimpsing through wispy cloud, he guessed that they were travelling along the eastern seaboard of the United States, probably above Linda's home state of Florida.

Wyatt turned back when Lieutenant General Bob Briscoe entered.

Briscoe said: 'Good morning, Mr President. I've finished collating the intelligence reports about the cruise missile attack. I'm sorry to keep you all waiting.'

President Joe Logan said: 'No problem, Bob. I'm happy to be alive to be kept waiting!'

Wyatt and the others chuckled politely at the President's quip. Linda Marquez was working with a laptop and did not respond. Briscoe stood in front of the large screen on the bulkhead and operated the remote control. A diagram of a cruise missile appeared.

Briscoe said: 'This is the BrahMos cruise missile. It was developed jointly by Russia and India. It has a range of about two hundred miles, travels at three times the speed of sound and is the only fully operational supersonic cruise missile in the world.'

Logan asked: 'You mean we haven't got anything like it, Bob?'

'There are projects under development but, at the moment, we have nothing to match the BrahMos, sir.'

'Umm,' Logan said. 'When I get back I'll have to ask the Joint Chiefs why we haven't got anything like it and speed things up until we have.'

'Sir, you might also like to ask the Joint Chiefs why our defences against this missile are so inadequate. Given enough time we could have brought it down but this thing doesn't allow that time. It's a fiendishly effective weapon. The warhead on the missile aimed at Spanish Head was set to detonate at approximately two hundred feet. It would have resulted in a massive fireball that would have destroyed every building. The main cause of death to humans would have been the shock wave. This weapon sucks out the atmosphere so that humans cannot breath and they suffer massive damage to internal organs. We might have got you to safety, Mr President, but everyone left behind, without exception, would have been killed. There is no escape from this sort of explosion, wherever you are.'

Wyatt gently nudged Linda and said: 'I told you.'

Linda did not look up from her laptop and said distractedly: 'Told me what?'

'Did you listen to anything that General Briscoe said?'

'No. What did he say?'

'Never mind. What are you looking for?'

'I'm on a dating website. I'm looking for a new relationship. Life with you isn't very exciting.'

Wyatt laughed. 'Good luck. I hope you find a dull mathematics professor from Iowa.'

'Umm, that sounds rather nice after all this gallivanting we've been doing.'

'Gallivanting? That's a good old-fashioned word.'

'Well, I'm a good old-fashioned girl.'

'You were very good in the long grass. If that's being old-fashioned then take me back.'

Wyatt and Linda looked up when President Logan coughed theatrically. He said: 'It would ill behove me to chide you two so soon after you saved us from the machinations of Dr Jaso, but if you could pay attention to General Briscoe he would be very grateful, and so would I.'

Linda closed her laptop and said: 'My apologies, sir.' Then under her breath: 'That was your fault, Wyatt. You got me into trouble.'

'I'd like to.'

'Shhh.'

General Briscoe went on: 'The navy have seized the ship, a small container vessel, from which the BrahMos was launched.'

Logan said: 'Any useful intelligence as to who supplied the missile or ordered the launch.'

'The ship was owned by one of Lord Philip Mountfitchet's companies. We don't expect to get much useful information from the crew, who all appear to be simply low grade technicians. We cannot, at this point, establish who supplied the weapon or who ordered the firing of the BrahMos.'

Wyatt said: 'You stated that this missile is a joint Russian and Indian co-production. I'd suggest that Yaroslav Blokhin might have supplied it. We're all aware of how the trade in arms from the old Soviet Union has mushroomed since it collapsed.'

Briscoe replied: 'That's exactly the line of enquiry we're already pursuing. It was extremely fortunate that this missile was jointly built by the Indian government. India realised that such a weapon could one day be turned against them, especially by such a volatile country as Russia, and installed in every missile a top secret coded device that could divert the course of the missile. That's how this guy Premendra Dhawan was able to divert it at the last moment. Apparently he found one of India's leading missile experts and practically dragged him out of his bed to help disable the missile.'

Logan looked at Linda and Wyatt and said: 'He's an interesting man, this friend of yours.'

'Indeed he is,' Wyatt said. 'Saved my life in London.'

Linda said: 'And saved my sanity when we were on the run and couldn't see a way forward.'

Briscoe said: 'Seems to me an odd sort of guy. We can't make out how he realised that Silk Fist would be using a cruise missile against us. I spoke to his commanding officer, a Colonel Chatterjee, and Dhawan had claimed that his dead wife had given him the answer in a dream. It was probably some tongue-in-cheek joke. I don't believe in all this eastern mysticism crap.'

Linda said: 'With respect, General, I believe it. I don't understand mysticism but Prem truly loved his wife and was desperate to find her killers. The human brain works in a strange and complex way. I believe that Rhea did give him the answer, but not in any way that we would understand.'

Wyatt added: 'I spoke to Prem earlier. There is a more down-to-earth explanation. When we interviewed Jaso he made some remark to the effect that when two rivers meet they can't be stopped. The name BrahMos is a combination of the names of two rivers, the Brahmaputra in India and the Moskva in Russia. Prem's brain was working on the problem while he was asleep, but I agree with Linda. I think Rhea was there to nudge him in the right direction.'

There was an uncomfortable silence. It was broken by President Logan saying: 'Anything else, ladies and gentlemen?' No-one replied so Logan said: 'Right, I'm going forward to my cabin for coffee and a doughnut.' He stood up.

Linda also stood up and said: 'Mr President, may I see you alone in private.'

'What? Now?'

'If you wouldn't mind, sir.'

'Is it important?'

'Yes, sir.'

'More important than my doughnut?'

'I'm afraid so, sir.'

'Well, come on then. You can have a doughnut too. Is it about Silk Fist?'

'Partly, sir.'

'Do you want Chris to come along?'

Linda looked at Chris Wyatt with an uncomfortable and apologetic expression. 'No, sir. This is for your ears only.'

63

Yellow Oval Room, White House, Washington DC, June 2nd

President Josiah Logan looked out over the Truman Balcony and the South Lawn to the soaring needle of the Washington Monument far in the distance. Beyond was the normal world, normality, a condition that Logan, for one of the few times in his life, earnestly desired.

Logan turned to Linda and said: 'Would you like to sit down?'

'I'd rather stand, sir, if you don't mind.'

'Not at all. That's what I'm going to do myself.'

Neither of them spoke for several minutes.

The door opened and Martina Logan entered. She said: 'Hello, Joe. I wasn't told you were back. I'm so glad to see you in one piece.'

Logan said: 'Hello, Marty. Please come and sit down on the sofa over here.'

Martina Logan did not move. She said: 'Hello, Linda. You're dressed as if you mean business.'

Linda could not look at her friend.

Martina Logan went on: 'The Yellow Oval Room is usually reserved for entertaining distinguished visitors. Are we expecting any?'

'Yes.'

Martina Logan waited for further information. It was not provided. 'Why are we meeting in this room, Joe?'

'Because it's neutral, secure and private.'

'So I shouldn't expect a social event any minute?'

'Come and sit down, Marty.'

This time Martina Logan did as requested. She said: 'Isn't either of you going to tell me what is going on?'

This time Linda found the courage to look at the First Lady. 'I'm sorry, Marty, but it became vital for me to inform the President about your relationship with the Vice President.'

Martina Logan sat back and sighed. 'Oh. I thought we had an agreement.'

'We did, but my allegiance to the President and the country takes precedence.'

'I thought we agreed that my affair is hardly a matter of national security.'

'Perhaps it wasn't a few days ago, but after what happened at the G20, and what I've discovered since, I could no longer remain silent.'

'Why? I didn't have anything to do with Silk Fist.'

President Logan said: 'I can't begin to tell you how hurt and betrayed I feel, Marty.'

Martina Logan nodded. 'Can we discuss this in private?'

'No,' Logan snapped. 'We talk about it now, with Linda present. Apparently she has something else to tell us.'

Martina Logan said: 'I do love you, Joe, but this job of yours has gotten in the way.'

'So instead of supporting me in a task vital to this nation you decide to go behind my back and sleep with my second-in-command.'

'I have supported you in public, Joe, in every way I can. Linda, you've seen what I do, day in and day out for years.'

Linda said: 'In public terms you are an exceptional First Lady, Marty, and a credit to the country.'

'Thank you, Linda. You see, Joe? I realise our private life has become a mess but I've always done my duty in a job I never asked for.'

President Logan nodded. 'That's a fair comment, and I accept my fair share of the blame. I accept that I haven't been the attentive husband I would have liked to have been, but the worry and responsibility of being President pounds the life out you, despite all the help and the power and the privilege. What do we tell the kids?'

Martina Logan was close to tears. 'Do we have to tell them, Joe?'

'I don't know yet, Marty. I don't know. I'm expecting a visitor. It depends on what he has to say.'

As if on cue there was a knock on the door.

'Come in!' Logan barked.

The door opened and Deputy Chief Isaiah Franklin stepped into the room. He looked around uncertainly. Then he said: 'Linda? What are you doing here?'

Logan said: 'She's assisting me on a personal matter, Stack.'

'Yes, sir. I mean, of course. I didn't mean to…'

'Is he here?' Logan asked.

'Yes, sir.'

'Then send him in.'

Stack Franklin held the door open as he turned and said: 'You can go in now.'

Franklin stepped aside to admit the visitor and then closed the door as he left the room.

Vice President Cleytus Kefalas said: 'Joe? I didn't think you were back yet. What's going on? I was about to leave for the meeting in Denver when I was told I had to report here.'

Logan said: 'Why don't you come and sit down next to my wife. I understand you've been getting very close to her recently. We were discussing your affair.'

The Vice President was wary and watchful as he sat down. 'Joe, you can't be serious. Marty, tell him there is nothing going on between us.'

'It's too late, Cley. I've already confessed.'

Kefalas bowed his head. Then he looked pointedly at Linda: 'Do we have to discuss this in front of the staff?'

Logan said: 'Linda is a friend of my wife and a friend of mine. A friend of the family if you like. Unlike you, I trust her.'

Kefalas said: 'That's harsh. I don't understand why you should say that, Joe. I've always supported you in the public arena, haven't I.'

'Yes, you've been a good Vice President, when you weren't banging my wife.'

Martina Logan winced.

Linda said: 'I hesitate to contradict you, Mr President, but Mr Kefalas is the worst Vice President in the history of the United States.'

Kefalas laughed sarcastically. 'Well, thank you for that, Sergeant Marquez. Such an appraisal from a jumped up rich girl who knows diddly squat about politics leaves me deeply wounded.'

'You're right, Mr Kefalas. I don't know diddly squat about politics but at least I didn't attempt to assassinate the President.'

'What?' Kefalas cried. 'Are you crazy? What are you saying? Joe, what is going on here? Are you going to let this low-grade secretary sit here and accuse me of treason?'

Martina Logan said: 'Linda, that's insane.'

President Logan said: 'I'm not sure what Linda is going to say but I promised that she could have her say. Linda, you've made the most serious accusation you could possibly make against a Vice President. You had better have some facts or some excuse for making such an accusation.'

'I have, sir. The Silk Fist conspiracy was started by Dr Anthony Jaso but it was hijacked by Vice President Kefalas for his own evil purposes.'

Kefalas said: 'That's ridiculous. What proof or evidence do you have for such an absurd claim?'

'Anthony Jaso told me.'

'Well, there's a reliable, honest and moral witness! What did Doctor Evil say about me?'

'When Sergeant Wyatt and I were interviewing Jaso, he concluded by saying that although he started Silk Fist he would not be the one to finish it, that it had been taken over by forces outside of his control. He said the finale was about to be played and that no-one could stop it. He was wrong. We did stop it. He also said that all solutions are contained in the head. I didn't understand what that meant. I thought it was a reference to Spanish Head, the resort where the G20 conference was held. Then I realised that Jaso had been sending us sly clues about who was responsible for the worst excesses of Silk Fist.'

'What clues?' Kefalas asked.

'Dr Jaso was brilliant but he was also vain and arrogant. He saw his own scheme gradually being taken over by an even more ruthless individual. Mr President, you'll recall that the Silk Fist perpetrators, at the moment they began their attacks, shouted a trigger word or code word that no-one could decipher or understand?'

'Yes, I do. Your husband shouted "kappa" and the Bishop of Carlisle shouted "bash" or something.'

'That's right, sir. One of the trigger words was "cop". We had assumed that it was spelt "c-o-p" as in policeman but when we were on Spanish Head it reminded me that the Afrikaans word for head is k-o-p. I've done more research and all the trigger words are names for the head in different languages. This was Jaso's little joke. He needed trigger words that were unusual, that would not come up in ordinary conversation and trigger action by the victim prematurely. So, my husband Mike was not saying "kappa" but "kapo", which means head in Esperanto. The bishop was not shouting "bash" but "bas", which means head in Catalan.'

'What are you getting at?' Kefalas interrupted. 'If you remember, Sergeant Marquez, the bishop was attacking me as well as Marty.'

'I remember it well. I'll never forget because I had to shoot him. That attack was a useful ploy to divert any suspicion away from yourself.'

Kefalas said: 'Joe, this is crazy. You can't listen to this nonsense.'

Logan said: 'Carry on, Linda.'

'Another couple of examples. The bomber who took the life of Premendra Dhawan's wife was supposed to be shouting "kaffir", a South African racist slur, but he was actually shouting k-a-f-a, which is Turkish meaning head. What we thought was "kisser" was actually "kichwa", Swahili meaning head. And when the Princess Royal was assassinated, Sergeant Wyatt and others thought that Dr Flaherty was shouting "ken". It is pronounced that way way but the Irish Gaelic word for the head is "ceann". I could go on with many other examples.'

President Logan asked: 'That's very interesting, Linda, but what has that got to do with the Vice President?'

'Sir, Mr Kefalas understands full well because "kefalas" is a Greek surname meaning head. That was Dr Jaso's hidden message.'

'Is that it?' Kefalas said. 'You are condemning me because of some riddle made up by a homicidal maniac. You're accusing the Vice President of the United States of treason because his name means "head"?'

President Logan said: 'Cley, do you deny that you had any involvement with the Silk Fist conspiracy?'

'I deny it emphatically, Joe. Can't you see how crazy this is? Linda, I don't understand why you're doing this to me. What have I done to deserve this?'

'Your conspiracy caused my husband to kill himself. How's that for starters? You were once the Director of the CIA. You had access to all the data about Project MKUltra and the drug now known as Hiatus.'

'All that data was destroyed by order of Congress.'

'That is not true. Congress ordered it to be destroyed but the order was not carried out. That possibility was investigated. The data still exists.'

'What if it does? During my time as Director I didn't see it or ask for it.'

'On the contrary. You became aware of what Jaso was doing and saw the perfect opportunity to make sure that you became the next occupant of the White House without the bother of winning a mandate from the American people.'

Kefalas said, with exasperation as if talking to a child: 'I was in charge of the battle against Silk Fist. Joe appointed me to that position.'

'So you were in the perfect position to suppress or divert the intelligence that was being gathered about Silk Fist.'

'That's not true.'

'I have statements from agents who suspect their reports were suppressed or lost.'

'Let me see them.'

'All in good time.'

'You're blowing smoke, Linda. Joe, how long are you going to let this go on for?'

'As long as it takes, Cley. Carry on, Linda.'

'When Sergeant Wyatt entered the country illegally to come and see me, it was you who advocated having him eliminated.'

'That was for your own safety, Linda, and now you are blaming me! I also advocated that Starfish Cay be bombed to blazes. Why should I do that if I was running Silk Fist?'

'You weren't running Silk Fist, Jaso was, but towards your evil purpose. Mr President, cast your mind back to the ultra-secret meeting you held to plan the raid on Starfish Cay. Only six people were present at that meeting and had knowledge of what the target was going to be, and yet Jaso had destroyed all the evidence before we captured Silk Fist headquarters. Jaso claimed that he thought Blokhin had betrayed him but I believe someone at that ultra-secret meeting tipped off Jaso. I know it wasn't me or Sergeant Wyatt, or you, Mr President, and it seemed extremely unlikely that General Briscoe and Captain Knighton were involved with Silk Fist. That leaves the Vice President. Mr Kefalas, you wanted Starfish Cay bombed to destroy any evidence that might lead back to you.'

'I wanted Starfish Cay bombed to save the lives of our boys. I hope you enjoy your next job in a burger bar, Marquez, because I'm becoming fucking angry and I'm going to ruin you. Jaso said that Silk Fist was about making money. Why should I want to get involved?'

'Because you saw a way to elevate Silk Fist from a low key money making scheme to a full-blown terrorist style panic, culminating in the attack on the G20 conference. President Logan would be killed, along with all the other heads of state. As prescribed by the constitution, you would automatically assume power, supported by President Logan's grieving widow. You would then take the credit for destroying Silk Fist, use the new powers that you would award yourself to suppress all proof of your involvement, and ride your popularity to an easy win at the next Presidential election.'

Kefalas said: 'Joe, this is pure insane fantasy.'

Martina Logan was pale with shock. She looked at Kefalas and said: 'You told me something would happen to change things.'

Kefalas shifted angrily. 'I didn't mean by killing Joe. I meant by some change in the political climate. The people might tire of Joe's old-style slow Southern charm and want something more dynamic.'

'Is that what you think of me?' Logan said.

'You know damn well it is, Joe, but it doesn't mean I want your job by murdering you. Come on, we're both politicians. I've been a loyal Vice President for the sake of the country but that doesn't mean I agree with everything you do.'

President Logan looked at his wife. 'Marty, you remember back last year when I told you where the next G20 conference was being held?'

'Yes.'

'I asked you not to tell anyone for the time being. Did you tell Cley?'

Martina Logan looked at her hands. 'I don't remember.'

'Marty? Look at me. Did you tell Cley?'

'Yes.'

Kefalas said: 'So what? What does that mean?'

Logan said: 'It means that Jaso needed many months to prepare his booby trap in the ceiling at the Alhambra on Spanish Head. His preparations began long before I announced the venue officially.'

'That's no proof that I was involved,' Kefalas protested. 'A few other people were informed of the venue in advance. Jaso could have got that information from anywhere.'

Logan said: 'That's true, Linda. A few other people were told of the G20 venue as soon as it was decided. You are making the most serious allegations that could ruin your career, if not your entire life. Think carefully. Do you have any solid proof of the Vice President's guilt?'

Linda said: 'Yes, sir. I wasn't sure who I could trust within the White House or the entire United States or British intelligence network, so I turned to the one man outside of both whom I could trust and who had the necessary resources to seek out the culprit.'

Logan said: 'You mean Premendra Dhawan of Indian intelligence.'

'Yes, sir. At my instigation, Prem has conducted his own investigation, concentrating on surveillance of the Vice President.'

Kefalas said: 'You mean to tell us that you connived with a representative of a foreign power to spy on the Vice President of your own country?'

'Yes, I did. Mr President, Premendra Dhawan's findings about the Vice President's guilt, known only to him, at my request, and not the Indian authorities, are on their way.'

'Findings such as what?' Kefalas challenged.

'Proof of how you ordered the launch of the cruise missile after you had received the news that President Logan had survived the ceiling bombing plot. The use of the cruise missile was your last resort back-up plan. It wasn't Jaso's idea, it was yours, probably in collusion with Yaroslav Blokhin. But, unluckily for you, Blokhin realised that his own Russian president, his friend and business partner, would also be killed in the blast, that's why he gave Sergeant Wyatt and I the information about Starfish Cay.'

For the first time a look of uncertainty crossed the Vice President's face, then he collected himself and said: 'Yaroslav Blokhin, eh. You mean the good friend of your pal Wyatt.'

Martina Logan said: 'Cley, swear to me that you had nothing to do with the Silk Fist conspiracy.'

'Of course I swear it, Marty. I don't understand why Linda is trying to destroy me. Perhaps she and Joe are in this together as some sort of weird revenge for the fact that we love each other. Don't listen to all this, Marty.'

There was silence, broken only by the quiet ticking of a long case clock.

President Logan said: 'Linda, have you anything else to say?'

'No, sir.'

'But you assure me that proof of the Vice President ordering the launch of the cruise missile is being sent by Premendra Dhawan.'

'Yes, sir.'

Logan gazed out of the window at that elusive normal world over the horizon. He did not speak for a long time.

Finally, Cley Kefalas asked: 'What are you going to do, Joe?'

Logan said: 'I'm making a decision in that slow Southern way that you detest so much. This is what is going to happen. Cley, you deny any involvement with Silk Fist?'

'I certainly do, sir.'

'But, Linda, you promise me that proof of Cley's guilt is imminent.'

'Yes, sir.'

Logan said, almost as if speaking to himself: 'Thanks to Silk Fist, this poor old beaten up republic of ours has had enough for the time being. There are millions of decent and honest Americans leading useful, loving and happy lives, paying their taxes. I would rather they never find out that their First Lady is a tramp.'

Martina Logan gasped. 'Joe, please, for God's sake.'

'And I would also rather they never find out that their Vice President is possibly a homicidally ambitious and ruthless fake who would commit mass murder to achieve his ends.'

Kefalas said: 'I've told you I'm innocent, Joe. I cannot…'

'Shut up, Cley. The President is talking. This is what is going to happen. Marty will continue to serve as my faithful and hard working First Lady for the remainder of my two years in office. Marty, you will smile and shake hands as if nothing untoward has ever happened. Then, after we have left the White House and after a decent interval, I will file for divorce.'

'Joe, please, let's talk about this first.'

Logan went on: 'The Vice President now has two choices. If he confesses his guilt right now, right this minute, I will grant him a Presidential pardon and allow him to eventually retire to private life where he will retain his wealth and his reputation. He will be required, in a few weeks time, to resign the Vice Presidency on the grounds of ill health. Apart from that he will be allowed to live out the rest of his life in anonymous comfort.'

Kefalas said: 'And if I don't admit my guilt now?'

'Then, after the evidence provided by Mr Dhawan has arrived, you will be dragged through the full process of the law, in the glare of the world's media, and end up imprisoned for life in the worst hellhole I can find, having trampled the reputation of your office and of this country into the mud. Make your choice now, Cley.'

Kefalas turned on Linda. 'You sneaky bitch. I never did like you, always sucking up to your Mexican boss here, both as tight as a pair of Tijuana whores, and being led by the nose by that British bastard Wyatt, betraying your own kind.' He turned back to Logan. 'Yes, I took control of Silk Fist because I saw a way of getting rid of you, President Logan, and taking over this country without the risk and bother of an election and governing in a way to make this nation great and strong again. Unlike you or Marquez I was born dirt poor. I've had to scrabble and scrap and fight for everything I've achieved. I served my country in the army, risking my life, and then I fought for the White House and saw you snatch it away from me because of your old Southern money and the power of your good old boy connections while I had to tour the country with a begging bowl. I've had to wait patiently for six years while that treacle slow mind of yours made decisions based on the law and American values. Our enemies take advantage because you're too soft and too respectful of so-called democracy and legal process. If Silk Fist proved anything, it proved how weak and vulnerable this country is without adequate force and adequate control.'

President Logan said: 'Vice President Kefalas, you will return to your office and write a statement admitting your culpability in the Silk Fist conspiracy and explaining exactly what you did and how you did it. That statement will be kept in a secure place, known only to me and my successors in the Presidency, as will the contents of that statement. You will be allowed to live out your life without repercussions but never again in public office. In the fullness of time, say after another one hundred years, your acts will be revealed to the American public and your name will go down by the side of Benedict Arnold and all other traitors. Now get out of my sight.'

Kefalas stood up. He opened his mouth to speak but President Logan commanded: 'Enough! Go!'

Kefalas left the room. The sense of shock at such a momentous event seemed to reverberate in the air. No-one spoke for several moments.

Finally, Martina Logan stood up and said: 'Joe, can we please talk?'

'Later, Marty. Go to the residence and wait for me. I need to speak to Linda in private.'

Martina Logan meekly left the room.

President Joe Logan slumped down in a chair. He held his head in his hands. He looked shrunken, careworn, defeated.

Linda said: 'Mr President, I'm so sorry.'

Logan looked up wearily. 'Why are you apologising, Linda? You are the one who was right, the one who is loyal to me and to the country.'

'I meant about Marty. I'm so relieved she was not involved in Silk Fist. Kefalas used her. If I may talk to you as a friend, sir, I plead with you not to be too hard on Marty. She has told me many times how much she loves and admires you.'

'She has a most peculiar way of showing it.'

'Sir, Marty is a bright and passionate woman. She deeply desires your love and attention. She couldn't get it because of your job and she's made a bitter mistake but she loves you. Don't throw that away.'

Logan waved his hand. 'Okay, you've said your piece, Linda. Let it go.' Then, cooling, he asked: 'Would you go on working for Marty after all this?'

'Sir, I truly think Marty is a great First Lady. She is also human, as we all are, and has made a mistake, which we all do. If Marty wants me to stay, I'd be happy to carry on working for her.'

Logan grunted. 'You're too good to be true, Linda. You shame me. I've made mistakes with Marty since I became President. I realise what you're thinking but daren't say to me. I've put on weight, let myself go, ignored her or not considered her needs and wishes. There was a time, before the Presidency, when merely the sight of her filled me with desire. I would dearly love to return to that state. I need time to think about all this.'

'Of course, sir.'

Logan suddenly smiled. 'Anyway, the bluff we worked out succeeded, Linda. When you first approached me with your suspicions about Kefalas I thought you had flipped.'

'It gives me no satisfaction to be proved right, sir.'

'But, Linda, this evidence from Indian intelligence. Why didn't you tell me about that beforehand? We could have simply waited and confronted Kefalas when we had the proof in hand.'

Linda shifted uncomfortably and did not reply.

Logan said: 'Answer me, Linda. Was that a bluff as well?'

'Sir, I was becoming desperate because Kefalas wouldn't crack. Jaso resented that Kefalas had used his power and influence to take over Silk Fist and wanted some form of revenge. Jaso, in his sick way, wanted all the credit for Silk Fist. Then Jaso found out he was dying and it was his little game, his little joke, to feed us clues about Kefalas, to take him down without actually giving the game away. But I didn't think Kefalas was going to crack and confess. The Indian evidence ploy was all I could think of to make him confess.'

'Well, as we discussed when you asked me to go along with this confrontation, if he hadn't confessed then I would have had to dismiss you from the service and prosecute you. If I hadn't then Kefalas would have done so.'

Linda said: 'I'm grateful and relieved that you came up with that tactic of offering Kefalas the choice between a comfortable anonymous life if he confessed and a living hell if he didn't. That forced his hand.'

Logan smiled wearily. 'I haven't played in the muck of politics for over thirty years without learning a few tricks to persuade people to do what I want. But I meant what I said. It's better that the people of America retain faith in the honesty and probity of their leaders. To reveal what Kefalas has done would be to give moral ammunition to our many enemies. They could point at us and sneer about our belief in the law and democracy and honest government. They would not see what you, and millions of other decent Americans do, to keep the world clean, safe and worth living in. May I ask you a personal question, Linda?'

'Of course, sir.'

'This Sergeant Wyatt, are you in love with him?'

Linda, for the first time in years, blushed.

Logan said: 'I can see the answer in your face, Linda. You're usually so composed and confident, it's a surprise to see you off balance. Perhaps I shouldn't have asked.'

'Why *did* you ask, sir?'

'Because of the way you were looking at him when we were coming back from Beef Island on Air Force One. I have a reason for asking the question.'

'Yes, sir, I am in love with him. I never expected it to happen. I must admit I'm a little guilty so soon after losing Mike, but there it is.'

'Don't feel guilty, Linda. It's a cliche but true, life has to go on. Sergeant Wyatt is a remarkable man and what makes him more remarkable is that he doesn't consider himself remarkable at all. It's better to fall in love with a courageous and honest man than a rich man.'

'You mean like Marty once did, sir?'

'You're very persuasive, and very kind to give me compliments I don't deserve.'

'Sir, I've watched you throughout your Presidency and I've always seen you act with temperance, honesty and a respect for the law and for other people. You've become President of the United States. That seems to me a pretty remarkable achievement and worthy of a compliment or two.'

Logan said: 'I asked about Sergeant Wyatt for a reason. Is he aware of what has been going on here today?'

'No, sir. Not a thing.'

'Do you intend to tell him?'

'No, sir. I love Chris and we have helped each other through some extraordinary events but some things transcend love. My duty is to you and to the country. I agree that what has happened today should remain unknown except for the four people involved. As far as Chris is concerned, Dr Jaso is the guilty party and will remain so.

I give you my solemn word that I will never tell a soul what has happened here.'

'Thank you, Linda. I'll be asking to see Chris, and Premendra Dhawan, in a few days time. I have what I hope will be some compensation for what they, and you, have done for me and the rest of humanity.'

64

Peredelkino Forest, near Moscow, Russia, June 11th

Yaroslav Blokhin was becoming weary. He had walked for miles and, although he loved the grand silence of the forest, his leg muscles were protesting and the shirt under his London-tailored hiking coat was soaked with sweat. His doctor had ordered him to lose weight and take more exercise. He was taking more exercise but his love of vodka and *haute cuisine*, cultivated during his years living in London and New York, was making weight loss a dread and impossible challenge. Time to return to his dacha, his beloved family, and a good dinner.

Blokhin stopped walking. The late afternoon sunlight slanted through the pine trees in wide sinuous beams that illuminated the grass with vivid intensity. The arrow straight pine trunks soared up to the canopy, slim ethereal pillars reaching up to heaven. The silence was awesome and overwhelming.

Blokhin had lost sight of his two bodyguards. He called out: 'Vladimir! Oleg! Where have you two idiots got to? I'm over here.' Blokhin muttered to himself: 'Should have sacked those two after Wyatt made fools of them in Switzerland.'

Blokhin turned and looked back up the winding track. The sunlight seemed to vibrate in the still air. No birds were singing. The silence was palpable, brushing his soul with dread. There was an icy chill in his heart. He turned back to see a tall man standing a few metres down the track. The man was wearing a ski mask and a black padded jacket. He was pointing a silenced pistol.

Blokhin said in Russian: 'Have you come to kill me?'

The man replied in English but in an odd guttural accent that Blokhin hardly understood. 'Where is Mountfitchet?'

'Mountfitchet is dead. Have you come to kill me?'

'Who killed Mountfitchet?'

'I ordered his execution. I had suffered enough humiliation. His body lies at the bottom of the Caribbean Sea. Have you come to kill me?'

The man nodded. 'Your family will not be harmed.'

Blokhin said: 'Why? Is this because of Silk Fist? I tried to help, to make amends. I have set up a trust fund to help the victims. Why do I have to die?'

The man said: 'I don't know. I am a professional hired to do a job. He who hired me said to tell you that I was sent by Durga, who also dwells in the forest.'

'What does that mean? I don't…'

A single shot crashed through the silence but Yaroslav Blokhin did not hear it. The silence, for him, would now last for eternity.

65

Cabinet Room, 10 Downing Street, London, June 15th

Prime Minister Murdo Montrose looked up from his papers and said: 'Ah, Christopher. Come and sit down opposite me. I often work in the Cabinet Room in the evening. This splendid Georgian ambience inspires me.'

Wyatt looked around at the lemon yellow walls, the elegant fireplace, the Corinthian columns, the gold brocade curtains. 'Very nice, sir.'

'When I'm faced with an insuperable problem I consider how the great Prime Ministers who have worked here before me might have solved it... Lloyd George, Baldwin, Churchill, Attlee, Thatcher.'

'Bonar Law, Chamberlain, Eden, Heath, Brown.'

Montrose said: 'I hardly dare ask but in which list would you place me?'

'In the former, sir, but right at the bottom.'

'I'll settle for that. You're an impertinent bastard with no respect for my position.'

Wyatt pulled out a chair and sat down at the Cabinet table. 'I respect character and personality, they are qualities imbued by nature and experience, not offices, ranks or titles that have mainly been gained by connivance, payment or bloodshed.'

'They can also be gained by talent and honest hard work. I trust I haven't spoiled your afternoon by summoning you here?'

'I hope this won't take too long. I'm going to have dinner with my sister and then take my nephews to the Bridge for the game against the Gunners.'

'I have only a vague idea of what the latter part of that statement means.'

'That's because like many champagne socialists who have moved from a privileged upbringing into Oxford University and then straight into politics, you have no idea of how working people live. You've read George Orwell and think you understand all about the so-called lower classes.'

Montrose could not control his annoyance. 'If you hadn't saved my life I'd break you.'

'You could take away my job but you couldn't break me. Why am I here, Prime Minister?'

'I have a couple of pieces of news. Assistant Commissioner Sherman will not be prosecuted for her part in the Silk Fist conspiracy, neither – as you requested – will she lose her pension rights. We accept that she was duped by Philip Mountfitchet and this government does not want the embarrassment of the world knowing that the third highest ranking officer in the Metropolitan Police was corrupt. Can I ask you to remain silent on her role in the Silk Fist affair?'

'You can, sir.'

'Another piece of news. Yaroslav Blokhin has been shot to death in a forest outside Moscow. You wouldn't know anything about that, would you?'

Wyatt was unprepared for the stab of genuine grief caused by the Prime Minister's stark announcement. 'Not a thing, but I'm not surprised. Yuri was a strange mixture of devious ruthlessness and affectionate foolery. I could not help liking him. Was his family harmed?'

'No, they are safe. On a much happier note, Premendra Dhawan has been named as the next head of the Research and Analysis Wing when Colonel Chatterjee retires in six months time.'

'That's excellent news. They couldn't choose a better man.'

'I'm glad you approve of something. Dhawan has also been awarded the Bharat Ratna.'

'What's that?'

'It's India's highest civilian award, given for the highest order of endeavour in any field.'

'I'm truly delighted for Prem.'

'Prime Minister Mishra was going to recommend you and Sergeant Marquez for receipt of the same award but I've asked him to wait. You've turned down a promotion and you have also indicated that you would not accept the award of our own highest civilian honour. I assume you would turn down the Indian honour.'

'Indeed I would, sir.'

'Your friend Dhawan had no qualms about accepting.'

'Prem is higher profile than me and such an award would boost his career enormously. He would be a fool not to accept. Whatever awards he receives, they won't compensate him for losing the love of his life.'

'Is that what your attitude is all about, some sort of survivor guilt?'

Wyatt shrugged. 'I don't know. I don't want to analyse it.'

'You were awarded the Conspicuous Gallantry Cross during your time with the Special Boat Service. You accepted that award.'

'That's because I was fighting with my comrades against equally brave men who simply happened to believe in something different to what we believe. It was what I would term a clean action, unlike taking on furtive sick psychopaths like Jaso and being forced to hurt innocent people on the way.'

'You were also in line for the Presidential Medal of Freedom from President Logan. I suppose you would turn that down?'

'Yes, I would.'

'Are you aware that Linda Marquez has also turned down promotion and the Presidential Medal of Freedom. Joe Logan, fond as he is of Linda Marquez, is as baffled as I am by your respective attitudes. Most people would be overjoyed to be awarded the highest honours bestowed by three separate nations, but you and Marquez turn them down. Did you influence Marquez to reject these honours?'

'No, sir, emphatically not. Linda Marquez is her own person. She is a serving officer and she understands the difference.'

'The difference between what?'

'The difference between being sent to openly and honestly use what courage you possess to combat an enemy in defence of your country as opposed to being pursued and duped and lied to by your own country and having to clean out a nest of roaches using whatever resources we could beg from a Harlem night club owner, only to find that our leaders are more than willing to grab the credit and glory after the dirty work is done. A serving soldier or policeman or Secret Service agent has a duty first to his or her country, then to their superiors, but the overriding duty of any human being, in the end, must be to humanity itself.'

'Umm, an impassioned speech, Christopher. Pious, in fact. You *are* being offered your share of credit and glory.'

'And I have the right to refuse it.'

Montrose shrugged. 'Very well, I will inform President Logan and Prime Minister Mishra that you are unable to accept their awards. I understand you have, however, accepted a reward from Brian Ransome for saving his Spanish Head resort.'

'Yes, he is paying for Linda and I to go on a grand tour of Spain, staying at the best hotels. Linda wants to study the culture and the architecture. I will study the paella and the sangria.'

Despite himself Montrose could not suppress a smile. 'When are you going?'

'As soon as we are granted a month's leave by our respective bosses.'

'As far as I am concerned you can go anytime you like. You've completed your report on the Silk Fist affair. There will have to be other investigations and inquiries but they will be months ahead. Take your holiday, you deserve it. Having read your report, and that of Sergeant Marquez and Premendra Dhawan, I think you all deserve a long break. Quite extraordinary.'

'Thank you, sir. May I ask about Vice President Kefalas?'

'What about him?'

'I'm puzzled by the nature of his sudden malady. He looked perfectly fit when I saw him last, now he has suddenly retired through ill health. That is quite a coincidence so soon after Silk Fist.'

'I asked President Logan the same thing but he insists there is nothing sinister behind the Vice President's resignation. Linda Marquez is very close to what goes on at the White House. Does she have anything to say about the resignation?'

'No. She won't tell me anything. Linda's loyalty, quite rightly, is to her President and her country. I will not ask her again.'

'But what do you think? Do you think Kefalas was somehow involved in Silk Fist?'

'It's possible. If he was involved then the Americans are wise not to make the fact public. You've made the same sort of decision about Assistant Commissioner Sherman. It shakes the confidence of a nation to find out that it's leaders are corrupt or evil. If the Americans made a decision to hide any crimes by their Vice President then I'll keep my mouth shut, especially if Linda Marquez supports such a decision by not telling me anything.'

Montrose studied Wyatt for several moments. Then he said: 'You saved my life, possibly my career, but I can't bring myself to like you, sergeant. You're a prickly and combative bastard with no understanding of the political mind or profession. You're also the most honest and courageous person I've ever met. I've been talking to President Logan and Prime Minister Mishra about you and Marquez and Dhawan. We've agreed that we might need you three to work together again sometime.'

'In what way?'

'Do you understand the Latin saying *Quis custodiet ipsos custodes*?'

'No, sir. I went to a North London comprehensive school, not Oxford.'

'It refers to a problem as old as power and politics itself. It was coined by the ancient Roman satirist Juvenal and means "who will guard the guardians?". If a situation similar to Silk Fist ever arises again, where the powers-that-be are being corrupted from the inside, we might need people of proven honesty, loyalty and courage like you three again.'

Wyatt smiled for the first time since entering the Cabinet Room. 'At last, Prime Minister, we're talking the same language. Sounds intriguing.'

66

Jumna River, Allahabad, Uttar Pradesh, July 12th

Premendra Dhawan stood on the new bridge and watched the sun setting over the sacred river Jumna. The water below took on the hue of molten gold to match the necklace of golden lights along the bridge. As the world darkened the sky was suffused with the rose and purple light of evening that Rhea had loved so much. Far below the last of the bathers, devotional adults and playing children, prayed and splashed and laughed at water's edge. Prem was consoled and comforted by the remembrance of Rhea's presence.

Prem caressed the wreath of flowers and talked to Rhea. 'You were a gentle and loving soul so I don't think you would approve of what I have done, not only for you but for Linda's husband and the Princess Royal and for all others who suffered. But mainly for you. I apologise for my murderous need for vengeance, for expiation. It is a need I would not have thought myself capable of, but losing you for such an unnecessary reason was too much to bear. Your boys are fine men living useful lives but your premature loss will affect them forever.

I also did what I did for India. Soon I must follow in the footsteps of Colonel Chatterjee, footsteps that will be difficult to emulate. India is a great nation, we have taken our rightful place, and we will not allow colonialism or terrorism to ever again deflect us from our true destiny. But the real battle is not between races and countries but between good and evil, between those who respect humanity, democracy and the law, and those who seek to destroy humanity with evil subterfuge and cruel criminal acts.

Christopher Wyatt and Linda Marquez are on our side and they are good people. I have learned a lot from them and they, I hope, have learned a lot from me about our common humanity. If the love they have found together is half as strong as we found together then they are blessed forever. I will be proud to work with them again if the need arises.

Mountfitchet is dead. Yaroslav Blokhin is dead. Christopher must never know that I ordered Blokhin's death. Christopher foolishly had a soft spot for that fat oligarch. Sangita Sherman and Francois Walden are spared. They were duped and did not realise what they were doing.

The Americans mourn the passing of their former Vice President, Cleytus Kefalas. Linda Marquez found out about Kefalas and caused his downfall. I do not know how she unmasked Kefalas and I will never ask. I respect her fine loyalty to her President and to her country, that is as it should be.

Kefalas made one mistake. If we had not intercepted his desperate telephone call from his home in Washington ordering the launch of the BrahMos missile then I would never have been sure that he was culpable, the vicious mastermind behind Silk Fist. Jaso began it but Kefalas perverted Silk Fist in the most evil way to serve his own purposes. Linda had asked me to intercept the Vice President's telephone calls but I did not tell her about this last desperate call. I bitterly regret withholding evidence from a respected colleague but I wanted Kefalas free, not out of my reach in prison. The Americans were told that their Vice President resigned because of ill-health. So be it. They played right into my hands. I could not allow Kefalas to live while you dwell in infinity. They said he was suffering from ill-health so that is what I arranged to give him, an illness short and lethal. You had to die because of evil men like Kefalas and Jaso but evil doers must always suffer the consequences of their actions.

Goodbye, my darling Rhea. You are no longer here but you are always new; the last of your kisses was even the sweetest; the last smile the brightest; the last movement the most graceful. You will always be in my heart and my mind.'

Premendra Dhawan threw the wreath down into the waters of the Jumna and watched it flow away towards the sunset and the eternal sanctity of the holy River Ganges.